Dinah Maria Mulock Craik

Nothing new

Tales

Dinah Maria Mulock Craik

Nothing new
Tales

ISBN/EAN: 9783337079130

Printed in Europe, USA, Canada, Australia, Japan

Cover: Foto ©Andreas Hilbeck / pixelio.de

More available books at **www.hansebooks.com**

NOTHING NEW.

Tales.

BY THE AUTHOR OF

"JOHN HALIFAX, GENTLEMAN," "AVILLION," "AGATHA'S HUSBAND,"

"THE HEAD OF THE FAMILY," "OLIVE,"

"THE OGILVIES," &c., &c.

NEW YORK:

HARPER & BROTHERS, PUBLISHERS,

FRANKLIN SQUARE.

1874.

BY THE AUTHOR OF "JOHN HALIFAX, GENTLEMAN."

LORD ERLISTOUN;

. A LOVE STORY.

CHAPTER I.

"Jean," I said, "Lord Erlistoun is coming."

"Is he?" said cousin Jean—not our cousin, I should add, but we called her so for convenience, to save telling the not-easy-to-be-told facts concerning her and her poor father.

"Jane, my dear, is that piano well in tune? Do see about it. And we must have the velvet furniture uncovered to-day; Lord Erlistoun's coming."

"Oh, yes, I'll remember, Mrs. Browne."

"Jean—oh, cousin Jean—Russell and I shall miss the rook-shooting. It is to be put off till Monday; Lord Erlistoun's coming."

This last of the various interruptions made Jean stop her practice. She was fond of the two lads, and they of her.

"Never mind, Algernon. The young rooks will have four more merry May days; and after all, I think I would rather see a worse fellow than you shooting them."

"A worse fellow? Eh? Lord Erlistoun?"

"Well, he may be; I don't know him."

"Jane—my dear Jane!" She never would remember to say "Jean."

"My dear Mrs. Browne." But mischief was too strong in the lass; her merry eye caught mine; she repeated solemnly out of last week's "Punch," which lay on the drawing-room table,

> "To H'Apsley 'ouse next day,
> Drives up a broosh and four,
> A gracious Prince sits in that shay;
> (I mention him with hor.)."

Of course, I knew as well as Jean that one of my good mother's few faults was a propensity to "mention with hor" any member of our British aristocracy. She had it, I have heard, from the time when honest Thomas Brown became clerk to Browne and Co., merchants, with many a true word spoken in jest about the possibility of changing the final e, which was the only thing in either his name or character that, in his progress upward, my father ever consented to alter. She was then Susan Steel, a young milliner and dressmaker; very pretty. As Mrs. Browne, of Lythwaite Hall, mother of many children—none now living but the three boys and myself—she was often pretty still; and she took a pleasure—very excusable, considering all the years she had kept herself neat and spruce in cotton and linsey-woolseys—in making the best of her good looks with handsome gowns.

She made the best, too, of every thing about her—house and carriages, servants and plate—even to "my sons at Cambridge," though I often thought they all bothered her at times, especially the latter. Poor dear! the only thing she never could make the best of was me.

I was new to the splendors of Lythwaite Hall. It was only lately that my father had bought it, and settled down among the landed gentry; only lately—probably through his active labors in the Great Exhibition, which that year mingled together all classes—that I had heard of his having Lords on his visiting acquaintance. I was not too pleased, moreover, that any visitors should break in upon this, one of my rare visits home, for I take a good while to become accustomed to new people; I did, even to cousin Jean. Jean and I were good friends now; yes, the best of friends.

We had taken a long walk that very morning —in the garden to the lily-of-the-valley bed, then across the park by the trout stream, and home by the rookeries, under the three horse-chestnuts; for Jean said, laughing, that when her "ship came home," and she owned a park, she would have it full of horse-chestnut trees. I remember the saying, since it quite convinced me that she and I had been, both in our speech and our silence, carrying on trains of thought, and plans for the future, as wide apart as the Poles.

Our "ships" rarely do come home, or are meant to come home, are they, cousin Jean?

I am but a plain man, I know. There is no poetry in me; if there ever was, the Liverpool docks and Liverpool 'Change beat it all out of me nearly twenty years ago. Whether it ever might revive depended upon certain things, which I had tried that morning to find out, without troubling any body, or making any talk in the family. I did find them out; or rather, I found out—in safe time—that there was nothing to find. So ended the whole matter, and I was once again Mark Browne, eldest son of honest Tom Browne, the merchant's clerk; belonging to a prior order of existence from Charles, Russell, and Algernon Browne, my brothers, born after a long interval, in days of prosperity. Nice, handsome lads they were; well-grown, well-educated, accustomed to ease and luxury. No wonder they got on so merrily with cousin Jean, and that Jean should have such a liking for the boys.

She was fond of my mother, too, and humored her peculiarities capitally; followed her this morning from chair to chair, taking the covers off with a most domestic and inexhaustible patience, worthy of a "poor relation," and then with a lively spirit, very unlike any poor relation, bursting into a song or two for her own entertainment.

"Just stop one minute, my dear;—don't you think Lord Erlistoun," etc., etc.

And having stopped and settled the important question, Jean was off again with her ditty:

"'O no, O no, says Earlistoun,
For that's a thing that maunna be:
For I am sworn to Bothwell Hill,
Where I maun either gae or dee.'

"Mark, who is Lord Erlistoun?"

"Just Lord Erlistoun; I know no more. What were you singing about him?"

"Oh, that Earlistoun was quite another person—an old ballad-hero of mine. Nobody you know—nothing you would care about."

Sometimes Jean was mistaken. She knew much that I did not know, but that was no reason why I should not care about it. True, my learning and my literature had been chiefly in ledger and cash-book, like my father's before me; and, until lately, in the incessant whirl of money-making, I had had little leisure for any other interests. Still, Jean was mistaken.

But I did not contradict her. I let her sing out her song, and watched her sitting at the piano in the green-shaded drawing-room, with one slender sunbeam sliding across the Venetian blind, and dancing to the music on the top of her head. Ah, bonny cousin Jean?

To return to Lord Erlistoun.

It had since struck me as one of those coincidences we afterward trace with some curiosity, that Lord Erlistoun should have first appeared at our house on this day. He was not expected till the morrow; and I had gone to my room. When my mother tried to open my door it was bolted, for a wonder.

"Mark, do go down; your father's out, the boys gone a walk with Jane, and I'm this figure. Oh, dear me, what shall I do, for Lord Erlistoun's come."

Yes, there I could see him from my window, lazily walking up and down in front of the portico—a tall, slight young man, in a gray shooting-dress and a Glengarry bonnet. Nothing very alarming about him, as I hinted to my mother.

"Nonsense, Mark—for shame! Only do go down stairs."

Usually I dislike strangers, and especially "fine" strangers, but this morning all things appeared the same to me and all people alike. The only thing worth doing seemed the simple necessity of small everyday duties, as they lay to my hand.

"Mother, don't vex yourself—indeed I'll go. How long am I to keep him out of the way?"

"Until dinner-time if you can. Mercy me! and there's no game to-day for dinner!"

I thought, what mere trifles do women, even the best of women, sometimes seize on to worry their lives out! But I went down.

"Lord Erlistoun, I believe?"

"Mr. Browne—I beg pardon, Mr. —"

"I am Mark Browne. I am sorry my father is not at home to welcome you."

"All my own fault, indeed—I mistook the day fixed for my visit. Still, may I intrude?"

His manner presupposed an answer—the only one possible. Probably his society was not usually considered an intrusion. I bade him welcome, and we shook hands, with a mutual covert inspection and dim recognition of having met somewhere, but no allusion was made to that prior acquaintance by either.

I remembered him distinctly. We hard-working classes seldom see even among our women, seldomer still among our men, that noble, yet delicate outline of face which is commonly called "aristocratic;" not unjustly either, for it is the best type of mere physical beauty. We rarely boast—we poor fellows, stunted in early growth by toiling in close offices and living in town homes—such lithe, tall figures, combining the strength of manhood and the grace of womanhood, even down to the long hands and almond-shaped nails—I remember noticing them. No; each rank has its own advantages—physical development rarely belongs to ours. It depends on chances frequently out of our power, or prior generations who bequeath us their personal type to start with; afterward, on rearing, education, and modes of life.

I saw at a glance what any sensible man must see, nor need be ashamed or afraid to see, that for certain qualities you might as well institute a comparison between a working cob and a race-horse as between Lord Erlistoun and Mark Browne. Perhaps the instinctive train of thought which led to that comparison, or rather distinction, indicated too much self-consciousness. But there are positions when a man will and does think of himself, and compare himself voluntarily or involuntarily with other men; such an one was mine this day.

"This is a very pretty place," said Lord Erlistoun.

He was correct; many a nobleman's I have seen not half so fine. My father took great delight therein; and it was not without a certain satisfaction that I did the honors of it to our guest, through gardens, conservatories, pleasure-grounds. There was a pleasant pride in showing to Lord Erlistoun that we also—we money-makers—could love nature and art, and expend wisely and liberally what we did not inherit but earned. And in going over the place, I was myself forcibly struck with the whole thing—with my father's princely style of expenditure, and with the contrast it formed to the little dark merchant's office in Liverpool which originated and maintained it all.

Sometimes I thought—but a son has no business to comment on a father—on so excellent a father.

Our walk came to an end, likewise our conversation. We talked over the state of Europe, the Great Exhibition, etc.—topics which were possible meeting points—until they successively fell dead. I am not a conversationalist myself, but I like to hear others; and am obliged to own that I found Lord Erlistoun's company rather uninteresting.

I left him safe in his apartments; whence, to every body's relief, he did not emerge till dinner-time.

He must have found it a dull meal; my father still absent—my mother, brother, and cousin being all I could introduce him to. I remember the boys, strong in Cambridge ease and "knowledge of the world," coming readily forward, till quenched by the grave politeness which it was impossible to make free with; and my mother, whose hearty apologies for "pot-luck," were met by a smile which expressed by its very reserve the most amiable ignorance of what "pot-luck" might be.

My dear good mother—hot-cheeked and hurried—a little too warm and too fat for her light-colored silk dress, and her white gloves, that would not come on properly—with her uneasy attempt at ease, and her incessant stream of talk, in which the "h's"—that unlucky letter which we had never yet succeeded in safely impressing on either her or my father—appeared and disappeared at pleasure—I wondered what Lord Erlistoun thought of his hostess.

Possibly nothing; for no outward indication testified that he ever had any thoughts at all. I have seen close-tempered men—iron-visaged fellows, whose faces were as hard as a locked chest—but then you guessed from that very fact that there was something inside; proud, sensitive men, who tried to wear a countenance like a mask, yet through which now and then, by some accidental flash of the eye, you felt sure it was a mask, with the natural flesh and blood behind it. But I never in my life saw such a smooth, courteous, handsome negation as Lord Erlistoun's physiognomy seemed, this first day of acquaintance.

"What do you think of him, Jean," I said, when, my father having returned late, I was free—free to settle myself in the usual corner, and watch Jean going about her usual evening's ways, which she did not alter, nor seem to intend altering, for our grand guest. She had merely bowed when I introduced him to "my cousin." She was not usually much noticed, and something in her manner rather evaded than attracted notice, when we had company. And yet it often seemed, to me at least, as if she, of the whole family, looked most at ease, most natural, in the beautiful rooms of Lythwaite Hall.

"What do you think of him?" I repeated, as she stood by the tea-table; ending a long discussion by persuading my mother it would be much better to let her make the tea, as she always used to make it, country fashion, in spite of Lord Erlistoun.

"What do I think of him!—wait a minute— (John, leave the lamp there). Yes, I think him very handsome, and remarkably well dressed."

"You are jesting?"

"Not at all—the latter quality is no slight one. Any man can dress like a dandy; but it takes a man of some taste to dress like a gentleman."

"And his manners?"

"I have seen worse and better."

"My dear Jane, how can you judge? So elegant, so polite! accustomed, as one might at once perceive, to the very highest society."

"But, mother, Jean has been accustomed to good society, too."

"I was accustomed for six-and-twenty years to my father's." She said this with pride, yet no unholy pride. I saw the tremble on her lip, and hastened to talk of other things.

Once in my life I had seen Jean's father. He was not a man ever to be forgotten, even by a young lad. Why he married into the Brown family, or whether the Emma Brown he chose had qualities in herself enough to make her his fit wife, and Jean's mother, I never could learn. She died early. We never heard of either father or daughter, save that occasionally we saw his name in newspapers and magazines, and my father would say, "That's surely poor Emma's clever husband," till we heard of him one day in a newspaper obituary. Authors usually die in poverty; but he left Jean enough to bring in fifty pounds a year. So, just for a visit, my father fetched her to Lythwaite, and then somehow we couldn't part with her. This was all her history that I knew of.

Of herself—she was a tall, dark-haired girl. People did not generally admire her; at least our sort of people; bright complexions, plump figures, well set-off by gay dresses, were their notion of beauty. If the Parthenon Athene (I have a head of her in my office-parlor over the bookcase, which I bought at an old curiosity shop, for some turn of the brow and hair which reminded me of Jean)—if Athene herself were to appear at one of their parties in a high black silk gown, a little white frill round her throat, and not a ribbon or jewel on neck, arm, or finger, they would doubtless have called the goddess a "rather plain young woman," as I have often heard Jean called.

A "young woman" she decidedly was—not a girl. She had seen a good deal of the world, in London and elsewhere; her character and manner were alike formed; that is, if she could be said to have a "manner," when, under all circumstances, she was so simply and entirely natural; not always the same—few people are, except the very reserved, the sophisticated, or the dull; but in all her various moods she was —as alone she cared to be—herself.

There was no pretense about her—no tendency to petty or polite humilities. I think she knew she was *not* plain; and was rather amused by the ill-educated taste of those who considered her so. I think, too, that in a harmless, womanly way, she took pleasure in her own classic features, large and noble, her father's features, and in her father's beautiful hereditary hands. For his sake, partly; she was the sort of woman to have something true and good at the root of her very vanities.

I describe her as she was to us who knew her—not to strangers. She rarely "came out" to strangers; or, except when she was really interested in them, made any show of appearing so. Nor, in the extremely quiet mood she was in to-night, was I surprised that Lord Erlistoun merely noticed her face (he, accustomed to art, must have seen it was handsome), as if it were picture or statue, and quitted it. She bore the look, or was unconscious of it, with those "level-fronting eyelids" of hers, full of other thoughts—sometimes thoughts evidently far away. She had had a hard life, you saw that; she had gone through a great grief, you saw that too, at least some might; but so much discernment was probably not to be expected from a young man like Lord Erlistoun.

"How old do you think he is, Jane?"

"Who? Lord Erlistoun? Really one can hardly judge so speedily. But 'Burke' will inform us, Mrs. Browne."

"I told you, my dear, that was by no means a useless purchase," said my mother, turning over with no displeasure our till lately unknown necessity; the book which some satirist calls the "British Bible." "Here it is—Nugent, Baron Erlistoun. Dear me, only twenty-four, just Charles's age—younger than you, Jane."

"Yes."

Here the subject of discussion unwittingly ended it by opening the drawing-room door, looking rather tired, but still listening, with the blandest courtesy, to every word of my father's. Now, my father's talk was always worth listening to; but then, like most old men, he had a trick of long-windedness, and it is trying to have the wisest sayings and the best of stories half-a-dozen times over. The young man turned, perhaps, a little too quickly, to my mother, when she came to the rescue; and there was just the slightest shade of personal interest, beyond his invariably polite interest in every thing, when among the long list of people whom he "had not the honor of knowing"—the *élite* of our friends, whom my mother had anxiously invited to a dinner party for his entertainment to-morrow, she chanced to light on some whom he did know. Lady Erlistoun ("my mother," he explained) "was acquainted with the bishop and his lady, very nice people."

"Charming people!" (ah, why so ecstatic, good mother of mine, for you had only dined there once, I know) "and that sweet little niece of theirs—she's not out yet though, the

heiress, Lady Emily Gage. You know her, of course?"

"Lady Erlistoun does. Allow me," and here Lord Erlistoun rose in a languid manner, to bring my mother's cup to the tea-table. It cost him some trouble, and her a thousand apologies; but Jean's eyes had a spice of mischief in them as she looked on.

"Don't stir, Mark. A little exercise won't harm him. Let him do at Rome as the Romans do."

He stood by, while she filled the cup, made some slight remark or acknowledgment, and retired. Then, in great dearth of entertainment, and with a dead, heavy atmosphere of restraint creeping over the room, he was set to whist with the parents and Charlie till bedtime.

Jean and I contemplated the party in silence; my mother's round, rosy, contented face—my father's, rather coarse and hard-featured, but full of acuteness and power—and between them this elegant young man, whose exquisite refinement was only one remove from, and yet just clear of, positive effeminacy.

"I wonder what on earth he came here for," Jean said, meditatively. "He must have had some very strong motive, or be sadly in want of novelty, before he—"

No, cousin, you need not have hesitated; I traced your involuntary thought; I, too, was aware of what our house was and its ways; also how they and we must necessarily appear to one so totally different from us as Lord Erlistoun. It is folly to disguise an abstract truth—I never do.

"I see what you would say, Jean; before he came among such inferior folk as we are—he, accustomed to the high breeding of fashionable life. That slow, listless, faultless manner of his, which, I perceive, is fidgeting my poor mother beyond expression, is, I suppose, high breeding? You know."

"No, I am glad to say I do not know. Mark, you ought to be ashamed of yourself" (and I was, seeing the indignant color flush all over her dear face); "I do not know, and never mean to know. What have I to do with fashionable life? I know how good you are—all of you—I love you."

Ay, Jean, speak up, frank and warm. Surely you loved us, every one and all alike.

After Lord Erlistoun had been lighted duly to his repose—and the greatest nobleman in the land, as his hostess secretly avowed, need not have desired a better furnished or handsomer chamber—we began to breathe. Of course we "talked him over" as families will among themselves—and thank Heaven, with all our increase of fortune, we had never ceased to be a family. Jean, stealing slowly into the place of the little daughters that had died, or else by the natural force of her character making a place for herself, took her due share in the discussion. She gave full merit where merit was, but was severe and sarcastic upon various small peculiarities which had struck the family with unacknowledged awe; namely, that under-toned, soft drawl, that languid avoidance of the letter R, and that nimini-pimini fish-mouthed "Oh."

"I should like to compel him for once into a good honest English round "O," of either pleasure or pain. Boy as he is, I wonder if he is still capable of either, or of the expression of them. I wish he may be."

"Not altogether a kind wish, Jean."

"Yes it is," she said, after a moment's thought. "Any pain is better than stagnation; any expression of feeling better than the elegant hypocrisy which is ashamed of its existence."

And then she turned laughingly to put her arm round my mother's neck, and tell, apropos of nothing, how twice that day she had been addressed in the village as "Miss Browne."

But no, Jean, you could never have been my mother's daughter. I saw clearer than ever to-night, the something in your mien, manner, and tone of thought, distinct from all of us. Perhaps you knew it too, much as you loved and respected us—honest, honorable Brownes. So thought I, and my thought had a truth in it; but was not the whole truth. "Each after his kind," was the original law of things; and that "like attracts like" is no less an absolute and never-to-be-ignored law. But sometimes we decide too hastily, and with mere surface judgment, upon what it is that constitutes similarity.

CHAPTER II.

LORD ERLISTOUN spent a whole week at Lythwaite Hall. Why he did so, or if he found any pleasure in it, we really could not tell. He deported himself agreeably to all; went meekly with my mother to various solemn dinner-parties; took his due share in our own company-keeping in his honor; at other times he shot or fished with Charles—Algernon and Russel having vanished—nay, even walked and talked amiably with me. With Jean, who had little leisure, and perhaps less inclination to spend it in doing nothing, his intercourse was chiefly confined to "Good-morning, Miss Jane" (having discovered that her name was not Browne, but being too courteous or too idle to find out what it was), and a brief, equally civil and indifferent, "Good-morning, Lord Erlistoun."

He did not seem to take any interest in one of us more than another—if indeed it was his habit to feel interest in any thing. The only occasional gleam visible in those soft, large, lazy eyes was once or twice over the post-bag, on getting an accidental letter or two: "My mother's letters"—as once, when my mother, in her homely way, ventured the ghost of a jest, he replied, with such overwhelming bland dignity that the dear old lady was quenched for evermore.

Still, as Jean observed, it was a good sign in

him to like—if he did always like, of which we were not sure—but at any rate to be interested in his mother's letters.

We knew—from "Burke" of course—who his mother was; a member of a noble, indeed, a truly noble family; also from that most useful book, and from various things he himself let fall, that she had managed a somewhat dilapidated property through his long minority, faithfully and well. There were some sisters, but he was the only son.

"I think," Jean observed, one night when, as usual, after he had gone to bed, the rest of us were sitting in committee upon him, making that domestic dissection of character which, as I said before, families and friends will make, and the only thing is to take care that it is made in good humor, justice, and charity, "I think much ought to be forgiven to an only son."

The next morning, during the garden walk, which, by mutual consent, had become a habit with my cousin and me, we being always the earliest risers in the household, the subject was again recurred to.

"Jean," I said, "if he stays over another week—and I think he will, for I heard him promise the Bishop to come to that child's party given for Lady Emily Gage—you really will have to take your turn in amusing him. He hangs heavy on my mother's hands, sometimes."

"Your poor dear mother!" half-amused, yet with a vexed air, no doubt at things which vexed me myself occasionally; but they were inevitable, and it was no use noticing them. "Mark," she added, seriously, "if a young man of four-and-twenty—handsome, well-educated, and by no means stupid—having been Lord Erlistoun from his school-days—having travelled a good deal, seen court life, common life, nobody knows what life, at home and abroad—his own master, possessing a good fortune, together with a mother and sister, whom he seems not to dislike, though to love them and own it might be a display of feeling quite impossible—cousin, if such a young man is not able to amuse himself, all I can say is, that it is a very great shame."

"I did not know you had reasoned so much and felt so strongly concerning him."

"Not him, but the simple right and wrong of the question, of which he is a mere illustration."

"Yet you appraised him categorically. You must have observed him a good deal."

"A little; one can not live in the same house with people without forming some judgment upon them."

"Do you dislike him, or his manner? His high-bred manner, I mean?"

"On the contrary, I like it; it is the external sign of those qualities which a few have and twice as many imitate. His case may be either the one or the other; I don't know yet. If we only could break this fine outside enamel and get at the real substance underneath, supposing there is any!"

"Do you think there is?"

"I am not sure. Mark, do you understand me? I like refinement; I love it! in every thing and every body. It is really charming to me sometimes to hear Lord Erlistoun's low-toned voice, and see his quiet way of doing little civilities, little kindnesses—especially to women. I give him credit for every thing he is, and would not wish to see him less, but more; I would like to make a man of him."

"Hush!" I said, for she was too much in earnest to notice, on the other side of the espalier, footsteps; also the top of a gentleman's hat. "'Tis himself; I think he heard you."

"I think he did." Jean set her lips together, and held her head erect. Nevertheless, she colored, as was not unnatural; still more deeply when, at the path's end, Lord Erlistoun crossed in front of us. Would he pass on? No; he turned and bowed.

"A fine day; you are walking early, Miss Jane," with a steady gaze, though he, too, seemed to have had those "hot cheeks" which are said to trouble people who are talked of behind their backs. "I have been stealing your lilies of the valley; may I restore some?"

Leisurely keeping a few and presenting her with the rest, with a matter-of-course air, as a mere "devoir" to her sex, he lifted his hat again, and sauntered on.

"Jean, I am sure he heard."

"I hope he did; it was the truth, and perhaps he does not often hear the truth; it may do him good."

That notion of "doing good" to a person, which women have, the best and sincerest women often most dangerously! Ah, Jean! I thought to myself, take care! But facing those eyes, bent forward meditatively as she walked—those eyes neither downcast nor passionate, neither a child's nor a girl's, but a woman's, with a woman's steady heart, I felt ashamed to say of what I wished her to "take care."

I was absent in Liverpool all day, but, with hard traveling, managed to return at night. We had a family party—postponed a little, waiting our guest's possible departure, till at last my father insisted on its being postponed no longer—a party of poor relations. By "poor" I mean not indigent, but less wealthy and in a less honorable position than ourselves, kindred whom, in climbing up the ladder, my father had passed one by one, and now stood toward them in the envied yet, perhaps, unenviable position of "the great man of the family."

An odd, heterogeneous gathering it was, as we were aware it would be under present circumstances. My mother had been seriously alarmed at the idea of it for days. "Mercy on us! what shall we do with Lord Erlistoun?" "What will Lord Erlistoun think of so-and-so?" and my father had invariably answered her with that dogged twist of the mouth which had helped him up to the top of the tree, and that merry twinkle of the little bright eyes which had kept some enjoyment for him when he got there.

"Molly"—he still said "Molly" sometimes in private, "I—don't—care."

So the good people came. I found them all in the drawing-room when I returned home.

Heaven forbid I should be hard upon poor relations, even the dozens that, lying *perdu* during a man's struggling days, spring up like mushrooms every where under his feet in the summer of his prosperity; and the scores, still worse and more trying, who, unable or unwilling to help themselves, expect always to be helped by somebody—him, of course; who, wherever he goes, cling like a fringe of burrs to his coat-tails, not a whit the better or greater in themselves for sticking there, and to the unhappy rich man neither a use nor an ornament. Yet, let every man do his duty, even to these; my father always did.

It was good to see him now and then, on occasions like this, fill his house with honest folk, who, no doubt, spent weeks after in commenting on the grand establishment of "cousin Tom;" to watch him, and even my mother, gradually warm up into old acquaintanceships and old recollections, till at last the very tones and manners, half worn-off, of earlier days would revive, and we would hear them both talking as broad Lancashire as any body present.

They did talk very broad, these "country cousins," or so it seemed to me to-night. I was accustomed to it pretty well in the way of business, and with men; but women! And then they dressed so showily, so tastelessly; those Liverpool ladies seemed so horribly afraid of being thought any thing less than "ladies," and so convinced that the only traveling patent of ladyhood consisted of clothes. They paid great court to my mother; there was always an admiring group of listening gazers round her ruddy velvet gown, and she was pleasurably and amiably conscious of it, too, dear soul! though, perhaps, just a thought too patronizing. But with all her pleasantness, and the pains she took to amuse them, they seemed at first to have ignored altogether, and then to stand a little in awe of my cousin Jean.

Must a man be blind with poring over a lifetime of ledgers? or deaf, from hearing the incessant rustle of notes and chink of sovereigns? I was neither.

Let me give all credit to those worthy people, my kindred; many of them good wives, good mothers, good daughters, lively and pleasant in their own homes, though a little awkward and ill at ease—more so than we were ourselves—in ours. But when Jean crossed the room, in her soft, rich, black dress; when Jean's low tones struggled through that awful Babel of loud voices, what a contrast! and yet she was of them, too—her mother was a Brown. But nature itself had made her what she was; different from these, possibly from all other women—oh, how different!

Some one else saw it besides myself; other eyes traced her, with slow observation, across the room and back again. Once or twice when she was talking, I saw him quit the books of prints in which he had taken refuge and listen.

Doubtless, Lord Erlistoun had spent a very dull day. My father, shrewd and wise—neither wishing to show off his titled acquaintance, nor thinking himself justified in mixing up heterogeneous classes against their will—had desired that his guest should be left entirely free to find his own level, and join in the society about him as much or as little as he chose. Perhaps for their comfort, if not their sagacity, some of our good relations did not even know that the young man who sat so quietly aloof, and talked so little, was Nugent, Baron Erlistoun.

"Ask him to play chess with you," said Jean, passing me toward the piano, where some of the old folk had begged for one of her old-fashioned songs.

I had intended asking him; so we soon sat down face to face to our mimic battle.

Let me do him justice, as I tried to do that evening. A finer face I have never seen; not a mean line in it. Something eclectic even in his way of handling the chessmen; balancing over a poor pawn, in doubtful choice, those white expanded fingers, laden with a ring that valued—(I know in a business capacity something about the value of diamonds)—nay, his every action, down to his way of lounging back on the crimson velvet chairs, had a freedom and repose—in addition to that last grace, the easy self-possession which gives the effect of entire unconsciousness—at once admirable and enviable.

Let me do myself justice now. I did *not* envy him. Physically I might have done a little — there are times when most men feel keenly Nature's niggardness; but spiritually, never! In any great moral battle—as in this sham one we were fighting, somewhat unequally, as I soon saw, I had an internal conviction which would be the victor—which would hold out toughest, strongest, and longest, Lord Erlistoun or I.

He lost, as I expected, but replaced the men, seeming to make no account of losing.

"Do you like the game, Lord Erlistoun? To enjoy chess requires a certain hard, mathematical, calculating quality of brain."

"Which I have not? Very probably. Nevertheless, it amuses: 'pour passer le temps.' Your move, I believe?"

He leaned back, and we began another game, keeping up the chess-players' solemn silence, nor distracted therefrom even by Jean's singing.

She rarely sang in public at Lythwaite. Either she disliked it, or her taste in music was too "old-fashioned" for our elegant friends. Now it struck home. People's songs they were, with the people's life in them; passionate or tender, merry or sad, but always fresh, warm-blooded life. One felt rather sorry for an age too refined to understand them.

"You like music, Lord Erlistoun?"

"Yes. You should have heard 'Ernani' last winter at La Scala. It was very fine."

"My taste in music is low. I had rather hear an English or Scotch ballad than a dozen operas."

"Chacun à son gout," said Lord Erlistoun, smiling.

Jean burst out again, like a mavis from a tree-top, with another of those ditties made for all time—such as "Huntingtower," "Robin Adair," or "The Bonnie House o' Airly." To see her—to hear her—with her heart both in voice and eyes—her true womanly heart—tried me. I could not play chess for it. Lord Erlistoun apparently could, for he won. Just as we were rising, Jean looked across at me, merrily and mischievously—I know she did it out of pure mischief—and began afresh—

"'O billie, billie, bonnie billie,
Will ye gae to the wonds wi' me?
We'll ca' our horse hame masterless,
And gar them trow slain men are we.
'O no, O no,' says Earlistoun.'"

Lord Erlistoun looked up quickly; Jean went on—

"'O no, O no,' says Earlistoun,
'For that's a thing that maunna be:
For I am sworn to Bothwell Hill,
Where I maun either gae or dee.'"

The ballad continued, verse after verse, in a wild, plaintive old tune, about this young laird's rising "i' the morn," his

"'Farewell, father, and farewell, mother,
And fare ye well, my sisters three;
And fare ye well, my Earlistoun,
For thee again I'll never see.'"

And so on, ending, I think, with

"Alang the brae, beyond the brig,
O many there lie cauld and still;
And lang we'll mourn, and sair we'll rue
The bluidy battle o' Bothwell Hill."

The last line fell in a faint echo, as if the singer herself were moved by the sweet old song. Lord Erlistoun rose.

"That ballad—I never heard it before—may I look at it?"

"You can not, unluckily; I sing it from memory."

"Will you sing it again?"

"Some time, but not to-night, I think."

Was Lord Erlistoun so surprised by being refused any thing by any body, that he did not ask again? Nevertheless, he still stood by the piano, talking to her.

"'The bluidy battle o' Bothwell Hill.' There was hard fighting in the days of our forefathers. We live an easier life now."

"Do you think so?"

"I mean—let me help you with that music-stand; I mean, there is a difference between the men of to-day and the hero of your ballad; Alexander Gordon, of Earlistoun, I think you said?"

"Certainly, a difference."

Lord Erlistoun was silent.

Presently he made another attempt at conversation

"I rather fancy I have a legitimate right in that pretty ballad of yours. We are descended collaterally, I believe, from those same Gordons of Earlistoun."

Jean's attention was caught. "Ah, indeed? Earlistoun near Dalry, a tall gray castle, among trees, in the bottom of a wide valley surrounded by low pastoral hills?"

"You seem to know the place better than I do myself. In truth, save the fact that the first Lord Erlistoun chose to take his title from the old castle, I know very little of those far-away Scottish ancestors of mine. I have been so much abroad; have become so thoroughly a cosmopolite."

"I perceive that."

"Do you?" as if he wished to discover whether the perception was favorable or unfavorable. "You are interested, I see, in those days of gone-by romance. Yet I thought you rather contemned old families?"

Yes, he had certainly overheard us this morning—Jean felt he had. Her color rose painfully even; but she was neither ashamed nor confused.

"I would be sorry to contemn any thing for being old; or, on the other hand, to value any thing merely because it was old."

"You believe, then, there is some little truth in the doctrine of race?"

He said it not without pride; but a pride too accustomed to its possessions to mind either condemnation or justification from others. Jean answered with something of the same feeling, though drawn from a different source.

"Thus far I do believe; that, seeing how fast races decline and families dwindle and die out—when a family has maintained itself notable above others for centuries, the chances are that its members must have sufficient fine qualities, and the whole race enough vitality, to keep it worthy of note."

"If so, can it be a mean thing to respect one's progenitors?"

"I never said that, Lord Erlistoun. Any one who ever honored a dear father can understand something of the delight of honoring remote forefathers—when they were deserving of honor. But"—and her great bright eyes flashed light and life enough to kindle a whole race—"I think it far, far beneath the honor of a living man to go trading all his days upon a heap of dead men's dust."

Perhaps never in all *his* days, among his noble English peeresses, his Russian princesses, his Paris "Baronnes"—had Lord Erlistoun seen a woman speak her mind out, with all her honest heart, in this way. Evidently simply because it *was* her mind; without any reference to or thought of her interlocutor. He looked certainly a good deal surprised. With some curiosity, if not admiration, his eyes rested on

the dark, glowing face—then he stooped to help her arrange her music.

"'Dowglas,'" reading the lettering on a volume; "'Jean Dowglas.' I beg your pardon —is that—"

"My name? Yes; my father was Scotch. My mother's name was Browne."

Ay, Jean, lift your head—speak up proudly of that poor young mother, who had no "gentle" blood, yet who left some of the bold plebeian energy of us Brownes in you, to help you after she died.

"Dowglas," repeated Lord Erlistoun. "Spelled, I see, with the *w*, as a very old branch of the Douglases still persists in spelling it?"

This was meant as a question, apparently; but whether she belonged to that "very old branch" or not Jean did not vouchsafe to say.

"Jean, too. Have I not always heard you called June?"

"My father called me Jean. Thank you. Do not trouble yourself any more with that music, pray."

She moved away, and busied herself for the rest of the evening in entertaining the poor relations. I did not see her speak again to Lord Erlistoun. He sat in his arm-chair, occupied with his book of prints, till at length finding some person worth talking to—as doubtless every one present was, if only one would discover the right key to unlock their hearts and lives—he began talking with a good will.

When we all separated for the night, I noticed that he held out his hand, which Jean had never touched before—in a manner that made it impossible for her to refuse it.

"Good-night, Miss Dowglas."

"Good-night, Lord Erlistoun."

CHAPTER III.

I WENT to Liverpool next day, but my mother made me promise to return every Saturday, remaining till Monday. I did not look well, she said, and she thought it was a curative measure; but I myself was not so sure of that.

A week in the office, with odd evenings spent in walking swiftly up and down the busy Liverpool streets, or taking a two-penny breeze on the river, to see the sun setting behind the Great Orme's Head, and coloring into something like beauty the long and sandy line of the Mersey shore; while all the while I knew it was lighting up wavy grass meadows, May hedges, and merry rookeries far away, in those lovely spring evenings, which I never knew so lovely any where as at Lythwaite Hall.

A clerk in our house, speaking of my father's new place one day, said he knew it well when he was a boy. He once spent a whole May month there with a cousin of his, who was dead now. He told me how they used to agree to rise early and stroll about the garden before any one else was up; go fishing in the trout stream, and rook shooting in the shrubberies—only she did not like that; how they generally went to church the field way, where he helped her over the stiles; and how he had still the clearest recollection of her face as she sat opposite to him listening to the sermon. She was dead now, and buried—had been for years. He thought he should like to get a holiday, and go to that village church again some Sunday.

Oh, Jean, my cousin Jean! if you and I had been girl and boy together, years ago—if we could be boy and girl still, and go hand in hand through the gardens and over the meadows of beautiful Lythwaite Hall!

When a man lives an exceedingly practical and busy life, when of necessity the one spot of —romance will you call it?—in his character must be reduced to a very small space of time and thought, daily, close pressed down, locked down, as it were—it is astonishing what vitality it preserves, and how, in the brief moment or two he allows it liberty, it appears to rule and sway his whole being.

I seemed to have lived a year in the short railway transit between Liverpool and Lythwaite Hall.

My mother was unfeignedly glad to see me. She had been worried about a good many things, she said, but that was nothing new. Poor body! she was always worried. "Could not Jean help her?" I asked.

"Oh, no! she did not like to say any thing to the poor dear girl."

"Mother, is any thing the matter?"

But that minute, through the dusk of the garden, I heard Jean's laugh, and saw two figures moving slowly up and down her favorite walk—our favorite walk.

"Don't go to them, Mark—please don't. It isn't Charlie—it's Lord Erlistoun."

"Not gone yet?"

"No; nor seems inclined to go. And I can t help thinking—though I wouldn't mention it to her or any body for the world—that this visit of his may turn out a very good thing for our dear Jane."

"A very good thing!" When women say that, they mean marriage—supposed to be the best possible thing for any woman. My mother —the worthiest creature alive, and not a bit of a match-maker—she also undoubtedly meant marriage.

Lord Erlistoun wanting to marry Jean Dowglas! Plain Jean Dowglas—the Brownes' cousin, Jean Dowglas. Things must have gone very far indeed for even my mother to take into her innocent head such a "very good thing."

It must be understood here that the matter struck me—who perhaps knew her better than my mother did, or any of us—solely in the light of Lord Erlistoun's wanting to marry Jean; a very different thing from her consenting to marry him.

"But if it does come to that," said my mother, after listening to all my excellent good reasons to the contrary, and then repeating her

own—"what will your father say? and what will his mother say about our having had him here—to entrap him, perhaps? and what will all the world say"—a little pleasure lurking in her lament—"our poor cousin Jane to be made Lady Erlistoun?"

"Hush, mother!"—for nearer came that little laugh—they two were in full and lively argument about something; they noticed nobody till we were close upon them, and then Jean turned with a start of surprise.

"Oh, Mark—I am so pleased!" with unfeigned pleasure.

Lord Erlistoun likewise, with extended hand and an air of real friendship, was "exceedingly glad" to see me.

We all joined company, and paced up and down the garden till nearly starlight. Jean linked her arm in mine, and, turning to Lord Erlistoun, went on with the argument. I don't remember what it was about—in fact, I did not hear much of it. I only recollect noticing the perfect frankness and freedom of her tone—mingled with a certain decision and independence which usually marks the intercourse between a woman and a man younger than herself, and possibly younger still in character.

Twenty-four and twenty-seven. Comparatively, a woman and a boy. Often a boy worships a woman, sometimes permanently, always devotedly, for as long as the passion lasts; but it is rarely that a woman's love goes backward on the dial of life, to expend itself in all its depth and power—as a true woman alone can and ought to love—upon a boy.

When starlight was exchanged for candlelight, and I had full opportunity of noticing them both, I saw nothing in any way to controvert this opinion. Not even when coming back into the drawing-room, after all the rest were gone, Jean found me still sitting over the fire, and stopped to talk a minute or two upon the nearest and most natural topic—Lord Erlistoun.

"He is here still, you see, Mark. He appears to like Lythwaite and our steady-going home ways. And, upon my word, I think they have improved him very much—don't you?"

"He certainly is a great deal altered."

"For the better?"

"Possibly—yes—I think, for the better."

"I am sure of it. Not all surface-politeness now, you may see his kind heart through it. And he is beginning to feel the useless waste of his life hitherto; thinks of dashing into politics, or public business, or literature. He longs for something to live for—something to do. He says he often envies you, Mark, that you have something to do."

"Does he?"

"Cousin"—after a pause—"I am afraid you don't quite like Lord Erlistoun, as indeed none of us did much at first; but we should be slow of judging. We never know how much good may lie hid in people, nor how good they may finally grow. I have great hopes of Lord Erlistoun."

I looked suddenly up at her, doubting for the

moment—only a moment—whether she, too, were playing off the usual feminine hypocrisy, or whether she was still her true self—my spotless Jean Dowglas. Ay, she was.

"Jean," I said, feeling somehow that now I ought to say it at all costs—"take care."

"Of what?"

Could I answer!—But she was no child. After a moment I saw she had answered the question for herself.

"I understand you; and, Mark, though it was not quite kind of you to say that, still, such friends as we are, I should be very sorry if for a moment you misunderstood me. No; I am not in the least afraid of—what you suppose."

"Why not?"

"Why not! Because I know myself, and trust myself. When we are girls," and she sighed—"out of our very innocence and ignorance we make mistakes sometimes; but not afterward. A young man must be blind indeed —very blind, and a little conceited too, if he can not discern at once from the manner of a sincere woman, whether she simply likes him, or *loves* him."

"That is true."

"So, cousin Mark," smiling. "do not be unjust again, either to me or to Lord Erlistoun."

No, I wished not to be. I made every effort to see things justly, and as Jean herself saw them; and, perhaps, her vision was clear then. Perhaps, had Lord Erlistoun left that day, or even the next, he might have merely carried away with him the remembrance of a noble and unworldly woman, who, in the totally opposite world in which he dwelt, might have been an element of purity and goodness, lasting at intervals all his life long. But in these things, people frequently go on safe and sure to a certain point—they cross that, on some idle hour, in some unconscious way, and there is no going back, ever again.

On the Sunday evening we took a walk, Jean, Lord Erlistoun, and I; through the same fields, which our old clerk in Liverpool had been talking of. It was such an evening as, perhaps, poor old fellow! he had enjoyed many with that little cousin of his; the sort of evening which always puts me in mind of Wordsworth's foolishwise rhymes—Jean repeated them, sitting on a stile, eating clover-honey—

> "'Oh, who would go parading
> In London, and masquerading
> On such a night of June,
> With that beautiful soft half-moon,
> And all these innocent blisses,
> Of such a night as this is?'"

"Who would indeed? But I am afraid I must soon." And Lord Erlistoun leaned against the stile, listening to the sad, sleepy, far-off "caw-caw" of the rookery—looking up at the face of the "soft half-moon," and then, at another face; also quiet, also rather sad—as if in the pathos of the hour Jean had gone back into former years—sanctuaries of her checkered life, whither no one could follow her.

"Miss Dowglass"—she started slightly; "I wish you knew my mother. You would like her, for many things—and I think likewise—" He stopped.—"I had a letter from her this morning; would you feel interested in reading it?"

"Thank you; you know my fancy for reading strangers' letters. Sometimes they let one into bits of character unknown to the correspondents themselves."

"I wonder what you will find out here!"— and he lingered over it—the delicate-tinted, scented envelope, with its exquisite handwriting and large coroneted seal, before he put it into Jean's hands. "Read it all, if you will, excepting, indeed, the crossed page. She has but one fault, this good mother of mine—like her one crossed page."

Jean read and returned the letter. "But I ought to tell," she said, smiling, "that I saw one word—I think the name of 'Emily or Emelia'—on this momentous page."

"Oh! no! quite a mistake!"—with one passing flash, fierce and bright, that showed what fire lurked in even Lord Erlistoun's eyes. He put the letter in his pocket and returned to the subject we had been lazily canvassing along the fields, as if in contrast to every thing around us, namely, London life, "high" life—as set forth in that most sparkling, hateful, and melancholy of fictions, whose very brilliancy tortures one like the phantasmagoria of disease—Thackeray's "Vanity Fair."

"The question seems," Jean said, "is it a true picture of that sort of life?—I would never shrink from any truth merely because it was painful—but, *is* it true? I have no means of judging. Is it true, Lord Erlistoun?"

"I am afraid, in a great measure, it is."

"Then, I would rather say to any sister of mine, like Hamlet, 'Get you to a nunnery; go, go, go,' than see her thrown out into the great world, to grow into the sort of woman you have described sometimes. I couldn't help thinking so, even in the cathedral this morning, when I looked across the aisle to the pretty baby-face of that little Lady Emily Gage."

Lord Erlistoun knocked the mud off his boots —he was not afraid of muddy boots now—saying, carelessly,

"Miss Dowglas, what is your opinion of that small school-girl?"

"Lady Emily? Indeed, I have no possible grounds for forming an opinion at all. I only now and then have felt sorry, looking at her, to think how soon her child-life will end. I always feel great pity for an heiress. She has less than the common chances of us women."

"How do you mean? that she is likely to be loved for any thing except herself?"

"Or if she were, she would be unlikely to believe it. Poor little Lady Emily."

"Don't waste your pity over Lady Emily. You might spend a fragment of it upon us men —men of the world—who never find a woman to believe in; who are courted, flattered, hunted down, as it were; afraid to look at a pretty face lost it should be only a bait to hook us with; afraid to trust a warm heart, lest it should turn out as hollow as this worm-cast under my foot. What chance is there for us men, when we have lost our reverence for women?"

"Not for all women," said Jean, gently; for he had spoken with passion, as certainly I never in my wildest thought expected to hear Lord Erlistoun speak. "You have told me of your mother."

"And what does my mother do, even *my* mother?" his tone was lowered, but I could not help hearing it. "She writes me that there is a charming creature just ready for me—one whose estate joins mine, and therefore will be a most suitable match, with a good fortune—and I am poor, you know—good birth, good looks, and in short, every thing convenient, except love. Shall I go in a year or so, propose to her, and marry her?"

"I thought you said that for ten or fifteen years to come you were determined not to marry?"

"So I was. I abhor matrimony. Of course after a time I must settle down, as others do, but I will have my liberty as long as I can. When I do sell myself, it shall be tolerably dear, even though it be to this young lady. I won't tell you her name, lest perhaps I might finally marry her."

Whether he was in earnest altogether, I know not, but Jean was. You should have seen her look of mingled pity and scorn.

"Lord Erlistoun, we will if you please discuss a less serious subject; on this, you and I could never think alike."

"Could we not?"

Perhaps he felt that, regarding sideways the dark, noble face, on which the last bit of sunset was shining, a pale face too, for she did not look either particularly well, or particularly young, while in his unwonted energy, stronger than ever I saw the distinction before spoken of, between the woman and the boy. Equally strong between the one who, living in the world, lived only for it, and its ideal of happiness; and the other who, also abiding in it, and enjoying it so far as fortune allowed her, had yet an ideal, a spiritual sense, far, far beyond it.

"You think, I perceive, that I am fit for nothing better than to turn out one of those people you hate so in 'Vanity Fair'—a Marquis of Steyne, perhaps?"

"I never said so or thought so, Lord Erlistoun."

"What would you have me do, then? What would you have me be?"

I, leaning on the other gate-post, apart from them, was struck by this speech. It is not a light matter when a man arrives at asking a woman "what she would have him be?" Perhaps Jean was struck too, for she replied, rather coldly—

"Indeed, you are the best judge of that; every man must be the keeper of his own conscience."

"But he may gain a better self, a purer conscience, to help him. Miss Dowglas, shall I take my mother's advice and marry?"

"No!" and the truth in her, the duty of speaking it, seemed to make Jean forget every thing else. "After the fashion of marriage you have told me of, undoubtedly no! For those who see no clearer—know no better—much may be allowed; but for you who do—nothing."

I saw Lord Erlistoun smile to himself. "You do not quite understand me."

"Yes, I think I do, but we see things from such opposite points of view. You have always been used to consider marriage as a bargain, a convenience, a matter of necessary respectability; I think it a sacred thing. There can be no medium in it, it must be either holy or unholy; entire happiness, or utter wretchedness and sin. For man or woman to marry without love—not merely liking, or decent respect, but downright *love*—is, to my thinking, absolute sin."

Lord Erlistoun replied never a word. All along the still twilight fields he scarcely made one observation. It was my hand that helped Jean over the stiles; he did not offer to do it. My hand, large and hard it might be, not like his; but a man's pulse beat in it—it could support, and it could hold fast, too.

"Will you take another turn up and down the walk, Miss Dowglas?"

"No, it is too late; I had rather go in."

She slipped away. Was it with the same sort of instinct that, whenever Lord Erlistoun came near her, for the whole remainder of the evening, she slipped away?

Well do I remember that evening and the look Jean had. Her face was a little flushed, and there was a certain unquietness in it. She sat at the piano a long time singing; it had become a custom, I found, that she should sing every night, and to no lack of listeners. What she chose, in spite of one or two hints to the contrary from Lord Erlistoun, who seemed a little surprised at our narrow notions about "Sunday" music, were songs of Handel and Mendelssohn, among which, I remember, were some of their solemnest and most spiritual— "I know that my Redeemer liveth," and "Oh rest in the Lord;" ending, at my father and mother's desire, with an old-fashioned Methodist hymn. We were Methodists when I was a child, and how the tune carried me back to the little hot chapel in Rathbone Street, where, after some fierce, coarse, strongly emotional sermon, the congregation rose, and their stout Lancashire voices threw the chorus backward and forward, women and men alternately.

> "For we're marching on Emmanuel's ground,
> We soon shall hear the trumpet sound,
> And we all shall meet at Jesus' feet,
> And never, never part again.
> No, never part again—no, never part again—
> Oh, never part again—no, never part again;
> For we all shall meet at Jesus' feet,
> And never, never part again!"

Oh, life!—life so full of partings! I have

often quieted the pain of it with a bit out of that old Methodist hymn; with the echo of that "never part again."

I was up early on the Monday, as usual, but my father caught and carried me off to look at some horses he had bought for the new brougham, so that I did not get my early walk with Jean. She had taken hers, though; for I met her in the hall laying her hat aside. She was late, and we waited some minutes for her, before she came down to make breakfast. All breakfast time she was exceedingly silent and grave.

Lord Erlistoun did not appear till the meal was nearly over. When he did, I noticed that Jean blushed burning hot—in trouble and pain —a very anguish of blushing. He did not speak to her, even to wish her good-morning, but took his seat near the foot of the table, and entered with my father into a long and energetic discussion on politics. In the course of it I overheard that he had some thought of standing for a small borough in the south of England, and to do so it would be immediately necessary for him to leave for London.

I breathed. Yes, he was going away at last. Maybe I could even feel sorry for the young man.

He did not seem much moved himself. He carried things with a high hand, and stood talking with energy and *empressement* of the great pleasure he had enjoyed at Lythwaite Hall; but I noticed he did not give any of us the slightest invitation to return the visit.

Ay, in a few hours he would be gone. The new element he had brought into our household—as he certainly had, since different characters and classes must necessarily act and react upon one another—would depart with him. My mother might cease to put herself and her house into full-dress every evening, and my father to bring out his claret every day as if for a dinner-party. We should go back to our old ways, and Lord Erlistoun to his. Could we? or could he? Can any new experience in any life be merely temporary, leaving no result behind? I doubt it.

Nevertheless, he would most probably vanish completely out of our sphere, as if he had dropped at Lythwaite from a balloon, and gone up again by the same ethereal conveyance. Would any body miss him? Would any body care?

Of this, too, I was not quite sure.

"Liking," not loving; used in opposition to loving, rather; but most certainly she had said the word, and she did not even "like" every body.

"Mark, are you going to walk to the station? I'll walk with you."

So once again went Jean and I under the chestnut trees, where the white flowers now lay strewn, soiled, and scentless, beneath our feet.

"Cousin, you had better reconsider the chestnuts that are to be in your park. You see ' it is not always May.' "

"Ah, no!" with a slight sigh. "Mark, you need not make public that foolish speech of mine."

"About owning a park? You never mean to own one, then?"

Whether, involuntarily, I put into this question some meaning below the surface, I know not; but Jean answered, seriously and emphatically, "No."

Still, as she walked along, though her head was erect and her footfall firm, and she talked easily and cheerily upon her usual family topics, I fancied I could trace at times the same unquietness of mien, as of a good and true nature not quite satisfied with itself. She was "out of sorts," as people say—out of harmony with herself and with the lovely June morning. It seemed almost to give her pain.

Waiting at the station—for she would wait —she took my arm to walk up and down the platform.

"Oh, Mark," clinging a little, "I wish you were not going away; there is some comfort in you."

I asked her, after some consideration, if any thing was troubling her—would she tell me?

"No, I had rather not. In fact, I ought not. It is, after all, really nothing. It will be quite over by-and-by. If I were not sure of that, as sure as— There's your train!"

"The next train goes at 2 40. Express, remember. Lord Erlistoun wished me to inquire. He goes by it."

"Oh, indeed!"

"Jean—one word. Are you sorry or glad he is going?"

"Very glad—heartily glad."

"But he may change his mind again—he has a trick of doing so. Ah, Jean, take care."

"I *have* taken care."

"You are not angry at my saying this?"

"No. Good-by!"

My sight rested on her there, for as long as the whirling train allowed, standing fixed and firm, with her shawl gathered tight round her, as if nothing in her or about her was to be left loose, subject to any stray wind of fancy, feeling, or chance.

CHAPTER IV.

BUSINESS kept me in Liverpool for three weeks, without intermission. My father could only find time to go down once to Lythwaite for a day and a night. The incessant burden and responsibility of money-making, money-turning, and money-spending—the cruel slavery of riches—sometimes weighed heavily upon even his stout heart.

"Oh, Mark!" he would sometimes say to me, when we were laying our heads together over business matters in the small parlor until long after office-hours, "I sometimes think I'd ha' done better to ha' left thee a clerk, as I was myself when thee wert a bit of a lad, going back'ards and for'ards twixt this and the little house at Everton. Heigho, my boy! I hope thee'll get more good than thy father gets out of Lythwaite Hall."

It did sometimes seem to me strange that he and I, working here in this musty room under the coarse flare of gaslight, sometimes lifting our eyes from the mass of papers and mazes of figures to exchange a word or two, then again silence; it seemed passing strange that he and I should have any part or lot in the splendors of Lythwaite Hall.

For its splendors, they might go to the winds, but then it had some sweetnesses too. Every Sunday—that being the only day I had time to let them come—I used to be haunted by wafts from the May-hedges, by the sound of rooks cawing, or the soft single twitter of young thrushes going to sleep in the rustling trees.

On Monday, when my father came back, I asked him if all were going on well at home.

"All well, and particularly quiet; your mother," with a twinkle of his keen eye, " your poor dear mother has quite given up telling folk how very much she misses Lord Erlistoun."

He was gone, then, safe and sure. Well, let him go, and prosperity go with him. He was a fine fellow in his way, but he could have done us little good, or we him. Why he came among us at all, whether from self-interest (yet, rich and influential as my father was, common justice condemned me for suspecting the young nobleman of that), or whether it was one of those mere idle adventures which an idle young man is prone to, I was still ignorant, and, to throw no further mystery over the matter, I remain ignorant to this day.

Sometimes, in the dull round of business, which chained my father and myself as effectually as if we were two horses in a mill, or two convicts working, hand-fasted, side by side, there would suddenly come across me a vision of that easy, enjoyable life, pictures from which Lord Erlistoun had given us at Lythwaite, and I had seen Jean's eyes light up on listening—pictures of summer sunrises in the Alps—of summer sunsets over the Euganean hills—of exquisite moonlights, brighter than our dull northern days, while lazily rocking on the blue Mediterranean seas, or skimming in and out among the lovely isles of the Grecian Archipelago. All pleasure, nothing but pleasure, bounded by no duties, burdened with no cares.

Yet would I have exchanged lives? No.

One Saturday afternoon, when I was just thinking of him, thinking, too, whether it would be possible to get away by the last train that night for a little, a very little "pleasure," my notion of pleasure, our housekeeper ushered into the back parlor " Lord Erlistoun."

I was surprised, and probably I showed it, for he looked rather awkward, that is, awkward for him.

Again—as I seem always to keep on saying—let me be just to him; let me not deny that delicate courtesy, that charming grace which made

B

the least thing he did well done, which, after the first, forced the little dark parlor and me to catch the influence of his company. He gave no reasons for his visit, except a slight apology for "interruption," but sat down as if determined to be friendly and at ease.

We talked upon ordinary topics; then, on his inquiring after my "family," about Lythwaite Hall.

"You go down every Saturday, I believe?"

Was that the reason of his coming? Was it only through me that he could hear, as, in spite of all his calm politeness, he seemed nervously eager to hear, any tidings of Lythwaite Hall?

At my age a man is seldom without some penetration, especially when his observation is sharpened by certain facts which concern no one but himself. I think I can detect falsehood in feeling or expression, and can likewise respect any feeling which is evidently honest and true.

Jean had "taken care," she plainly said. Perhaps one might even afford a little temporary regret for the temporary pain of young Lord Erlistoun.

I told him I did not go every Saturday, but intended to be at home to-night.

"Ah! indeed! It must be a pleasant thing to be able to say, as you say it, that thoroughly English word, ' home.' "

Thereupon we diverged, in an abstract way, upon different branches of this same subject. I detected in Lord Erlistoun's conversation many turns of thought, nay, even of phrase, which I recognized as my cousin Jean's. I have often noticed this fact—how one person will involuntarily imitate, not merely the tone of mind, but slight peculiarities of word or gestures belonging to the one other person who has most influence over him or her.

Again, I say, both on this account and from a certain restlessness which, well as he disguised it, pervaded his whole manner, thoughts, and plans—for he poured out to me, unwilling and unresponsive confidant, a great many of these—I could not help feeling sorry for Lord Erlistoun.

Rising to leave, he said, suddenly, " You are going home to-night; might I burden you with these?"

Two letters, one addressed to my mother, the other to Miss Dowglas. Probably he noticed my surprise, for he continued—

"They are, you perceive, from Lady Erlistoun. She wished them delivered to-night, and I think—I have reason to believe—your Lythwaite post is uncertain. May I ask of you this favor, on the part of my mother?"

He always spoke somewhat haughtily when mentioning the word "favor;" and yet to-day there was a hesitating humility about him, too.

"I was not aware of any shortcomings in the Lythwaite post; but I will deliver these safely."

"Thank you. And you return on Monday?"

"I really can not inform you, Lord Erlistoun."

All these miles the letters seemed to lie burning in my pocket. Men, especially young men, visit about as they will, in circles lower or higher than their own. If honorable in themselves, there is no reason why they should not be accepted and acceptable; but with women it is different—or society thinks so. What on earth did Lady Erlistoun want with my mother and my cousin Jean?

I reached home late: they had not expected me. The drawing-room windows were dark; however, in the little breakfast-room I found them both, presiding over a large heap of new household linen, my mother looking busy and pleased, as she always did when on any excuse she could put off the fine lady and be the housewife once more; Jean rather pale and anxious, but she brightened up when she saw me at the door.

"Ah, cousin Mark!"

"Mark, my dear boy!"

Lord Erlistoun had said truly; it was pleasant coming home. I did not for an hour or more deliver the two letters. My mother opened hers in a flutter of curiosity.

"Dear me! Bless my heart! Why, Jane."

But Jean had taken up hers and gone out of the room.

When she came back it was merely to say "Good-night, Mark;" and she said it hastily. Two hot roses burnt on each cheek, but her hand was very cold. It struck to my heart.

I am no advocate for the romantic dignity of silence—that is between two people who, however much or little their mutual regard, understand and believe in one another. With such, silence is often no virtue; merely cowardice, selfishness, or pride.

"Don't go," I said, "I want to speak to you."

"I can't! I must not stay."

"Only a minute; sit down"—for she was trembling. "Lady Erlistoun is coming to call here on Monday. Did you know?"

"Yes, he told me."

He!—that little momentous word! But I passed it over; it would not do to stand upon trifles now.

"Cousin, I should like to know—not that I have the smallest right to ask, and you must not answer if you have the slightest objection, but I should just like to know, in explanation of something he let fall, whether you have heard, since he left, from Lord Erlistoun?"

She paused a moment, and then said slowly and sadly, "He has written to me almost every day, but I have never answered a single letter."

No need to ask what the letters were about; no need to guess what their effect must have been, coming thus, every day—and strong must have been the impulse to make Lord Erlistoun do any thing regularly every day—coming from a young man fresh in all the passion, the poetry, the energy of his youth.

I stood silent by the chimney-piece; meeting in the mirror over it, a familiar face—well known in Liverpool warehouses and on the Liverpool 'Change. Seeing, too, in the distance beyond, that poor flushed face of Jean's. At last she turned and hid it on the sofa-pillow.

"Do help me, Mark! I have been so very miserable."

I took a chair and sat down; opposite the grate, with my back to her; and said something or another. I waited—and waited in vain. My mother called from the stair-case "Mark, it's bedtime—see that the house is locked up"—and I answered from the parlor-door, to prevent her coming in.

"Now Jean, tell me?"

She told me; just what I had feared—nay, expected. There is no necessity to give her precise words; indeed, she explained no more than the bare fact that she might have been Lady Erlistoun.

"I thought you said you had 'taken care?'"

"Ay, that's the thing. It was my pride, my wicked self-reliance. I thought I was doing him good; I wanted to do him good; I liked him to like me. But I never thought—Oh Mark, if I did wrong, I have been punished."

Punished! Then, even though his letters came day after day; even though by some unaccountable means he had persuaded his lady-mother to visit and condescendingly investigate his choice—there was no fear. I had judged her rightly. Our Jean would not marry Lord Erlistoun.

"I know it will not last—he is too young. After a little it will seem to him no more than a dream. And I may have done him some good after all. Was I so wrong, Mark?"

I did not attempt, from any false kindness, to compromise the truth. I said, it was likely that she had been in some way wrong, since, as she had herself acknowledged, under similar circumstances, the woman is rarely free from blame.

"Ay—that is it—that is my self-reproach and fear—Yet oh, Mark, if you knew what it was to feel your youth going—to feel, too, that you never had had its full value, that there had been no happiness in it, and now it was going, gone; and if some one came and loved you, or thought he did; said you were the only creature in the world who could make him happy, make him good; if you saw, too, that there was some truth in what he said; that if you had been younger or he older, or if other things had been more level between you both—you might—"

"Jean," I said, startled by the expression of her eyes, "do you love Lord Erlistoun?"

"I am afraid I do."

So in a moment the whole face of things was altered; so, in less than a moment, that "ship" which Jean used to laugh about, as being with most people so long in "coming home"—went down, down, without the flapping of a sail, or straining of a mast, to the bottom of the sea!

Otherwise, I might have perceived something unnatural in those five slow words, something not right in any ear except the lover's being the first to hear them. As it was, I simply heard them in all their force and significance to both our lives, and, so recognizing them, entered upon the duty of mine.

This was plain as daylight. There are none who feel so sacredly the absolute right of love for love than those to whom fate has denied its possession.

Jean came behind me and laid her hand on my shoulder. She might! Henceforward, I could no more have touched it—except cousinly or brotherly, than I could have put out my own to steal the crown jewels.

"Well, Mark."

"Well, Jean."

"I think 'tis time we said good-night."

"Good-night, then." A look up into her bending face—which was pale, drawn, and hard. "You will be happy, never fear."

"No, what I told you has no reference to—to that. If any thing, it prevents it; and makes easier what I did upon instinct, for his good as well as mine. No, Mark; I shall always remain Jean Dowglas."

With a smile, that made her face saint-like in its sadness—she passed out of my sight.

But we can not be in a state of saint-hood always. Certain facts which four dun walls might that night have borne witness to, till such time as the rookery was all astir in the weary dawn, gave me a clew to certain other facts, which Jean's exceeding paleness, next morning, and that alone, betrayed.

There was, happily, no one at home but us three. I kept my mother safe out of the way the best part of Sunday, and on Monday forenoon.

My good mother! she behaved admirably. Only a few nods and winks in confidence with me, and an affectionate lingering over Jean, indicated her perception of what was going on—or her prophetic vision at what was undoubtedly coming. After the first expression of pleasure, she did not even refer to Lady Erlistoun's visit, and, moreover, gave me a hint to the same purport.

"You see, she doesn't like to be noticed. Very natural—I was just the same myself when your father was courting, Mark, my dear."

Monday came. My mother was rather fidgety—dressed herself directly after breakfast in her gayest silk gown, and strongly objected to Jean's, of some soft gray stuff—mouse-color—her usual morning dress.

"Oh, don't, please," Jean answered, in a weary tone, "what does it signify?"

"Well!" my mother commented, after watching her stand arranging the drawing-room flowers, her customary daily duty, and then sit down to work in the far window, "Well, I don't think it does signify. Poor Emma Brown! I wonder what she would have thought of her daughter."

And my mother wiped her eyes, for all she seemed so proud and pleased.

Not many minutes after, she rushed back into the drawing-room, all in a flurry—Lady Erlistoun's carriage was coming up the avenue.

"Who is in it?" I asked. Jean did not stir.

"Only herself. Dear me—how very odd of Lord Erlistoun!"

I thought differently.

Lady Erlistoun was a very handsome woman. You saw at once where her son had inherited his delicate profile, his full soft eye. The likeness might have been stronger when she was young, or would be, as he grew old. In their world, the years between twenty-four and forty-four effect much.

She resembled her son in manner too. She paid various elegantly implied compliments to my mother on the exceeding beauty of Lythwaite Hall, and her own desire to see it—then went on graciously to explain how she happened to be staying a night at the Bishop's, and was unwilling to return North without having had the pleasure of making Mrs. Browne's acquaintance, and so on, and so on—never alluding to any particular object of her visit, nor noticing, except by the customary acknowledgment, the lady who was presented to her as "Miss Dowglas."

Nor when, after this formal introduction, Miss Dowglas slowly retreated to her seat, could a less sharp eye than mine have detected the occasional wandering of Lady Erlistoun's—keenly inquisitive as women are of women—anatomizing her at a glance from top to toe.

Jean sat still—proudly quiet, unmistakably fair.

"Miss Dowglas, will you take me to see your rosery? Erlistoun has spoken much of your beautiful roses." This was the first time she had mentioned her son's name.

Jean crossed the room. Lady Erlistoun watched her—every step, every trick of gesture and action of hands, as she showed the flowers in the vases; listened attentively to every word that fell from her lips, dropped easily in that low-toned, pure English—not, alack! as my dear, good Lancashire mother talked.

Let another mother meet equal justice! She, who had been used all her life to these external refinements, valuing them far beyond their worth, and yet they are worth no little, as indications of greater things—let her be judged fairly! Nay, I doubt now, if even my mother's son and Jean's cousin had a right to feel his heart so hot within him, while this noble lady stood conversing with and investigating the other lady—(yes, she recognized that self-evident fact, I saw)—whom her only son desired to set in her own place, as Lady Erlistoun.

And for Jean?

Once or twice, at the bent side-face, at some accidental family tone, which you can detect in most voices, I could see Jean's composure stirred; otherwise she was, as she was sure to be, simply herself. Her mind she could disguise—or rather conceal—and in degree her feelings, but her character never. To attempt it would have been to her an ignoble hypocrisy.

I followed them as they moved slowly up and down the garden, talking of books, pictures, continental life—as Jean could talk if necessary, and did so. In no way could I detect in her the least faltering—the least paltering with what she owed to herself, or to us Brownes.

Us Brownes. Though Lady Erlistoun was extremely gracious, though she had too much self-respect not to fulfil to the last letter whatever courtesy she had evidently set herself to perform—still one felt, if one did not see, the soft, intangible, but inevitable line she drew between Jean Dowglas and "us Brownes."

In leaving, she held out her hand—"I trust we shall meet again, Miss Dowglas?"

"You are kind to wish it, Lady Erlistoun."

And so they parted. When, after seeing her to her carriage, I returned to bid my mother and cousin good-by, for I was starting, I found Jean had gone up at once to her own room.

Two days after, my father showed me a letter from Lord Erlistoun, inclosing another from his mother, and from himself a formal application for Miss Dowglas's hand.

A very extraordinary thing, the old man said—quite unaccountable. If he had known what was going on, he should have set his face against it—he didn't like those sort of marriages. But in this case, when the other party had shown such respect and consideration toward the dear girl, and toward us likewise, when it must be a thoroughly disinterested affair, for he remembered telling the young fellow himself, that, except her fifty pounds, Jean had not a penny; —why, he hardly knew what to say about it.

I suggested that none of us ought to say anything. Jean was her own mistress—she must decide.

"You're right, my dear boy—of course she must." And not sorry to have the responsibility lifted off his shoulders, my father, in his own honest way, wrote to that effect.

In four days more I learned, or at least judged from obvious evidence, that she had decided;—Lord Erlistoun was again my father's guest.

That Saturday I did not go down to Lythwaite Hall.

*   *   *   *   *

Youth and love—first love;—let not those who have passed them by turn back and deny either: they are glorious things.

In time I became accustomed to the new order of circumstances—could go home and see those two pacing the garden of mornings, or talking of evenings in the summer Sunday twilight, without feeling that their position toward each other was unnatural or wrong.

This came easier, perhaps, because I saw Jean looked happy. Not at first; but when she saw how happy her lover was—how gradually, under her influence, his whole tone of mind seemed changed, how his character settled and deepened, the fine qualities in him strengthening and the frivolous ones vanishing away—then Jean likewise became at ease and content. She evidently loved him; and love alone will make people happy—for a time, not permanently, at least not that sort of love ·

Even now, sometimes I fancied—could it be only fancy?—a slight shade of doubt—like as when she had asked me so pitifully that night, "Was I so very wrong?" We had never spoken together confidentially again; indeed it was an understood thing in the family, that Jean did not like to be spoken to on the subject of Lord Erlistoun. When and where she was to be married, my mother said she herself had not the least idea—it seemed "rather odd of Jane."

But, either from the inherent weakness of human nature, or something different in the girl herself, every body in the household treated her with great consideration, and offered not the shadow of a reproach to the future Lady Erlistoun.

I was not of them, and had no call to be. Their Jean Dowglas was not mine—never had been. It was a very different thing. And one day, when she was mentioning something she intended to alter in the Lythwaite garden "next year"—I determined to find out the truth about her engagement.

"Next year?—you forget"—and I looked at her left hand, where, as I had noticed, she wore no ring.

With a rather sad smile she turned to me. "No, I did not forget—I know what you are thinking of, but you are mistaken. I told you the truth that night."

"That you should always remain Jean Dowglas?"

"I believe I always shall."

I could not just then find words, or her manner stopped me. She went on—

"Mark I wish to tell you one thing—which is all that any body has a right to know, and I have said it from the first, only nobody here seems to believe it—that Lord Erlistoun is not engaged to me."

"Jean," I cried, for it was hard to think her less than the woman I had always thought her, and yet keep silence, "for the third time I say, Take care! You are attempting a dangerous game—you are playing with edged tools."

"Am I?"

"Beware! Two people may go on together easy and friendly for a long time; but after love is once confessed, or even suspected, they must be lovers, or nothing. I speak as a man. You women know not what you do; you are toying with burning coals when you play fast and loose with a man's heart. It is worse than folly—wickedness. Let there be no half-measures—take him, or reject him—love him, or let him go."

I spoke hotly, out of the bitterness of my soul; but she was neither hurt nor angry. A little reproach there was in her eyes, as if in me, at least, she had looked for something she did not find.

"Mark, can not you understand the possibility of loving *and* letting go?"

CHAPTER V.

Toward the end of the season, which lasted longer than usual that year, we all went up to London for a month, not with any great show, or to enter on expensive gayeties—my father, without assigning any reason, forbade that. He went back to Liverpool, leaving the family under my charge, at a handsome lodging in Baker Street. There was only my mother and Jean, Charles (now the Reverend Charles—we were very proud of that " Reverend") having gone to his curacy and promised living; and Russell and Algernon being away, on a reading tour.

Lord Erlistoun called at Baker Street almost daily; in the Park I had continually to lift my hat to that handsome carriage, where, placed beside Lady Erlistoun's smiling fashionable face, was one I knew; not altered—no outward circumstances could alter Jean, except that, by the contrast, it seemed sometimes a little graver than it used to be.

Well, she had chosen her lot; she was old enough to know her own mind, and to be the arbitress of her own destiny.

Frequently, in my duty as temporary head of the family, I took my mother and cousin to the receptions at Erlistoun House. There, having nothing better to do, I used to moralize on the sort of life they led—this noble old family—nobler in strict purity of blood than many modern Dukes and Earls. And, theirs being a type of many others, though of none other had I any experience—I often, in that whirl of society, which makes a centre of contemplative solitude for any man who chooses, took notes of a few facts that we *parvenus*, we daring swimmers, who have struggled into unknown waters by the main strength of our hands, are rather slow to learn.

It seemed to me, that we are looked down upon, not so much for what we are as for what we assume; that the secret of "aristocratic" ease, is its conscious possession of so much that assumption becomes needless. Alas, if we in our generation were as wise as these children of the world, if we valued our sterling ore, our honest manhood and womanhood, as much as they their lovely filagree-work of external refinement, if we were never ashamed of ourselves, I think these, our "betters" in breeding and education—if such they be, the only tangible betterness they possess over us, would be shamed into acknowledging that nobility which worth alone possesses—that power which needs no asserting, since it "cometh not from man but God."

I know that night after night I, Mark Browne, whose father was a clerk and whose mother was a milliner, have gone among the best of the land, the high, the wise, and the fair; the higher I went being the more courteously entreated; that there, amidst velvets and diamonds, I have watched Jean Dowglas, always Jean Dowglas, in her simple attire and free, noble manners; speaking as she chose, dressing as she chose; for she obstinately refused to spend a shilling more than her own humble income; different from all, fearless of all; yet compelling for herself and more than herself, an invariable, instinctive reverence.

Let no one bely truth by doubting the power of it. In the foolish strife between patrician and plebeian, jack-daws and jays, it is only our sham feathers that make us despised, and deservedly, because all shams are despicable. We that keep our own honest plumage shall always be respected and respectable birds. I never heard one sneer, or saw one covert smile against either poor Miss Dowglas or "those wealthy Brownes."

This was one view of the subject, but I noted another.

Splendid as this sort of life was, having apparently no aim beyond that of the old Athenians, "to tell or to hear some new thing;" to seize on some new plan of beauty or delight—it seemed to me exceedingly sad and strange. Not for people in their first youth, when the faculty of enjoyment is so intense that it must needs be right rationally to enjoy—but afterward. I dwell not here on the dark under-side of such a life, but simply on its brightness—a glare like living in a house all glass, with no shadowy corners in it—or tossing from wave to wave with a dazzling sunshiny sea, without anchorage or rest.

Sometimes coming from one of those assemblies, where in the whole of Erlistoun House you could not find a single nook to make a fireside of—not a single bare jeweled neck where you could fancy a child nestling to and lisping "mother," I would catch from Jean's corner in the dark carriage, a faint, half-involuntary sigh.

No wonder Lord Erlistoun had been struck by the pleasantness of our middle-class "home." In his sphere, except as an order to the coachman, they seemed hardly to know the meaning of the word.

Lord Erlistoun came to us—or rather to Jean, as I have said, incessantly. And now, catching an occasional flicker of the fire that smouldered in his dark eyes—indicating the "substance underneath" which Jean had once said she should like to get at—ah, foolish Jean! I began to perceive some reason why, for his own sake, it was better that he should be allowed to come.

His mother never hindered him. All her plans for him seemed to have vanished in air, conquered or made void by his own impetuous will. She was a wise woman—Lady Erlistoun; something better than a mere woman of the world, too; for Jean always said when questioned that she "liked" her.

One forenoon Jean and I sat together, in total silence, for I had business letters to attend to; and the present surfeit of "pleasure" made me feel business to be even a respite and rest. Jean was by the window, watching the rattling confusion of the London street; she hardly looked like the rose-cheeked, active Jean Dowglas, who used to loiter about with me, of early spring mornings, before Lord Erlistoun had ever been seen or heard of at Lythwaite Hall.

Those far-away days were never mentioned now. Happily, I can put aside times and seasons, thoughts and feelings, when I will—that is, when my conscience wills. Not destroying aught—nothing save evil may be destroyed—but locking all up and keeping the key. I never contest any thing with any body—I simply resign. Absolutely and utterly; let small rights go with the great ones; I never would claim, or beg, or struggle for one iota that was not freely and solely mine.

Thus, Jean and I rarely talked to one another more than habit made necessary; thus, to-day, hearing a knock at the door, I merely observed that it was doubtless Lord Erlistoun, and began putting aside my papers.

"No, it is Lady Erlistoun; I was expecting her. Mark, do not go; I wish you would not go."

Of course, I obeyed.

Lady Erlistoun had never before called at this early, familiar hour, rarely alone, as now. She saluted Jean, French fashion, in her lively loveless way, thanked her for admitting herself so early, hoped she was not weary with her exertions last night.

"But really, ma chère, your singing is perfection. Mr. Browne, why did you not tell me of it before? Such charming simplicity, and yet thorough finish of style! Your cousin might have studied under Garcia himself."

"I did for a little while"—Lady Erlistoun look surprised—"At one time I meant to be a professional singer."

"Oh, indeed."

"It would not have been quite the life I would have chosen, but it appeared necessary I should earn my own living. I had only my voice, and I would thankfully have used it. However, I had no need, and may not have."

"No, certainly not," and the visitor began talking graciously to me—would have talked me out of the room if she could—for that was the usual result of her benignity toward me. But Jean's directness ended all difficulty.

"I believe, Lady Erlistoun, you had something to say to me? Need I banish my cousin Mark, who is as good as a brother to me who have none?"

Lady Erlistoun bowed a negative. "My communication is very simple—possibly Erlistoun had told you, his lady confessor? Nay, he said his decision depended on yours. Truly there could not be a more devoted worshiper than my son, at this fair shrine."

Her light recognition, implying the lightness of the bond—did it hurt Jean? However, she replied, steadily.

"Lord Erlistoun is kind; nor could he leave any decision concerning him in safer hands; but as you both knew, I claim no right to influence his plans."

Lady Erlistoun smiled. "I see. He must make his own confession, implore his own absolution."

"I trust he knows me better than to do either."

Jean's earnestness surprised the mother into something of the same. She asked in a low tone,

"Miss Dowglas, am I to understand that no tie exists between you and my son? Is the engagement broken?"

"There never was any on his side, as I thought he had long since told you. He has always been free—perfectly free."

A glitter in Lady Erlistoun's eyes—faint reflex of that in her son's sometimes. "Do not let us argue nominal points; I will tell you this plan of mine, which I have long desired to carry out. It is, that my son and I should take a tour together through Italy, Greece, and the Holy Land. A charming country, the Holy Land?"

This last remark, addressed to me, I answered by one or two more, to give Jean time. Presently she said,

"Would it be a long tour, Lady Erlistoun?"

"Only two or three years, or a little less."

"And when should you start?"

"Immediately."

Jean inquired no further, but sat quiet. Something—it could not be color, for she was now always pale—faded out of her face, like the light cast on a window when the sun goes down—faded too gradually to indicate that it was unexpected, or in any sense a sudden loss; still it was a loss; a something that had been, and was not.

"Tell me, what do you think of this plan, Miss Dowglas?"

"I think, if Lord Erlistoun wishes it, and since his mother wishes it, he will—there can be no doubt that you ought to go."

"'Ought'—your favorite word. Nay, you have ingrafted it on a certain young friend of ours. He is always talking of what he 'ought' to do. Seriously"—and there was a kindliness under her sportive air—"a mother owes thanks for any good influence which at a critical time of his life is exercised over her son."

Jean's mouth trembled.

"I am really sorry to take him from you for this tour; but you know him as I know him, my dear Miss Dowglas—a noble fellow—the soul of honor, both in principle and practice; but a little—just a little—however, that will amend."

What would amend? Jean must have known, for she answered slowly and firmly—"I believe it will."

"Once—I may speak before your cousin, I know? once I wished Erlistoun to marry early; and even now, I think"—hesitating, with a passing survey of the face and form, less fresh and fair than it was under the first maternal investigation in the Lythwaite drawing-room—"I think sometimes if you would listen to him—"

"No," Jean interrupted hastily, "he had better not marry early. It would not be for his good that he should marry me."

"Have you told him so?"

"From the first. But he will not hear it. He will not let me go. He loves me, *now*."

Oh, what depths of meaning lay in that half-uttered—I know she did not mean to utter it—that quickly smothered "now."

Lady Erlistoun might have heard it, or might not. I suspect she did, and understood it likewise. Taking Jean's hand, she said, out of the heart that may have beat truly, or even passionately some time, possibly, since she married at twenty, for another Lord Erlistoun, "I never wish my son to love a nobler woman."

From that day I ceased to avoid Jean's lover so much as I was accustomed to do. The lover in him interested me in spite of myself; this persistent pursuit and absorbing worship of the woman who had taken hold of his best self as well as of his imagination, and had become to him higher and purer than a passion, an ideal. Yet, there was no lack of passion either—quick jealousies, brief angers; all that sparkling and crackling of a fire which burns fierce, bright, and *fast*; but one can not readily detect that while it is burning.

A young man, passionately, deeply, and disinterestedly in love, has always in him something worthy of respect. Nor, while women are still women, and to be loved touches and ennobles their nature as to love ennobles a man's, did it seem any marvel or shame that this devotion of his was not altogether wasted on a mere idol, marbly cold. For all Jean said, I, catching many a look and tone less sedulously guarded now that the time of parting drew near, began to feel sure that, though she might test her lover's faith, or, for his own sake, refuse to bind him by a formal engagement—still, soon or late, she would marry Lord Erlistoun.

The day before his departure, his cab was at the door before nine o'clock. I heard his quick footstep springing up the stairs and his familiar entrance into the back drawing-room, where Jean stood watering her flower-stand; of all the gifts he would have loaded her with, she refused every thing but flowers.

"I am come to stay all day—may I?"

Jean smiled; she was busy over a sickly heliotrope, withering in London air—"I can't keep it alive, you see."

"Never mind it—keep it while 'tis worth any thing, and then throw it away. But you did not answer me. Say, may I stay? or do you wish me to go?"

"No!" her hand slipped into his. "This last day? No."

He had never spent a whole day in Baker Street before—he soon became very restless, pacing up and down the dull drawing-room suite, which was all our establishment. No charming nooks to sit and talk in, as at Erlistoun House—no sunshiny gardens to make love in, as at Lythwaite Hall. If, indeed, Jean had allowed any "love-making;" which she did not. Only in the eyes that, however quiet she was,

seemed always to take note of him and his enjoyment, you could see the utter unselfish love, which, abhorring all coquetry, found its best demonstration in silence.

At last, when he had sat listening amiably to my good mother's long-winded confidences of our lodging-house woes—Jean put her work away, and proposed we should all go once more to our frequent haunt, the Crystal Palace.

"But it is Thursday—one of the people's days?"

"I am one of the people: I should like to go."

So she went.

Already it is half forgotten—soon it will become a mere tale to tell our children—that People's Palace of 1851. Yet, oh! the beauty and wonder of it, when you came out of dusty London, and stood in the lofty nave, with its captive trees, green but motionless—its lines of white statues—its crystal fountain. The fairy-land it was! Till, advancing, you caught the "hum innumerous" of the moving crowd, which thenceforward never left you. Such a grand, touching, infinitely human crowd: its huge mass giving an impression of solitude—its confused incessant noises producing the sense of silence.

I liked to be carried along by that living sea, or else, from one of the end galleries, to watch it rolling on, each atom bearing its unknown individual burden of pleasure or pain. I liked to recognize, by my yearning over them, that every one of these was my brother or my sister—noble or ignoble, rich or poor, learned or unlearned, sinful or innocent—no less my brother and my sister; and as such, never to be overlooked by me, since not one of them was forgotten before God.

Sometimes, too, when the great organ began to sound, I would try to solve many a troubled problem concerning myself and these, by thinking of them, not as now, the most of them laden with useless sorrow, or tainted with apparently irredeemable sin—but as that "great multitude, which no man can number," which, out of all "nations, and kindreds, and people, and tongues," shall yet make the innumerable company of the Church of the First-born.

Feelings like these dwarfed all minor ones, and caused me, when every hour or so I saw emerging from or disappearing in the throng its only two units in which I had any personal interest, to look on them much as I should have done on meeting in that wondrous company, where, we believe, we shall have lost all personality that is not too pure to suffer pain.

I think they enjoyed that day. I myself can still see, as then, Lord Erlistoun's tall head and Jean's slender, sober-hued figure, moving down the long transepts or loitering in the gorgeous courts. And once, fixing a rendezvous, I found them sitting among "the people"—who were dining out of big baskets and filling clumsy drinking-cups at the crystal fountain—nay, Lord Erlistoun rose and took much pains to do the same for some cross, child-laden woman, whose sole answer was a gruff "Thank'ee; you be civiler than most o' the young gentlemen."

Would he have done it of himself? I thought, or only for Jean's smile? Any how, it was better done than undone.

Day waned: a semi-twilight shadowed the courts, while quaint refractions of sunshine flitted about the many-colored carpets and motionless banners of all nations hung along the aisles.

"Let us all come and sit quiet somewhere until the bell sounds."

They two went and sat in the alcove—many will remember it, made of iron-work from Coalbrookdale. They talked earnestly—of what I did not hear, nor ever wish to know. Let no one ever desire to break the sanctity of another's past.

I can think of Jean, even now, as sitting there, her hands crossed, her eyes declined on her lap, listening; or speaking, with sweet eyes lingering on his face—a face beautiful in itself, and beautiful to her, Heaven knows. I will not deny it, or him. God love him! he was Jean's first love.

The gong of dismissal sounded. It made her start—she was often nervous now. That dull, heavy boom seemed to pierce her through and through; when she rose from her chair she could hardly stand.

"She is worn out," I said; "we must take her home."

"Yes, yes. Only five minutes more, for one last walk through the beautiful nave—can you, Jean?"

She smiled assent.

So, leaning on Lord Erlistoun's arm, she walked slowly through, till at the door she stopped, and turned to look back.

Last year, crossing to Kensington Gardens, I, too, stopped, as it might be, on that very spot, and called to mind how we three stood and looked back on that fairy palace, with all its glory of color, form, and sound. What was left of it? Nothing, save (and I thought, happy for those to whom this is left, after the clearing away of their youth's crystal palaces!) free space, light, and air; where the sun may still shine and the grass grow.

Coming home, Lord Erlistoun found a note from his mother, which, with a gesture of annoyance, he passed on to Jean.

"But I will not go—I wonder she can expect it. This, my last night, to be wasted at the Bishop's; she knows I hate going there. Jean, if you knew"— He stopped.

"I know one thing." said Jean's persuasive voice, "that you will not refuse your mother—it is her right."

"And have you no right? Not even this last night! you are cruel."

"Am I?" Jean took out her watch; her hand shook much, but she spoke decisively— "You will have time enough for both. See—one, two, three hours longer with us, then you shall go."

A few more restless reproaches, such as she often had to bear and to smile down, as now. But her smile always calmed him, and—another of those facts which sometimes set me pondering as to the future—her will always ruled.

A quiet hour or so in the slowly-darkening drawing-room, I read at the window for as long as I could, my mother dozed on the sofa. Lord Erlistoun protested against lights; so we had only the fantastic glimmer of the street gaslamp dancing on the wall. By it I could just trace Jean's motionless figure leaning back in the arm-chair—another figure sitting beside her —lastly on the hearth-rug at her feet. One would have smiled, remembered the dignified behavior of Lord Erlistoun at Lythwaite; but it was a matter beyond smiling at, now.

"Will nobody talk?" said Jean, after a long silence.

Some desultory conversation ensued, about people and books, and then his thoughts deserting him, or assuming lover-like forms that were necessarily limited in expression, though on the whole he observed little restraint in the presence of my mother and me—Lord Erlistoun took to repeating poetry.

What a voice it was—rich, deep, and low; how—stealing through the dark, with intentional emphasis, it must have gone direct to any heart that was young and loved him. Even me it touched in a measure; some fragments in particular; because I afterward found them in a book, and because of the deeper meaning they carried than I then wist of. It was a love poem, of course.

"In many mortal forms I rashly sought
The shadow of this idol of my thought;
And some were fair, but beauty dies away,
Others were wise, but honeyed words betray;
And one was true—Ah, why not true to me!
Till, like a hunted deer that could not flee—"

The young man goes rambling on, in language intoxicating with its loveliness, half earthly, half heavenly—till he finds *the* one—the last—and thus describes her:

"Soft as an incarnation of the sun
When light is changed to day, this glorious one
Floated into the cavern where I lay,
And called my spirit, and the dreaming clay
Was lifted by the thing that dreamed below
As smoke by fire, and in her beauty's glow
I stood, and felt the dawn of my long night
Was penetrating me with living light;
I knew it was the vision veiled from me
So many years; that it was—"

"Emily;" supplied Jean, with a little soft laugh, "why did you pause over it? 'tis one of the sweetest names I know."

"I hate it."

Lord Erlistoun started to his feet and would say no more poetry. Certainly, it had struck me as odd that a lover on the eve of parting should expend his feelings in another man's words, or indeed in any words at all. But love takes so many forms, that what seems false to one nature may be essentially true in another.

He continued his old restless walk up and

down the room; Jean sighed, and then went and opened the piano.

"Do you remember this, Mark? you used to like it, though you do not care for music."

Not every body's music; but this, it was a "song without words"—Mendelssohn's. She had played it with the sunbeam dancing on her head that May forenoon at Lythwaite. Before many bars it was broken in upon by Lord Erlistoun.

"'Tis too tame, too quiet. Jean, play something *I* like, or rather do not play at all. Hark!"—the church clock struck—"only one hour now."

He seized her left hand, the other moving vaguely over the treble keys, and began talking to her in a low voice, as lovers do.

I went back to the window. In the middle of the street, singing in a high voice, cracked now, yet not without the ghost of former tunefulness—stood a woman with a baby in her arms, and a boy at her side. Clustering round the gin-palace, farther down, was a knot of still wretcheder women—some with children likewise—dragging in or out refractory husbands—or worse; while appearing and disappearing under the doctor's red lamp opposite our door, passed score after score of all sorts of faces—hardly one in the whole number a contented or good face—which make up the phantasmagoria of London streets of a night.

Without, such sights as these; within, those two, repeating delicious poetry and whispering together over soft music! God help us! I said to myself, is there nothing in the world but love, nothing to live for but happiness?

Oh, Jean, I was hard to thee! Hard even at that moment—and blind, as we almost always are, when we severely judge. I caught Lord Erlistoun's voice, so impetuous that it was impossible not to hear.

"At last you will write to me? you will not forbid my writing to you as often as I please?"

"Did I not promise, long ago?"

"I know, you have made me every promise I could desire, though you will take none from me. Once, again, why will you not? Do you think me changeable?"

Jean repeated, half-jesting, half-sadly, the lines:

" In many forms I rashly sought
The shadow of this idol of my thought."

"I was not the first of these, you know."

"But you will be the last. Oh, Jean, do you not believe I love you?"

"I do—yet—"

"Stop, I know what is coming—the old argument; that your experience and mine have been so different; that you have lived for work and I for enjoyment; that my youth is but just begun; while yours—"

"You brought me back my youth," she murmured. Oh, yes—I have been very happy!"

"Have been! 'Tis always *have been;*" and he said something more, rapidly—incoherent-

ly—his manner being fierce and tender, by turns.

"No," Jean replied, "it is not these things I am afraid of. External differences are nothing with union at the core—love and trust, and—faithfulness."

"Enough; I know," he said, bitterly. "I am not one of your 'faithful' temperaments. You judge me—most wise woman! by the tinge of my skin, and the color of my hair."

"Lord Erlistoun!"

"No—I deny it not, I am a very different person from your cousin Mark there. I am southern to the very core: my blood seems to run like fire sometimes—and you set it alight —you stand by and watch it burning. Jean, you do not love me, you never loved me!"

Jean did not answer for a minute. "Then you think when I promised—you know what —I was false to myself, and worse, to you, after the cruelest falseness any woman can show?"

"Forgive me—oh, forgive me! I love you —yet I am always grieving you."

Again Jean paused before replying. "I take the grief with the love, and would have done the same, twenty times over, because I have hope in you."

She did not say "faith;" faith, the very root and foundation of love; but he never noticed that. "Yes," Jean repeated, "great hope. That is the way with us women, we care less for your loving than for what you are; we can be content if, quite apart from us, we see you every thing that you ought to be. I could."

"Jean, I will be any thing, every thing, if you will be my Jean."

He tried to clasp her, apparently—for she shrank visibly from him.

"Oh, do not!" in an accent of pain, "I feel as if it were not right; I could not unless"— she dropped her face upon her hands. "I know we shall never be more to one another than we are now."

What he replied I can not say; nor what farther last words passed between them. Let all rest sacred, as last words should.

When Jean called me from my room to bid him good-by, Lord Erlistoun was standing by the now lit lamp, exceedingly pale; but proud; more like the Lord Erlistoun of Lythwaite times than as we knew him now. My mother, out of her dear warm heart, extended her hand with a good wish and blessing; when, very much to her surprise, he lifted the hand and kissed it.

"Thank you all for all your kindness; I hope to return it one day, two years hence. Two years, and remember"—he turned to me; whether he liked me or not I think he trusted me—"however free she holds me, I hold Jean Dowglas as my wife. Take care of her, until she is my wife. Good-by."

*   *   *   *   *

He had not been gone a month when there befell our family what, as I am not writing our history but that of Lord Erlistoun, I will state

"Lady Emily Gage—how strange!"

"Not so strange, it's being herself, as that she should have remembered me. She did."

"At the Cathedral?"

"No—but last year—at Erlistoun House. If you recollect, they knew her."

This, then, caused Jean's brightness of mien; this sunny rift out last year's history, which, but for the foreign letters, often seemed no more than a dream, to us at least. Such security must end.

"Jean," I said, "you should have told me before you took such a step as this. For you to teach at all is, to my mind, ill-advised—to become governess, or singing-governess, or whatever you call it, to the Bishop's niece, strikes me as simply impossible."

"Hardly; since I have already promised."

Here my mother, catching my meaning, followed it up loudly.

"My dear, what have you gone and done! what will Lord Erlistoun say?"

Jean was silent.

"If you had been Miss Anybody, it would have been hard enough, my poor child! But for you to turn singing-mistress—you, Jean Dowglas, that is to be Lady ——"

"Oh don't—don't." Her expression of acute pain silenced even my mother. "Let me say a word, and then you and Mark must let me alone. Being Jean Dowglas, I must act as Jean Dowglas, without reference to any body. I believe—" her voice shook a little, "no man would think the less of me he cared for, for doing any thing or every thing that she thought right. It is right for me to help to earn money; I can do it, and wish to do it; this is the easiest way. Besides, I have promised. Don't let us talk any more."

She then gave us a detailed account of her proceedings, and described Lady Emily, now nearly grown up, and one of the loveliest creatures ever seen.

"There is a curious simplicity about her, too, like a plum with the bloom on it. She said she knew my face quite well, and used to creep into dark corners to listen to my singing. Afterward, she had often wondered who I was, and what had become of me."

"What, doesn't she know?" broke out my mother.

"You forget, nobody knows, nor must know. It is much better thus, and much easier for me."

It stung me, the idea of her going among these people with "nobody knowing." The whole position of matters indicated something jarring—something not right. True, Jean's own will had governed every thing—there was, strictly speaking, none to blame; yet I was irritated and sore. The feeling did not wear off for some time.

Yet good rather than evil apparently accrued from this plan. Money was the least thing Jean gained. She soon taught out of love, also—which is a teaching that makes happy. It filled up a certain blank in her life that I had

already begun to notice between the somewhat irregular and lengthening spaces, when those foreign letters came; and supplied the lack of many wants that in our narrow humdrum way of existence a young woman, constantly occupied in tending an old and friendless one, was sure to feel—refinement, cheerful sympathy, associations with those after her own kind.

These explanations I used to make, regarding her ardent delight in this new interest, foreign to us and ours. But mine was an external judgment, as those of mankind often are.

One Sunday Lady Emily alighted, like a bird of Paradise, on the mundane regions of Pleasant Row; and then I found out, or thought I had, a good deal.

"Jean, that 'child,' as you call her, is just like a little lover to you."

Jean smiled—"Well, am I not better, certainly safer than a lover to her? Don't laugh, Mark. Girls often choose their 'first loves' among women—I did myself. What do you think of Lady Emily? Is she altered?"

"I forget what she used to be; but I think she is growing very like you."

Jean laughed in merry incredulity. "What, dark and fair, thin and soft-rounded, seventeen, and nearly twenty-nine. How old I am growing!" She turned grave for a moment, then went back to the argument in question.

Yet my observation had a truth in it. That similarity, either natural or acquired, which I have before noticed is often discernible in people attracted to one another, already showed itself between these two. The stronger nature of course made the impression; in twenty different ways I could trace in Lady Emily the influence of Jean.

I remarked one day, "that she seemed to go to Pleasant Row a good deal."

"Yes, they trust her with me, and she likes coming."

"Truly, I think she would come to Newgate if you were there."

"I know she would," Jean answered, with a soft, grateful tenderness in her tone. "Mark, I am neither Quixotic nor romantic—now; yet it goes to my heart that this child loves me. She has been brought up like a nun, almost; she is as harmless as a dove, and as sweet as a flower. I want to keep the dove her 'silver wings,' to let nothing soil the lovely white flower."

"You can not. Her lot is cast in the world—she must meet it."

"I feel that, and I would not wish to keep her from it. But I would like to make her strong for her perilous place—safe in it, and worthy of it. I want—"

"To 'do her good?'"

Had I thought that phrase would have so wounded Jean, I would have cut my tongue out before I uttered it. Her lip quivered with pain as she answered,

"Do not say that. I shall never say it again."

"Perhaps it is safest not said, or thought, but you need not cease to do it. One like you has only to live in order to do people good."

"Thank you, cousin." Her eyes swam in tears; she sat down silent.

I had brought her a letter that day, which I think she had been expecting a long time. Correspondence seemed more difficult to Lord Erlistoun in the capitals of civilized Europe than to the amateur Bedouin in the Syrian desert.

We men, accustomed to take our sweetest draughts in small gulps, during the intervals of our busy or ambitious lives, can never fully understand how women actually live in letters. They may not own it, even to their own hearts; when the deep root of love—and safer than love, *trust*—is there, you may cut it down over and over again, and it will blossom up afresh; but —'tis cruel handling.

I found this out, when, during an absence of Lady Emily's, her fond, girlish letters came regularly once a week—never missing a day. "As sure as the sun," my mother observed, "real lovers' letters."

Jean turned away.

When her pupil returned there was a gratefulness almost pathetic in the way Jean responded to this love—childlike in its demonstration still, though in most other things the young lady had ceased to be a child. She had learned to have a will and a judgment of her own, and to exercise both in the innumerable ways with which one of her rank and fortune can use a a woman's best "rights"—personal influence. A lovely and lovable creature she was; beside her exquisite fresh bloom, I sometimes fancied even Jean looked faded and old.

Jean, faded?—Jean, growing old? I pondered. Would a man—say any man—regarding the face he loves, think with alarm, or with a solemn and yearning tenderness, of how it will look when it is growing old?

Another winter passed—another summer; in the autumn my father would have been dead two years.

Two years. Was it with another chronology than this of death that Jean now laid aside her black gowns? Her looks and her step lightened; voluntarily or involuntarily, she was evidently hoping, if not believing.

About this time I myself received a letter from Lord Erlistoun.

It stated his extreme regret that circumstances of which Miss Dowglas was aware—he had written to her by the same mail—prevented his immediate return to England. That he must leave in my charge for a few months longer, "his best treasure in the world."

I gave Jean the letter without comment, and she made none. Her time was just then fully occupied, for Lady Emily was going on a tour, to Switzerland I believe; and it was hard for Jean to refuse her "little lover's" earnest wish for her companionship.

"I can't," she said, when I urged too—promising to remove all scruples on account of my mother—"I can't go abroad. Oh, no! I was never fit for any thing but quiet and home."

And after Lady Emily was gone, she seemed to turn more than ever to what, if peace, unity, and affection could make it so, was indeed, with all its narrowness, a "home." I can see her now, as she used to sit on Sunday afternoons, crouching down with her arm across my old mother's lap, and her great wistful, weary eyes fixed opposite on me, as I tried to amuse them and make them merry. Sometimes, after listening and laughing a little, she would end with a sigh of relief:

"Oh, Mark, how comfortable you are!"

These "treasures," which some are readier to prate of than to prize, yet others must neither covet nor steal! Thank God, I was always true to myself, and to both of these.

Day by day I watched Jean's round cheek straighten into the line which marks youth's departure. Once, stooping her head as she sat, she said, "Mark, see here!" and in an under lock of her hair were distinct white threads, too many to count.

I hardly know the sort of feeling it gave me, except that it was not altogether one of pain.

CHAPTER VII.

"In a few months" had been Lord Erlistoun's date of return—indefinite as most of his dates were. During November, December, January, February, March, I brought his letters to Pleasant Row, at the usual uncertain intervals, and with the usual variable post-marks—then they paused.

It was again spring. I think there is a time of life before we learn to recognize and acquiesce in the mysterious law of mutation, in ourselves as in the external world, when the return of spring is intensely painful. Walking with her by the railings of budding suburban gardens, catching at street-corners bits of soft white and blue spring skies—I could trace in Jean's profile an expression that went to my heart.

Not a word she said; but often a knock at the door would make her start and tremble; and I noticed that she never went out or came in without leaving the careful message, "I shall be back at such and such an hour," or the question, studiedly careless—"Has any body been?"

No! There never was any body; and she used to walk up stairs, slowly, wearily; then, after a few minutes, come out of her own room with her bonnet off and her hair smooth—pale and quiet; that day and its chances were over.

I broke through my customary rule, and used to come up to Pleasant Row almost every evening. One day I got a holiday, and invited myself to dinner with them, laden with a nosegay and "many happy returns" to my cousin Jean.

The tears started involuntarily as she said,

"Thank you, Mark; you remembered it."
Alas, no one else.

I had formed my plan, a little to lighten the heaviness of this day; I laid before her two green tickets inscribed with "Sacred Harmonic Society, Exeter Hall." It did one good to see the brightening of her eyes.

"To-night! and it is the 'Lobjesang' and 'Requiem.' Oh, Mark!"

"You'll go then, madam? In an omnibus, with your bonnet on, and sit all in the crowd among the people? with an individual who doesn't understand music?"

"Cousin Mark!" She laughed, which was all I wanted.

So cheerily out into the spring evening, then shutting the omnibus-door upon the sunset, and jolting into the gas-lit London streets, we went together, my cousin Jean and I. Her hand on my arm, her voice talking at my side, her bright look turned back every minute as I put her in front of me and tried to keep her safe amidst the waiting crowd, thankful to my heart that for ever such a little while I could have her to myself, and make her happy; that this night, at least this hour, should be marked with a white stone.

I suppose nowhere in the world are music meetings like these at Exeter Hall; counting musicians by hundreds, and audience by thousands. Nowhere, probably, can a true music-lover feel keener pleasure than to be among that sea of heads, looking up the sloping hill of music-stands, gradually appropriated, till on the sweet discords of universal tuning booms out the solid, majestic C, of the great organ. Then the murmurous human waves calm down—the feast begins.

Mendelssohn's "Hymn of Praise." Every body knows it, its noble opening symphony which musicians love; and the chorus, "*All that hath life and breath, sing to the Lord.*" Jean turned to me—her eyes beaming. The great music-flood came pouring out, rolling and rolling round us; with a happy sigh, she plunged in it, and was swallowed up and lost.

And to me, better than music it was to watch her absorbed listening face, as the soft notes of "*I waited for the Lord,*" dropped like oil into her troubled heart, till after "*Watchman, will the night soon pass?*" burst the chorus "*The night is departing—departing!*"—then it brimmed over. Large tears gathered and fell, washing away the hard lines of pain, and leaving her dear face as peaceful as a child's. I knew it would do her good; and though the features quivered, and tears were dropping still, I saw that her spirit, as well as her voice, was joining in the line which makes the beginning and end of this "Lobjesang"—"All that hath life and breath, sing to the Lord."

I let the healing dew fall, and would not talk to her. In the interval I stood up, vaguely noticing the people round us; intelligent, expressive countenances, as one mostly sees in an audience at Exeter Hall; then across the division to the ten-and-sixpenny "reserved" folk, who probably did not enjoy it near so much as we. It amused me to glance along row after row of those bright-colored opera cloaks and bare decked heads; and then think of the bent head beside me—*the* one among all those thousands, every hair of which, poor gray hairs and all! was more precious than gold to—one other.

I think—I am sure—for that moment, in its silence fuller than whole months of my usual life, I had quite forgotten Lord Erlistoun. It was a shock almost like seeing a ghost rise from the dead; or, better simile, like the quiet Elysian-dwelling dead being suddenly confronted by an apparition of flesh and blood—that out of these rows I saw a young man's tall head rise. The height, the carriage, the impetuous toss back of the hair—I could not be deceived; it was Lord Erlistoun.

Lord Erlistoun, here in England?—going to concerts, sitting gayly among his own friends—his mother, and two other ladies were with him. And what of Jean Dowglas?

I sat down doggedly, without a word or sign; placing myself so that when she turned to me she must turn from him. I need not; for she never stirred, only said, with a soft comfortable sigh—

"Oh, Mark, this has been such a happy birth-day!"

That decided me. Come what would, this day—perhaps the last, should be hers; and mine. So I sat by her, careful and close, and heard in a sort of dream, Mozart's Mass for the dead—the crash of the "Dies Iræ"—the "Rex tremendæ"—the "Agnus Dei," with its heavenly close, like the shutting of the peaceful gates of the grave upon all human pain—"*Dona nobis requiem.*"

Then the evening was over.

Very quietly, close, arm and arm, Jean and I went out with the press; just one minute, and I should have had her safe out into the street, but it was not to be.

There is a spot at the foot of the stair-case, just where the two streams of audience mix. Here, direct face to face, we met Lord Erlistoun!

Smiling and talking, with that air of absorbed attention which it was his habit to bestow on any woman, as if she were to him, for the time being, the only woman in the world; with his handsome head stooping over and his careful chivalric arm protecting the lady in his charge—undoubtedly, Lord Erlistoun.

He might have passed us by unperceived, but this lady's eyes were quicker. "Miss Dowglas! my dear Miss Dowglas!" cried the happy voice of Lady Emily Gage.

So—a pause and a greeting. It lasted only a moment, for there was a call of "Lady Erlistoun's carriage," and they two were pressed onward in the crowd; Jean and I being left together. She hung heavily on my arm. I said, "Shall we go home?"

"Yes."

We had scarcely got clear out into the Strand, when some one touched me.

"Mr. Browne! where is she ?"

Jean leaned slightly forward; he sprang to her side and caught her hand.

"I must go home with you—where is your carriage ?" He had forgotten, doubtless, but recollected soon. "It will be pleasanter walking. You must allow me," taking firm possession of Jean's passive arm, he hurried her on, as if hardly knowing what he said or did.

"My mother is gone home with them—we are staying there; we have not been in England more than a day or two. This meeting is so strange, I can hardly believe it. Jean, oh, Jean!" — with a sudden alarmed glance, for hitherto she had not uttered one word.

I called a vehicle; Lord Erlistoun almost lifted her into it. He sat opposite, holding both her hands, and gazing at her, till slowly the color came back into her face. She took her hands gently away, saying, in a tremulous voice—

"You are welcome home."

We reached Pleasant Row. The narrow door and dark stair-case—the little parlor, with tea laid out, and the kettle singing on the fire, seemed considerably to surprise Lord Erlistoun. When my mother came forward, in her widow's cap and altered looks, he was more than surprised—moved.

"My dear Mrs. Browne—my dear Mrs. Browne," he kept saying; greeting her with a friendly sympathy that was even affectionate, and by its unexpectedness startled the dear old lady into a few natural tears.

"You find us sadly changed, indeed, Lord Erlistoun."

"No, no, no," he repeated several times; replacing her in her arm-chair, and taking his seat by her, with an air of earnest friendliness.

And Jean Dowglas? She stood looking on, forgotten for the moment—yet her pale face was all radiant. When at last Lord Erlistoun turned round in search of her—she had gone. Several minutes, and various though brief explanations, passed before we heard her hand on the door.

Lord Erlistoun rose, took that hand and kissed it, openly. "Jean, I have been hearing a great deal which you never told me. In all those long good letters of yours, you never once told me ?"

Half-reproachfully he spoke; and again, with a sort of tender deference, kissed her passive hand.

Then, her manner being equally passive, though composed, Jean took her place and began to pour out tea.

Lord Erlistoun was certainly altered. Younger-looking if possible, as a man in his settled prime is often younger than an unsettled *blasé* boy. His impetuosity was lessened; and there was about him a new atmosphere of repose which in itself is strength. He talked as much as or more than he used to do—chiefly of his travels;

mentioning incidentally, in reply to a question of mine, that they had traveled home with the Bishop and Lady Emily, whom they met in Switzerland: but his conversation was on the whole general rather than personal, and interspersed with fits of gravity and silence.

Thus we all sat till very late; Lord Erlistoun and Jean side by side, like lovers. Yet I noticed not one lover-like whisper—not one glance of discontent at the presence of my mother and me. He was evidently satisfied with things as they were; content to have her sitting by him, himself unengrossed and unengrossing; testifying none of those exquisite sweet selfishnesses, that passionate personality of right, which marks the line, often so fine as to be all but imperceptible, between mere affection, however trusting and true, and love—absolute lordly love, that, giving all, requires all, and will have it—or nothing.

Did Jean see this, or seeing feel it ? Did she understand as a man would, that to any true lover it would have been torment to have to sit looking at her sweet face—two other faces looking on ? That after this long parting, to part from her again, though but for twelve hours, with that quiet good-night, that easy lifting of her cool fingers to cool lips, would have been intolerable—impossible ?

Where was all his passion gone to ? *His* passion ? Pshaw! A petty flame

"That doth in short, like paper set on fire,
Burn—and expire."

What had he known—this boy "in love"—of the real passion, strong as silent—capable of any endurance, daunted by no opposition; like the fire in the heart of a mountain, out of its very fervency growing pure; patient under loss —yet content with no medium between total loss and total gain; exacting, perhaps, yet supplying all that it exacts; the love that swallows up all other petty loves, and rises sole and complete, unalienated and unalienable—the love that a man ought to have for his wife ?

Again, for the hundredth time, I was unjust to Lord Erlistoun. Once more, as I paced the solitary street, till the moon set behind the terrace opposite, and Jean's long-lingering candle went out in the attic-story of Pleasant Row, I judged hastily, uncharitably, as we always must when measuring other people by our own line and rule. I forgot—alas, that we less seldom forgot!—how Providence never makes any two trees to grow after one pattern, or any two leaves of the same tree exactly alike.

This was Friday—or rather Saturday—for I did not reach home till dawn. On Sunday morning I rose and walked ten miles out into the country to a little church I knew; not appearing at Pleasant Row till evening.

Jean was out. They had called for her in the carriage—Lady Erlistoun and Lady Emily Gage; the latter was to return with her after dinner.

"Does Lady Emily know ? I think she ought," I said, after a long pause.

"About Jean's engagement? Most likely. But I take no notice, Jean is so very particular."

"He was here yesterday?"

"Oh, yes, and Lady Erlistoun likewise. They treat her with great respect, you see. Poor Jean, how I shall miss her when she is married—"

"Hush, I hear carriage wheels."

They entered all together, Jean, Lady Emily, and Lord Erlistoun. The latter, of course, was invited by my mother to remain.

Lady Emily looked surprised, but said nothing; except afterward, with a pretty childish willfulness, observing that "if he staid he was not to interrupt the thousand-and-one things she had to say to her dear Miss Dowglas."

No; it was plain the happy, innocent creature did not know; Jean had not told her. I thought—was it right or wrong of Jean?

She gave them, Lord Erlistoun and Lady Emily, the guests' places at either corner of the old-fashioned sofa, and herself sat opposite, at the tea-table. The smile, always ready to answer Lady Emily's, though exceedingly soft was very grave, as if she were a great deal older than either of these.

A strange evening—I often now look back and wonder at it; at the mysterious combinations of fate that arise, not only among evil but good people—placing them in positions where right seems hardly distinguishable from wrong; where every step is thick with netted temptations, every word, even of kindness or affection, like the whipping of another with a rod of thorns.

Lord Erlistoun comported himself blamelessly. If in Lady Emily's artless admission it came out that they had been incessantly together, dreaming over art and poetry in Italian cities—learning great lessons, and forming noble plans of life under the shadow of the Alps—it also came out that this bond had hitherto never passed the limits of simple "friendship." Likewise that its foundation had evidently been in a certain other friend, whom, without naming, he said she resembled, but whom she in her humility never thought of identifying with that dear friend of her own, who used to talk to her "just like Lord Erlistoun."

"'The noblest woman he ever knew,' he said you were"—whispered she with her arm round Jean's waist. "I might have guessed it could be none other than my own Jean Dowglas."

Jean kissed her. They were standing at the window—where, far over chimneys and roof-tops, spread the bright soft sky.

"What a lovely evening! Lord Erlistoun was saying on Friday morning, at Richmond—that he never remembered so beautiful a spring."

No? Not that at Lythwaite Hall? He had forgotten it. He was gazing, with an uneasy air, at the two faces, strongly contrasted, and yet bearing a shadowy likeness each to each, the woman's and the girl's.

Steadily, with the manner of one not startled into very sudden conclusion, but to whom pre-

vision has been already preparation, Jean looked down into those happy eyes.

"My child, at your age, and Lord Erlistoun's —every thing is, and ought to be, beautiful spring."

He heard, as she must have meant him to hear. Shortly afterward I noticed that he took occasion to sit by her side, and talk desultorily but pointedly to Miss Dowglas, and her alone. Jean listened.

People think they can be generous hypocrites, and hide their feelings marvelous well; but they can not. All vain tenderness, conscience, pride of honor, fear of giving pain, can not swaddle up a truth. Through some interstice of glance or action it will appear, naked and cold, yet a tangible, living truth.

Thus, though he sat by her side, paid her every observance, though in every tone of his voice was unfeigned regard, even tenderness, as if conscious of some involuntary wrong, still to one who knew what love is and is not, it became clear as daylight that Lord Erlistoun's present feeling for Jean Dowglas was no more that of two years since—than the wax simulacra he was now eloquently describing to her, set in church niches and dressed up with flowers, compared with the warm breathing womanhood, adored yet beloved, of the saint that once had been.

His reverence, his esteem, remained; but his love had died. Of natural decay? or, perhaps, at his age and with his temperament, of an equally natural change—substitution? If so, that fact had been carefully and honorably concealed. He was neither coxcomb nor brute—he was a gentleman. His attentions all that evening, without being marked, remained sole and undivided, and the object of them was undoubtedly Jean Dowglas.

Once or twice I saw Lady Emily glance at them both with a flitting troubled suspicion; then smile her happy smile. No, it was not possible.

This young man, in the full glory of his youth, toned down by a maturer wisdom, learned—no matter how or from whom; his career just opening before him—a career worthy of a true English nobleman, in his hands the triple power of rank, wealth, and education, and the will worthily to use all three. And Jean Dowglas, a woman past her prime—youthful pleasures having ceased to be her pleasures—having been beaten to and fro in the world till even in her brightest moods her very enjoyment was grave, and you could trace at times a certain weariness of aspect, which betokened that the haven she sought was less happiness than rest.

No! love might exist, or that lingering regard which assumed its name; but unity, that oneness of sympathy in life and life's aims, which alone makes marriage sacred or desirable —between these two, was no longer possible.

Lady Emily departed—Lord Erlistoun put her in the carriage; then, instead of returning, asked me if I would walk with him for half an hour?

We strolled up the road together; at first in silence, then, as with a tacit right, he asked me various questions concerning our family and Jean. Finally, in a manly, serious way he thanked me for my fulfillment of my "charge," and hoped I should ever remain his "good cousin."

Returning, we found Jean sitting by the newly-lit lamp, a book open before her. She had been reading to my mother the Evening Psalm. She looked up as we entered. "Did you think I was gone?" said Lord Erlistoun.

"No; oh, no."

He sat down by her, and began to enter more fully into his plans about attempting the sole vocation which is readily open to young men in his position—politics. All his remarks were clear and good, evidently the result of much thought and a deep sense of responsibility for all the blessings of his lot.

"They are many," Jean said, gently.

"Do you think so?" He sighed. "Yes, you are right. Surely you did not imagine I thought otherwise?"

"I should not be likely to imagine anything unworthy of you."

"Thanks—thanks." He then asked if she approved of his plan of life. "I used to call you my conscience, you know. Are you satisfied?"

"I am satisfied."

Something in her manner struck him. He gave a quick glance at her, but under the shadow of the long, thin hand, the mouth which spoke looked not less sweet than ordinary.

Still Lord Erlistoun seemed not quite at ease. He began to move about the parlor, taking up one or two things that ornamented the chimney-piece—small relics saved out of the wreck, which Jean had bought in at the sale.

"I think I remember this vase. It used to stand on the side-table at —"

"Oh, do not!" At the sharp pain of Jean's voice, he turned—took her hand.

"Did you think I had forgotten Lythwaite?"

"No, no—you will not, you could not. If you wished ever so, you could not forget."

"I hope," he began, but Jean had recollected herself now.

"It hurts me to talk of Lythwaite; we will not do so any more."

"As you please."

And I saw that either she had removed her hand, or it had slipped from his. He did not attempt to take it again. They sat talking, side by side, as friend with friend, until the time that his carriage arrived.

Lingering about, still restless, he began turning over Jean's little book-shelf.

"Ah, did I give you this? how fond I was of it once! Here is my mark, too;" and he ran over the lines to himself, warming over them as he went. They were the very same he had re-

peated with such fervid passion the night before he left England. With the same intonation, yet different, he repeated them now, up to the same close—

"I knew it was the vision veiled from me
So many years—that it was—

" 'Emily.' "

Again, for the second time, Jean had supplied the word, in a low, steady voice, as conveying the simple statement of a fact—no more. Lord Erlistoun started violently, crimsoned up to his very brow, shut the book, and pushed it away, saying, hurriedly—

"I must take to blue-books now — I have done with poetry. Good-night, all — good-night, Jean."

———

CHAPTER VIII.

LIFE, like love, has its passive as well as active phase—its season of white winter, when all external vitality ceases, and the utmost exercise of reason and faith is necessary to convince us that any vitality exists at all. We walk on, darkly and difficultly, as far as each day will carry us—no farther.

Thus, for many days, I know not how many, did I go to and fro between my lodgings and Mincing Lane, pleading press of business to excuse my absence, if excuse were needed, at Pleasant Row. In all there happening I was as powerless as if I abode at the North Pole. It was better to keep away.

But as firmly as I believe in the life of nature, sleeping under the snow, so I believe, and did then, in the everlasting vitality of truth, of right, and what is in one sense lesser than, yet in its purest form identical with both these—love. Yes, I believe in love. Despite its many counterfeits and alloys, some so like it that for a time they may even pass current for it; with all its defilements and defacements, too pitiable to be unpardonable—I doubt not that at the core of every honest man's and woman's heart lies that true coin which, its value found, is a life's riches, and if never found, is yet a life's possession; being still pure gold, and stamped with the image and superscription of the Great King.

I had learned much in these few years; I, Mark Browne, was no longer the Mark Browne whose rough-built castle in Spain crumbled down at a word or two, lightly uttered under those chestnut-trees. It fell as, being baseless, it perhaps deserved to fall; the sole architectural effort of a too-late developed youth; we men build differently. It seemed now as if I had never been thoroughly a man till the responsibility of those two dear women fell on me, making me conscious at once of my weakness and my strength.

Ay, my strength; "magna est veritas et prevalebit," as runs the little Latin I ever had opportunity to learn. A man who has truth in himself must be very dim-sighted not to detect

C

the true from the false in others, and he who can trust himself is not afraid to trust fate—that is, Providence—for all things.

My poor Jean! my sorely-tossed, tempted, long-tried Jean, with neither father, brother, nor friend; not a heart, that she knew of, to lean against for counsel or rest! Sometimes I thought I would go to her; and then—No. My old doctrine, that silence may be lawful, hypocrisy never, took from me the possibility of being Jean's counselor. Besides, all she did must be out of her own unbiased rectitude; all she had to suffer must necessarily be suffered alone.

Oh, no, Jean, not alone! If people could tell, afterward, the burdens they have borne for others, secretly and unasked, the days of sickening apprehension, the nights of sleepless care, when, rationally or irrationally, the mind recurs with a womanish dread to all possible and probable evils, and racks and strains itself, beating against the bounds of time, distance, or necessity, when it would give worlds only to arise and go.

At last, one evening, I snatched up my hat and went.

A carriage was driving from the door of Pleasant Row; I turned up the next street. There it passed me again, and I saw leaning back in a thoughtfulness that was absolute melancholy, the sweet face of Lady Emily Gage. My cynical mood vanished in an abstract sort of pity for four persons who shall be nameless, but whose names, no doubt, ministering angels knew.

Lord Erlistoun I found sitting with my mother: both started, and "thought it was Jean."

"Is Jean out alone, and in this pouring rain?"

"I can't help it, Mark—she will go. But I forget you do not know she has taken fresh pupils, and works as hard as if all her life she intended to be a poor singing-mistress."

Lord Erlistoun sprang up, and went to the window. There he stood, till the knock at the door announced Jean.

Dripping, muddied, with a music-book under her arm—pale, with the harassed look that all teachers gradually get to wear—she stood before this young man, by nature and education so keenly sensitive to external things. Perhaps she felt the something, the intangible something, which all his courteous kindliness could not hide; she flushed up, and with a word or two about "never taking cold," went to her room.

Contrasts are good, but not such contrasts as these. Yet different from them, and more momentous, were other things that throughout the evening incessantly arose, making Jean start like one who, trying to walk steadily, is always treading here on a thorn and there on a sharp stone; those little things which, involuntarily, unconsciously, are the betrayal of love's decay.

She took her work, Lord Erlistoun sitting by her, idle; she asked him, mechanically, where he had been all the week; and he answered, in

a sort of apology, giving a long list of engagements "impossible to avoid."

"I did not mean that; I know you must be very much occupied. You were at the drawing-room on Thursday?"

"Yes; it was necessary, returning from abroad and expecting soon to return, on the diplomatic business I told you of."

Jean bent her head. "Lady Emily was there. I saw her dressed. She looked very beautiful—did she not?"

"I believe so."

Here my mother broke in with Lady Emily's message, and how, finding Lord Erlistoun here and Jean absent, she would not stay. "She was rather cross—if so sweet a creature could be cross. I fancy her gay life does not suit her; she looks neither so well nor so happy as she did six months ago."

Lord Erlistoun's was a tell-tale countenance at best; it told cruel tales now, and Jean saw it. Hers expressed less of doubt or pain than infinite compassion; but when he looked up he started as if he could not bear her eyes.

"What are you so busy about? You are always busy."

"I am correcting counter-point exercises of my pupils."

"Those pupils," he repeated with irritation. "Mr. Browne, can not you, whose influence here seems at least equal to my own, represent how unnecessary, how exceedingly unsuitable it is for Miss Dowglas to continue taking pupils?"

"She never had any, until now; with the exception of Lady Emily Gage."

He was silent.

Jean said gently, "My pupils do me no harm but good. To work is necessary to me. I have worked all my life; I believe it always will be so."

"What do you mean?"

"I will tell you another day."

"Jean—Miss Dowglas—I trust that you—"

"Hush, pray—I said another day."

Lord Erlistoun somewhat haughtily assented. For the rest of the evening he talked chiefly to my mother and me—scarcely to Jean at all. But just before leaving he drew her a little aside.

"I have never, in the short time since my return, been able to have speech with you alone. May I call to-morrow? and, in the mean time, will you please me by accepting this?"

He placed on the third finger of her left hand a ring blazing with diamonds. Before she could speak, he was gone.

During the short time I remained after him, Jean sat where he had left her, the ring still flashing on her hand—which was now beginning to lose its shapely roundness, and grow thin and worn-looking, like an old woman's hand.

Next day, a carriage and pair astonished Mincing Lane, and in the dim office which, at this time of the afternoon, I usually had all to myself, entered Lord Erlistoun. He was evidently in much agitation.

"Pardon me, I will not detain you two minutes; but I wished, before waiting upon your cousin, to ask if you had in any way counseled or influenced this letter?"

My surprise was enough to testify my total ignorance.

"I thought so; I always knew you for a man of honor—you would suggest nothing that could compromise mine. Read this, and judge between us."

The idea of a third party judging between two lovers!—I hesitated.

"I beg you to read it; you being in some sense her guardian, I claim this as my right."

A brief letter:

"MY DEAR FRIEND,—With this, I return your ring. Some day, I may take from you some other remembrance, as from a friend to a friend, but—no ring.

"What I have for some time wished to say, I now think it better to write; namely, to ask you to remove from your mind any feeling of being engaged to me. The reasons which made me always resist any formal engagement on your part have proved just and right. You were always free—you remain free. I knew you better than you knew yourself, and I do not cast upon you the shadow of blame.

"I believe that once you loved me dearly; that, in some degree, you will always love me; but not with the full and perfect love that you owe to your wife, or that alone I could ever consent to receive from my husband. Therefore, I am determined to remain, as I shall be always,

"Your sincere and affectionate friend,
"JEAN DOWGLAS."

"Well, Mr. Browne?"

My heart beat horribly; yet I could not but answer him.

"I am sure my cousin means what is here written, and that in the end it will be better thus for both."

"And by what right— But I forget, I requested your opinion. Now it is given, will you further favor me by accompanying me to Pleasant Row?"

The young man's state of mind was so obvious that, as Jean's nearest and only friend, I resolved to go. We scarcely exchanged a word till we were in her presence.

Lord Erlistoun advanced haughtily, "Miss Dowglas, I intrude, in consequence of a letter received"—but at sight of her he broke down. "Jean, what is your meaning? What have I done to offend you?"

"Nothing."

"Then explain yourself. I must have an explanation."

At his violence, Jean turned as white as marble; but once more, with the feeling, higher than any thing that women call "proper pride," which had made her from the very commencement of his passion consider him and his good first—she controlled herself.

"Before I answer—answer me one word truly; I know you would never either say or act a falsehood. Do you love me as you did three years ago?"

He did not reply; he dared not.

"Then, whatever men's code of honor may be, in the sight of God it would be utter dishonor in you to marry me."

My mother left the room; I would have followed—but Lord Erlistoun called me back. "Stay! my honor, which this lady calls into question, requires that at this painful crisis I should have witnesses."

He then addressed Jean. "I am to understand that you consider my hand unworthy of your acceptance?"

"I did not say unworthy—but you know," steadily regarding him, "you know well, there does not now exist between you and me the only thing which makes marriage right or holy."

"What is that;—if I may ask you to name it?"

"Love. Understand me; I never doubted your honor. I know you would marry me, be to me most faithful, tender, and kind; but that is not all—I must have love. No half heart, charitably, generously given. My husband's whole heart—or none."

"Is it the old complaint, of my 'faithless temperament?'" said Lord Erlistoun, bitterly. "Because you were not my 'first love,' as the phrase is?"

"No, I am not so foolish—most men's last love is safer than their first; yours will be. But it must be the last. I had best tell you the whole truth." Jean spoke quickly and excitedly, as if out of long pent-up endurance: "You used to call me an angel, but I am a mere woman—a very faulty woman too. I know what jealousy is; hard to bear in friendship, worse in love, but in marriage I could not bear it. It would madden me—it would make me wicked. Therefore, even for my own sake, I dare not marry you."

"Dare not?"

"Do not be angry; I blame you not; but let us not shut our eyes on the truth. Love can change, and does; better in a lover, where it is still remediable and excusable, than in a husband whom even to forgive would be, in some measure, to despise."

"You despise me? oh, Jean!"

At the anguish of his tone her composure melted away in a moment.

"No, no, you could not help it; it was I that ought to have known—I was a woman, you were only a boy—it was natural, it was almost right you should change." She knelt down by the table where he leaned, his hands before his face —"I did not mean to hurt you so. Nugent, Nugent!"

"You despise me," he repeated, "and you have reason, for I despise myself. No, Jean, I can not tell you a falsehood; I do not love you —in that way."

Perhaps the truth, hitherto verbally unconfirmed, had not, till then, come upon her in its total irrevocableness, for Jean slightly shivered. Lord Erlistoun went on, passionately:

"I know not how it came about; I do not know myself at all; but it is so. For months

I have been a coward and a hypocrite; every day has been a torment to me. To escape I was going to make myself a hypocrite for life. Jean, don't despise me—pity me!"

"I do."

"Will you help me?"

"I will."

She separated, and took fast hold of one of his clenched hands, a lover's hand no longer; then looking round, with a faint movement of eye and lip, she dismissed me from the room.

Once the bell rang to send away Lord Erlistoun's carriage; and once afterward Jean came to the door and called my mother.

"I want a piece of bread and a glass of wine."

When we came in, Jean was standing by him, while he ate and drank this last sacrament of parting. He needed it, for he was ghastly pale, and his hands shook like a person in ague. What he had told her must have cost her much, but evidently every thing was told.

Jean spoke. "Aunt and cousin Mark, Lord Erlistoun wishes to bid you good-by. He is going abroad again immediately. When he returns, I have told him he will find us all his faithful *friends*," with unmistakable emphasis on the word. No farther explanation.

He staid a little longer, resting his head back on the sofa, while Jean sat watching him. Oh, what a look it was! Scarcely of love, but of inexpressible tenderness, like a mother's over a suffering child. Passion burns out; personal attachment dies out; the desire of individual appropriation altogether vanishes away; but I believe this tenderness over any thing once loved to be wholly indestructible. Shame upon any man or woman who would wish otherwise! for to kill it would be to kill the belief in love itself, to doubt which is the very death of the soul.

Lord Erlistoun rose. Jean said she would walk with him a little way, and he sat down again without opposition. He seemed totally guided by her. Only once, as if some irritating thought would not be controlled, I heard him whisper,

"It is useless; I can not consent. You must not tell her."

"I must; it is only right. Nothing is so fatal in love as concealment. I must tell her every thing."

"Jean!"

"You are not afraid of me? Of *me*, Nugent?"

At that, the only reproach she had ever made, he yielded utterly. "Only write to me. This suspense will be intolerable until you do."

"I will write—once."

"Not again?"

"Not again."

He looked up; just a little he saw—if a man ever could see into a woman's heart.

"One word. Say you are not unhappy!"

Jean paused a moment, then replied, "I believe it is not the will of God that any one of His creatures should have the power of making another permanently unhappy."

"And you forgive me?"

Jean stooped over him as he sat, and kissed him on the forehead—the first kiss she ever gave him, and the last.

They went out of the house together, walking slowly arm in arm along the quiet streets, where lamps were being lit in snug parlors, children fetched in from play to bed, and hard-working husbands waited for, late coming home.

There is here a burying-ground—surrounded with houses now, but then only shut in by a railing, through which one could catch both sight and scent of the flowers which grew luxuriantly over and about, bordering the graves. At the corner of this railing I saw Jean Dowglas and Lord Erlistoun pause, stand a minute, as if with clasped hands; then their ways parted. He went on toward town; she walked slowly back, without turning.

No; in the pathway which with her here ended, we return no more! One heart, at least, bled for thee, Jean; *my* Jean!

At safe distance, I followed her to Pleasant Row; but she passed the door. Thence, up streets and down streets, with a pace sometimes rapid, sometimes heavy and slow, along the familiar places that had been, as I once called them, her "Holy Land"—keeping out of her sight, but never losing sight of her—I followed my cousin, Jean Dowglas.

At last she went back to the corner of the cemetery, the spot where Lord Erlistoun had left her. There, for many minutes, she stood leaning on the railing, looking across over the graves.

I let her stand. Better that she should bury her dead out of her sight. Who is there among us that has not at some time done likewise? Who is there that, in all this busy world, does not own some graves?

At length, I crossed over and touched her on the arm.

"Jean!"

"Oh, Mark, take me home—take me home!"

I took her home.

CHAPTER IX.

I TOOK Jean home.

Saying this, it seems as if I had included all —as if it were the sufficient explanation of our two lives, external and internal, from that day forward. Knowing my cousin as well as I now did, I was fully aware that, even among her own sex, her character was a peculiar one. Their petty daily provender of work or play was not enough to satisfy the hunger of her spirit, active and restless as a man's, yet burdened with those especial wants and weaknesses that we are wont to designate as "women's nature." She might have conquered them all in time, and survived to dwell in that paradise of peace, lit with the reflected glory of the next world, which is possible even here; but in this world there was but one thing that her heart could ever recognize and rest in as *home*.

I loved Jean Dowglas. She was the only woman I ever did love. She came and stood over my life like a star; clouds arose between me and it; I "wandered in night and foulest darkness," as the man sings in that "Lobgesang"—how its tunes haunt me to this day! —but my star never faded, never fell.

With us, as Jean said it was with her sex, the test of a true attachment—hear it, ye coquettes, ye selfish mean prudes, who think to make us the better lovers by making us the greater fools—is, when we prize a woman less for her love than for herself; for what she is, and what she does; for that image of bright excellence, which every man born of woman ought to see shining before him all his life through, attained or not—like a star in the sky. If it falls, God help him! for its falling is like that of the star Wormwood, which draws a third of heaven after it.

I loved Jean. At first, after this fashion of abstract worship; then nearer, nearer—recognizing all her foibles; not blind even to her very faults; yet never losing the reverence, the sense of tender mystery, which all who love should have for one another, else, by a violent or a natural death, the love most assuredly dies. And so it happened that in the time of her trouble I took her "home."

She was perfectly ignorant of this; ignorant as a child; she looked to me for every thing with a tacit pitiful simplicity, also like a child. But I was a man, and strong as a man ought to be when Heaven apparently gives his destiny—perhaps more than his, into his own hands.

Young, self-presuming simpletons may waver —I never did; cowards and passionate may shrink back, afraid of their fate or themselves —I was afraid of nothing. Fortune's vicissitudes, lapse of years, trouble, suspense, uncertainty—all these things are as nothing, and less than nothing, to a man who truly loves a woman whom he esteems worth his winning. Either she is not, or he does not deserve to win her, unless he can conquer them all.

So much of myself, which here I shall leave; as it is a subject which concerns myself alone.

Lord Erlistoun quitted England; not immediately; but he never came again to Pleasant Row. Lady Emily did, more than once; pale and sad-looking, my mother told me, but more tenderly loving than ever to our Jean. Shortly, she too disappeared from London, and I heard of her no more. If Jean did—she kept a passive silence, which it would have been cruelty to break.

At midsummer we left Pleasant Row; left it to the shriek of the engines and the curl of the gray, spectral steam. They will never tell any tales--those two bare walls, roofless, open to the sky.

I found a little cottage, some miles out of London, where I established my mother and Jean. Algernon likewise; that he might have every chance of keeping up health in the work from which he must not shrink. Poor lad! but we all of us have something to endure.

"Oh, how pleasant!" sighed Jean, beholding the cottage, the fields, and the flowers. "Only my pupils—"

"You must give them up."

"Must?"

"If you please—at least for the present while you honor me by taking charge of my mother and that obstreperous boy. They will give you quite trouble enough."

"Oh, Mark!" She smiled and consented.

Sunday by Sunday I found her cheeks looking less wan and her step lighter. There is hardly any trouble which can not be borne easier in the country, among fields and flowers.

About this time I had a sort of calenture myself; a desperate craving that was granted to my cost. I fell ill; and was a month absent from Mincing Lane.

I had seen Jean's care over others; her watchful tenderness, her power of entire devotion to those who needed her, but I had never experienced it myself till now. Every trivial circumstance of every day and hour of that month still remains vivid in my memory. I may yet bless Heaven for it. I did even then at times; not always.

When I recovered, it was winter; then, rapidly as time seems to gallop when one has fairly left youth behind, it was spring. For nearly a year the trains had been passing and repassing through our old parlor at Pleasant Row.

Not a syllable heard I of Lord Erlistoun. He might have been dead—or married, as was indeed more likely. Caught, doubtless, by the next fair face that crossed his way, since, apparently, some retributive fate had swept from him that sweet fond one of Lady Emily Gage. As for Jean, hers, dear heart! was to him no more than dust and ashes now.

So thought I, but I was mistaken. One day I found on my table a packet addressed "Miss Dowglas."

How dared he even to write her name!

I carried the letter in my pocket all Saturday, half of Sunday, in the village church, up and down the peaceful fields. Jean's spirit seemed peaceful as they; she was a little more silent than usual, perhaps, but with an inexpressible calm in her and about her. I could not give her the letter.

After tea, when Algernon had gone out and my mother was asleep, she said,

"Mark, I wanted to tell you something. You sent me this '*Galignani*' on Friday last, did you know what was in it?"

"No."

"See."

I read. "*Married at the British Embassy, Paris, Nugent, Baron Erlistoun, to the Lady Emily Gage.*"

I folded up the paper slowly and returned it; as I did so, it was my hand that shook, not Jean's.

"You see," she said, "all is as was right to be. I knew it would happen so in the end. I am very glad. Only, somehow, if they had told me themselves—"

I gave her Lord Erlistoun's letter.

Two letters I saw were inclosed. She read them one after the other without moving from her place, without even turning aside: then took up and unfolded a little packet which accompanied them. It was a ring made of hair, a dark lock and a fair one, set in gold, with their two names engraved inside; "Nugent"—"Emily."

Jean put it on her finger, looked at it, twisted it up and down, till slowly her eyes filled—ran over.

"It was very kind. God bless them. God bless them both!"

This was all.

For another year our life flowed on, without change or prospect of change. At least, to three of us, my mother, Jean, and me. The boys were all grown up, Charles even contemplating matrimony, though he had faithfully educated Russell and started him as a private tutor before indulging in that luxury. Algernon had been transferred to a situation in Liverpool, where still lingered in good repute our honest name of Browne.

"They tell me, if I were to start as a merchant, on my own account, I might make a fortune yet, Jean."

"Should you?" She answered me with that open smile which showed at once her total ignorance of for whom alone the fortune would be worth making; and so, without referring to the matter again, I turned my ways back to Mincing Lane.

And still, in rain or sunshine, green leaves or snow, I came, on Sundays, to look after "my household," as I called my mother and Jean.

A quiet household—though dear and home-like. At least as much so as the just law of nature and possibility allows two solitary women, of different ages, opposite in character, and unallied by blood, to make, to themselves a home, or rather a habitation. Sometimes I wondered if Jean felt this distinction; if her present life were sufficient to her; or, supposing her Monday morning thoughts ever followed me from the sunshiny jessamine porch into the shadows of Mincing Lane, whether she thought my life was sufficient to me?

I was no coward. I did not complain of my lot, nor dash myself to pieces against its stony boundaries. If Heaven had set them, let them stand! if not, mine was a strong hand still.

Once only, I confess to have been beaten by fate, or the devil, or possibly both. I was hurrying down Cheapside, anxious to shut up the office, the business of which the firm now left almost entirely in my hands. I wanted to catch the last breath of an autumn afternoon down the

river; less for pleasure than for health, which a man whose sole capital it is has a right to economize; and mine had somewhat dwindled of late.

There was a "lock" in the street, which detained and annoyed me; I was apt to be irritable at little things now. That pair of prancing grays which stopped the crossing, what right had they and their owners caracoling lazily along the smooth ways of life, to come and balk us toiling men out of our only possession, our time?

I just glanced at the occupants of the carriage —only two, a lady and gentleman, talking and smiling to one another; young, handsome, happy-looking. When they had passed I knew them; Lord and Lady Erlistoun. They did not see me, and I was glad of it. I am afraid the devil was uppermost for many minutes after then.

So they were in England again? Would they seek us? would Jean wish it? would she dare wish it? I could not tell. I racked myself with conjectures; trying to measure a woman's nature by a man's; arriving at what is usually the only safe and wise conclusion, viz., that we know nothing about the sex at all. My sole certainty was in her own words—that Heaven never allows to one human being the power of making another "permanently unhappy."

How a few quiet words, spoken naturally, as we were crossing the Sunday fields, settled all! I could have smiled.

"Mark, I had yesterday an invitation that I should like to accept. Will you try to take a day's holiday and go with me to see Lord and Lady Erlistoun?"

"Certainly."

I called for Jean early one forenoon. She was sitting quite ready, in her bonnet and shawl, reading; but she looked up at my entrance—that bright involuntary look which, caught unexpectedly, is worth untold gold.

The lanes to the station were sunshiny and dewy; Hollingbourne, the chief property of the heiress Lady Emily, was about thirty miles down our line of railway. We walked briskly, rejoicing in the pleasant day. Jean said, she believed none but those who rarely had it, could fully appreciate the deliciousness of a holiday.

"Then a life of labor is the best. Do you think so, Jean?"

"I do. Far the highest and noblest."

"More so, for instance, than that of Lord Erlistoun?"

I felt almost reproved at her grave and soft reply.

"Lord Erlistoun's is, and will be more so as he grows older, a noble life too. I always felt sure of that. He was like a good ship, gallant and true, but blown about hither and thither for want of an anchor to hold by. He has found it now, in his wife's heart."

"Do you think a man's life is never complete without a wife?"

" Some men's are not—he is one. He needs to be happy in order to be good. I used to think the same myself once. Now it seems to me that those characters are nearer perfectness in whom to be good is the first aim ; who, living in and for the All-good, can trust Him with their happiness."

I said, looking at her sideways for a moment, " I think so too."

Thus talking we reached the station, and Jean put her purse into my hand with a wicked little trick of independence she was prone to, however unavailing.

" Well, second-class, of course," she warned me.

" No. I never mean to let you travel second-class again."

Jean laughed and submitted. When we were in the carriage she leaned back, watching the whirling landscape in silence ; but my landscape was her face.

No longer, by the utmost flattery, to be called a young face ; roundness and coloring gone, the large aquiline features distinctly, not to say harshly marked—it was noble still, but beautiful no more ; unless for that mellowness, like the haze of autumn which never comes until the summer of life is altogether gone by. A sweetness, a repose, indicating her total reconcilement to youth's passing away—her perpetual looking forward to that which alone gives permanent content in earthly pleasures—the rest which is beyond them, the pleasures which are for evermore.

The train stopped at a small wayside station. A carriage was waiting, and a gentleman.

" Miss Dowglas !"

" Lord Erlistoun ?"

They met—not quite without emotion ; but only so much as old friends might naturally meet with, after long absence. No more; not a particle more.

" Emily is here too. She is longing to see you," and he hurried Jean to the little waiting-room, where Emily fell on her neck and shed a few tears. She seemed more affected than either of them, this fortunate, happy, loving and beloved Emily.

That day passed like a dream ; in and about Hollingbourne, which was a spot lovely as dreamland, and with those two, fit owners of it all, who seemed in their position and themselves, familiar and yet strange, known and yet unknown, as people are whom one has to do with in dreams.

" We asked no one to meet you," said Lord Erlistoun, " we wanted this first visit to have you all to ourselves ; and besides we do not intend to be swamped in society just yet ; we feel as if we never could have enough of solitude."

His natural, unconscious " we,"—his evident delight in this same " solitude,"—at least so much of it as was possible in a house like a palace, and an estate like half a shire,—ay, Jean was right. His last love had been the true one ; he had cast anchor and found rest.

" Yes, she looks well, and happy too," I overheard him say ; his eyes, fonder than any lover's eyes, watching his young wife, as she flitted about her splendid conservatory, a flower among the flowers ; " and, I think, Jean, every day she grows more like you."

This was the only time he called her " Jean," or that in speaking to her his voice dropped into any thing of the old tone. The only time that Jean's countenance altered—though for no more than an instant. No angel in heaven could have worn a happier smile than Jean Dowglas now.

They both walked with us to the station—they seemed to be in the habit of walking together a good deal. Our last sight of them was standing on the platform, arm in arm ; Lord Erlistoun lifting his hat in adieu, with his peculiar stately air—Lady Erlistoun leaning forward to catch one more look, in her fond childish way, of her " dear Miss Dowglas."

Jean closed her eyes, as if to shut in the picture and keep it there. Opening them a few minutes after, she met mine and smiled.

" Have you liked your holiday ?"

" Yes ; and you ?"

" I have had a happy day. I was very glad to see them."

" Shall you go again often ?"

" No, I think not. Their current of life runs so widely different from mine. I do not wish it otherwise. I think, Mark, I am coming to that time of life when one's chief happiness is home."

We happened to be alone in the carriage ; the lamp shone dimly on Jean's figure—leaning back, with her hands crossed : outside all was pitch-black nothingness. There might have been nothing and nobody in the wide world but her and me.

" Jean, something happened to me last week that I should like to consult you about. Shall I now ?"

She turned and listened.

I told her how, this Michaelmas, my salary had been doubled. How, then speaking to the head of our firm upon Algernon's conviction that the good name of " Browne and Son" was still enough to launch " Brown, Brothers," and float them into smooth water, if they had only a handful of capital to start with—the worthy old fellow, once a creditor of my father's, had offered me as a loan the amount of his long paid debt.

" ' Use it, or lose it, or give it me back any time these ten years. 'Tis as good as thine own, lad, for nobody would ever have paid me a penny of it, except thy honest father.' "

Jean's eye sparkled as I ended my tale.

" Would you like me to accept it and start afresh ? You think it would not be too late ?"

" Nothing right to do is ever too late. And this seems right, for Algernon's sake. Also," her voice dropping tenderly, " for the sake of your father."

" Yes—he would be happy, if he knew his

memory could help us still—my dear old father!" And for the moment I thought only of him, and of the pride of once more building up our honest name in my native town, and among my own people.

Jean asked, if I had any hesitation in accepting this loan, for which I might pay interest shortly, and repay the whole in ten years?

"But what if I do not live ten years?"

"Nonsense."

"So you think me immortal, as those seem to be whose life is valueless to themselves and every body else?"

"That is not my cousin Mark—as you well know."

After a while, I asked her if she could not understand my fear of taking this loan, and perhaps failing, and leaving the debt as a legacy to Algernon.

"But is it not for Algernon's sake that you would undertake the risk?"

"Not entirely, Jean," and out came the bitterness of years—"I have never in my life had any thing to live for except duty and honor. At least let me hold these until the end."

Jean sat thinking for some time; then she turned to me.

"Mark, I also feel that the only things worth living for are duty and honor. Will you trust me with yours?"

"What do you mean?"

"You asked my advice—this is it. Accept this good man's money; use it well: repay if you can. If not, and I live, I will. Otherwise at my death I will take care that it is paid. Now, shall you be content?"

Probably few men ever feel as I did then. Not for the matter of "generosity," "obligation,"—there was that in my heart which counterbalanced both, nay, smiled at the thought of their existing at all, between Jean and me—but the goodness, the tenderness, which, whether or not indifferent to my personality, understood and cherished, and was ready to guard to the death, the true me, which I valued above all things else,—my conscience and my honor.

"Will you be content?" she said again.

"Will you trust me? I would you, and always did."

"Do you trust me, Jean?"

"More than any body in the whole world."

Doubtless she wondered that I replied nothing, that I did not even touch her extended hand, that I lifted her out of the railway carriage, and walked with her through the solitary star-lit lanes, almost without a word. That when we found my mother gone out with Algernon, not to be back for an hour, I sat down stupidly by the parlor fire mute—as death, if you will. "Hold the last fast," says the proverb.

When Jean came down stairs, with her bonnet off, in her white collar and braided hair, she made a discovery of a change in the parlor, which indeed I had myself forgotten. She looked at once to me, and I attempted no denial.

"Yes, I thought the hired tin kettle had been strummed enough in its day, and merited superannuation. Do you like your new piano, even though I chose it?"

"How kind you are!"

Not another word. No folly of "obligation." If there had been, if she had not taken it quite naturally, as I would have wished to see her take a mountain of diamonds, were it mine to offer her, I also should probably never have said another word.

She sat down and played for some time, I sitting over the fire.

"Mark, have you forgotten this? you have not asked for it for a long time."

—My tune, which always brought back my cousin Jean, in the Lythwaite drawing-room, with the sunshine on her hair. Also, because this "Lied ohne worte" seemed to my fancy to tell a whole life's story; a duet in which you can hear distinctly the man's voice and the woman's; separate; together; then wandering apart again in troubled involved phrases, but always in extremity comes back the tune in the bass, sweet and firm; at last the treble air is caught up with it, and both fall into a melody more "comfortable"—to use Jean's word—than any bit of music I know. Ending in two notes several times recurring, which say, as plain as notes can say it, "Come home, come home, come home."

Sometimes, when a vase is brimful, a touch, the shadow of a touch—and over it runs.

"Did you like your tune?"

"Yes—but come and sit by the fire, Jean."

She did so—one on each side the hearth; making two of us. Only two. Supposing it had been "my ain fire-side!"—I, who never in my life had had a fire-side of my own—my very own.

"How pleasant a wood fire is, Mark! But when you go to Liverpool, we shall cease to have one fire-side to sit over and talk together."

"We never had, except on Sundays. You forget, I have only had you for my Sunday blessing."

"Have I been a blessing? I am glad. It is something to be a blessing to somebody. It is more than I deserved."

She shaded her eyes from the fire, which blazed and crackled as if it knew winter was coming, but burned cheerily and was not afraid.

Now or never.

"Jean," I said, "if I go to Liverpool, and can make a fortune there, or at least a competence, will you come home?"

"Your mother and I?"

"My mother, if she chooses, but I meant you. I can not do without you. I could once, five years ago, because it was necessary and right; but now I can not. 'Tis not worth making a home—I will not do it—except for you."

"Me! me?"

She looked steadily into my face, and found

out all. She drooped her head lower and lower, almost into her lap, and burst into tears.

I said no more. It may be months, years, before I say any more. I would not take my life's ransom unless it were a free gift.

———

Algernon and I—"Browne Brothers"—are working our best. We have hardly any holidays, except an occasional evening stroll, with a western breeze blowing in the tide, and the sunset throwing colors, beautiful as Paradise, along the sandy flats of the Mersey shore.

I write either to my mother or Jean every Sunday. Now and then, Jean writes to me, only a line or so, expressing little or nothing; and so it may be for God knows how long, or forever.

But sometimes I think—

ALWYN'S FIRST WIFE.

CHAPTER I.

Yes—she loved him.

It was a thing which has happened over and over again—which will happen while the world endures; almost the saddest thing which can occur in the life of a woman: he only liked her—she *loved* him.

I use these impersonals in commencing, because they seem to come naturally in writing of the two concerned. "He" and "she" were then, and for years after, the most important objects in my circle of existence—my brother, Alwyn Reid, and Marjory Blair. He lived with me, earning his bread as a teacher of languages in our country neighborhood; she was his pupil. At least this was the tie between them at first; gradually I found he had gained the footing of a friend in the house. Old Mr. and Mrs. Blair were simple people; fonder even than grandparents are proverbially allowed to be. They liked every body who liked Marjory.

And Alwyn told me—as I doubt not, both in word and manner, he had openly expressed at the farm, for he was a warm-hearted, impulsive, and demonstrative fellow—that he liked Miss Marjory very much indeed.

She was the first woman he had known intimately—that is, the first who possessed youth, grace, and a cultivated mind; and at his age all women are angels. I feel sure that, for a little space, his fancy had thrown the glamour of a poetical ideal over the simple manners and mild expressive face of Marjory Blair. For a day and a half he even contested with me that she was handsome. However, that notion faded away, and he contented himself with avouching that it was her soul which made her beautiful, since in her were combined the finest intellect and the highest moral nature he had ever found in a woman. He used to talk of her qualities, taking her to pieces, anatomizing her, as it were, by the hour together, proclaiming continually her perfection, and how very, very much he liked her.

At first I was uneasy for his sake, remembering that Mr. Blair was a rich farmer, and my brother a poor teacher of languages. Afterward, on keener observation, I grew satisfied on his account.

Thus things went on for a whole summer; it was not until the fall of the year that I myself was formally invited to the farm.

Coming home, after having for a long evening watched Miss Blair and Alwyn, I just drew from my own mind the conclusion, which afterward became only too clear, thinking it sadly over to myself—in almost the same words which head this chapter.

Ay, Marjory loved him. Poor little girl! I could not think he was to blame; he was a very honorable fellow. He did not "make love," as the saying is, in the slightest degree. The "love" made itself—sprang instinctively in response to his goodness, his kindness, his tenderness. For she was a feeble and delicate creature; and for Alwyn to feel and to show a protecting fondness over such an one, was as natural as the breath he drew. Then he was so totally different from all other young men in our parts. He had nothing to do but to be himself—his natural, true self—without any seeking to please—to make almost any woman care for him.

And so this fate befell poor Marjory, who was simple and lonely, and perhaps, from her weak health, too much given to look to the dreamy and romantic side of things. Also, the cup—the universal cup—being held to her lips rather later than to most, for she was four-and-twenty—six months older than Alwyn—she drank—drank; thinking, perhaps, that it was his beloved hand which held it, when, in fact, it was the hand of the angel of doom.

I was very sorry, indeed, for poor gentle Marjory.

She did not betray her feelings in any unmaidenly way; in fact, they were scarcely betrayed at all, except by accidental flushings and tremblings; a certain restless wandering of the eye toward any corner of the room where he was; a certain intentness of ear whenever he was speaking, however hard she tried to keep up conversation with me the while. For all things else (these little things no one would notice, or did notice, save me) she was just what I expected to find her—graceful, simple, retiring. He had painted her correctly, which no lover would have done.

"Well, what do you think of her?" said he, eagerly, as we walked home.

"All that you think of her, and something more."

"That is right; I felt sure you would like her. She is the very sweetest girl we know. If she were only a little prettier, and—don't you agree with me?—just a trifle less pale; a degree more of rounded outline."

"I thought you hated fat women."

"Ugh!—so I do. But she is so very thin.

Ah, she will never live. She is too good for this world."

He sighed, and then began talking of how far she had got in Italian, and how in their lessons this morning, Petrarch's description of Laura had seemed to him exactly like Marjory. "Did you tell her so?"

"I don't remember; yes, I think I did. Why not? It really was very like her. I could not help it; could I now?"

I glanced up at his fine earnest face, so free from all a young man's self-conceit with regard to women. "Oh no," I said; yet my heart sighed "Poor Marjory!"

All love stories are more or less alike; it is just the same thing repeated in different forms—very often the same form—to the world's end. The world would weary of it sorely, save that the perpetually throbbing universal heart of the young generation attracts the history to itself, and makes it always new.

People who have seen around them a lifetime of loves rise and set, climax, change, and cease, sometimes ended by the will of fate, sometimes going out like faint candles in vapor, rarely, if ever, growing to be a light to lighten the world, as a happy and pure mutual love ought always to be—learn to view these things differently, and it often seems both idle and rather mournful to write about them at all.

This innocent, sad love-tale of Marjory Blair I watched, week by week, till the year closed. No one else seemed to notice it at all. Whether or no the parties concerned suspected the truth, of themselves or of each other, it was quite impossible to divine. Marjory was so very quiet, composed, and silent, that at times I was doubtful whether my too anxious pity had not exaggerated the danger. Perhaps she was not in love at all?

For Alwyn, he went on praising her to me in the most indefatigable and earnest way; but then he had done the same, or nearly the same, of at least six young women, all of whom he warmly admired, but without loving a single one.

I repeat, he was not to blame—I, his sister, who he declared loved him best and judged him hardest of any one alive, say so. He was handsome, gay, ignorant of care. His was, in the highest degree, the poetic eclectic temperament, which being exceedingly sensitive and difficult of choice, is successively attracted by what is grand in one woman, rare in another, and lovely in a third, but wholly satisfied by none. It is therefore set down by the mere matter-of-fact half of the world as essentially false and inconstant.

I do not join in that hue and cry. It is constant to the one inward truth of its nature—its ideal of abstract perfection constantly pursued and seldom found.

Let me not be supposed to excuse willful faithlessness—the capricious fancy that wearies of an imaginary idol as soon as it finds the least flaw in it; the selfish cruelty which enjoys all the sweetness of a pleasant bond, yet evades its responsibilities, duties, and burdens.

All that I mean is to defend my brother Alwyn, and all men of his type, from wholesale blind accusations of fickleness and heartlessness in love. The error is in using the word "love" at all, to such mere dreams of the imagination. I used to count on my fingers Alwyn's "sweethearts," and smile at his fancied adorations, as, year by year, they rose and sank like waves in the tide. It was only a tide; ebbing and flowing; I knew that the great deep sea of his manhood's love lay calm and still below them all.

The question was whether the time were now come, and the woman. Would Miss Blair be she?

I doubted. In the first place, she was not beautiful enough—a man like Alwyn, more than most men, requires a degree of absolute beauty in a wife. Poor Marjory, with her small sickly face, was often almost plain. Then she changed so. A word or look of his would sometimes, for an hour or two, transfigure her into another being—a creature of brightness and joy; again another chance word, and all the light was gone out of her; she became a pale, spiritless, ordinary girl.

At such times, on going home, Alwyn would say to me, "Really I never saw a woman alter like Miss Blair. How very plain she looked to-night!"

Poor little Marjory!

For my brother, he was utterly unconscious—utterly! Never was there a young man more simple-minded, more free from self-conceit. "I am only a poor teacher of languages," he would say. "I can't marry; every body knows it. It will be at least ten years before I can venture to love any woman, therefore I am quite safe."

And I truly think he believed so. It never crossed his mind that, from his pure goodness and singleness of character, to say nothing of his other qualities, some unlucky woman might come to love him.

Have I not said enough—I hope so! to prove unto any one, calmly and impartially viewing the story, that no wrong could be laid at Alwyn's door?

Thus the year went round.

CHAPTER II.

Alwyn and I spent a rather dreary Christmas. We knew not how it was, but his pupils had fallen off, and so had mine. Ours was a thinly populated district, and I found no new children replacing the little boys who, one after the other, were transferred from me to grammar and foundation schools. I speculated beginning what was always my great aversion, a girl's boarding-school.

"But then I should have to get rid of you, Alwyn?"

He looked surprised, and colored like a maiden, when I showed him how impossible it was that so good-looking and attractive a young man could abide, as a disguised hawk, in a dovecote of young ladies.

But this vague idea of mine, foolishly thrown out, worked deeper than I dreamed. He became troubled, restless—the dull home life grew irksome to him; he wanted to try his fortune in a wider sphere.

Finally, after much argument, after looking at our future on every side, and seeing it grow paler and cloudier as we gazed, one winter day, when we sat at home from morn till eve, shut in gloomily by the incessant snow, he made his determination.

It was to go back to Germany, where for a year he had once studied, and try to settle there permanently, as a teacher in one of the universities.

The pang of parting was not small—but one gets inured to pangs. And none could be sharper than to see him wasting here the prime of his youth; sinking into a mere idle dreamer, if nothing worse. I wished to see him a man in the world of men. I consented that he should go.

The day after, the snow ceased, and over a beautiful white fairy world rose up the first January sun.

"I will begin a new life with a new year," said Alwyn, as he gayly ate his breakfast, and planned a journey into the nearest town, to make all arrangements for his departure. He would be absent till evening.

"Have you forgotten Miss Blair was to come to us on New-Year's morning?"

"I declare I had!" He looked disappointed.

"And your pretty New-Year's gift that you took such pains to get for her?"

"Well, you can give it, Charlotte; it will be all the same."

"Do you think so?"

"No; by-the-by, not quite. Besides, I like to see her face when she receives a present: it is so childlike, with such a wondering gratefulness in the innocent eyes. No," laying down his great coat; "no, Charlotte, I must stay."

"As you choose."

"I wonder," said he, after half an hour's reading over the fire, "I wonder what Marjory will say to my going away. I shall miss her very much; she has been such a pleasant friend." He mused for another five minutes. "But then she will write. I wonder how she does write, by-the-by. If there is one thing I like more than another, it is a real, natural woman's letter. It is almost better than conversation. Do you think she will write to me, Charlotte?"

"How can I tell, my dear?"

"I am afraid she will be sorry to part: so shall I. Perhaps, on the whole, you had better tell her instead of me. I must not think of these good-bys that are coming, or I shall waver in my purpose, as you sometimes say I have a habit of doing."

"Only in little things, Alwyn."

In this—which was a greater thing than it seemed, as I well knew—he wavered for a good hour at least. Finally he departed, leaving the field open to me. I saw the idea of telling Marjory of his departure pained him, nor did he hesitate to show it. He had a very tender heart.

I sat and waited uneasily. Of late Marjory had got into a habit of coming about my little house and me, generally on the days when she knew Alwyn was absent on his rounds of teaching. I had become used to see her enter, timidly lay aside her bonnet and shawl, and sit down for a chat, just as if she belonged to me. She was never very loving to me—always rather shy; but I felt she liked me for myself individually, with a feeling quite different from the showers of affection which Alwyn's sister had had the honor of receiving from a great many other young ladies, and which the said sister, with an amused complacency, set down at their true value accordingly.

But I liked this girl, she was so gentle, so thoroughly true. And if in her half-avowed liking for me crept in some tenderer alloy—why, that was sincere too. When I saw it, it only made me smile, or sigh. We women ought not to be hard upon one another.

It was noon before she came. I took off her bonnet and her wet shoes; she had very dainty little feet. I made her put them on my lap to warm them, which she long resisted, but finally received the perhaps unwonted fondling with a blushing, beaming smile, and sat chatting merrily until some sound in the house made her start and slip into a formal attitude.

"You need not move; Alwyn is away. He was obliged to go out on business for the whole day. He hopes you will excuse him."

"Oh, yes."

"He left this book as a New-Year's gift. He would have liked to have given it to you himself, but thought I should do it as well."

"Oh, yes."

"He hopes you will read it sometimes, and not forget what good friends you and he have been all this old year."

"Oh, no."

Her fingers could not untie the string; she was trembling.

"Suppose, my dear, we put the parcel by till you go home."

She obeyed, not unwillingly; but many, many times I saw her innocent eyes turn, with a glad light in them, to the shelf where it lay. Somehow I wished he had not given it to her. But it was his habit. Half the poetry-books in the neighborhood owed their distribution to Mr. Alwyn Reid. However, Marjory did not know this.

We spent a quiet morning. She looked so happy that I could not tell her any thing. I felt all day like a smiling executioner with a dagger under his sleeve. I wished Alwyn had not chosen me to communicate the unpleasant fact of his departure for Germany—too unpleasant for him to do it himself. Yet, perhaps, considering all things, it was best. I was a woman, and—once—I had been young.

The early gloaming came; and all the winter Marjory was forbidden to be out after dusk. I wrapped her delicate chest well, and myself put on her little shoes. The executioner-like feeling was upon me stronger than ever. I postponed my melancholy duty till the last minute, when—a poor substitute for Alwyn—I slipped her arm under mine, and saw her home.

It was along a field-path; on every side, in smooth white waves, the deep snow lay. There was a little bridged brook we had to cross, where she stood and looked down.

"How merrily the water gurgles on between the two shelves of ice! This stream never wholly freezes, your brother told me. He talked so beautifully about it, one day lately."

"Did he?"

"I wanted him to write a poem on the subject, and he said he would. He promised me faithfully to finish his book, and come over and read it to us regularly every evening this spring."

"Ah, this spring!"

She looked up quickly, very tenderly, in my face. "Is any thing amiss with you, Miss Reid?"

"Amiss, my dear?" I was putting her off, when something whispered me that now was the best—the only time to do what I had promised. And it must be done. "Yes, I fear I am rather dreary."

"Is it about—" She stopped, coloring intensely.

"About my school falling off? Well, partly; partly about—about Alwyn. He is too clever a fellow to rust here in a country village. I wish he were away."

She started, then reassumed her usual monosyllabic answer, "Oh, yes."

"I think—it is possible—nay, very probable—that he will go away."

No answer. She was leaning on the rail of the bridge. She held it very tight and firm.

I felt I must be firm, too. No paltering, for present pity or fear of present pain, with the truth—which I knew was the truth. No unsteady holding of the knife—its stroke must be sharp, swift, and keen. It was safest so.

"He has no ties here—none, he says. He wishes to go out into the world, and make his way there for himself. I think any friend of Alwyn's must be glad that he should go. His sister is, though it will cost her much—much."

The little hand made a slight motion toward mine, but stopped half-way. She said, in a low, carefully guarded tone,

"It is very hard for you. Will he be absent long?"

"Indefinitely. He is gone to-day to complete his plans. He thinks of proceeding at once to Germany."

"Oh, to Germany! It is a—a fine country, Germany. Shall we walk on, Miss Reid?"

"If you please, my dear."

She did not take my arm, but moved on alone, with a slow but unfaltering step.

I was very thankful the disclosure was so well over. I would not trust myself to any more speech on the subject, but went on pointing out the red frosty sky, the white tracery of the trees, and every thing that could make a conversation.

She answered—just answered, and no more. "Take care, Miss Blair: the road is all ice —you will fall."

"Shall I?"

"Let me help you. You shiver."

"I am so cold."

With one slight moan, she slipped from my hold and dropped into a snow-drift in the ditch bank, as white as the snow that buried her.

I carried her in my arms across the field home. She came to herself just as we reached the farm-gate, and insisted upon walking.

"Don't tell any body. It was only the cold."

And then she lost consciousness again. Hours passed before she spoke another word. The doctor said it was the shock of the fall in the snow acting upon her nervous system, sensitive in the highest degree. She must be kept very quiet indeed, or he would not answer for the consequences.

I went home to Alwyn with a heavy conscience. I felt as if between us we two were conspiring the death of that poor child. Even I—how wrong it was of me to let her come, to let him go to and fro, when I might, perhaps, have found excuses to keep them asunder! Or why did I not give some hints—surely it was in the power of a woman and a sister so to do—to save her, poor innocent, from building her love palace upon such shifting sands? For such, alas! I felt sure they were.

Still, I thought I would sound Alwyn. He was so full of his German plans that it was not till tea was over that he thought of asking about Miss Blair.

"Did she like her present?"

"Very much, I believe."

"Did you tell her of my going away? How did she receive the news?"

"Very quietly."

He looked rather disappointed. Ah! poor human nature. Alwyn loved so to have people liking him—harmlessly liking him, as he liked them—especially women. He had very few male friends.

"But surely she said something—some little hint of regret? What passed between you? Tell me, word for word."

"I believe she said 'that Germany was a fine country.'"

"Nothing more?"

"Why should you desire more?"

He laughed. "Oh! I can't tell; only I like my friends to care for me a little. I thought she did. Perhaps I was mistaken. That is all."

"Alwyn," I said, looking earnestly at him across the tea-table, "do you really wish Marjory Blair to care for you?"

"In a friendly way—yes!"

"In any other way?"

"No."

After a silence, during which he gulped his scalding tea and asked for another cup, he said, "Charlotte, what could put such a question in your head? You know I never meddle with those sort of things. I can not—I dare not—'make love,' as the phrase goes, to any girl; or if I could and dared, Marjory Blair—sweet, gentle creature—is not the girl for me."

"I was sure of that."

"She is too pure, too meek," he continued; "I want a woman, not an angel. I should feel myself black by the side of her. Also, she is so very small and pale, and she has just a little —a little red tinge in her hair. Couldn't marry a girl whose locks were any thing but dark! Quite impossible."

I did not smile. I was very restless and miserable. My brother called me "rather cross" more than once that evening. As for telling him what had happened, the hours of anguish I had passed on Marjory's account, I found it simply impossible.

It was a real relief when about nine o'clock the young doctor, Alwyn's sole associate in the village, came in for a game at chess. He had been again sent for to the farm, he said; Miss Blair was very ill indeed—dangerously so.

Alwyn sprang up—"Charlotte, what's this? You never told me she was ill."

"It was only a fall she had—a slip in the snow," said I, sullenly.

"Nay, more than that, I suspect," observed the young doctor. "She has had a great shock of some kind — something here, or perhaps here," and he touched successively his forehead and his left side, with a suspicious glance at Alwyn.

My brother did not notice it, he was too much grieved.

"O Charlotte, you should have told me. What can have befallen her? What shock can she have received? Poor gentle little soul! Poor dear Marjory!"

"I dare say she will be better soon," said the young doctor, with an expressive smile. "Come, Reid, we shall have more chess playing. I don't believe you will go to Germany."

After that I was quite prepared for the news which met me on every hand in our village next day, that Miss Marjory Blair was dying for love of my brother Alwyn. In my agony of remorse and pain I told, God forgive me! to half a dozen gossips at least half a dozen absolute lies.

I went to see the poor child afterward. Her grandmother received me very frigidly indeed. Marjory did not know me at all. She kept talking incessantly about the snows—"the cold, cold snows"—whispering now and then in a low, fond, frightened voice the word "Alwyn."

I felt like a guilty thing when her grandparents took me solemnly into the chilly state parlor and shut the door.

"I wish to speak to you, Miss Reid," said the old man. "Confidentially it must be, and candidly. Will you answer in the same way?"

"If possible."

"It is about our poor child."

"Our darling, our only one," echoed the grandmother, weeping.

"We are old folk, or we should have been wiser. We have found it out now. It is not her fault, poor pet! Though we could have wished things different; she might have looked higher."

"Sir!" A momentary flash of sisterly haughtiness, which was gone as soon as I looked at the sorrowful old couple, and thought of the almost dying girl up stairs.

"But he is a fine young fellow, and, on the whole, we are content. She loves him—her words betrayed her when she did not know what she was talking about; she shall marry him if she likes. Miss Reid, will you tell us how long your brother has been courting our Marjory?"

"I can not tell. This is so sudden."

"Perhaps he has not told you," said the grandmother, kindly. "Yet he ought—so good a sister. And he must be so proud of being chosen by our Marjory."

I rose; I hardly knew what I was about. I muttered something about going home and explaining all to-morrow.

"Yes, go tell him we forgive him. He shall see her as soon as she is better. Her old grandfather will not have her fretting. Say, he shall marry her at once, and he need not go to Germany."

Homeward through the snowy fields I ran, feeling drawn around me an inexplicable net of sorrow, and gloom, and wrong.

CHAPTER III.

"Is she very ill, Charlotte?"

"Very ill, indeed."

Alwyn looked thoroughly miserable, as he had done all day. Had he shown his grief less, or struggled against it more, I would have been more satisfied. As it was, I felt to a horrible degree that uncertainty of action in which right and wrong seem to change places, till one hardly knows the one from the other.

Fate, or circumstance, or his own error, had led my brother into a position whence his next movement must inevitably create misery and wrong to some person—doubtless to more than one. A choice only lay of the lesser misery— the lesser wrong.

If he had then, or ever had had, any prior attachment, if his temperament had been sterner, and not, as I knew it to be, inclined to love every human being who cared for him, there could not be the slightest doubt that he was not bound—in fact, it would have been an absolute sin—to marry Marjory Blair. As matters stood, I wavered. He was fond and yielding in his nature, his conscience tender, his sense of honor keen, and to be loved was a necessity of his existence. Besides, he would need so much devotion, so much forbearance throughout life; safer, I thought, for him to marry a woman who loved him, than a woman whom he loved.

Whether my theory grew out of evidence, or I found evidence to suit my theory, I can hardly tell, but I reasoned thus: No one will question the fact that a man's love, however passionate and intense, must, from its very nature, after marriage become calmed and settled down, often temporarily cooling, until the new bond, which has in it more of affectionate friendship than passion, is formed between the pair—this bond which, once formed, endures forever; while, on the other hand, almost invariably, the wife's love grows, becomes more deep, more patient, more fond than ever the girl's could be. Romance changes into household tenderness, exacting caprice is merged into the humblest devotedness. Out of ten men who have married in a state of maddest adoration, I would engage to find, at the end of the second year, at least eight couples where the wife loved the husband more than the husband the wife.

I began to question whether my brother might not do worse than save from lasting sorrow the foolish, faithful heart of Marjory Blair.

"What are you thinking of?" said he to me, when for half an hour I had been pretending to sew and he to read, till on looking up we found it was pretense on either side.

I paused a moment, then dashed at once into the honest truth: "I was thinking of poor Marjory."

"So was I."

"What about her?"

"That she must be of even more delicate constitution than I feared. Such a trivial thing—a mere slip in a snow-drift—to produce this dangerous illness."

I was silent.

"Are you quite sure it was nothing more serious? Did you not tell me it was that, and only that?"

"No, I never did. It would have been telling a falsehood."

"Charlotte, you are cross with me about something."

"Not cross with you, only very miserable on account of you. Oh, Alwyn, why did not nature make you an ugly, commonplace, harmless fellow, like the generality of mankind?"

And putting back his hair, I looked into his noble, handsome face, with a vague sense of pity for all womankind. The more so as he looked up in real unconsciousness of my meaning. One could not but forgive him, for half the mischief he did sprang from his own entire humility.

"Don't talk nonsense, Charlotte; I am far too sad for that. Talk of poor Miss Blair. How soon will she be herself again?"

"God knows!"

"Surely in a week or so she will be well, at all events. I must see her before I leave."

"Why so? To grieve her, torture her, break her heart? Brother, you shall not. You men have no more feeling than a stone. I would give the world if you had never exchanged a word with that poor child."

"Charlotte!"

"Do you know what has come of it, your daunderings up to the farm, your Italian readings, your walks in green lanes, looking at the moon? I feared how it would end—I saw it coming weeks ago."

"Sister Charlotte" (angrily), "don't be a fool."

"I wish to Heaven I were! Would it were all my fancy, and no one were to blame! She is not—poor, fond darling! I don't know that you are either. You could not help it, Alwyn. But you have done a cruel thing. You have broken a girl's heart."

"I?—"

"Now don't look so astonished and innocent. You know it too—or it is high time you did. I have spoken the simple truth. Her friends asked me to day 'how long my brother had been courting Marjory?'"

"I protest, I never said a word of love to her in my life!"

"Foolish boy, do you think that love is expressed and won only by words?"

He hung his head.

"But, whatever you did, or whatever you said, the case stands thus — you have made that poor girl's life miserable, and now you are going away and taking her peace with you. She loves you to the very bottom of her soul."

"Loves me? Oh, Charlotte?"

His head dropped on the table; he turned as pale as death.

We remained silent for many minutes. I sewed on fast till I could not see for crying.

"God forgive me," he said at last, "I meant no harm. What am I that she should care for me? Poor Marjory! Sweet, gentle angel!" He actually wept.

"Charlotte, first tell me all that passed."

I told him, disguising nothing. He was greatly affected.

"Oh, my unworthiness, my unworthiness! To make so many people miserable. What a wretch I must have been!"

I tried to comfort him, but the case was too clear. He must have erred in some degree, perhaps more than I knew, or a modest, shy maiden like Marjory would never have so blindly thrown her heart away. Also, other observers would never have been so deceived as to the relation existing between them.

Still he had done no more, in fact much less, than hundreds of young men do, and pass unblamed through the world, while the foolish young women are only laughed at. But his sensitive conscience exaggerated the folly into the blackest crime. He was overwhelmed with remorse.

"Charlotte, tell me, what must I do? How can I atone? If the most complete, heart-broken—"

"Your broken heart will not exactly heal hers."

"Do you think hers will never heal? Do women never get over these—these things?"

"Get over! as a horse leaps a hedge, either falls staked in the middle or limps for life afterward. Oh yes, certainly they get over it. It is a case of kill or cure, according to the patient's strength. For my part, I think poor little Marjory will be returned among the 'killed.'"

"Oh, hush! Sister, you ought not to speak in that light, unfeeling manner"—(unfeeling? I?) "What should I—what can I do? Ought I to—to marry her?"

"Ask your own heart that question."

I left him, went to lock the house and dismiss our maid Mary's jo, who was courting assiduously by the kitchen fire. How much simpler and happier these affairs are often carried on in kitchens than parlors!

"Alwyn, take your candle; it is time for bed."

"Sister, come here. Give me some help—advice. I feel half crazy."

I came, smoothed his hot forehead and kissed him. My poor boy! He was paying dearly for all his follies.

"Tell me, Alwyn, did you ever for any moment feel a spark of love, not mere sentimental friendship, but downright love, for that gentle creature, whom many men would really adore?"

"Would they? Yes, I know it. At times, even I have fancied—but then I smothered the feeling down. I dared not love, you know. And to think of her loving me—me that am not worthy, not half worthy, of a girl like her!"

"You might grow worthier. She might help you to conquer your faults and become a noble man. You may never in your whole life find such love again, and from such a woman."

"I feel that."

"Are you quite sure that, honoring and liking her, you do not in some vague fashion love her?"

"As a friend, a companion, a comforter, yes; as my wife, no!"

"Then she had better, ay, and if she knew it she would rather a thousand times, suffer any anguish—struggle with it—beat it down—outlive it—or, if that may not be—die of it—than live and be married to you."

I took up my candle and went to bed.

It was two o'clock before I heard Alwyn quit the parlor and go up stairs. As he passed my room I called him. He answered, opened the door and stood a minute outside. He had a paler, more resolute, and calmer face than I ever saw him wear.

"Do you want any thing, Charlotte?"

"Yes—no. Alwyn, dear, what time do you wish to breakfast?"

"Early. I am going to London. Probably shall be away a week. Meanwhile will you send me news of—the farm, every day?"

"I will."

"And you will manage to let them know that I am not—at least not yet—going to Germany?"

"Thank Heaven for that! Yet, Alwyn—"

But he had closed the door and vanished.

CHAPTER IV.

Two days after he wrote me a long letter, full of tenderness.

He said, "he ought to be grateful everlastingly for the love of two such women as myself and Marjory. That he would try to deserve and keep both to the end of his days."

"He should not be able to live with me again," he added, "having got employment in London, which would at least keep him above want; but he would try to visit me as often as was practicable."

For what had passed between him and me on that unhappy evening (he mentioned the date), he begged me never to reveal it to any human being. "He had quite made up his mind now. She was a noble creature, worthy of all love. She should never know to her dying day that he had married her from *gratitude*."

The last sentence was written on a half-sheet; his letters were always careless and fragmentary.

So my brother would be married. Of what had been all my own—I should henceforth have only a part. Of all his many confidences in me this must necessarily be the last, or nearly the last. For the future, himself and all belonging to him must be shared with her, who had the deepest, tenderest, most solemn right to him and to all his secrets.

But there was one secret which, as he said, must be kept from her forever—one trust which must forever remain mine, or rather kept faithfully and silently between my brother and me. To no conceivable chance must be left the possibility of Marjory's finding out "that he had married her from *gratitude*."

I was a lone woman. Any accident happening to me would leave all my papers in the hands, and open to the inspection of—my only brother hitherto—now, of my brother's wife—or betrothed wife.

Being of a nervously cautious temperament, I never like to leave any thing that must be done, undone for a single day. That very night I determined to look through Alwyn's accidental letters for the past year, and destroy all which bore the slightest reference to Miss Blair.

This entailed considerable sacrifice. Yet his letters—and he wrote many—were beautiful in themselves, and I had been used to keep every scrap of his writing—naturally precious to me.

So I resolved on not burning the whole, but merely cutting out passages here and there—especially *the* passage. Having done so, and, as I believed, seen it safely in ashes under the grate, I felt easier in my mind.

The remainder of the lad's dear letters, many of which he had written to me quite in his boyhood, I tied up, not without some natural emotion, which rather hurried my fingers and blinded my eyes, and put the packet by against the time when my brother and his wife would have the examining of the papers of me—the "dear sister departed."

I sent Alwyn daily tidings of Miss Blair; but in one thing I acted contrary to his desires. Knowing him, perhaps, better than he knew himself, I thought it safest to say nothing at the farm about him.

Marjory slowly recovered. By the week's end she was able to sit up and be carried down stairs. No one talked to her concerning her sudden illness, or even mentioned my brother's name. But she saw me about her continually, tending her and watching over her, as if with a sort of right. She seemed to feel it and be glad.

Yet there was in her a great change—a quiet recognizing of her inward wound, and setting herself to meek endurance of the same. The struggle was altogether silent. If it lasted long, it would, I foresaw, speedily destroy the frail tabernacle of such a loving spirit, which loved the more intensely from its total unselfishness and its want of that useful quality called Pride.

She was one of those fortunate beings who find it "not so difficult to die."

On Sabbath afternoon, when all the house was quiet, she came down into the parlor, and sat reading her Bible; then leaned back musing, with her hand on a bunch of snowdrops, the first out of my garden borders. She looked as frail and fair as they.

All of a sudden, without giving any notice of his approach, and so quietly that the grandparents were not even roused from their doze on either side of the fire, my brother walked into the room.

He was a great deal more agitated than Marjory. After the first minute she sat calm in her chair, and answered his questions about her health in the most ordinary way, as in his many, many visits beforetime. It is astonishing what even the weakest of women can do when need compels.

Mrs. Blair woke, looked pleased, and asked him to stay to tea. Alwyn staid. He was a trifle less gay than his wont, but there was about his manner a tender repose infinitely more attractive.

He paid very little formal attention to Marjory; only I saw him earnestly looking at her sometimes, at which she would start, and grow the color of a rose.

After tea, Mrs. Blair asked me to come and see the chickens—chickens in January!—but I

D

humored the open ruse, and coaxed the old man after us to the kitchen fire.

"We must leave the young folk together, you know, Miss Reid," said the grandparents.

It was a very, very long hour, and I do not remember in the least what the worthy old couple talked to me about.

Later, the farmer observed, with a chuckle, that he was sure, if ever so much in love, the young folk must want their supper, and somebody ought to summon them. "Do you go, Miss Reid."

I went, previously making an ingenious clatter at the handle of the parlor door.

Idle precaution! My brother, who was sitting with his arm round Marjory's waist, did not remove it when I entered. He testified no annoyance at my intrusion, no shyness at the fond attitude in which I found them. Alas! he was doing only that which it was his duty to do.

"Come here! Nay, don't shrink, dear Marjory. Charlotte, here is your sister. Take her, and love her always."

The young betrothed ran into my bosom, and wept out her happy heart there.

Poor Marjory!

CHAPTER V.

THEY were married early in the summer, and went to live in London. Marjory had a little fortune of her own; but my brother, through the situation he had obtained, was sufficiently independent to have married without it. They began life prosperously enough.

Both wished me to live with them; but I believe this is usually a great mistake: that husband and wife are better beginning life alone together. So I kept firmly to my school: though many a time, when the noisy little lads were gone, I sat by my still fireside and thought of theirs.

Often I used to get Marjory's letters. They were very frank and free. She was freer with me even than with her husband. She loved him so, it made her afraid of him.

The honeymoon letters were as happy as a bird singing in a May-bush. He was so kind and so tender over her, she said: almost like a mother or a sister. He watched her every step; it made her often wicked enough to feel glad she was not strong, that she might have his fond care perpetually around her. As for the joy of being near him, doing little things for him, knowing that she utterly and entirely belonged to him, now and forever—there could be nothing like it in this world!

Love! — that incomprehensible, wonderful thing, intangible as air, a mere modicum of which suffices to some excellent, cold-blooded creatures, but which to others is the sole atmosphere in which they live and move, without which they suffocate and die—poor Marjory;

love was to her the very breath of life. Beyond it was nothingness.

It is a mournful thing, seeing we are not yet angels, whose sole existence is love, and that we have not yet arrived at that angelic development which is wholly satisfied with, and absorbed in, the Love Divine; it is, I say, a very mournful thing when any human being is constituted thus.

At Christmas-time Alwyn wrote to me, "Sister, you *must* come." So I packed up my trunk for a month, and went.

It was the oddest thing imaginable for me to be knocking at my brother's own door, and to have to inquire in a formal manner for "Mr. Reid." Neither of them knew the precise hour of my coming; so I appeared at the new house as a stranger. It was about five: their dinner hour. I saw the cloth laid as I passed. From the drawing-room floor a figure came fluttering—nay, flying down.

"Alwyn! you are in capital time to-day."

Then seeing me, the little mistress of the house discovered her mistake. Her sisterly welcome was very fond—tearfully so.

"I am sure—if we had known—I am so sorry Alwyn is not here to meet you."

"Never mind; I dare say he will be home in a minute."

"Oh, yes!" Her old monosyllables.

She brightened up, and busied herself about me in a thousand ways, as if she could not sufficiently impress upon me the sweet fact that now, and for always, I had got a sister.

It was sweet—there could be no doubt of it. Sweet to have her flitting round, insisting on doing twenty little things that I never let anybody do for me before; to feel that I had a right to her love and care—that she was my own property, my sister—my Alwyn's wife. Then we came and sat down by the drawing-room fire, and I admired the pretty house most indefatigably.

Nevertheless, conversation paused, flagged, sank into that lull which always oppresses those closely united, who, meeting after a long absence, during which much has happened, have so many things to say that they can not say one.

Marjory's eyes wandered continually to the clock on the mantle-piece.

"You must not mind it, though, Charlotte; it is always too fast. Those pretty French clocks rarely go well. But Alwyn liked it. He has exquisite taste."

"He always had. He has a perfect passion for the beautiful."

"Oh, yes!"

Just the faintest shadow passed over her face, making me vexed at the remark I had innocently made.

Mrs. Reid—how strange the name seemed—was many degrees further from being beautiful than Marjory Blair. London air did not suit her—she was grown paler than ever. Dark circles underneath them seemed almost to take away the light of her soft, dove-like eyes—the only really pretty feature she had. She looked much older than before her marriage.

When seeing me gaze earnestly at her, she asked me with a smile, "If I thought her altered?" I was very much puzzled what to reply.

"Come, you must be hungry," she said, after listening and starting at every foot in the street. "Shall we ring for dinner?"

Of course I said no; but we shared between us a piece of bread, and sat quiet.

More weary waiting, with fragments of talk between, till a church-clock near struck loudly seven. Then Marjory rose.

"Some business must have detained my husband. He is sure to be at home before we have done dinner."

But she ate with a sick, sad face, and could hardly keep up the ordinary civilities of the table.

"Is Alwyn often late?"

"Not oftener than he can help. He is much engaged, and his occupation"—(he was secretary to a fashionable author)—"leads him into a great deal of acquaintance. He is so much admired—you can't think—in every circle into which he goes."

"Do you go with him?"

For I had heard somewhere of the difference in this respect between literary men and literary men's wives.

"Sometimes I do—when my health allows. He is very careful over me—too careful, almost. Ah! Hark!"

His quick run up the steps, I knew it well! his loud, rapid knock. The wife was another creature in a moment.

"Is that you, my dear? Really Marjory, why will you open the street-door?"

He came in, threw down his hat, shook back his curls. He was the same fine handsome fellow as ever—or handsomer. *She* was a mere pale shadow by his side.

"Bless my soul—Charlotte! Why, Marjory, what a pleasant surprise!"

"Yes, indeed. We had begun dinner, you see. She has been here ever since five."

"What a pity! I would have come home half an hour earlier had I known."

"I knew you would."

Marjory, thou wert truly of the angel kind! For worlds I could not have uttered those four words with that perfect smile.

We sat round the fire, my brother, my sister, and I. Alwyn was unfeignedly glad to see me. Whatever might be the vagaries of his imagination, and the attachments pertaining thereto, his affection for me was always firm and sure.

He told me of all his plans, aims, and hopes, which had taken a far wider range within the last year. His marriage had, unconsciously to himself, been the maturing of his character, the stepping-stone to his future—a future which to me and his fond wife seemed limitless.

Marjory did not talk much. She sat idling over some light sewing, often laid down, that from under her shading hand she might look across the table at Alwyn, with a fullness of admiring love. She did not hover about him, or try to win from him those little attentions which young wives rejoice in and expect; it seemed as if she neither were used to nor required them. His mere presence in the room was sufficient to her; she desired no more.

I never, save this once, saw an instance of a creature solely wrapped up in another human being, whose love was too humble to be exacting, too self-existent to burden the recipient. Alwyn was very kind and tender to her, with the sort of tenderness which springs from habit. He would go on talking for hours in his brilliant, charming manner, without seeming conscious of her at all; but whenever he wanted any thing, it was "Marjory—where's Marjory?"

On the whole, if I had been a person satisfied with the outer surface of things, I should have said they were a very happy married couple,—happy in the sort of calm content, which generally comes after ten years of union; a content which ten more years would probably add to rather than diminish.

But for that wild dream of youth, the perfect love which of two makes one flesh, the satisfied mutual love which in riper years becomes more and more a vital necessity of existence, which, receiving as much as it gives, is a rest, and stay, and blessing, beyond any other blessing which earth can afford: if Marjory ever thought of or longed for this, God help her!

These were my meditations when I lay down to sleep for the first night in my brother's house. The next night slumber was forbidden to my eyelids. Poor, simple, countrified me! I was plunged into the very midst of that whirling Maelstrom—a London literary party.

It was a gathering of lions at a great lion's house. A lion of twenty years ago, when they roared much louder than they do now, when they used to meet exclusively among themselves for the express purpose of using their lungs, and proving how much greater they were than the minor beasts.

I never much liked literary people; they talk so fast and so continually about themselves. They seem to think it is the grandest thing in the world to handle a pen, to write about virtues instead of showing them, to narrate noble lives instead of living them. Alas! I fear me the former is often supposed to preclude the necessity of the latter.

Thus I thought, when Alwyn for the first hour kept me on his arm, bless him! he was not the least bit ashamed of his countrified old sister; pointing out to me one after another, the clever people, the celebrated people, the people who were hung out as lanterns in the world; adding to each description various biographical or personal comments, frequently so caustic and severe that they made me regard him amazed, and caused Marjory's half remonstrating, half pathetic whisper, "Oh, Alwyn!" After a time he left us to take care of one

another, and we watched him, brilliant among the most brilliant, noticed even among the most noticeable, in the very centre of the throng. Marjory's eyes followed him continually with the fondest, proudest gaze. Few people came to speak to her, indeed no one would have guessed she was his wife; she sitting in a corner with her pale face and plain high silk dress —her wedding-dress, the boast of our village dressmaker, but quite old-fashioned here.

"Marjory, my dear, how tired you look! Had we not better go home?"

"Hush! he likes to stay late. Don't mention such a thing."

But I did mention it, being a very daring and determined person, and not in the least afraid of my brother. Why should I? He was but flesh and blood. His wife and his sister need not be always his humble, obedient slaves. So I represented the case.

"Go home, my dear Charlotte? To be sure I will, immediately. She is not ill, I hope, poor child? She is too delicate for these crowded rooms, I must go alone next time. Come, Marjory."

He led her out, leaning on his arm. They could hardly get through the throng, he was so beset by acquaintances. She seemed quite a stranger to most of them.

"Who is she?" I heard asked behind them.

"Only Reid's wife."

"What a fine clever fellow he is! How could he marry such an ordinary little thing!"

By the start Alwyn gave, by the deep flush on Marjory's cheek, I think both the young couple heard that comment. He answered it by the most pointed and tender care over her until we reached home. There he said,

"Now, Charlotte, I put my wife into your charge. I am going back, just for one half hour."

He did not return till long, long after midnight.

A little figure all in white glided past my half-open door, and let him in.

"I could not help it, Marjory," he was saying, as they repassed up stairs. "I would not have kept you sitting up on any account, if I had only thought of it. But then they were so very entertaining."

CHAPTER VI.

IT is strange, how differently strikes on us the atmosphere of different households. Some are so warm, fresh, and clear, we bathe in them as in the light of a May-day. In others, the air hangs heavy and close, as if always threatening a storm. Of many the atmosphere is still, cold, and pale; you can neither stir it to a tempest, nor brighten it into sunshine. You walk in it, and feel that if you lived there you would pine and wither like a plant in a dark room, which barely exists, and can never either blossom or grow.

This was somewhat the impression that Alwyn's home made on me. Ay, even though it was a very beautiful, kind, quiet home, with no disturbing element, but there was little brightness in it; no laughing round breakfast tables, no running to and fro, busy, merry, meeting at intervals for a few minutes of cheerful chat, and ending by a fireside circle, into which all the cares and joys of the day are brought, thrown in the midst, and danced round, till all mingle happily together, and the veriest witch's caldron of pain becomes a wholesome family brew of sweetest savor.

We had no such circle; my brother was almost always out of evenings.

I think—and my thinkings spring out of some experience—that one of the saddest descriptions one can give of a household—a virtuous and not disunited household—is, that the master of it "generally goes out of an evening."

Marjory, when I hinted a little surprise at his so doing, said decidedly—very decidedly for her—"that it was London ways. All clever men did the same, and Alwyn's friends were most of them celebrities. She was quite accustomed to sit alone of an evening. She rather liked it."

Of course I made no further remark.

So she and I used to sit together, five nights out of the seven, occupied in our women's work and desultory women's talk—she seemed to talk less than ever. But there was always a blank, a want of the cheerful face we both loved best, of the voice that, reading or talking, would have been sweeter to us than any music in the world.

I remained a month in my brother's house, and came home with a vague feeling that there was much satisfaction in living alone in the country and teaching school.

When I left, Marjory hung about me affectionately. I said, "Remember, if you are at all ill or unhappy, you must come down to your sister, my dear. Mind that she does, Alwyn." Marjory's eyes turned to her husband, who had been particularly tender over her the whole of that day, for she was weak and ailing this winter time. "I unhappy?" she answered, with a smile of the fondest incredulity. "You must not wait for that, Charlotte, or you will never see your sister."

So I hoped that an old maid's notion of married life was a ridiculous Utopia, and that they were really a very happy couple after all.

In the spring I received from my sister-in-law a parcel of little clothes. She said she was too ill to make them herself. I made them for her, nearly all; sewing late and early, sometimes merrily, oftener still with tears.

At midsummer, on the breaking-up day, when my little pupils were making such a clatter that I could hardly hear my own voice, I received a letter from Marjory.

It contained more of herself than her letters usually did. They were generally all "Alwyn —Alwyn," from beginning to end.

She said her husband was away on a short journey, and she felt very lonely. She dreaded more particularly a longer absence he was about to make; a tour in Switzerland with his patron, the titled author, who, she added, found it utterly impossible to travel without the agreeable companionship of Alwyn Reid. And it would be a great treat to Alwyn himself. Meantime she wanted to come "home" (which word was carefully erased, and "to the farm" substituted), to be with her grandparents and me.

She came. Alwyn brought her. The same afternoon they appeared at my wicket-gate, just as they used to appear when he went and fetched her over to take tea with us.

That time might have been yesterday, so like all seemed. The same yellow ribes was in flower against the wall—the same standard rose-tree, large white roses with waxen petals, of which he once gave her one, saying it was the very picture of herself.

She stood and gazed, evidently with an overflowing heart.

"Oh, Alwyn! do you remember?"

"Remember what, my dear?"

"Every thing. In our courting days, you know."

He sighed, half sadly.

"I fear I never 'courted' much, Marjory."

"No: I should not have liked it if you had; I could not have endured being 'made love to.' But we were so happy—I was so happy. I did not know that I loved you, or you me—only I felt so very happy!"

"Mayst thou always be happy, my little white rose! Not one of us all deserves happiness so much."

He staid with her at the farm for a few days: then he went away; and I had my little sister entirely to myself.

I saw a great deal of her; penetrated fold after fold into the pure calyx of the white rose, and wondered at its rare perfectness.

There are two distinct classes of our sex—women whom men love, and women whom women love. Marjory was of the latter, and, though it be treason to mankind to say it, the higher order. Her attractions were wholly distinct from those "of the earth, earthy," which gain a young woman many lovers. Hers would be more likely to win her only friends; but all she did win she won forever.

Watching Alwyn closely, during the few days of his stay, it had seemed to me, when the London rust was rubbed off him, that his nature was growing purer and purer—that toward his wife, especially, a deep tenderness was springing up. As if his love, omitting the passion-time, had seized on the friendship-stage of married life, and was blossoming out; like an auricula of mine which obstinately refused to flower at the proper season, but in the middle of August astonished me by putting forth the prettiest bud in the world.

I augured that my brother's marriage would some day become one of the many instances of how almost impossible it is for a truly good man not to love a noble and lovable wife who loves him.

We spent a very happy month, my sister and I, in talking of his future, in which was included both of ours. And a little—a very little—of another future, so dim, yet so near—so strange, yet so wondrously beloved, which as yet lay in the Almighty's hand among unborn souls.

On the last day of the month, the day before Alwyn was expected home, Marjory came to drink tea with me. She was restless with joy —could not sit still for five minutes—kept on smiling and talking, turning over and over again my books and work. At last she came to my desk, where I had been making out my mid-summer school-bills, and began to amuse herself with its contents.

"I may, Charlotte? You have no secrets, I suppose? At least none from me."

"None, my child."

And I thanked Heaven it was so—that every trace of the only secret I ever had to keep from her had long since become dust and ashes under my grate.

"Your correspondence is small. Only my letters and Alwyn's—mine the most plentiful by far. Are these all that Alwyn has written to you since his marriage?"

"Do you want to read them, Mistress Jealousy?"

"No, thank you; I have read them all beforehand. He generally gives me his letters to read. You don't mind that, sister, dear!"

"My pet, no!"

"Jealous"—she went on moralizing. "Charlotte, what a strange feeling that jealousy must be! Did you ever know what it was?"

"A little—once."

"I never did. Of course not? I could never feel it concerning any one but Alwyn. And to be jealous of him, how impossible—how wicked it would be!"

"Don't you think so?"

"Certainly."

"I can understand people being jealous before they are married, or engaged—but afterward! Why, such an idea would never come into my head. How could it, when once I was sure, perfectly sure, that Alwyn loved me; that he must have married me simply for love — since there was nothing else in me he could marry me for."

"Foolish girl!"

"No, I repeat—nothing. I am not hand-some—or clever, or accomplished—no more to compare with him than the night with the day. Sometimes when I see what other women are— the women he daily meets with, without caring for any of them—I sit and marvel at my bless-edness—at the infinite mercy of Heaven which made Alwyn love me. Charlotte, do you re-member the day I fell in the snow."

"I do remember it."

"I thought—no, at the time I thought no-thing. It was as if somebody struck me — stunned me. Something kept saying as loud

as a trumpet, 'Alwyn is going—Alwyn does not care for you. You had better die.' And I verily think I should have died."

" And been buried in the church-porch,
And Alwyn buried in the quire ;
And out of her bosom there sprang a red rose,
And out of his bosom a brier."

I quoted this, adding, "Marjory, are you not ashamed of such sentimentality? You—a wife, and—you know! There, take your beloved's letters, which he wrote me years before you married him, and which were a great deal more foolish and rhapsodical than any he ever writes now. Quick, take them!"

And I gave them to her, with this hand— "this accursed right hand," as old Cranmer moaned. So could I also moan! Oh, would it had rather been consumed in flames!

I left her reading, and went about my house-hold business, entering and re-entering several times. She always looked up with a smiling or an admiring comment, and once I heard her laughing heartily to herself at some quaint pas-sage. There was no fun like Alwyn's fun, we both thought.

The last time I came in, after a little longer absence from the room, my sister did not turn round and smile. She was sitting, with the letters carefully tied up on her lap—her head thrown back against the wall. She was fright-fully pale.

"What have you been doing, Marjory, child?"

"Oh, nothing. Only laughing too much, I think. I felt sick. I am better now."

I gave her a glass of water. Soon she look-ed up in my face with a smile—such a soft, sad smile, like that of a dying person.

"Thank you ; you are very kind. I think you love me, Charlotte ?"

"Not a bit of it ; only on Alwyn's account. Shall I put by his letters? You have read them ?"

"All."

"They are very beautiful letters !"

"Very beautiful letters."

"Then having praised them as much as duty requires, let us put them away and talk of some-thing else."

"Oh, yes !"

She turned her chair round to the window, and sat leaning out till it grew dusk. Soon after I took her home as usual. Passing the little bridge, she clung to my arm for a minute. I asked her if any thing was the matter.

"It turned me sick again—the water. How fast it runs—how fast it runs!"

I left her sitting at the supper-table with her grandparents. I have in memory a perfect pic-ture of her there; white' as a statue—but then she was always pale—with her light hair partly dropping down, just as she had taken her bon-net off; her eyes looking straight forward, with a melancholy blankness in them; her thin hands folded over each other on the table-cloth, one finger tightly pressing the wedding ring.

Oh, my sister—my poor Marjory !

CHAPTER VII.

In the middle of the following night I was roused by a message from the farm. The pains of motherhood had prematurely come upon Alwyn's wife, and Alwyn was not here—would not be here till morning!

I rose, prepared to run across the fields at once, without waiting for daylight. In passing out, I stumbled over my desk. A horrible idea flashed across my mind. I *must* be satisfied.

Ay, even before I went to her, I must be satisfied.

I struck a light. I dragged out the packet of Alwyn's letters—looked them over separately and carefully. Inside one, with which it had no connection, and into which it must have slipped by the merest, the most fatal chance, I found the small half sheet in which he had said, "*she should never know till her dying day that he had married her from gratitude.*"

Then I felt sure that she had read it. Likewise that, in a different sense, alas! to that in which they were written—those words had and would come true.

Going across those meadows, in the dawn, with the dull stolid step with which one goes to meet the Inevitable, I felt as certain as if I saw it written in the red lines along the east, that the day then breaking would be my sister's "dying day."

She was perfectly calm. She smiled when I entered, saying, "I knew you would come, Charlotte."

I remember once, when her throes were hard, she spoke of Rachel at Ephrath, and said, "If it were a boy, she might almost call the child Benoni."

"But his father called him Benjamin," whispered the old grandmother, scarcely knowing what she was saying. "Look how Marjory shivers! Don't fret, darling; Alwyn will be here in an hour or two. Isn't it fortunate, Miss Reid, that she should never have asked to see her husband?"

I motioned silence, for Marjory continued shuddering convulsively. At last she drew my head down to hers, and put her lips to my ear.

"Do you think—tell no one I said so—but do you think he will love my child, his own, own child?"

Very soon she grew delirious, and talked incoherently and fast, every sentence ending with some thing about "gratitude."

When Alwyn came to the farm, he heard her voice thus sharp and wild. He was not allowed to see her.

If she had seen *him*—his intolerable remorse and agony! But it was too late; I do not think any human power, any human love could then have saved her.

Alwyn rode off like a madman in search of all the medical help in the country. When he came back, no frightful ravings met his ear. I was waiting for him at the door.

Marjory was lying, very still and beautiful—more beautiful perhaps than he had ever seen her—with her little dead baby beside her. We put it there.

He had no longer wife nor child—only his poor heart-broken sister.

CHAPTER VIII.

After my brother became a widower, I gave up my little school and went to keep his house.

He had nobody but me; for he had grown an altered man. The brilliant London society dropped from him—he could amuse it no longer. A few people called once or twice to do the civil to me, to inquire after "poor Mr. Reid," and confide to me their hopes that he would soon get over it and marry again—all men did so. Gradually, however, they ceased their visits, for they never saw him; and were not particularly attracted by his sister. So we two were left in solitude.

His literary patron discovered that it was useless to have a secretary who could not be entertaining; so he aided Alwyn in getting the secretaryship to an insurance company. Thither, day after day, Alwyn, who once hated business, now patiently trudged—disappearing after breakfast, appearing again at five—then settling down with interminable office papers before him until bedtime.

He never now went out of an evening.

Sometimes he would lift his eyes, and for five minutes at a time, stare with a fixed, sad gaze on the chair opposite, where she used to sit—I always took care to sit at the other side myself—but from the day she was buried he never mentioned Marjory's name.

Many months after, he happened to have a short but sharp illness, and, unlike most men, illness always made Alwyn gentle, loving, childlike, and good.

I had been sitting up with him till late at night, till after he had dropped into his first sleep. Suddenly he started out of it, moaning drowsily, "Don't go—don't go, Marjory."

I roused him, "It is only a dream, Alwyn, dear."

He answered sharply, "You are mistaken—I wish you would leave me. She will not come because you are in the room."

I was afraid he was delirious. My looks must have grieved him; for after a minute he held out his hand.

"I did not mean to be cross with you, Charlotte. You are very good to me. Nobody ever loved me like you, except—"

I knew whom he meant.

After a while, lying broad awake, and speaking in a rational tone, without any excitement, he said to me: "Sister, I will tell you something which I never intended to tell any one. It might be thought a delusion, a piece of down-

right insanity on my part, but it is as true as
that you are sitting here. You will not mention
it again.

"Is it likely, when you desire me not?"

"Well, then, listen. Every night since the
first night we came back into this house I have
seen, the moment I put the candle out, her—
Marjory"—(he stopped)—"my dear wife Marjory, sitting where you sit, with her hand laid
on her own pillow—what used to be her own—
looking at me. If I move, she vanishes—but
if I lie quiet, she sits there; sometimes all night
long. Now do you believe me?"

I paused a minute, then said, "Yes, I do.
That is, I believe it to be *possible.*"

I think any woman who knows what it is to
love as Marjory loved my brother, will likewise
allow that such a thing is at least possible.

"What does she look like?"

"Herself, exactly. But more as she used to
look as a girl, before—before I married her."

"Does she ever speak?"

"Never."

He lay quiet a few minutes, then broke out
into a sort of moan, "Oh, my poor Marjory,
what a blind fool was I! Sometimes, I fancy,
she *felt* the truth—though, thank God! she
never knew it."

For I had not dared to tell him the terrible
fact, which, in spite of the doctor's positive
declaration that she must inevitably have died
in childbirth, often made me feel as if I were
my sister's murderess.

"Charlotte, do you think she knows I love
her now?"

"I do think it."

I wept; I could not but weep. It seemed so
sad and strange that this love, the one hope
and desire of her existence, should only have
come after she had died. Yet, poor Marjory,
she might have thought it worth living for!

Our conversation ceased. My brother never
recurred to it, any more than if it had happened
in a dream of the night or a delirium during
his illness.

I do not know how long this delusion or
visitation—whichever it may be called—lasted.
In a few months my brother had become such
a quiet, grave man, wholly absorbed in business,
that any one would have thought him the last
person in the world to be subject to a superstitious fancy.

His character totally changed. From having
been transparent as daylight and gay as sunshine, he grew reserved, subdued, sometimes
even cold—but cold only toward strangers.
Toward any one who liked or loved him, he
seemed morbidly anxious to return every grain
of that liking or loving. He was solicitously
kind, even to a fault. No creature heard from
him a sharp or angry word—none ever knew
him pursue his own comfort or pleasure in preference to theirs.

We lived in the house at Kensington—the
house where he had first brought his bride, and
where he had come back, a solitary widower—

for seven years. A peaceful life it was, without any events of any kind.

My brother was now thirty-two years old.

CHAPTER IX.

I URGED Alwyn to pay the visit. Ockham
was a beautiful place. Sir —— —— (his former patron, who was still as much a friend to
him as a shallow, sentimental, fashionable *lit-
terateur* can be) eagerly pressed him to go. He
had been toiling at that insurance office early
and late, without any holiday, for seven years;
except that once a year, so long as Mr. and
Mrs. Blair lived, he used to go down to the
farm, generally in the winter time. But that
stay was in the original, not in the corrupted
and pleasurable sense—a keeping of holy-day.

We always came up to London better and
calmer after this visit—not exactly to his wife's
grave, for we both held that the revisiting and
mourning over graves is a needless, almost a
sinful, thing to those who believe in the immortality and perpetual presence of the beloved lost
—but to the places sanctified by Marjory's living presence, and Marjory's love.

It did not make him sad now. Human nature is human nature; and God's providence
allows not that there should ever be in any human heart a continual unhealed wound.

The snowdrops of seven winters had grown
over all that was mortal of Marjory and her
little babe. The widower, though never forgetting either, lived on calmly and was comforted.

I was glad when he at last consented to mingle again for a brief season with the circle to
which he had once brightly belonged, and to
revisit Ockham Tower.

There was some slight bustle of preparation,
for his habits had become simple even to home-
liness. As delicately as I could I started the
question whether he should not put off his deep
mourning, which he had worn all these years.
But he absolutely refused.

However, a handsome man never looks so
well as in black, and my brother was a very
handsome man still. His voice had a graver
tone—his face was somewhat sharper—with a
slight baldness over the forehead. Every trace
of boyish sentimentalism had become absorbed
in the maturity of middle age. You would
hardly recognize the Alwyn Reid of former days,
save from those "gentle manners" which had
won the heart of poor Marjory Blair.

I admired him very much myself, and thought
it probable that other women would do the
same.

While I was packing his portmanteau, he
said, hurriedly,

"Charlotte, do you think this is quite safe?"

He showed me the wedding-ring—hers, which
he had always carried at his watch-chain, it being too small for any of his fingers.

"It is worn thin, you see. I am afraid of losing it."

"You had better give it to me to keep until you come back."

I took it. It lies in my desk now.

My brother's letters from Ockham Tower were almost like his letters of ten years ago. Certainly in description, in humor, in the rare and exquisite tact which, without effort, says precisely what the recipient of the epistle likes to hear, I never knew a correspondent like Alwyn. His were not "show" letters, written as if the author were fully conscious that every line was, or deserved to be, preserved in adamantine record for the edification of posterity; nor were they those formal, cold documents which very clever and good people sometimes indite—mummied epistles, with no more of the writer's true soul in them than there is in the body of a defunct Egyptian. No. Alwyn was the prince of correspondents. He wrote, not for himself or too much of himself, but from himself to you. Wrote, because he loved you, and liked to write to you, because he knew you loved him, and liked to hear about him. His letters were himself—his best, tenderest, noblest self. It was a bright day whenever the postman brought one to the door.

He told me a good deal about the people who were staying at Ockham—very pleasant company, as it seemed. Among the rest—of two lovely little girls, named Rossiter, with whom he was greatly charmed. In his young man's time he had been particularly fond of children. These tiny playmates, of from four to six, were apparently great favorites of his.

They had a mamma who, he said, "was an agreeable and lady-like woman."

In the three following letters, which came on three several days when I had vainly expected him, he having fixed to return home, he did not mention the Rossiters. His tone of mind seemed different from what it had been in the early part of his visit—restless, perplexed, with a slight touch of sadness.

I had begun to be uneasy, when suddenly, without giving me notice, he came back. He had been absent a full month.

Though it was late, we sat down to talk over the fire. He seemed in high spirits—very communicative about every body and every thing, with one exception.

"Alwyn, you have forgotten to tell me any thing about the Rossiters."

He turned toward the fire. "Oh, they are very charming little girls."

"And their mother, I suppose the same adjective may apply to her?"

"Certainly."

"Are they her only children?"

"Yes."

"Is she a middle-aged person?"

"About my age, or a little younger."

"And who is Mr. Rossiter?"

"Really, did I not tell you? Mrs. Rossiter is a widow."

An "agreeable" widow, of thirty, with two "charming and lovable" little girls! If the subject had been one that allowed jesting, I might have taken this excellent opportunity for a little harmless joke at his expense. As it was, I only laid my hand upon his arm, and looked at him, smiling. His color rose, I thought.

"What are you staring at me for, Charlotte?" spoken all but angrily.

I drew back, and sat gazing into the fire for a long time. Thoughts, many and fast—possibilities which I had long believed impossibilities, traversed my brain, with dull, steady tramp, like a regiment going to battle. Finally, they fought the battle out—other and softer thoughts took their place.

I looked sideways at my brother. He was the last of our race. Youth, energy, hope, were still strong within him. Life is often only begun at two-and-thirty; and a man can not live forever upon a dream or a memory, as a woman can.

Still the idea which had entered my mind was painful. I was rather glad not to know the whole truth at present.

"Brother, it is growing late."

"Stay—just ten minutes—I want to talk to you."

We sat down. It struck me forcibly, almost with a chill of pain, how exactly we were sitting as we sat one winter night in my cottage, before he married Marjory.

He dashed into the matter with a desperate plunge—

"Mrs. Rossiter is a very agreeable woman."

"So you said."

"You would like her very much, Charlotte. She wishes—in fact, I wish—that you should visit her."

"Does she live in London?"

"In the season; otherwise at her jointure-house, Manor Place, in Shropshire."

"She has property, then."

"A good deal."

"And you think I shall like her. Do you like her?"

"Very much indeed."

"Alwyn, I am going to put to you a plain question; answer it or not, as you will."

"Go on."

"You know what I think of second marriages, at least for men; that they are natural, justifiable, often even advisable. I never should object to—I mean regret—your making a worthy second choice. Will it be Mrs. Rossiter?"

"Not yet; oh! Charlotte, not yet. Don't talk of my marrying—yet." And with one wild, mournful glance at *the chair*—we had never moved it—he dropped his face between his hands.

"Have you any hesitation in telling me how the matter stands between you—the engagement?"

"Good Heavens! there is none. How could I form one without telling you? Only she loves me, Charlotte—loves me. I found it out quite by chance."

"And you (the word 'love' stuck in my throat), you return her feelings?"

"I admire her. I have thought sometimes I could be happy with her, if I could only make her happy. Something in me cries out, 'Atone, Atone!' Charlotte, remember, she loves me. I can not, I dare not, break another loving heart."

Break the heart of a handsome widow of thirty, rich, with two charming children?—I could have smiled at the notion; but it was a sore point, made sorer by the never-ceasing stings of conscience. Either he truly believed what he said, or he deceived himself, led away unconsciously by his long dormant and now suddenly aroused craving after the refined and the beautiful: his perpetual necessity of being loved.

When I saw Mrs. Rossiter—he took me to pay her a visit next day—I was by no means certain whether he loved her, with the high, pure love that few men feel more than once—but I was convinced that he desired to marry her.

Let me do justice to this lady, who, as I detected almost immediately, was deeply and generously attached to my brother. But what marvel in that?

She was what people call a "gentleman's beauty;" that is, a beauty who attracts and dazzles immediately. Of person rather large and Juno-like; cheerful, even brilliant in conversation, though not the least of the "intellectual" stamp; a thoroughly sensible, open-hearted woman, accustomed to, and rather fond of, but not spoiled by the world.

We dined with her. Coming home, Alwyn did not ask me, as in that far day in a buried life—buried from us as completely as the young face which had then looked from under the roses at the gate of the farm—he did not ask me "how I liked her?" He only made the careless observation, "that I seemed to like the children."

"Yes, they are extremely pretty little girls."

We parted in a very friendly manner, and with a sort of silent understanding, on the staircase. He kissed me before he went into his room.

I marveled whether that night he saw the figure sitting watching him, with its hand on the vacant pillow that had been Marjory's.

Yet surely had she known she would have felt, as I did, that whatever makes the justifiable happiness of the beloved can never be the grief of those who love.

Mrs. Rossiter became Mrs. Reid. It was a grand wedding; St. George's, Hanover square; a dozen carriages; ten bridesmaids, including the two graceful children, in India muslin flounced up to the waist; and a Champagne breakfast afterward. Nothing at all that could remind the bridegroom of that dim village church where, through the soft rain of a May

morning, we had walked; just we five, the betrothed pair, old Mr. and Mrs. Blair, and I. Alwyn looked very well; composed, dignified, rather grave. Returned from the church, the little girls jumped on his knee, and called him "papa." He started; then kissed them fondly, saying in a smothered tone, "that he hoped always to keep and to deserve that name."

I have often thought those pretty innocents had a great deal to do in making the marriage.

Well, it was all over quickly, like a dream. I woke alone in my brother's old house, of which I had so long been the mistress; of which a large "To be Let" in one window, and a "To be Sold by Auction" in another, revealed that he was no longer master, nor I mistress, any more.

But he had spent the last evening alone with me, going quietly and solemnly through all the rooms, choosing the furniture which she had happened to like, and the little knick-knackeries which had belonged to her in her maiden days, or been wedding-presents afterward. All these he gave to me, though without once mentioning her name.

Likewise, he made a settlement upon me of the little fortune which Marjory brought him, the principal of which he had never once touched.

All these gifts made me quite a well-to-do woman. I half hesitated to receive the last; but he imperatively bade me be silent.

"You know, sister, it is exactly what she—" The sentence was never finished.

CHAPTER X.

My old cottage near the farm being to let, I took it. It seemed a kind of satisfaction now that some one who had been fond of Marjory should live near the village church she was married in, and (though that was against my creed, yet instinct is often stronger than opinion) near the white head-stone on which was her simple name, "Marjory Reid," and which was —I mourned—the sole memento left on earth of such a pure and beautiful soul.

I erred. The Giver and Claimer of souls knows His work better. Evil perishes; it has done its work as a purifying and chastening agent; it dies, according to its natural tendency, which is to die. But Good is from its very nature and origin immortal.

Every Sunday I used to say to myself, passing by the head-stone, "Poor Marjory! what wert thou sent on earth for? Only to love, suffer, die, and be forgotten?"

Oh, purblind unbeliever that I was! As if, in the wondrous mechanism of God's universe, wherein nothing is ever wasted, He should suffer innocence and love to pass away into oblivion, having apparently done no work, effected no good, and only lived less to enjoy than to endure!

If we could but see a little forward toward the end!

It so happened, from various counteracting chances, that my brother and I did not meet for several years. I was always disinclined to travel, and he was fast bound at the estate in Shropshire of which his marriage had made him master.

An excellent master he proved; filling admirably the difficult position of the husband of "a woman of property." He became a noted man in the county; a large agriculturist, a member of parliament, a justice of the peace. Children sprang up, one after the other, round his board: he was to all appearance a prosperous and happy man. Nay, he himself told me so. His letters—for we maintained a steady correspondence—gradually changed their character into the business-like gravity of middle age. I hardly knew it, till I happened to read one of those, long ago, from Ockham Tower, and lay it side by side with these.

Alwyn was not my only Shropshire correspondent. Mrs. Reid favored me rarely; she was not a ready penwoman; but various minor scrawls came to hand from the young Misses Rossiter. One day I received a few lines of wide-ruled pen-over-pencil writing, as if some one had guided the little hand: ah, bless that little hand! it was of my own flesh and blood:

"DEAR AUNT,—I love you, and some of these days I am coming to see you. Your affectionate niece,
"MARGARET REID."

She was Alwyn's eldest child.

I will not confess to how many people in our village I triumphantly showed that document. I was growing a very weak-minded old woman.

On the day fixed—it was a day in winter, just after the New Year—I sat awaiting my brother and my niece. All was trim in my cottage, over the appearance of which I was morbidly anxious, considering what the Misses Rossiter had told me of the splendors of Manor Place. There was holly on the mantle-piece, and holly on the piano that no living fingers had ever touched—ah, I remember! The garden was trim and green; and I knew by the snow-drops in my borders what a number Alwyn would find—where I supposed he would not think of going now.

There drove up grandly a post-chaise and four. A gentleman leaped out; I could hardly believe it was my brother Alwyn.

Those who live alone are prone to think that the world stands still, and that the people therein cherish memories and feelings which belong only to solitude. Living here I had naturally lived wholly in past days. I expected the Alwyn Reid who married Marjory: I found Alwyn Reid, Esq., of Manor Place, magistrate of the county of Salop, husband of Mrs. Reid, father of a large and rising family. At first I was disappointed. Not afterward. Not when I had his daughter on my knee, and him by my side, and saw the love between them.

Margaret was a very sweet-looking child; but I vainly traced any family line. Yet it seemed as if she belonged to me familiarly—as if she had come out of the far-back period of a forgotten life. I found it almost impossible to believe she was Mrs. Reid's daughter.

She made herself quite at home immediately; strayed about the house; talked to Mary (who had married her jo, buried him, and come back to me); examined all the furniture, and especially the piano.

"It is locked. May I open it?"

"It has not been opened for many years, my dear."

"Oh, please, aunt!"

I could not resist the name. I began fumbling among my bunch of keys.

"Whose piano was it?"

"It belonged to—a lady—who is dead."

The child colored—interchanged a glance with her father. He said, gently, "Yes, it was hers, Margaret!" and walked, first to the window, then quietly out of the room.

"Aunt, I know who that lady was. Papa has told me about her. She was my half-mamma; I love her very much."

"Bless thee, my dear child."

"Don't cry now, aunt. Papa and I never do, and we often talk about her. I know her quite well. Papa says I am just a very little like her sometimes. Am I?"

"It may be."

"Oh, I wish I were! She was so good. Papa loved her so. He says, the more I grow like her, the more he shall love me every day."

I could hardly speak. Oh, Marjory, thou wert living still—thou couldst not die.

"Aunt, now may I open her piano?"

The next day I had it put in tune. Margaret was very happy; she sat all the evening playing her pretty, simple music by the firelight, her father and I listening. It seemed as if the spirit of the lost had come back to us in that child.

It was a strange thing—which, while they were staying here, struck other people besides myself—that little Margaret was very like Alwyn's first wife. Not in face exactly, but in manner and ways. As she grew older, the likeness rather increased than diminished. Year by year—for from this time I visited my brother's household nearly every summer—I watched her bloom into womanhood. They were a handsome family; she was at once the least handsome and the flower of them all.

She was her father's right hand. He loved her better than all his other sons and daughters.

I do not think Mrs. Reid minded this, being a kind-hearted, business-like woman, to whom life was an easy, active, bustling affair. She brought up her family well, and from their cradles began settling how she should put out her sons in the world, and marry her handsome daughters. She was affectionate to her husband, but always wondered what he could see so especially charming in that little plain Margaret.

How Mrs. Reid would have smiled—a calm, good-humored, incredulous smile—if any one had told her that all the good influence in house, the higher spiritual influence, in opposition to the very strong tide of worldliness which was always setting the other way, came from "little plain Margaret," and through her from one whom perhaps the good lady had hardly thought of a dozen times, "Mr. Reid's first wife, who died in childbirth, poor thing!"

CHAPTER XI.

My brother had nearly reached his threescore years. The latter half of them he had had a peaceful, uneventful life. I will pass it over rapidly, for it seems to me now as if the years had fled like lightning, and as if it were but yesterday that he was a young man—the young man who married Marjory.

And now he was an old man, wheeled about in a garden chair, looking for all his pleasures, amusements, comforts, to the one companion who never failed him—his daughter Margaret.

Until the age of sixty he was a brave, sturdy English gentleman; the boldest hunter, the keenest shot, the most active and the *justest* justice in the whole county. Sickness came and changed his whole existence. He became an invalid for life. His family gradually grew accustomed to the fact, and all went on as if he were a mere adjunct of the household, to be tenderly treated, and paid great attention to when they could spare time. But the true head of Manor Place was Mrs. Reid.

They were rather a fractious family, especially when the sons and daughters grew up; and between them and the energetic mother storms often arose. Never with the father. His study, with Margaret and his books beside him, was the sanctuary of the house.

Margaret has often told me, that did the children bring never so many complaints, his constant command was—for his least entreaty had the weight of a command—"Respect your mother!" "Obey your mother!" "Bear with your mother, *she* has much to bear." And to the mother herself—though, well as she loved him, she tried him sometimes—none ever heard him give a harsh word.

I believe through all his life, in all his conduct to her, the one idea pursued him—of his duty to atone to this woman, who loved him, for all the anguish he had caused to the other.

"Charlotte," he said to me, one day looking after Mrs. Reid as she sailed smilingly from under the walnut shade where we were sitting, "I think I have made *her* happy."

"Papa," murmured Margaret's fond voice behind, "you make every body happy."

It was true. One I knew—one who had been dead more than thirty years—would have rejoiced to see into what perfection his character had grown—how the faults of his youth had melted away, and his virtues shone out clearer, year by year. And could she have seen all this, surely her true heart would have said, what matter if he were no longer hers? What matter if she and her poor life were totally forgotten, so that he thus nobly fulfilled his life, faithful to himself and to his God?

But she was not forgotten—Alwyn and I often talked of her when we were alone. Ay, and sometimes to his children—to his eldest and dearest child, he would speak (without any sacrilege to their mother, and his own good wife) of the girl who was his friend when he was little more than a boy—of the woman who had loved him so faithfully, and died years before any of them were born. Margaret said to me once, she always felt as if her true mother—the mother of her heart and soul, whose influence had formed her mind and moulded her character, had been her father's first wife.

CHAPTER XII.

THE end must come. Let me hasten to it.

I sit once more in my little cottage; Margaret sits opposite. We are very silent; we have not got used to that change which our black dresses show. She will put off hers in due time for marriage white; I shall wear mine until I dress—that is, until they dress me—in the simpler garment which no one ever lays aside.

We have lost him—I have lost him, for a little while, "a little while!" It is so comforting, so comfortable to repeat the words, that I shall not dwell upon the loss itself, except to narrate a circumstance which occurred on the night before his departure, which I have often thought of afterward.

It was my turn to sit up with Alwyn; there was no one in the room but me. He was not sleeping, but lay quite still, with his eyes open, looking earnestly on the curtains at the foot of the bed. They were looped up, with just space enough between for a person to stand.

He lay so long, with his eye steadily fixed, that at last I spoke.

"Alwyn, if I move the night-light, would you try to sleep?"

"No. Hush!"

"What are you looking at?"

He made no answer for a minute; then turning, heaved a deep sigh. "You should not have spoken. She is gone now."

"Who?"

"Marjory."

I was greatly startled. Not that I disbelieved the statement; I have already declared that I hold such visions or visitations to be at least possible. But in this illness, though it was not a more severe attack than he had several times recovered from, it seemed almost like a supernatural warning.

"Are you sure it was no fancy? Have you seen her before?"

"Not for thirty years, until now. These five nights she has come and stood there." He pointed to the foot of the bed. "She looks so calm, smiling, and glad. She is as young as ever, while I—"

Alas, his white head, his withered, palsied hands!

While he was speaking, Mrs. Reid and Margaret came in, and we ceased talking.

They wished me to go to bed; but a foreboding, impossible to conquer, kept me in Alwyn's room during the night.

At six in the morning my brother died.

His wife, his sons, and daughters, were all surrounding him on either side the bed. At its foot no one was standing. Just when we thought he was gone, he opened his eyes and fixed them steadily there.

"Mar— Mar—" He tried in vain to utter the name.

"Go to him, Margaret, my love!" sobbed Mrs. Reid. "Go and kiss your dear father."

He heard, and faintly turned to receive the embrace of his wife and daughter. Then, turning away from both, he stretched his hands with a bright dying smile to the place where no one stood, and faltered out distinctly, as if answering to a call, the words—

"Yes, Marjory."

He never spoke again.

M. ANASTASIUS.

CHAPTER I.

I will relate to you, my friend, the whole history, from the beginning to—nearly—the end.

The first time that—that it happened, was on this wise.

My husband and myself were sitting in a private box at the theatre—one of the two large London theatres. The performance was, I remember well, an Easter piece, in which were introduced live dromedaries and an elephant, at whose clumsy feats we were considerably amused. I mention this to show how calm and even gay was the state of both our minds that evening, and how little there was in any of the circumstances of the place or time to cause, or render us liable to—what I am about to describe.

I liked this Easter piece better than any serious drama. My life had contained enough of the tragic element to make me turn with a sick distaste from all imitations thereof in books or plays. For months, ever since our marriage, Alexis and I had striven to lead a purely childish, commonplace existence, eschewing all stirring events and strong emotions, mixing little in society, and then, with one exception, making no associations beyond the moment.

It was easy to do this in London; for we had no relations—we two were quite alone and free. Free—free! How wildly I sometimes grasped Alexis's hand as I repeated that word.

He was young—so was I. At times, as on this night, we would sit together and laugh like children. It was so glorious to know of a surety that now we could think, feel, speak, act—above all, love one another—haunted by no counteracting spell, responsible to no living creature for our life and our love.

But this had been our lot only for a year—I had recollected the date, shuddering, in the morning—for one year, from this same day. We had been laughing very heartily, cherishing mirth, as it were, like those who would caress a lovely bird that had been frightened out of its natural home and grown wild and rare in its visits, only tapping at the lattice for a minute, and then gone. Suddenly, in the pause between the acts, when the house was half darkened, our laughter died away.

"How cold it is!" said Alexis, shivering. I shivered too; but not with cold—it was more like the involuntary sensation at which people say, "Some one is walking over my grave." I said so, jestingly.

"Hush, Isbel," whispered my husband, and again the draft of cold air seemed to blow right between us.

I should describe the position in which we were sitting; both in front of the box, but he in full view of the audience, while I was half hidden by the curtain. Between us, where the cold draft blew, was a vacant chair. Alexis tried to move this chair, but it was fixed to the floor. He passed behind it, and wrapped a mantle over my shoulders.

"This London winter is cold for you, my love. I half wish we had taken courage, and sailed once more for Hispaniola."

"Oh, no—oh, no! No more of the sea!" said I, with another and stronger shudder.

He took his former position, looking round indifferently at the audience. But neither of us spoke. The mere word "Hispaniola" was enough to throw a damp and a silence over us both.

"Isbel," he said at last, rousing himself, with a half smile, "I think you must have grown remarkably attractive. Look! half the glasses opposite are lifted to our box. It can not be to gaze at me, you know. Do you remember telling me I was the ugliest fellow you ever saw?" "Oh, Alex!" Yet it was quite true—I had thought him so, in far back, strange, awful times, when I, a girl of sixteen, had my mind wholly filled with one ideal—one insane, exquisite dream; when I brought my innocent child's garlands, and sat me down under one great spreading magnificent tree, which seemed to me the king of all the trees of the field, until I felt its dews dropping death upon my youth, and my whole soul withering under its venomous shade. " Oh, Alex!" I cried once more, looking fondly on his beloved face, where no unearthly beauty dazzled, no unnatural calm repelled ; where all was simple, noble, manly, true. " Husband, I thank Heaven for that dear ' ugliness' of yours. Above all, though blood runs strong, they say, I thank Heaven that I see in you no likeness to—"

Alexis knew what name I meant, though for a whole year past—since God's mercy made it to us only a name—we had ceased to utter it, and let it die wholly out of the visible world. We dared not breathe to ourselves, still less to one another, how much brighter, holier, happier, that world was, now that the Divine wisdom had taken—*him*—into another. For he had been my husband's uncle; likewise, once my guardian. He was now dead.

I sat looking at Alexis, thinking what a strange thing it was that his dear face should not have always been as beautiful to me as it was now. That loving my husband now so deeply, so wholly, clinging to him heart to heart, in the deep peace of satisfied, all-trusting, and all-dependent human affection, I could ever have felt that emotion, first as an exquisite bliss, then as an ineffable terror, which now had vanished away, and become—nothing.

" They are gazing still, Isbel."

" Who, and where ?" For I had quite forgotten what he said about the people staring at me.

" And there is Colonel Hart. He sees us. Shall I beckon him ?"

" As you will."

Colonel Hart came up into our box. He shook hands with my husband, bowed to me, then looked round, half curiously, half uneasily.

" I thought there was a friend with you."

" None. We have been alone all evening."

" Indeed ? How strange !"

" What ! That my wife and I should enjoy a play alone together ?" said Alexis, smiling.

" Excuse me, but really I was surprised to find you alone. I have certainly seen for the last half hour a third person sitting on the chair, between you both."

We could not help starting ; for, as I stated before, the chair had, in truth, been left between us, empty.

" Truly our unknown friend must have been invisible. Nonsense, Colonel ; how can you turn Mrs. Saltram pale, by thus peopling with your fancies the vacant air ?"

" I tell you, Alexis, said the Colonel (he was my husband's old friend, and had been present at our hasty and private marriage), " nothing could be more unlike a fancy, even were I given to such. It was a very remarkable person who sat here. Even strangers noticed him."

" Him !" I whispered.

" It was a man, then," said my husband, rather angrily.

" A very peculiar-looking, and extremely handsome man. I saw many glasses leveled at him."

" What was he like ?" said Alexis, rather sarcastically. " Did he speak ? or we to him ?"

" No—neither. He sat quite still, in this chair."

My husband turned away. If the Colonel had not been his friend, and so very simpleminded, honest, and sober a gentleman, I think Alexis would have suspected some drunken hoax, and turned him out of the box immediately. As it was, he only said : " My dear fellow, the third act is beginning. Come up again at its close, and tell me if you again see my invisible friend, who must find so great an attraction in viewing, gratis, a dramatic performance."

" I perceive—you think it a mere hallucination of mine. We shall see. I suspect the trick is on your side, and that you are harboring some proscribed Hungarian. But I'll not betray him. Adieu !"

" The ghostly Hungarian shall not sit next you, love, this time," said Alexis, trying once more to remove the chair. But possibly, though he jested, he was slightly nervous, and his efforts were vain. " What nonsense this is ! Isbel, let us forget it. I will stand behind you, and watch the play."

He stood—I clasping his hand secretly and hard ; then, I grew quieter ; until, as the drop-scene fell, the same cold air swept past us. It was as if some one, fresh from the sharp seawind, had entered the box. And just at that moment, we saw Colonel Hart's and several other glasses leveled as before.

" It is strange," said Alexis.

" It is horrible," I said. For I had been cradled in Scottish, and then filled with German superstition ; besides, the events of my own life had been so wild, so strange, that there was nothing too ghastly or terrible for my imagination to conjure up.

" I will summon the Colonel. We must find out this," said my husband, speaking beneath his breath, and looking round, as if he thought he was overheard.

Colonel Hart came up. He looked very serious ; so did a young man who was with him.

" Captain Elmore, let me introduce you to Mrs. Saltram. Saltram, I have brought my friend here to attest that I have played off on you no unworthy jest. Not ten minutes since, he, and I, and some others saw the same gen-

tleman whom I described to you half an hour
ago, sitting as I described—in this chair."

"Most certainly—in this chair," added the
young captain.

My husband bowed; he kept a courteous
calmness, but I felt his hand grow clammy in
mine.

"Of what appearance, sir, was this unknown
acquaintance of my wife's and mine, whom
every body appears to see except ourselves?"

"He was of middle age, dark-haired, pale.
His features were very still, and rather hard in
expression. He had on a cloth cloak with a
fur collar, and wore a long, pointed Charles-the-
First beard."

My husband and I clung-hand to hand with
an inexpressible horror. Could there be another man—a living man, who answered this
description?

"Pardon me," Alexis said, faintly. "The
portrait is rather vague; may I ask you to re-
paint it as circumstantially as you can?"

"He was, I repeat, a pale, or rather a sal-
low-featured man. His eyes were extremely
piercing, cold, and clear. The mouth close-
set—a very firm but passionless mouth. The
hair dark, seamed with gray—bald on the
brow—"

"Oh, Heaven!" I groaned in an anguish of
terror. For I saw again—clear as if he had never died—the face over which, for twelve long
months, had swept the merciful sea waves off
the shores of Hispaniola.

"Can you, Captain Elmore," said Alexis,
"mention no other distinguishing mark? This
countenance might resemble many men."

"I think not. It was a most remarkable
face. It struck me the more—because—" and
the young man grew almost as pale as we—"I
once saw another very like it."

"You see—a chance resemblance only. Fear
not, my darling," Alexis breathed in my ear.
"Sir, have you any reluctance to tell me who
was the gentleman?"

"It was no living man, but a corpse that we
last year picked up off a wreck, and again com-
mitted to the deep—in the Gulf of Mexico. It
was exactly the same face, and had the same
mark—a scar, cross-shape, over one temple."

"'Tis he! He can follow and torture us
still; I knew he could!"

Alexis smothered my shriek on his breast.

"My wife is ill. This description resembles
slightly a—a person we once knew. Hart, will
you leave us? But no, we must probe this
mystery. Gentlemen, will you once more descend to the lower part of the house, while we
remain here, and tell me if you still see the—
the figure, sitting in this chair?"

They went. We held our breaths. The
lights in the theatre were being extinguished,
the audience moving away. No one came near
our box; it was perfectly empty. Except our
two selves, we were conscious of no sight, no
sound. A few minutes after Colonel Hart
knocked.

"Come in," said Alexis, cheerily.

But, the Colonel—the bold soldier—shrank
back like a frightened child.

"I have seen him—I saw him but this
minute, sitting there!"

I swooned away.

CHAPTER II.

IT is right I should briefly give you my history up to this night's date.

I was a West Indian heiress—a posthumous,
and, soon after birth, an orphan child. Brought
up in my mother's country until I was sixteen
years old, I never saw my guardian. Then he
met me in Paris, with my governess, and for the
space of two years we lived under the same roof,
seeing one another daily.

I was very young; I had no father or brother; I wished for neither lover nor husband;
my guardian became to me the one object of
my existence.

It was no love-passion; he was far too old
for that, and I comparatively too young, at
least too childish. It was one of those insane,
rapturous adorations which young maidens'sometimes conceive, mingling a little of the tenderness of the woman with the ecstatic enthusiasm
of the devotee. There is hardly a prophet or
leader noted in the world's history who has not
been followed and worshiped by many such
women.

So was my guardian, M. Anastasius—not his
true name, but it sufficed then, and will now.

Many may recognize him as a known leader
in the French political and moral world—as
one who, by the mere force of intellect, wielded
the most irresistible and silently complete power
of any man I ever knew, in every circle into
which he came; women he won by his polished gentleness—men by his equally polished
strength. He would have turned a compliment
and signed a death-warrant with the same exquisitely calm grace. Nothing was to him too
great or too small. I have known him, on his
way to advise that the President's soldiers should
sweep a cannonade down the thronged street,
stop to pick up a strayed canary-bird, stroke its
broken wing, and confide it with beautiful tenderness to his bosom.

Oh, how tender! how mild! how pitiful he
could be!

When I say I loved him, I use, for want of
a better, a word which ill expresses that feeling.
It was—Heaven forgive me if I err in using the
similitude!—the sort of feeling the Shunamite
woman might have had for Elisha. Religion
added to its intensity, for I was brought up a
devout Catholic; and he, whatever his private
opinions might have been, adhered strictly to
the forms of the same Church. He was un-
married, and most people supposed him to belong to that Order called—though often, alas!
how unlike Him from whom they assume their
name—the Society of Jesus.

We lived thus—I entirely worshiping, he guiding, fondling, watching, and ruling by turns, for two whole years. I was mistress of a large fortune, and, though not beautiful, had, I believe, a tolerable intellect, and a keen wit. With both he used to play, according as it suited his whim—just as a boy plays with fire-works, amusing himself with their glitter—sometimes directing them against others, and smiling as they flashed or scorched—knowing that against himself they were utterly powerless and harmless. Knowing, too, perhaps, that were it otherwise, he had only to tread them out under foot, and step aside from the ashes, with the same unmoved, easy smile.

I never knew—nor know I to this day—whether I was in the smallest degree dear to him. Useful I was, I think, and pleasant, I believe. Possibly he liked me a little, as the potter likes his clay and the skillful mechanician his tools —until the clay hardened, and the fine tools refused to obey the master's hand.

I was the brilliant West Indian heiress. I did not marry. Why should I? At my house —at least it was called mine—all sorts and societies met, carrying on their separate games; the quiet, soft hand of M. Anastasius playing his game—in, and under, and through them all. Mingled with this grand game of the world was a lesser one—to which he turned sometimes, just for amusement, or because he could not cease from his métier—a simple, easy, domestic game, of which the battledore was that same ingenious hand, and the shuttlecock my foolish child's heart.

Thus much have I dilated on him, and on my own life, during the years when all its strong wild current flowed toward him; that, in what followed when the tide turned, no one may accuse me of fickleness, or causeless aversion, or insane terror of one who after all was only man, "whose breath is in his nostrils."

At seventeen I was wholly passive in his hands; he was my sole arbiter of right and wrong—my conscience—almost my God. As my character matured, and in a few things I began to judge for myself, we had occasional slight differences—begun, on my part, in shy humility, continued with vague doubt, but always ending in penitence and tears. Since one or other erred, of course it must be I. These differences were wholly on abstract points of truth or justice.

It was his taking me, by a persuasion that was like compulsion, to the ball at the Tuileries, which was given after Louis Napoleon Bonaparte had seized the Orleans property—and it was my watching my cousin's conduct there, his diplomatic caution of speech, his smooth smiling reverence to men whom I knew, and fancied he knew, to be either knaves or fools—that first startled me concerning him. Then it was I first began to question, in a trembling, terrified way—like one who catches a glimpse of the miracle-making priest's hands behind the robe of the worshiped idol—whether, great as

M. Anastasius was, as a political ruler, as a man of the world, as a faithful member of the Society of Jesus, he was altogether so great when viewed beside any one of those whose doctrines he disseminated, whose faith he professed.

He had allowed me the New Testament, and I had been reading it a good deal lately. I placed him, my spiritual guide, at first in adoring veneration, afterward with an uneasy comparison, beside the Twelve Fishermen of Galilee —beside the pattern of perfect manhood, as set forth in the preaching of their Divine Lord, and ours.

There was a difference.

The next time we came to any argument— always on abstract questions, for my mere individual will never had any scruple in resigning itself to his—instead of yielding I ceased open contest, and brought the matter afterward privately to the one infallible rule of right and wrong.

The difference grew.

Gradually, I began to take my cousin's wisdom—perhaps, even his virtues—with certain reservations, feeling that there was growing in me some antagonistic quality which prevented my full understanding or sympathizing with the idiosyncrasies of his character.

"But," I thought, "he is a Jesuit; he only follows the law of his Order, which allows temporizing, and diplomatizing, for noble ends. He merely dresses up the truth, and puts it in the most charming and safest light, even as we do our images of the Holy Virgin, adorning them for the adoration of the crowd, but ourselves spiritually worshiping them still. I do believe, much as he will dandle and play with the truth, that not for his hope of heaven would Anastasius stoop to a lie."

One day, he told me he should bring to my saloons an Englishman, his relative, who had determined on leaving the world and entering the priesthood.

"Is he of our faith?" asked I, indifferently.

"He is, from childhood. He has a strong, fine intellect; this, under fit guidance, may accomplish great things. Once of our Society, he might be my right hand in every Court in Europe. You will receive him?"

"Certainly."

But I paid very little heed to the stranger. There was nothing about him striking or peculiar. He was the very opposite of M. Anastasius. Besides, he was young, and I had learned to despise youth—my guardian was fifty years old.

Mr. Saltram (you will already have guessed that it was he) showed equal indifference to me. He watched me sometimes, did little kindnesses for me, but always was quiet and silent—a mere cloud floating in the brilliant sky, which M. Anastasius lit up as its gorgeous sun. For me, I became moonlike, appearing chiefly at my cousin's set and rise.

I was not happy. I read more in my Holy Book,

and less in my breviary; I watched with keener, harder eyes my cousin Anastasius, weighed all his deeds, listened to and compared his words. My intellect worshiped him, my memoried tenderness clung round him still, but my conscience had fled out of his keeping, and made for itself a higher and purer ideal. Measured with common men, he was godlike yet—above all passions, weaknesses, crimes; but viewed by the one perfect standard of man—Christian man—in charity, humility, single-mindedness, guilelessness, truth—my idol was no more. I came to look for it, and found only the empty shrine.

He went on a brief mission to Rome. I marveled that, instead as of yore, wandering sadly through the empty house, from the moment he quitted it, I breathed freer, as if a weight were taken out of the air. His absence used to be like wearisome ages—now it seemed hardly a week before he came back.

I happened to be sitting with his nephew Alexis when I heard his step down the corridor—the step which had once seemed at every touch to draw music from the chords of my prostrate heart, but which now made it shrink into itself, as if an iron-shod footfall had passed along its strings.

Anastasius looked slightly surprised at seeing Alexis and myself together, but his welcome was very kind to both.

I could not altogether return it. I had just found out two things which, to say the least, had startled me. I determined to prove them at once.

"My cousin, I thought you were aware that, though a Catholic myself, my house is open, and my friendship likewise, to honest men of every creed. Why did you give your relative so hard an impression of me, as to suppose I would dislike him on account of his faith? And why did you not tell me that Mr. Saltram has, for some years, been a Protestant?"

I know not what to reply he made; I know only that it was ingenious, lengthy, gentle, courteous, that for the time being it seemed entirely satisfactory, that we spent all three together a most pleasant evening. It was only when I lay down on my bed, face to face with the solemn Dark, in which dwelt conscience, truth, and God, that I discovered how Anastasius had, for some secret—doubtless blameless, nay, even justifiable purpose, told of me, and to me, two absolute Lies!

Disguise it as he might, excuse it as I might, and did, they were Lies. They haunted me—flapping their black wings like a couple of fiends, mopping and mowing behind him when he came—sitting on his shoulders, and mocking his beautiful, calm, majestic face—for days. That was the beginning of sorrows; gradually they grew until they blackened my whole world.

M. Anastasius was bent, as he had (for once truly) told me, on winning his young nephew back into the true fold, making him an instrument of that great purpose which was to bring all Europe, the Popedom itself, under the power

of the Society of Jesus. Not thus alone—a man may be forgiven, nay, respected, who sells his soul for an abstract cause, in which he himself is to be absorbed and forgotten; but in this case it was not—though I long believed it, it was not so. Carefully as he disguised it, I slowly found out that the centre of all things—the one grand pivot upon which this vast machinery for the improvement, or rather government, of the world, was to be made to turn, was M. Anastasius.

Alexis Saltram might be of use to him. He was rich, and money is power; an Englishman, and Englishmen are usually honorable and honored. Also there was in him a dogged directness of purpose that would make him a strong, if carefully guided, tool.

However, the young man resisted. He admired and revered his kinsman; but he himself was very single-hearted, stanch, and true. Something in that truth, which was the basis of his character, struck sympathy with mine. He was far inferior in most things to Anastasius—he knew it, I knew it—but, through all, this divine element of truth was patent, beautifully clear. It was the one quality I had ever worshiped, ever sought for, and never found.

Alexis and I became friends—equal, earnest friends. Not in the way of wooing or marriage—at least, he never spoke of either; and both were far, oh, how far! from my thought—but there was a great and tender bond between us, which strengthened day by day.

The link which riveted it was religion. He was, as I said, a Protestant, not adhering to any creed, but simply living—not preaching, but living—the faith of our Saviour. He was not perfect—he had his sins and shortcomings, even as I. We both struggling on toward the glimmering light. So, after a season, we clasped hands in friendship, and with eyes steadfastly upward, determined to press on together toward the one goal, and along the self-same road.

I put my breviary aside, and took wholly to the New Testament, assuming no name either of Catholic or Protestant, but simply that of Christian.

When I decided on this, of course I told Anastasius. He had ceased to be my spiritual confessor for some time; yet I could see he was surprised.

"Who has done this?" was all he said.

Was I a reed, then, to be blown about with every wind? Or a toy, to be shifted about from hand to hand, and set in motion just as my chance master chose? Had I no will, no conscience of my own?

He knew where he could sting me—and did it—but I let the words pass.

"Cousin, I'll answer like Desdemona.

'Nobody; I myself.'

I have had no book but this—which you gave me; no priest, except the inward witness of my own soul."

"And Alexis Saltram."

Not said in any wrath, or suspicion, or inquiry

—simply as the passive statement of a fact. When I denied it, he accepted my denial; when I protested, he suffered me to protest. My passionate arguments he took in his soft passionless hold—melted and moulded them—turned and twisted them—then reproduced them to me so different that I failed to recognize either my own meaning or even my own words.

After that, on both sides the only resource was silence.

CHAPTER III.

"I wish," said I to my guardian one day, "as I shall be twenty-one next year, to have more freedom. I wish even"—for since the discovery of my change of faith he had watched me so closely, so quietly, so continually, that I had conceived a vague fear of him, and a longing to get away—to put half the earth between me and his presence—"I wish even, if possible this summer, to visit my estates in Hispaniola?"

"Alone?"

"No; Madame Gradelle will accompany me. And Mr. Saltram will charter one of his ships for my use."

"I approve the plan. Alexis is going too, I believe?" How could he have known that which Alexis had never told me? But he knew every thing. "Madame Gradelle is not sufficient escort. I, as your guardian, will accompany and protect you."

A cold dread seized me. Was I never to be free? Already I began to feel my guardian's influence surrounding me—an influence once of love, now of intolerable distaste, and even fear. Not that he was ever harsh or cruel—not that I could accuse him of any single wrong toward me or others; but I knew I had thwarted him, and through him his cause—that cause whose strongest dogma is, that any means are sacred, any evil consecrated to good, if furthering the one great end—Power.

I had opposed him, and I was in his hand—that hand which I had once believed to have almost superhuman strength. In my terror I half believed so still.

"He will go with us—we can not escape from him," I said to Alexis. "He will make you a priest and me a nun, as he once planned—I know he did. Our very souls are not our own."

"What, when the world is so wide, and life so long, and God's kindness over all—when, too, I am free, and you will be free in a year—when—"

"I shall never be free. He is my evil genius. He will haunt me till my death."

It was a morbid feeling I had, consequent on the awful struggle which had so shaken body and mind. The very sound of his step made me turn sick and tremble; the very sight of his grand face—perhaps the most beautiful I ever saw, with its faultless features, and the half-melancholy cast given by the high bald forehead and the pointed beard—was to me more terrible than any monster of ugliness the world ever produced.

He held my fortune—he governed my house. All visitors there came and went under his control, except Alexis. Why this young man still came—or how—I could not tell. Probably because, in his pure singleness of heart and purpose, he was stronger even than M. Anastasius.

The time passed. We embarked on board the ship *Argo*, for Hispaniola.

My guardian told me, at the last minute, that business relating to his order would probably detain him in Europe—that we were to lie at anchor for twelve hours off Havre—and, if he then came not, sail.

He came not—we sailed.

It was a glorious evening. The sun, as he went down over the burning seas, beckoned us with a finger of golden fire, westward—to the free, safe, happy West.

I say *us*, because on that evening we first began unconsciously to say it too—as if vaguely binding our fates together—Alexis and I. We talked for a whole hour—till long after France, with all our old life therein, had become a mere line, a cloudy speck on the horizon—of the new life we should lead in Hispaniola. Yet all the while, if we had been truly the priest and nun Anastasius wished to make us, our words, and I believe our thoughts, could not have been more angel-pure, more free from any bias of human passion.

Yet, as the sun went down, and the sea-breeze made us draw nearer together, both began, I repeat, instinctively to say "we," and talk of our future as if it had been the future of one.

"Good-evening, friends!"

He was there—M. Anastasius!

I stood petrified. That golden finger of hope had vanished. I shuddered, a captive on his courteously compelling arm—seeing nothing but his terrible smiling face and the black wilderness of sea. For the moment I felt inclined to plunge therein—as I had often longed to plunge penniless into the equally fearsome wilderness of Paris—only I felt sure he would follow me still. He would track me, it seemed, through the whole world.

"You see I have been able to accomplish the voyage; men mostly can achieve any fixed purpose—at least some men. Isbel, this sea-air will bring you back your bloom. And, Alexis, my friend, despite those clear studies you told me of, I hope you will bestow a little of your society at times on my ward and me. We will bid you a good-evening now."

He transferred to his nephew my powerless hand; that of Alexis, too, felt cold and trembling. It seemed as if he likewise were succumbing to the fate which, born out of one man's indomitable will, dragged us asunder. Ere my guardian consigned me to Madame Gradelle, he said, smiling, but looking me through and through,

E

"Remember, my fair cousin, that Alexis is to be—must be—a priest."

"It is impossible!" said I, stung to resistance. "You know he has altogether seceded from the Catholic creed; he will never return to it. His conscience is his own."

"But not his passions. He is young—I am old. He will be a priest yet."

With a soft hand-pressure, M. Anastasius left me.

Now began the most horrible phase of my existence. For four weeks we had to live in the same vessel, bounded and shut up together—Anastasius, Alexis, and I; meeting continually in the soft bland atmosphere of courteous calm; always in public—never alone.

From various accidental circumstances, I discovered how M. Anastasius was now bending all the powers of his enormous intellect, his wonderful moral influence, to compass his cherished ends with regard to Alexis Saltram.

An overwhelming dread took possession of me. I ceased to think of myself at all—my worldly hopes, prospects, or joys—over which this man's influence had long hung like an accursed shadow, a sun turned into darkness, the more terrible because it had once been a sun. I seemed to see M. Anastasius only with relation to this young man, over whom I knew he once had so great power. Would it return—and in what would it result? Not merely in the breaking off any feeble tie to me. I scarcely trembled for that, since, could it be so broken, it was not worth trembling for. No! I trembled for Alexis's soul.

It was a soul I had gradually learned—more than ever, perhaps, in this voyage, of which every day seemed a life, full of temptation, contest, trial—a soul pure as God's own heaven, that hung over us hour by hour in its steady tropic blue; and deep as the seas that rolled everlastingly around us. Like them, stirring with the lightest breath, often tempest-tossed, liable to adverse winds and currents; yet keeping far, far below the surface a divine tranquillity, diviner than any mere stagnant calm. And this soul, full of all rich impulses, emotions, passions—a soul which, because it could strongly sympathize with, might be able to regenerate its kind, M. Anastasius wanted to make into a Catholic Jesuit priest—a mere machine, to work as he, the head machine, chose!

This was why (the thought suddenly struck me, like lightning) he had told each of us severally concerning one another, those two lies. Because we were young; we might love—we might marry; there was nothing externally to prevent us. And then what would become of his scheme?

I think there was born in me—while the most passive slave to lawful, loving rule—a faculty of savage resistance to all unlawful and unjust power. Also, a something of the female wild-beast, which, if alone, will lie tame and cowed in her solitary den, to be shot at by any daring hunter; whereas if she be *not* alone—if she have any love-instinct at work for cubs or mate—her whole nature changes from terror to daring, from cowardice to fury.

When, as we neared the tropics, I saw Alexis's cheek growing daily paler, and his eye more sunken and restless with some secret struggle, in the which M. Anastasius never left him for a day, an hour, a minute, I became not unlike that poor wild-beast mother. It had gone ill with the relentless hunter of souls if he had come near me then.

But he did not. For the last week of our voyage, M. Anastasius kept altogether out of my way.

It was nearly over—we were in sight of the shores of Hispaniola. Then we should land. My estates lay in this island. Mr. Saltram's business, I was aware, called him to Barbadoes; thence again beyond seas. Once parted, I well knew that if the power and will of my guardian could compass any thing—and it seemed to me that they were able to compass every thing in the whole wide earth—Alexis and I should never meet again.

In one last struggle after life—after the fresh, wholesome, natural life which contact with this young man's true spirit had given me—I determined to risk all.

It was a rich tropic twilight. We were all admiring it, just as three ordinary persons might do who were tending peacefully to their voyage-end.

Yet Alexis did not seem at peace. A settled, deadly pallor dwelt on his face—a restless anxiety troubled his whole mien.

M. Anastasius said, noticing the glowing tropic scenery which already dimly appeared in our shoreward view.

"It is very grand; but Europe is more suited to us grave Northerns. You will think so, Alexis, when you are once again there."

"Are you returning?" I asked of Mr. Saltram. My cousin answered for him, "Yes, immediately."

Alexis started; then leaned over the poop in silence, and without denial.

I felt profoundly sad. My interest in Alexis Saltram was at this time—and but for the compulsion of opposing power might have ever been—entirely apart from love. We might have gone on merely as tender friends for years and years—at least I might. Therefore no maidenly consciousness warned me from doing what my sense of right impelled toward one who held the same faith as I did, and whose life seemed strangled in the same mesh of circumstances which had nearly paralyzed my own.

"Alexis, this is our last evening; you will sail for Europe—and we shall be friends no more. Will you take one twilight stroll with me?"—and I extended my hand.

If he had hesitated, or shrunk back from me, I would have flung him to the winds, and fought my own battle alone; I was strong enough now. But he sprang to me, clung to my hand, looked wildly in my face, as if there were the sole light of truth and trust left in the world; and as if even there, he had begun—or been taught—to doubt. He did not, now.

"Isbel, tell me! You still hold our faith—you are not going to become a nun?"

"Never! I will offer myself to Heaven as Heaven gave me to myself—free, bound by no creed, subservient to no priest. What is he, but a man that shall die, whom the worms shall cover?"

I said the words out loud. I meant M. Anastasius to hear. But he looked as if he heard not; only when we turned up the deck, he slowly followed.

I stood at bay. "Cousin, leave me. I wish to speak to Mr. Saltram. Can not I have any friend but you?"

"None, whom I believe you would harm and receive harm from."

"Dare you—"

"I myself dare nothing; but there is nothing which my Church does not dare. Converse, my children. I hinder you not. The deck is free for all."

He bowed, and let us pass; then followed. Every sound of that slow, smooth step seemed to strike on my heart like the tracking tread of doom.

Alexis and I said little or nothing. A leaden despair seemed to bind us closely round, allowing only one consciousness, that for a little, little time it bound us together! He held my arm so fast that I felt every throbbing of his heart. My sole thought was now to say some words that should be fixed eternally there, so that no lure, no power might make him swerve from his faith. That faith, which was my chief warranty of meeting him—never, oh never in this world! but in the world everlasting.

Once or twice in turning we came face to face with M. Anastasius. He was walking at his usual slow pace, his hands loosely clasped behind him, his head bent; a steely repose—even pensiveness, which was his natural look—settled in his grave eyes. He was a man of intellect too great to despise, of character too spotless to loathe. The one sole feeling he inspired was that of unconquerable fear. Because you saw at once that he feared nothing either in earth or heaven, that he owned but one influence, and was amenable but to one law, which he called "the Church," but which was himself.

Men like M. Anastasius, one-idea'd, all-engrossed men, are, according to slight variations in their temperaments, the salvation, the laughing-stock, or the terror of the world.

He appeared in the latter form to Alexis and me. Slowly, surely came the conviction that there was no peace for us on this earth while he stood on it; so strong, so powerful, that at times I almost yielded to a vague belief in his immortality. On this night, especially, I was stricken with a horrible—curiosity, I think it was—to see whether he could die—whether the grave could open her mouth to swallow him,

and death have power upon his flesh, like that of other men.

More than once, as he passed under a huge beam, I thought—should it fall? as he leaned against the ship's side—should it give way? But only, I declare solemnly, out of a frenzied speculative curiosity, which I would not for worlds have breathed to a human soul! I never once breathed it to Alexis Saltram, who was his sister's son, and whom he had been kind to as a child.

Night darkened, and our walk ceased. We had said nothing—nothing; except that on parting, with a kind of desperation, Alexis buried my hand tightly in his bosom, and whispered, "To-morrow?"

That midnight a sudden hurricane came on. In half an hour all that was left of the good ship *Argo* was a little boat, filled almost to sinking with half-drowned passengers, and a few sailors clinging to spars and fragments of the wreck.

Alexis was lashed to a mast, holding me partly fastened to it, and partly sustained in his arms. How he had found and rescued me I know not; but love is very strong. It has been sweet to me afterward to think that I owed my life to him—and him alone. I was the only woman saved.

He was at the extreme end of the mast; we rested, face to face, my head against his shoulder. All along to its slender point, the sailors were clinging to the spar like flies; but we two did not see any thing in the world, save one another.

Life was dim, death was near, yet I think we were not unhappy. Our heaven was clear; for between us and Him to whom we were going came no threatening image, holding in its remorseless hand life, faith, love. Death itself was less terrible than M. Anastasius.

We had seen him among the saved passengers swaying in the boat; then we thought of him no more. We clung together, with closed eyes, satisfied to die.

"No room—off there! No room!" I heard shouted, loud and savage, by the sailor lashed behind me.

I opened my eyes. Alexis was gazing on me only. I gazed, transfixed, over his shoulder, into the breakers beyond.

There, in the trough of a wave, I saw, clear as I see my own right hand now, the upturned face of Anastasius, and his two white, stretched-out hands, on one finger of which was his well-known diamond-ring—for it flashed that minute in the moon.

"Off!" yelled the sailor, striking at him with an oar. "One man's life's as good as another's. Off!"

The drowning face rose above the wave, the eyes fixed themselves full on me, without any entreaty in them, or wrath, or terror—the long-familiar, passionless, relentless eyes.

I see them now; I shall see them till I die. Oh, would I had died!

For one brief second I thought of tearing off

the lashings and giving him my place; for I had loved him. But youth and life were strong within me, and my head was pressed to Alexis's breast.

A full minute, or it seemed so, was that face above the water; then I watched it sink slowly, down, down.

CHAPTER IV.

We, and several others, were picked up from the wreck of the *Argo* by a homeward-bound ship. As soon as we reached London I became Alexis's wife.

That which happened at the theatre was exactly twelve months after—as we believed—Anastasius died.

I do not pretend to explain, I doubt if any reason can explain, a circumstance so singular —so impossible to be attributed to either imagination or illusion; for, as I must again distinctly state, we ourselves saw nothing. The apparition, or whatever it was, was visible only to other persons, all total strangers.

I had a fever. When I arose from it, and things took their natural forms and relations, this strange occurrence became mingled with the rest of my delirium, of which my husband persuaded me it was a part. He took me abroad—to Italy—Germany. He loved me dearly! He was, and he made me, entirely happy.

In our happiness we strove to live, not merely for one another, but for all the world; all who suffered and had need. We did—nor shrunk from the doing—many charities which had first been planned by Anastasius, with what motives we never knew. While carrying them out, we learned to utter his name without trembling; remembering only that which was beautiful in him and his character, and which we had both so worshiped once.

In the furtherance of these schemes of good it became advisable that we should go to Paris, to my former hotel, which still remained empty there.

"But not, dear wife, if any uneasiness or lingering pain rests in your mind in seeing the old spot. For me, I love it! since there I loved Isbel, before Isbel knew it, long."

So I smiled; and went to Paris.

My husband proposed, and I was not sorry, that Colonel Hart and his newly-married wife should join us there, and remain as our guests. I shrunk a little from reinhabiting the familiar rooms, long shut up from the light of day; and it was with comfort I heard my husband arranging that a portion of the hotel should be made ready for us, namely, two saloons *en suite*, leading out of the farther one of which were a chamber and dressing-room for our own use—opposite two similar apartments for the Colonel and his lady.

I am thus minute for reasons that will appear.

Mrs. Hart had been traveling with us some weeks. She was a mild, sweet-faced English girl, who did not much like the Continent, and was half shocked at some of my reckless foreign ways on board steamboats and on railways. She said I was a little—just a little—too free. It might have seemed so to her; for my southern blood rushed bright and warm, and my manner of life in France had completely obliterated early impressions. Faithful and tender woman and true wife as I was, I believe I was in some things unlike an English woman or an English wife, and that Mrs. Hart thought so.

Once—for being weak of nature and fast of tongue, she often said things she should not—there was even some hint of the kind dropped before my husband. He flashed up—but laughed the next minute; for I was his, and he loved me!

Nevertheless, that quick glow of anger pained me—bringing back the recollection of many things his uncle had said to me of him, which then I heard as one that heareth not. The sole saying which remained on my mind was one which, in a measure, I had credited—that his conscience was in his hand, "but not his passions."

I had known always—and rather rejoiced in the knowledge—that Alexis Saltram could not boast the frozen calm of M. Anastasius.

But I warned tame Eliza Hart, half jestingly, to take heed, and not lightly blame me before my husband again.

Reaching Paris, we were all very gay and sociable together. Colonel Hart was a grave, honorable man; my husband and I both loved him.

We dined together—a lively *partie quarrée*. I shut my eyes to the familiar objects about us, and tried to believe the rooms had never echoed familiar footsteps save those of Mrs. Hart and the Colonel's soldierly tread. Once or so, while silence fell over us, I would start, and feel my heart beating; but Alexis was near me, and altogether mine. Therefore I feared not, even here.

After coffee, the gentlemen went out to some evening amusement. We, the weary wives, contented ourselves with lounging about, discussing toilets and Paris sights. Especially the fair Empress Eugénie—the wifely crown which my old aversion Louis Bonaparte had chosen to bind about his ugly brows. Mrs. Hart was anxious to see all, and then fly back to her beloved London.

"How long is it since you left London, Mrs. Saltram?"

"A year, I think. What is to-day?"

"The twenty-fifth—no, the twenty-sixth of May."

I dropped my head on the cushion. Then, that date—the first she mentioned—had passed over unthought of by us. That night—the night of mortal horror when the *Argo* went down—lay thus far buried in the past, parted from us by two blessed years.

But I found it impossible to converse longer with Mrs. Hart; so about ten o'clock I left her reading, and went to take half an hour's rest in my chamber, which, as I have explained, was divided from the salon by a small boudoir or dressing-room. Its only other entrance was from a door near the head of my bed, which I went and locked.

It seemed uncourteous to retire for the night; so I merely threw my dressing-gown over my evening toilet, and lay down outside the bed, dreamily watching the shadows which the lamp threw. This lamp was in my chamber; but its light extended faintly into the boudoir, showing the tall mirror there, and a sofa which was placed opposite. Otherwise, the little room was half in gloom, save for a narrow glint streaming through the not quite closed door of the salon.

I lay broad awake, but very quiet, contented and happy. I was thinking of Alexis. In the midst of my reverie, I heard, as I thought, my maid trying the handle of the door behind me. "It is locked," I said; "come another time." The sound ceased; yet I almost thought Fanchon had entered, for there came a rift of wind, which made the lamp sway in its socket. But when I looked, the door was closely shut, and the bolt still fast.

I lay, it might be, half an hour longer. Then, with a certain compunction at my own discourtesy in leaving her, I saw the salon door open, and Mrs. Hart appear.

She looked into the boudoir, drew back hurriedly, and closed the door after her.

Of course I immediately rose to follow her. Ere doing so, I remember particularly standing with the lamp in my hand, arranging my dress before the mirror in the boudoir, and seeing reflected in the glass, with my cashmere lying over its cushions, the sofa, unoccupied.

Eliza was standing thoughtful.

"I ought to ask pardon for my long absence, my dear Mrs. Hart."

"Oh, no—but I of you, for intruding in your apartment; I did not know Mr. Saltram had returned. Where is my husband?"

"With mine, no doubt! We need not expect them for an hour yet, the renegades."

"You are jesting," said Mrs. Hart, half-offended. "I know they are come home. I saw Mr. Saltram in your boudoir not two minutes since."

"How?"

"In your boudoir, I repeat. He was lying on the sofa."

"Impossible!" and I burst out laughing. "Unless he has suddenly turned into a cashmere shawl. Come and look."

I flung the folding doors open, and poured a blaze of light into the little room.

"It is very odd," fidgeted Mrs. Hart; "very odd, indeed. I am sure I saw a gentleman here. His face was turned aside; but of course I concluded it was Mr. Saltram. Very odd, indeed!"

I still laughed at her, though an uneasy feeling was creeping over me. To dismiss it, I

showed her how the door was fastened, and how it was impossible my husband could have entered.

"No; for I distinctly heard you say, 'It is locked—come another time.' What did you mean by that?"

"I thought it was Fanchon."

To change the subject, I began showing her some parures my husband had just brought me. Eliza Hart was very fond of jewels. We remained looking at them some time longer in the inner-room where I had been lying on my bed; and then she bade me good-night.

"No light, thank you. I can find my way back through the boudoir. Good-night. Do not look so pale to-morrow, my dear."

She kissed me in the friendly English fashion, and danced lightly away, out at my bedroom door and into the boudoir adjoining—but instantly I saw her reappear, startled and breathless, covered with angry blushes.

"Mrs. Saltram, you have deceived me! You are a wicked French woman."

"Eliza!"

"You know it—you knew it all along. I will go and seek my husband. He will not let me stay another night in your house!"

"As you will"—for I was sick of her follies. "But explain yourself."

"Have you no shame? Have you foreign women never any shame? But I have found you out at last."

"Indeed!"

"There is—I have seen him twice with my own eyes—there is a man lying this minute in your boudoir—and he is —not Mr. Saltram!"

Then, indeed, I sickened. A deadly horror came over me. No wonder the young thing, convinced of my guilt, fled from me, appalled. For I knew now whom she had seen.

*   *   *   *   *   *

Hour after hour I must have lain where I fell. There was some confusion in the house —no one came near me. It was early daylight when I woke and saw Fanchon leaning over me, and trying to lift me from the floor.

"Fanchon—is it morning?"

"Yes, madame."

"What day is it?"

"The twenty-sixth of May."

It has been he, then. He followed us still. Shudder after shudder convulsed me. I think Fanchon thought I was dying.

"Oh, madame! oh, poor madame! And monsieur not yet come home."

I uttered a terrible cry—for my heart foreboded what either had happened or assuredly would happen.

Alexis never came home again.

An hour after, I was sent for to the little woodcutter's hut, outside Paris gates, where he lay dying.

Anastasius had judged clearly; my noble generous husband had in him but one thing lacking—his passions were "not in his hand."

When Colonel Hart, on the clear testimony of

his wife, impugned *his* wife's honor, Alexis challenged him—fought, and fell.

It all happened in an hour or two, when their blood was fiery hot. By daylight, the colonel stood, cold as death, pale as a shadow, by Alexis's bedside. He had killed him, and he loved him!

No one thought of me. They let me weep near my husband—unconscious as he was—doubtless believing them the last contrite tears of an adulteress. I did not heed nor deny that horrible name—Alexis was dying.

Toward evening he revived a little, and his senses returned. He opened his eyes and saw me—they closed with a shudder.

"Alexis—Alexis!"

"Isbel, I am dying. You know the cause. In the name of God—are you—"

"In the name of God, I am your pure wife, who never loved any man but you."

"I am satisfied. I thought it was so."

He looked at Colonel Hart, faintly smiling; then opened his arms and took me into them; as if to protect me with his last breath.

"Now," he said, still holding me, "my friends, we must make all clear. Nothing must harm her when I am gone. Hart, fetch your wife here."

Mrs. Hart came, trembling violently. My husband addressed her.

"I sent for you to ask you a question. Answer, as to a dying person, who to-morrow will know all secrets. Who was the man you saw in my wife's chamber?"

"He was a stranger to me. I never met him before, any where. He lay on the sofa, wrapped in a fur cloak."

"Did you see his face?"

"Not the first time. The second time I did."

"What was he like? Be accurate, for the sake of more than life—honor."

My husband's voice sank. There was terror in his eyes, but not *that* terror—he held me to his bosom still.

"What was he like, Eliza?" repeated Colonel Hart.

"He was middle-aged; of a pale, grave countenance, with keen, large eyes, high forehead, and a pointed beard."

"Heaven save us! I have seen him too," cried the Colonel, horror-struck. "It was no living man."

"It was M. Anastasius!"

My husband died that night. He died, his lips on mine, murmuring how dearly he loved me, and how happy he had been.

For many months after then I was quite happy, too; for my wits wandered, and I thought I was again a little West Indian girl, picking gowans in the meadows about Dumfries.

The Colonel and Mrs. Hart were, I believe, very kind to me. I always took her for a little playfellow I had, who was called Eliza. It is only lately, as the year has circled round again to the spring, that my head has become

clear, and I have found out who she is, and—ah, me!—who I am.

This coming to my right senses does not give me so much pain as they thought 'it would; because great weakness of body has balanced and soothed my mind.

I have but one desire: to go to my own Alexis; and before the twenty-fifth of May.

Now I have been able nearly to complete our story, which is well. My friend, judge between us—and *him*. Farewell.

ISBEL SALTRAM.

CHAPTER V.

I THINK it necessary that I, Eliza Hart, should relate, as simply as veraciously, the circumstances of Mrs. Saltram's death, which happened on the night of the twenty-fifth of May.

She was living with us at our house, some miles out of London. She had been very ill and weak during May, but toward the end of the month she revived. We thought if she could live till June she might even recover. My husband desired that on no account might she be told the day of the month; she was, indeed, purposely deceived on the subject. When the twenty-fifth came, she thought it was only the twenty-second.

For some weeks she had kept her bed, and Fanchon never left her—Fanchon, who knew the whole history, and was strictly charged, whatever delusions might occur, to take no notice whatever of the subject to her mistress. For my husband and myself were again persuaded that it must be some delusion. So was the physician, who nevertheless determined to visit us himself on the night of the twenty-fifth of May.

It happened that the Colonel was unwell, and I could not remain constantly in Mrs. Saltram's room. It was a large but very simple suburban bedchamber, with white curtains and modern furniture, all of which I myself arranged in such a manner that there should be no dark corners, no shadows thrown by hanging draperies or any thing of the kind.

About ten o'clock at night Fanchon accidentally quitted her mistress for a few minutes, sending in her place a nursemaid who had lately come into our family.

This girl tells me that she entered the room quickly, but stopped, seeing, as she believed, the physician sitting by the bed, on the further side, at Mrs. Saltram's right hand. She thought Mrs. Saltram did not see him, for she turned and asked her, the nursemaid—"Susan, what o'clock is it?"

The gentleman did not speak. She says he appeared sitting with his elbows resting on his knees, and his face partly concealed in his hands. He wore a long coat or cloak—she could not distinguish which, for the room was rather dark, but she could plainly see on his little finger the sparkle of a diamond ring.

She is quite certain that Mrs. Saltram did not see the gentleman at all, which rather surprised her, for the poor lady moved from time to time, and spoke, complainingly, of its being "very cold." At length she called Susan to sit by her side, and chafe her hands.

Susan acquiesced—"But did not Mrs. Saltram see the gentleman?"

"What gentleman?"

"He was sitting beside you not a minute since. I thought he was the doctor, or the clergyman. He is gone now."

And the girl, much terrified, saw that there was no one in the room.

She says Mrs. Saltram did not seem terrified at all. She only pressed her hands on her forehead, her lips slightly moving—then whispered: "Go, call Fanchon and them all, tell them what you saw."

"But I must leave you. Are you not afraid?"

"No. Not now—not now."

She covered her eyes, and again her lips began moving.

Fanchon entered, and I too, immediately. I do not expect to be credited. I can only state on my honor what we both then beheld.

Mrs. Saltram lay, her eyes open, her face quite calm, as that of a dying person; her hands spread out on the counterpane. Beside her sat erect the same figure I had seen lying on the sofa in Paris, exactly a year ago. It appeared more lifelike than she. Neither looked at each other. When we brought a bright lamp into the room the appearance vanished.

Isbel said to me, "Eliza, he is come."

"Impossible! You have not seen him?"

"No, but you have?" She looked me steadily in the face. "I knew it. Take the light away, and you will see him again. He is here, I want to speak to him. Quick, take the light away."

Alarmed as I was, I could not refuse, for I saw by her features that her last hour was at hand.

As surely as I write this, I, Eliza Hart, saw, when the candles were removed, that figure grow again, as out of air, and become plainly distinguishable, sitting by her bedside.

She turned herself with difficulty, and faced it. "Eliza, is he there? I see nothing but the empty chair. Is he there?"

"Yes."

"Does he look angry or terrible?"

"No."

"Anastasius." She extended her hand toward the vacant chair. "Cousin Anastasius!" Her voice was sweet, though the cold drops stood on her brow.

"Cousin Anastasius, I do not see you, but you can see and hear me. I am not afraid of you now. You know, once, I loved you very much."

Here, overcome with terror, I stole back toward the lighted stair-case. Thence I still heard Isbel speaking.

"We erred, both of us, cousin. You were too hard upon me—I had too great love first, too great terror afterward of you. Why should I be afraid of a man that shall die, and of the son of man, whose breath is in his nostrils? I should have worshiped, have feared, not you, but only God."

She paused—drawing twice or thrice, heavily, the breath that could not last.

"I forgive you—forgive me also! I loved you. Have you any thing to say to me, Anastasius?"

Silence.

"Shall we ever meet in the boundless spheres of Heaven?"

Silence—a long silence. We brought in candles, for she was evidently dying.

"Eliza—thank you for all! Your hand. It is so dark—and"—shivering—"I am afraid of going into the dark. I might meet Anastasius there. I wish my husband would come."

She was wandering in her mind, I saw. Her eyes turned to the vacant chair.

"Is there any one sitting by me?"

"No, dear Isbel; can you see any one?"

"No one—yes"—and with preternatural strength she started right up in bed, extending her arms. "Yes! There—close behind you—I see—my husband. I am quite safe—now!"

So, with a smile upon her face, she died.

THE WATER CURE.

" Having our hearts sprinkled from an evil conscience, and our bodies washed with pure water."

CHAPTER I.

" Now, if I knew—Lord help me! I often feel as if I did not know—whether the next life be any better than this, whether getting rid of the body be any advantage to the soul—I would gladly die to-morrow!"

"By Jove! Alick, *I* haven't the slightest wish of the kind."

We two—Austin Hardy and Alexander Fyfe—as we sat over the fire in my lodgings, in Burton Crescent, were not bad types of two classes of men, not rare in this our day, who may stand convicted as moral suicides—mind-murderers and body-murderers.

We were cousins, but at the opposite poles of society—he was rich, I poor. The world lured him, and scouted me; its pit of perdition was opened wide for us both; but he was kissed, and I was kicked, into it. Now we both found ourselves clinging to its brink, and glaring helplessly at one another from opposite sides, wondering which would be the first to let go, and drop to—where?

It was the 1st of November. I had sat hour after hour, the MS. of my last book before me; the finished half on my left hand grinned at the unfinished half on my right—to wit, a heap of blank sheets, at least two hundred. Two hundred pages that, by Christmas, *must* be covered—covered, too, with the best fruit of my soul, my heart, and my brains; else my dear friend the public would say, compassionately, "Poor fellow! he has written himself out;" or, sneeringly, "If these authors did not know when to stop!"

Stop?—with life and all its daily needs, duties, pleasantnesses (pshaw! I may draw my pen through *that* word), hammering incessantly at the door! With old Age's ugly face, solitary and poor, peeping in at the window—Stop, indeed!

I had been in this agreeable frame of mind, when my cousin Austin lounged into my room.

" Do I interrupt you?" he said, for he was a kindly-hearted fellow, though not over-burdened with brains, and wholly uninitiate in the life of literature.

" Interrupt! no, my good fellow. I wish you did," said I, with a groan. " There is nothing to interrupt. One might as well spin a thread-of-gold gown out of that spider-line dangling from the ceiling, as weave a story out of this skull of mine—this squeezed sponge, this collapsed bladder; it's good for nothing but to be a dining-hall to a select party of worms."

" Eh ?" said he, innocently uncomprehending.

" Never mind. What of yourself, Hardy? How is the hunting and the shooting, the betting and the play-going, the dinner-parties, the balls?"

" All over."

He shook his head, and a severe fit of coughing convulsed his large, strong-built frame.

" I'm booked for the other world. I wish you were my heir."

" Thank you; but, for so brief a possession, it wouldn't be worth my while."

I lit a candle, and we stood contemplating one another. Finally, we each made the remark with which I have commenced this history. Let me continue it now.

" Why do you want to die, Alexander Fyfe?"

" To escape the trouble of living. Live !—it's only existing; I don't live—I never lived. What is life but having one's full powers free to use, to command, to enjoy? I have none of these. My body hampers my mind, my mind destroys my body, and circumstances make slaves of both. I look without—every thing is a blank ; within—"

I beg to state to the reader, as I did to Austin the next minute, that I am not used to whine in this way; but I was ill, and I had sat for five hours with a blank page before me, upon which I had written precisely five lines.

Austin's face expressed the utmost astonishment.

" Why, I didn't know any thing amiss with *you*; you always seem to me the happiest fellow alive. A successful author, with only yourself to look after—no property, no establishment, no responsibilities; just a little bit of writing to do each day, and be paid for it, and all's right."

I laughed at his amusing unsophisticated notion of an author's existence.

" Then, so hermit-like as you live here, all among your books. My poor dear aunt herself if she could see you—"

" Hush! Austin."

" Well, I will; but all the world knows what a good woman she was, and you take after her. You live like a saint, and have no temptation to be otherwise. Now, I am obliged to go post-haste to destruction, if only to save myself from dying of *ennui.*"

Another fit of coughing cut him short. I forgot my own despair in pitying his, for he seemed to hold that cheating vixen Life with such a frantic clutch, and she was so visibly slipping from him. There, at least, I felt myself better off than he. This world was all my terror; of that to come, dark as its mysteries were, I had no absolute fear.

"You're hard up, Austin, my boy. What are you going to do?"

"Nothing. It isn't consumption, they say. It will turn to asthma, most likely. All my own doings, the doctors say—would have knocked up the finest constitution in the world, which I had ten years ago"—with a piteous groan.

"Well, confess. What has done it?"

"Smoking, late hours, and," after a pause, "hard drinking."

"Whew!" It was a very dolorous whistle, I believe.

"What is a fellow to do?" said Hardy, rather sullenly. "Life is so confoundedly slow? You want excitement—you take to the turf or the gaming-table. If you win, you must drink and be jolly; if you lose, why drink, and drown care. Then other perplexities—womankind, for instance: you run after an angel, and find her out something on the other side of humanity; or she's sharp and clever, makes a mock of you, and marries your friend; or she tries to jump down your throat, and you might have her so cheap, she isn't worth the winning?"

"Is that the fact in your case?"

"My lad, you'd find it so, if you had ten thousand a year."

This was a doubtful compliment, certainly; but he meant it in all simplicity. Besides, I knew enough of his affairs to be aware that the circumstances he mentioned in this impersonal form were literally true.

"I wonder, cousin, you are not weary of this hunting after shadows. Why don't you marry?"

"Marry! I?—to leave a wife a widow next year. Though *that* would raise my value in the market immensely. Seriously, Alick, do you think there is any woman in the world worth marrying? I don't, and never did."

I was silent. Afterward he said, in an altered tone—

"I did not quite mean 'never.' Was she fifteen or sixteen when she died, Alexander?"

I knew he was thinking of his old child sweetheart, my little sister Mary.

"No, no; marrying is out of the question. Whether I die early or late, I shall certainly die a bachelor. Shall you?"

"Very probably."

And, as I glanced at the two hundred blank pages, and the two hundred more scrawled over, I hugged . yself in the knowledge that, if it came to starvation, there was only one to starve —no pale wife, fading slowly from a dream of beauty into a weak slattern, peevish and sad; no sickly children, wailing reproaches into the father's heart, not only for their lost birthright, but for their very birth. "No," I thought, with set teeth and clenched palms, as if the time of my youth were a bitter fruit between my lips, or a poison-flower in my hands, and I were grinding both to powder—"No, as old Will hath it, '*Tis better as it is!*"

"Still," cried I, rousing myself, for poor Austin's case was worse than mine, and he had more responsibilities in the world—"still life is worth a struggle, and you know you hate your next heir. Once more, what are you going to do?"

"I don't know."

"Have you any doctor?"

"Three."

"Then you are a dead man, Austin Hardy."

"So I believe."

Again a long pause.

"I can't leave you this estate, Alick, you know, and I have spent most of my ready money; but I have left you my cellar and my stud—they will be worth a thousand or two; so you needn't kill yourself with this sort of work," pointing to the MS., "for a few years to come. That will be one good out of my dying."

"My dear boy, if you say another word about dying, I'll—you see Corrie's Afghan cutlass there—I'll assassinate you on the spot."

"Thank you."

"By-the-by," and a sudden brilliant thought darted into my mind, "did you ever meet my friend Corrie?"

"No."

"The finest, wholesomest, cheeriest fellow, with a head big enough to hold two men's brains, and a heart as large as his head. I had a letter from him this morning. He gave up army service some time since, began London practice—searched fairly and honorably into all the nonsense going—tried allopathy, homœopathy, kinesopathy, and, Heaven knows, how many pathies besides; and has finally thrown them all aside, and, in conjunction with his father, Dr. Corrie, has settled in ——shire, and there set up a water cure."

"A what did you say?"

"A hydropathic establishment—a water cure. Have you never heard of such places?"

"Ah, yes, where people sit in tubs all day, and starve on sanitary diet, and walk on their own legs, and go to bed at nine o'clock—barbarians!"

"Exactly. They cut civilization, with all its evils, and go back to a state of nature. Suppose you were to try it; you have so long been living 'agin nature,' as says our friend Nathaniel Bumppo—but I forget, you don't read—that if you were to return to her motherly arms, she might take you in, and cure you—eh?"

"Couldn't—impossible."

So many possibilities frequently grew out of Hardy's "impossible" that I was not a whit discouraged.

"Here is Corrie's letter, with a view of his house on the top of the page."

"A pretty place."

"Beautiful, he says; and James Corrie has visited half the fine scenery in the world. You see, he wants me to go down there, even without trying what he calls 'the treatment.'"

"And why don't you?"

I laid my hand on the blank MS. leaves—

"Impossible."

Austin soon after went away. I shut the shutters, stirred the fire, rang for the student's best friend—a cup of hot tea, no bread therewith. Yes, though rather hungry, I dared not eat; we head-workers are obliged to establish a rigorous division of labor between the stomach and the brain. Ugh! that one piece of dry toast would spoil at least four possible pages—can't be! And that uncut magazine, with a friend's article therein, how tempting it looks! But no; if I treat myself with his fiction I shall lose the thread of my own; and if I sit thus, staring into the cozy fire, I shall go dream and then—. Now for it. Approach, my MS., that I used so to love—you friend, you mistress, you beloved child of my soul! How comes it that you have grown into a fiend, who stands ever behind me, goading me on with points of steel, ready to pierce me whenever I drop! But many a human friend, mistress, or child does just the same.

Now, surely I can work to-night. Come back, dreams of my youth! I am writing about folk that are young; so let's get up a good love scene—a new sort of thing, if I can—for I have done so many, and reviews say I am grown "artificial." Reviews! Ten years ago what cared I for reviews! I wrote my soul out—wrote the truth that was in me—fresh, bursting truth, that would be uttered, and would be heard. To write at all was a glory, a rapture—a shouting out of songs to the very woods and fields, as children do. I wrote because I loved it—because I could not help it—because the stream that was in me would pour out. Where is that bright, impetuous, flashing, tumbling river now? Dwindled to a dull sluice, that all my digging and draining will only coax on for a mile or two in a set channel—and it runs dry.

Well, now for the page. These five lines—rich day's work—what driveling inanity! There it goes into the flame. Let's start afresh.

Once, twice, thrice, four times, a new page flies, in fine, curling sparkles, up the chimney. Thank Heaven, I have sufficient wit left, at least, to see that I am a dull fool. Try again.

This time comes nothing! My pen makes fantastic circles over the white page—little birds' nests, with a cluster of eggs inside—or draws foolish, soft profiles, with the wavy hair twisted up Greek fashion, as I used to scrawl over my bedroom walls when I was a boy. My thoughts go "wool-gathering"—wandering up and down the world, and then come back, and stand mocking and jibing at me.

How is it all to end? I can not write. I have no more power of brain than the most ar-rant dolt—that especial dolt whom I hear whistling down the Crescent—

"Cheer, boys, cheer, the world is all before us!"

Oh, that it were! Oh, that I were a back-woodsman, with a tree and a hatchet, and the strength of labor in these poor, thin, shaking hands! Oh, that I had been born a plow-lad, with neither nerves nor brains!

My head is so hot—bursting almost. This small room stifles me. Oh, for one breeze from the old known hills! But I should hardly feel it now. I don't feel any thing much. My thoughts glide away from me. I only want to lie down and go to sleep.

There! I have sat twenty minutes by the clock, with my head on my hands, doing nothing, thinking nothing, writing nothing, not a line. The page is as blank as it was three hours ago. My day's work—twelve golden hours—has been absolutely nothing.

This can not last. Am I getting ill? I don't know. I never do get ill. A good wholesome fever now—a nice, rattling delirium—a blistering and bleeding, out of which one would wake weak, and fresh, and peaceful as a child—what a blessing that might be! But I could not afford it—illness is too great a luxury for authors.

But—as I said to poor Austin some hours since—what is to be done? Something must be done, or my book will never be finished. And, oh, my enemy—oh, my evil genius, that used to be the stay of my life—with a sad yearning I turn over your leaves, and think it would grieve me, after all, if you, the pet babe of my soul, were never to be born alive!

If any thing could be done! I do not drink; I do not smoke; I live a virtuous and simple life. True, I never was very strong, but then I have no disease; and if I had, is not my soul independent of my body? Can not I compel my brain to work—can not I? for all you used to argue, my sapient friend, James Corrie, M.D. And his known handwriting, looking me in the face to-day, brings back many a sage, practical warning, disregarded when I was in health and vigor, mentally and physically—when it seemed to me that all authors' complainings were mere affectations, vapors, laziness. I know better now. Forgive me, my hapless brethren, I am as wretched as any one of ye all.

Can any thing cure me?—any medicine for a mind diseased? James Corrie, what sayest thou?

"For any disorder of the brain—any failure of the mental powers—for each and all of these strange forms in which the body will assuredly, in time, take her revenge upon those who have given up every thing to intellectual pursuits, and neglected the common law of nature—that mind and body should work together, and not apart—I know nothing so salutary as going back to a state of nature, and trying the water cure."

I sat pondering till midnight. It was a desperate chance, for each day was to me worth so much gold. Yet what mattered that? if each day were to be like this day, I should go insane by Christmas.

At nine A.M., next morning, I stood by my cousin's bedside, in his chambers at the Albany. He was fast asleep. His large, white, sculptured profile, with the black hair hanging about, was almost ghastly. I sat down, and waited till he awoke.

"Hollo! Alexander! I thought you were a water-demon, waiting to assist me into a bottomless bath out of which I was to emerge at the South Pole. Well, I'm meditating a similar plunge."

"I likewise."

"I am going to try the water cure."

"So am I."

"Bravo!" cried he, leaping out of bed. "I am delighted to find there will be two fools instead of one. We'll start to-morrow."

"I'm ready."

CHAPTER II.

"Give me the whip, Fyfe. Who would have thought of finding such a place, so near London! That's a very decent hill; and that moorland wind reminds one of your own Scotland."

"Ay," said I, gulping it down—drinking it like a river of life.

The free, keen breeze; the dashing across an unknown country—made dimly visible by a bleak, watery November moon; the odd curves of the road, now shut up by high rocky sides, now bordered by trees, black and ghostly, though still keeping the rounded forms of summer foliage—above all, the entire solitude, when, not two hours ago, we had been in the heart of London. That drive has left a vivid impression on my mind. It always seems like a journey in a dream. It made a clear division between the former life and that which was at hand.

I said to myself, in a dreamy sort of way, as, passing under a woody hillside, the little footboy sprang down and opened the lodge-gate, and we drove in front of a lighted hall door, between two white shadowy wings of building—I said, vaguely, "Old things are passed away; behold, all things are become new."

It is only in the middle of life, or when its burden has become heavier than we can bear, that one comprehends the stretching out of the spirit, as it will yet stretch out of the husk of the body into a fresh existence. It is not till then that we understand the feeling which created the fabled Lethe of Elysium—the full deliciousness of oblivion—the thirsty craving after something altogether new.

Therefore, except to such, I can never explain the ecstacy of impression which this place made upon me, as producing that involuntary cry, "All things are become new."

Except its master! That is, its real master; for Dr. and Mrs. Corrie were in the decline of life, and nearly all the burden of the establishment fell upon their son, their only child. No, James Corrie, I would not for the world have any thing new in thee. Change could not improve thee, nor novelty make thee more grateful to an old friend's heart.

If I were to describe him literally as he stood to welcome us, I fear the effect made would be but small.

He was not a woman's man, my lady readers! He had no smooth blandness or charming roughness—the two opposite qualities which make the fortune of fashionable physicians. You would hardly take him for a physician at all. His well-built figure; his large, well-balanced head, broad-browed, with a keen intellectual eye, but with a pleasant humanity smiling about the well-turned mouth—all indicated the wholesome balance between the mental, moral, and physical organization which made James Corrie, more than any person I have ever known, give one the impression of a true man.

Not a mere poet, or a visionary, or a philosopher, or a follower of science, made up of learning and dry bones, or a man of the world, to whom "the world" was Alpha and Omega; but a combination of all these, which resulted in that rare character which God meant us every one to be, and which about one-thousandth of us are—a man.

Dr. James Corrie was about forty. He had married early; it was an unhappy and childless union. He had now been a widower about five years. I do not know if womankind thought him handsome, but it was a very noble and good face.

"I like him," said Austin, decisively, when he had left us in our apartments—a sitting-room dividing two cheerful bedrooms—in each of which the principal feature was a large shallow bath, standing on end in a corner, like a coffin with the lid off.

"Tea at seven, bed at half past nine," I heard Austin maundering drearily to himself, as he brushed his curly hair, and reattired his very handsome person. "How the—. But I suppose one must not swear here—eh, Alick? Your Dr. James is not in that line."

I laughed; and we went down stairs.

It was a large, old-fashioned house, baronial-like, with long corridors to pace, and lofty rooms to breathe freely in. Something of the old feudal blood in me always takes pleasure in that sort of house, especially after London lodgings.

A dazzle of light, coming from a large bright table, of which the prominent ornaments were two vases of winter flowers, and a great silver urn. But abundance of delicate edibles, too; nothing implying future starvation, as Austin indicated by the faintest wink of the eye to me; and then, with an air of satisfaction, resumed his customary gentlemanly deportment.

We were introduced to Mrs. Corrie, a tall, spare, elderly lady, who sat, "frosty but kindly," at the head of the table; beside her the old Doctor ; at the foot, our friend, Dr. James. There was also a Miss Jessie Corrie, a niece, lively and good-looking, though not so young as she might have been. A score of heterogeneous patients, of both sexes and all ages, in which the only homogeneity was a general air of pleasantness and pleasure, completed the circle. Its chief peculiarity seemed, that, large as it was, it had all the unrestrainedness and coziness of *home*.

"That is exactly what we want to make it—isn't it, father?" said Dr. James, when, the meal over, the Corrie family, we two, stood round the wide, old-fashioned, fagot-heaped hearth. "We want to cure not only the body, but the mind. To do our patients real good, we must make them happy, and there is no happiness like that of home."

"True." I said, with a sort of sigh.

"And have you not noticed that one-half of the chronic valetudinarians we see are those who have either no home or an unhappy one? To such we try to give, if not the real thing, at least a tolerable imitation of it. And in so doing we double their chances of cure."

"I believe it ;" and, turning into the cheery drawing-room, we gave ourselves up—Austin thoroughly, I partially—to the pleasure of being pleased.

"Well." said he, when we retired, "for a sick hospital, this is the jolliest place I ever knew. How do you feel?"

I could hardly tell. I was stupid-like, so great was the change to me, after months of hard work and almost total solitude ; besides, Corrie and I had been talking over old times. As I lay dozing, with the glimmer of the fire on the tall, upright, coffin-like bath, there seemed to rise within it a mild, motionless figure, beautiful, as a young man's first love, in soft white dead-clothes, with shut eyes, and folded hands, and an inward voice kept repeating my favorite saying—in its simplicity one of the truest and most religious that Shakspeare ever wrote—" 'Tis better as it is!"

CHAPTER III.

WE began "the treatment" next day, in a November morning, by the light of a candle. I will not betray the horrors of the prison-house. Of course, it was a trial. My turn over, I could hardly help laughing when I heard afar off the "roar of waters," and Hardy's smothered howl. And when I found him out of doors tramping the hoar frost, and gazing lugubriously over the dim, bleak, misty hills—for it was before sunrise—he, who was usually waked at eleven A.M., to find a valet, silken dressing-gown, coffee, hot rolls, etc., etc., I could not hide an uncontrollable fit of mirth.

He took it good-humoredly ; he was a capital fellow ; but he shook his head when I proposed to climb the hillside—the lovely hillside, with its carpet of fallen leaves, which left still foliage enough to dress the trees, like Jacob's youngest darling, in a robe of many colors, yellow, brown, red, dark-green—I never beheld more glorious hues. Sick and weak as I felt, they stirred my soul to something of its old passion for beauty.

"Very well; and then I must go up the hill alone. It is thirteen years since I saw the country in November; it is fifteen years since I watched the sun rise."

So on I trudged. I was free! free! I had not to walk as I did in weary London, but the mere motion might stir up some new thoughts in my sluggish brains. Thoughts, not for the mere pleasure of thinking, but that each might be woven out for use and coined into gold.

My demon, with its two hundred white, blank faces, was fifty miles away.

I did not see the sun rise. Who ever did when he climbed for it? But I found a sea of misty moor, sweeping in wave on wave of brown heather—how purple it must once have been ! —over which the wind blew in my face, as it used to blow over the hills at home.

I met it—I who two days since had cowered before the slightest draught. My throat choked, my eyes burned. I walked rapidly on, howling out at the top of my voice fragments out of Victor Hugo's song, "Le Fou de Tolède."

"Gastibelza, l'homme à la carabine
    Chantait ainsi :
Quelqu'un a-t-il connu Donna Sabine ?
    Quelqu'un d'ici ?

Dansez, chantez, villageois, la nuit gagne
    Le mont Falù :
Le vent qui vient à travers la montagne
Me rendra fou, oui, me rendra fou !

Dansez, chantez, villageois, la nuit tombe!
    Sabine un jour
A tout donné, sa beauté de colombe,
    Et son amour,

Pour l'anneau d'or du Comte de Saldagne,
    Pour un bijou—
Le vent qui vient à travers la montagne
M'a rendu fou, oui, m'a rendu fou."

Breakfast early; rosy looks; cheerful greetings; every body seeming to take a kindly interest in one another; the Corrie family taking an interest in each and all; the wholesome give-and-take system of life's small charities going on around, so that, perforce, strangers joined in the pleasant traffic.

These were my first daylight impressions of Highwood. Austin's seemed the same. He was busily engaged in doing the agreeable to the bright-eyed Jessie Corrie and three other ladies ; his public devotion to the sex being very polytheistic in its tendencies.

I sat aloof and made professional "studies."

"Are these all the patients now with you, Corrie?"

"All but one."

Here I saw Miss Jessie, filling a small tray with comestibles, take a chrysanthemum from the centre vase, and lay it by the toast.

"Ellice likes white chrysanthemums."

"Is Ellice your sister, Miss Corrie?"

"I have none."

"Your cousin, then?"

"No," half laughing, half blushing; so I concluded it was a man's name, and owned by the invisible patient in whose floral tastes the lady took an interest.

After breakfast, the dining-room was left deserted; every body had something to do or suffer; we nothing. Stay—nothing, did I say? Enter John the bath-man.

"Gentlemen, will you please to be ready for me at twelve, and half past?"

"There's something to suffer, at least," said I, as Austin pulled a long face. Then we settled, he into languid, I into restless dreariness.

"I shall go and smoke, Fyfe."

"And I shall take to my writing."

"I'll sit with you; come along."

I had not meant that, being of those owl-of-the-desert authors who can best ply their trade alone. But there was no help for it. Despite my resolutions, and the magnum opus left behind, a miserable restlessness drove me to commence some small operetto, so as anyhow to steal a march upon my enemy, Time.

I was cutting folios preparatively, and inwardly execrating the unwelcome company of my cousin, who puffed gloomily over the fire, when in walked James Corrie.

"Welcome, doctor; take a cigar?"

"Against Highwood rules, my good sir," said Corrie, pleasantly.

"Indeed; but I never kept to a rule in my life. Quite impossible; couldn't give up my cigar."

"So thought I once. Nor my glass of ale. Nor my brandy-and-water at supper-time."

"Yet you did. What cured you?"

"Necessity first. I became a struggling man. I had real wants enough; I could not afford an artificial one. Now cigars cost me, besides a hearty dyspepsia, thirty pounds a year; and thirty pounds a year will keep one man, or two children from starving. It seemed a pity, in this over-populated country, that I should be slowly killing myself with what would save two other human beings alive."

Austin dropped his weed, and paused a little ere he lit another.

"And your strong drinks?"

"Once in my life, Fyfe, I knew what it was to want water."

"When?" asked Austin, lazily, still irresolutely poising his unlit Havana.

"Four years ago, on the Atlantic, in an open boat, for five days."

"How many of you?"

"Six men and one woman, all dying of thirst. I have never touched any thing but water since."

The doctor became silent. Austin looked at him with a dawning interest. The second cigar still remained in its case.

"Come, Mr. Hardy, I am sure, since you have put yourself under my care, you will allow me to confiscate these contraband articles. I belong to the preventive service, you know."

"But, doctor, how am I to drag through the day without my cigar?"

"Leave that to me and mother Nature, or, as our friend here would poetically say, the goddess Undine. By-the-by, Fyfe, what is this I see? MS.?"

"Only an article I want to finish in the intervals of my courting this said goddess of yours."

"Can't be, my friend; she will not take a divided heart. In her name I must seize all this. Best to be 'off with the auld love before you are on wi' the new.'"

"If Hardy will set the example. Come, old fellow, we have only to fancy ourselves at school again, with James Corrie instead of Birch for our Tyrannus. Let's submit."

"I know it will be the death of me," groaned Austin. But he met the doctor's cheerful, comical smile, and smiled too. Somehow the cigar-case vanished, likewise my MS., and I rather think the two great pockets of Corrie's shooting-jacket entombed both.

Making no more remarks on the subject, he continued talking; upon common topics, the Eastern war, Highwood, its neighborhood, and lastly, its inmates.

"What odd varieties of humanity must come under your hands, doctor! How ever do you manage to guide, control, and amalgamate them all?"

"By two simple rules—the law of truth and the law of kindness. Sick people are not unlike children." Here we both slightly winced, but the doctor took no notice. "Have we not high authority for trying to become 'as little children?' That, it seems to me, is the principle of the water cure; that is how I strive to carry it out."

"You certainly succeed. I have rarely beheld more cheerful and happy faces. It is quite a treat to look round at meal times. We have seen all the patients, I think you said?"

"Except the one I mentioned."

"Who was that?"

"Miss Ellice Keir."

"I have heard about her," said Austin, languidly. "Something in your line, Fyfe; the high, heroic dodge. For my part, I don't fancy your middle-aged, strong-minded, self-devoted females."

"Miss Keir would be as much surprised as any one of her friends to hear herself put under that category. Indeed, Mr. Hardy, you quite mistake," said the doctor, quietly.

"What is she then?"

"She has been, and still is, a great sufferer."

Something extra-professional and dignified in Corrie suppressed my cousin. Besides, he was too kind-hearted to make game of any "great sufferer."

"But when our medico was gone, I scrupled not to question what Austin had heard about the 'high, heroic dodge.'"

"It might come in, you know. Any scrap

of an idea is valuable to such addled brains as mine. I might put her into my next book."

"Do you put people in your books?" said Austin, with an open mouth of slight alarm.

"Never, my good fellow. That is never *in toto*, never to their injury, and never when I think they would dislike it. I only make studies of 'bits,' heads and feet, noses and eyes, as a painter would. I wouldn't 'show up' any body. It's mean. But," for I saw I was talking miles over Austin's head, "what of Ellice Keir?"

"She is an American."

"Stop! a Yankee? Then I don't wish to hear another word."

CHAPTER IV.

No, it was useless trying to get up an interest in any body or any thing. Chronic ill-health of mind, or body, or both, is not cured in a day.

True, the charm of change lasted for some eight-and-forty hours or so, and I began greatly to enjoy the morning bath, the moorland walk to meet the sun, the cheery breakfast, where food tasted well, and one was not afraid to eat; where conversation was pleasant, and one did not tremble to use one's brains, nor to waste in mere talk the thoughts which were one's stock in trade, valuable as bullion gold.

But as the day crept on all this brightness faded, and life became as dull and pale as it was every where to me.

And still in solitary walks, amidst the soft droppings or wild whirlings of dead leaves, and the rustle of the dying fern; in the still deeper solitude of parlor circles, merry and loud, I found myself moodily and cynically commenting with the preacher, "Vanity, vanity, all is vanity." And out of the intolerable weight, the leaden-folded cloak, which seemed to wrap me round, or else to hang like a pall between me and all creation—sometimes, a twitter of a bird, or sound of moorland wind, or hand-breadth of rosy, winter sunset lighting up the dull sky, I used to stretch out my hands, long-ing to sob out like a child, yet able only to sigh, "Oh, for the dreams of my youth!"

For Austin, he succeeded better. His soul did not trouble him much, or the dreams of his youth either. His fine animal nature responded to this uncorrupt animal existence. He grew rapidly better, and lived apparently a very jolly life, though at intervals still complaining of its being so "slow."

CHAPTER V.

I SAT by the dining-room fire, alone, for it was the forenoon. Let me draw the picture of that day.

A gloomy day. True November; damp and raw. The terrace and the lawn was strewed with dead leaves; and more kept falling, flut-tering down one by one, like shot birds. The only bit of warm color the eye could seize on was a tall cedar, between whose branches shone a beech-tree beyond, making alternate lines of dark-red and dark-green. Every day at break-fast I used to look at it, often thinking, childish fashion, that if I had to choose a vegetable ex-istence I should like to be a beech, with its ever-moving leaves, so vocal in their prime, so rich in hue, to the very minute that they fall.

Maundering thus, thus "mooning" up and down the lone room, my hands in my pockets, thinking how long it was since I had been a child—wondering whether in the next form of existence I should be a child again.

Hark! a harmonium! I did not know there was one in the house. In the next room, prob-ably. Somebody playing it well, too.

Now, I do not care for music in general—not the music one gets "in society." It is too flimsy for me. The love-songs sicken me; the sad, plaintive songs, badly sung, are atrocious; well sung, they tear one's heart; and at thirty, one begins to find that a very unnecessary piece of laceration.

"What is life, that we should moan—
Why make so much ado?"

In Heaven's name, troll a merry stave and have done with it. As for piano-forte playing, I had rather hear my aunt's kitten run over the keys—at least, almost always.

But I like an organ; an l, second best, a harmonium. I liked this one. Corrie found me pacing up and down, or listening, rapt in a state bordering on sublimest satisfaction.

"What a lovely tone—calm, liquid, grand! Dreamy, too—like the dreams of one's youth, with all the passion and pain burned out of them. How exquisitely smooth and delicate the touch! and it isn't easy, for I have tried—listen!"

"Yes—she plays very well."

"Who is it, doctor?"

"Miss Keir."

"Miss Keir! She with her Yankee fingers and Yankee soul!"

"My good friend, you mistake; even if Yan-kee were the terrible adjective you make it, which I beg leave to deny, having myself a great respect for Brother Jonathan. But Miss Keir is a Canadian. She was born at Montreal. Come, I will introduce you."

We entered—a lady rose from the instrument; a very little lady, almost elfishly small; hands and feet so tiny, you would have crushed them with a touch. Dressed in black, of some soft material that did not rustle, but caused her to move softly and airily, without a sound. She was neither young nor handsome in the least; but—and that "but" contradicts both assertions —she had very dark Canadian eyes.

I say Canadian, because I have only seen them in Canadians by birth or descent. They are neither Eastern nor Southern, neither fiery nor voluptuous; but large, soft, calm, swimming and trembling in a tender passionateness, or breaking at times into a flash of the wild Indian blood—worth all your placid, pale-colored English eyes.

"Mr. Fyfe—Miss Keir. He is a very old friend of mine."

Miss Keir offered her hand, her pale little hand, soft as a bit of snow, only it was so warm.

Now, that is one of my crotchets—the *feel* of a hand. Some it is martyrdom to me to touch. I hate your fishy, your skinny, your dumpling, your flabby hands—a hand that is afraid—a hand that clutches. I like a woman who comes and lays her soft, pure palm in mine, knowing I am a man and a gentleman, that I prize the little passing angel and will entertain it honorably and well.

Another crotchet I have—the tone, *i. e.*, *timbre* of a voice. Venus herself would be intolerable to me if she had the voice of some women I have known. A voice is the test of character—you can detect at once the true ring in it, or the false ; of temper—however education and the decorums of society may soften it down—in critical moments, out it comes. I think I never yet knew a thoroughly lovable woman who had an ugly voice.

Miss Keir's voice was beautiful. Among other women it sounded like a thrush's note among a congregation of sparrows—as rare, too. Yet her manner and looks were so expressive, so *spirituelle*—nay, rather let me use the English word spiritual, for that more truly indicates the way in which her soul seemed to be shining through and glorifying her little frail body—that she required language less than most women.

We had all three a very long conversation. We dashed at once in *medias res*—tried our several hands at solving some of the great world-questions of our day—some of the greatest problems of the universe. We grew earnest, excited—that is, I did—then calm. She calmed me. What she said I know not. I can not tell if she explained any thing, because the most formidable of our spiritual, like our physical mysteries, are utterly incapable of explanation ; but she calmed me down—like as a man in great mental anguish is quieted by being suddenly brought out into the open daylight, the summer air.

I have great faith in instinctive attraction and repulsion. I believe there are people—I am one —who know at first meeting whom they will love and whom they will hate, who will do them harm, and who good. I believe this sensation is placed in them for warning and guidance. I myself have never run counter to it, except to my after peril.

It was blindly obeying this attraction, when, on leaving, I requested permission sometimes to join the Corries in Miss Keir's apartment.

She looked at the doctor; he answered, smiling—"You are so much better now, that you may safely be allowed a little society—especial-ly that of so celebrated a literary character as my friend Mr. Fyfe."

Literature! faugh! I had forgotten the very word.

"Why did you tell her I was an author?" I said, as we turned out of doors ; Corrie remorselessly exacting the walk before the noonday bath. "Why could you not let me stand for once upon my own footing? let her judge me not by what I do, but what I am. Yet"—and a bitter conviction of what a contemptible specimen of manhood I had sunk to, forced itself upon my mind—"Yet a hard judgment that might have been."

"Not from her. She knows that some characters, sorely tried, must be judged, not solely from what they are, but from what they aspire to be—and one day may be. Why should I have kept *incog.* your best self—your books? She has read them all."

"Has she? I am sorry. No—glad. For after all, with all my shams, she will find the real Alexander Fyfe by snatches there. But enough of myself. I want to talk about her."

"You seem greatly pleased with her. Yet few take to her at once, she is so very quiet."

"But her quietness gives one a sense of rest, and her soft way of moving throws a harmony over the room. She is not unlike the instrument she plays. You can not fancy her attuned to the drawing-room ditties and ball-room jigs of life—you can not conceive of her either beautiful or young."

The doctor silently smiled.

"I mean, there is in her that which transcends both youth and beauty—a cheerful sacredness—a wholesome calm. She seems to do me good. I should like to know more of her."

"That is very easy, if her health keeps improving."

"Has she been long an invalid?"

"Four years."

"How did you meet her?"

"Literally, at the gates of death. In the boat I told you of, after our ship went down—"

"Was she that one woman saved?"

"She was. She had a brother and sister with her, bringing them to Europe. I got them into the boat. For six days she was the strength of us all. Then the little sister died on her lap. The brother survived."

James Corrie cleared his throat ; we walked on a few yards—

"Such a quiet creature—who would have believed it of her?"

"Nobody does, and nobody need ; such deeds are not done for the world, and she has been quite as heroic—if you will use the word—in her illness since, as at the time of the shipwreck."

"How is she affected?"

"With almost constant neuralgic and rheumatic pains ; it is only within the last few months that she has been able to walk—or even to stand."

"And the brother?"

"He is walking the hospitals in Edinburgh. She struggled on with him for six months till she fell ill—fortunately in my mother's house. She has never quite recovered."

"Do you think she ever will recover?"

"Certainly. That is—if it be the will of God. Now, Fyfe, your hour is come—to the 'dripping-sheet'—away!"

I left him; and he walked rapidly up the hill.

CHAPTER VI.

"SMALL—plain—and not young! Very attractive description, truly. But the patients here seem all middle-aged. What with baths and walks to cut up the day, and your friend Corrie to look after one, what with his awfully honest, righteous eyes, one can't get the least bit of harmless amusement."

"Except with Miss Jessie. You flirt enough with her."

"Put that verb in the passive voice—do, my good fellow. I merely respond. What a wild devil it is—just like pepper and mustard—French mustard. It's the only bit of spice left in your terribly wholesome hydropathic diet. I might amuse myself really with it if it were only young."

"Le besoin de s'amuser, seems the only possible element in your affairs of this sort."

"Exactly so."

And he sauntered back into the drawing-room, where, our aquatic duties all done, there was usually a most merry circle till bedtime—into which circle my friend Hardy had dropped like a god-send, and even by his third night made himself acceptable to everybody there, and especially to Miss Jessie Corrie.

Yet I had no qualms on her account; if, indeed, I could have felt enough interest in life to suffer qualms about any thing. The lady was—like Isopel, in Borrow's "Lavengro" (you see, unlike many authors, I do read other books besides my own)—"large and fierce, and able to take her own part." I did not think she had a heart; anyhow, it did not matter it's being broken—most people's are, else where would all the poems and novels come from?

"As you will, my good friends," thought I, watching them lounging, flirting, and laughing. "It's a case of diamond cut diamond. Skim away over life's shallows in your painted jolly-boats. You'll swamp no one—not even each other; or, if you did, it's no business of mine."

But just at that minute I paused; I caught a tone of the harmonium down stairs.

"Now," thinks I to myself, "I wonder what those eyes down below would say if they were looking on instead of mine. Would they have my cynicism—my contemptuous laissez-faire? But, 'Physician, heal thyself!' How can I be bold enough to pull the mote out of another's

eye, when I am still blinded by the beam in my own? Blinder than ever—or else coming into the light makes me feel it more—since morning."

Our fourth day at Highwood—Sunday; Austin escorted a carriage full of ladies to church; he thought it more "respectable." For me—Oh, thou one Father of the universe! one infinite and unapproachable Wisdom! one all-satisfying and all-perfect Love! when wilt Thou visit me? when wilt Thou enlighten me? when wilt Thou comfort me? I stand under the pine-wood on the hill-top, where the air is so rare, and the wind so wild, it seems nearer to Thee. I long to die and learn Thy mysteries—to die and be filled with Thy love. My soul cries out unto Thee with an exceeding great and bitter cry, which is often the only evidence it has of its own existence. I do not believe in myself at all, my worthless, aimless, broken-spirited, miserable self; but I believe in Thee.

"The fool hath said in his heart, There is no God." But only the fool, or, perhaps, he who pays a guinea toll to heaven on a silver charity-plate, or keeps a bishop to pray for him. I prefer the hill-top and Parson Breeze.

Descending the hill I met Corrie, and went in with him to speak to Miss Keir. He told her what I had been saying.

She pointed to a line she had been setting as a copy for the lodge-keeper's lame daughter, whom she usually taught to write of a Sunday:

"In every place he that loveth God, and worketh righteousness, is accepted of Him."

That was the best sermon after all. That was what the Divine Preacher on the mount would have said to us, Ellice Keir!

CHAPTER VII.

"WATER-CURE! I think, doctor, your system is directed not only to the body but the soul. Mine feels cleaner than of yore."

"Does it?"

We were pacing the terrace walk, Miss Keir and Miss Jessie watching us from the window. It had become a matter of custom that I should always spend a morning hour or two in her room. They were the best hours of the day.

"What a calm, clear mind hers is, purified by suffering, full of inward faith! How she looks through all shams right down into truth—God's truth! Like—if the simile were not as hackneyed as Piccadilly in May—like a steadily-eyed astronomer looking down into a well. We see only the glaring noon without, or the black, incrusted sides. She sees the stars at the bottom. She knows where to look for them, because she believes they are there."

"You are quite poetical again."

"Yes, I think I could write my book, if you would let me."

The doctor shook his head.

"And sometimes I could almost fancy that

Alexander Fyfe's boy-heart was only buried with the old knight's under that sun-dial, and that a trifle of digging would bring it to the surface again, slightly decayed, perhaps, but a human heart still."

"Are you thinking of marrying?" said the doctor, very gravely.

"No; nor of loving, in that sense. It isn't in me. But simply of resuscitating from fast corruption that aforesaid portion of human anatomy, which we authors trade in so much that we leave no material for home use."

"Do speak plainly; I am but a plain man."

"For the which thank Heaven! Merely, Corrie, that we authors are liable, above most people, to the danger that, while preaching to others, ourselves should become castaways. We persuade ourselves that to paint high virtue is to exemplify it. We like to act leader and chorus instead of principal—to talk rather than to work. In brief, we write when we ought to live."

"Possibly. But what are you driving at?"

"This. Here have I been lauding up the ideal these thirteen years; have scribbled folios on moral power, heroism, self-denial, and that sort of thing."

"You have, indeed; your writings are beautiful."

"My *writings!* And what am I? A self-engrossed, sickly, miserable, hypochondriacal fool."

"My dear fellow!"

"It is true! And that woman, Ellice Keir, who never wrote a line in all her days, she lives a poem. Such a one as in all *my* days I will never be able to write."

"I'll tell her what you say," answered the doctor, smiling. "Come along."

He told her almost word for word. She looked in his face, and blushed up to the eyes—a vivid, tremulous, happy blush.

"Mr. Fyfe is quite mistaken, you know."

"I know he is mistaken in one thing. We need only judge ourselves, as we trust we shall be judged, according to our gifts. He whose gifts it is to write great books, though himself far below his own ideal, is, when not false to it in his life, a means of ennobling other lives; and though to my mind a great life is nobler than any book, still, to have written a great book is—to have done something. Never let a rose-bush despise itself because it is not an oak."

"Yes," Miss Keir added, her eyes turning from Dr. James to me, "it should rather abide in peace, and grow to the utmost perfection its own roses. They are very dear and sweet."

She held out her hand. It was better to me than a laurel crown.

Henceforward I began truly *to live*; the first time I had lived for years. Up ere daylight, instead of that stupor of body and soul which used to last till near mid-day. The baths, out of which one comes merry as a child and strong as a Hercules. The walks, clasping nature like

F

a mistress; nature, always lovely and beloved, even when she pelted me with rain-storms, frowned at me through leaden skies, soaked me with her soft, perpetual tears.

I will not say what it was to be, every day, and many hours in the day, under the heavenly darkness of light—if I may coin the paradox—of the eyes of Ellice Keir.

She never grew, in mine, any younger or any handsomer; in truth, I hardly thought of her physical self at all. It was a pure, abstract recognition of my ideal of moral beauty—more perfect than in any woman I have ever known.

Pardon, pardon, O first love of my youth! Thine eyes are closed—closed!

CHAPTER VIII.

"Well, if you ask me for my opinion (I don't think one man has a right to give it to another man—hardly even one friend to another friend, without)—I consider you are not acting like that most sensible, upright, gentlemanly youth I knew ten years ago—Austin Hardy."

"Pshaw! don't bring up ten years ago. Our virtues wear out like our clothes. We can't go shabby. Best get another suit."

"But let it be, at least, as decent as the former."

"If it can, *i. e.*, if there's any cash to get it with. But let's talk plain English. What have you to say? Do you think I shall get into a scrape?"

"Not a bit of it. Miss Jessie is a wise one, and a sharp one, too. She isn't the least likely to break her heart for you. She only coquettes a little."

"Mighty little. Your friend the doctor keeps such a steady look-out, one would think he wanted her for himself. Then the old people; I suppose it's their duty to watch black sheep for the credit of their establishment. Never was there a fellow who had so few opportunities of love-making, even if he chose. But I don't choose. I only want to amuse myself."

"That is—you find yourself in a world where people live, work, struggle; and all you can do is to amuse yourself! Tired of all other shams, you put on the largest sham of all—the highest, strongest feeling a human being can have—love—just 'to amuse yourself.'"

"You're civil, Alexander."

"I'm honest."

"Don't fly into a passion; you know I always listen to you. Why did you not give me this sermon a week ago?"

"Why, indeed!"

"There's something changed about you, my boy. You don't talk such rigmarole as you used to do, nor in such a savage tone. Also, you grow quieter—not so nervous. You will grow into a 'show case,' as our friend Corrie would say. It is really the water-cure."

"Probably. But never mind me. I'm talking about you, and Miss Jessie likewise. Mark me, Austin, that young woman—"

"Hold there. Middle-aged. Twenty-seven, at least; else I might have thought seriously of her—for a quarter of an hour. She is a good figure, large and lady-like—very decent requisites for Mrs. Hardy. More I can't expect. Well, what about 'that young woman?'"

"Merely, that she never had any heart at all; or, if she had, she has worn it on her sleeve, till the daws have pecked it away."

"Just like mine."

"I wonder you'll even condescend to play it fully—still worse, at mock sentiment, with her. She who is all false, from top to toe, without and within."

"Heigho! So am I."

"You're not, Austin Hardy. You think it fine to sham vice; you're too lazy to struggle through to virtue; but you're an honest fellow at heart."

"Hold your tongue, Alick," said he, in a gruff voice. "Here comes the lovely young Jessie. Welcome! She is just in time to spread her petals to the sunrise, my fair Flower of Damblane."

For—and let me promise that this is a most original scene for a tryst, and quite peculiar to a hydropathic establishment—I ought to have said that we were taking our morning walk, all things being yet dusky, in the cloudy winter dawn. Though in the east, and up even to the zenith, the sky was catching a faint rosy tinge; and between the two pinewoods one vivid sulphur-colored cloud showed that somewhere, far below the visible horizon, the sun was beginning to shine.

I maintain, from personal experience at Highwood, that sunrise in general is what a school-boy would call "a great humbug"—"a dead take in." But still it has a peculiarity of its own, especially on a winter morning. The worthy old sun seems to climb up so doggedly pertinacious, so patiently strong, though shorn of his beams—struggling through mist and damp to smile upon a poor earth, who is too weary, ragged, and wan to welcome him. But steadily he rises—like a high honest purpose dawning in the hopeless winter of a man's days, when time is short and weather bleak; yet steadily he rises, and comes at last to daybreak—daylight—ay, unto perfect noonday.

I began to think sometimes on this wise—as if even though it was but yesterday that I had sat and watched my sun go down—watched stoically, with open eyes that never blenched or moistened; yet every morning at this hour, it seemed as if it *might* rise to-morrow.

And Austin?

CHAPTER IX.

"BLESS my life! Is that your wonderful Miss Keir? What a very plain woman!"

It was her first appearance in the evening circle, and I had offered Hardy to introduce him. Of course, receiving this reply, I immediately turned, and left him to his own devices.

A "plain woman" was she? Perhaps. I could not tell; I had scarcely thought about it. If I did now, it was only vaguely, thinking of an observation once made on a lady, a friend of mine. Its object told it me herself, with a simple, grateful pleasure, touched even to tears: "He said, he never knew whether I was pretty or not; he only knew that he loved me."

And I loved Ellice Keir, in that sort of harmless way, with a tender friendship which, when both are well advanced in life, so as to make it safe and free, it does a man good to bestow, and is sweet for a woman to receive. So I reasoned. Oh! fool, fool, fool!

She sat in the fireside arm-chair, the same little black-stoled figure, the sound of whose voice was seldom heard, yet whose mute smile created around her a circle of brightness. Sunlike, she appeared to draw from the various calyx of every human heart some perfume—usually the best perfume it had.

Gradually nearly all the party gathered around her; and a few stragglers only were left apart, including Hardy and Miss Corrie. At last I heard him behind me.

"How glad everybody seems to have Miss Keir back here again!"

"That is not wonderful."

"There is a general seceding to her. I suppose I must e'en follow the herd. Come, you may introduce me, if you like."

"By no means. How could you be expected to do the civil to such 'a very plain woman?'"

"'Pon my life, and so she is. But there's something odd about her. Those eyes—I felt them at the farthest corner of the room. They seem to be finding me out. Confess—have you been telling her any of my misdeeds?"

"Austin Hardy!"

"Well, it would not be like you. Now for it; lead the victim to the horns of the altar. I'm prepared."

But Miss Keir was already retiring. A mere introduction passed—no more.

"Ah!" said Austin, drawing a deep breath, and giving me a slight wink, as Miss Jessie came on in full sail up to the chair where he was lounging. "No matter; I shall go back to my old silly ways. It's easier now that woman is out of the room."

Hardy held out for one evening—two—the beginning of the third; said she was clever, and he hated clever women; quiet, and he liked to be amused. Afterward, I saw him listening, with polite, abstracted smile to the large dose of "amusement" Miss Jessie always furnished; but his eyes were riveted on the fireside circle, now a brighter circle than ever, since Miss Keir was its centre. No, not its centre; for her attraction in society was more of the passive kind. She did not shine herself, but she created a fresh, clear atmosphere, in which every one else shone brighter than before. Finally, Hardy was discovered leaning behind the velvet arm-chair, attentive to the discussion. It was something about Northumberland mines, and the improvement of the miners.

"Miss Keir is speaking to you, Mr. Hardy." It was really droll to see him bend forward with that eager, pleased face, to "such a very plain woman."

"Yes, my property does lie among the mining country, but I never troubled my head much about it. I have had no time."

"No time?"

"That is, I fear I have never had energy enough to make time. I am a very lazy fellow, as Fyfe would tell you."

She smiled again, and said something more which I did not hear. Austin brightened up.

"Ay, my cousin has always a good word for me; but, indeed, I am not fit for any thing of the sort. I couldn't take the trouble. My property is the greatest burden of my life."

Here Jessie Corrie tittered out some very commonplace remark, to which he replied with one of his usual fulsome speeches to women; but still kept talking to Miss Keir—

"Duties of property did you say? Dreadful word, 'duty!' Quite out of my line. Besides, it's too late now. With my ill-health—"

Here he seemed conscious of her amused look resting on his brawny figure and ruddy face—

"Well, I fear you and the doctor must find out a better man for the carrying out of your philanthropic plans. I have been too long given up to the do-nothing system."

Yet he lingered and listened, gradually with some real interest gleaming through his elegant languor; now and then joining in the conversation with a word or two of the capital good sense he could furnish at will, though he was not cursed to any heavy degree with that commodity called "brains." At parting, Miss Keir shook hands with him, with a friendly word or two.

"By Jove, Fyfe, that isn't a bad sort of woman, just for a change. I'm rather tired of beauties. One is obliged to think before one speaks to her, just as if she were a man."

"Her sex is indebted to you."

"Pshaw! she is not a bit of a woman."

"Altogether a woman, I think."

"Well, have your own way."

He stood long meditating, a rare fact for Austin Hardy.

"There is some sense in those schemes of hers. When I was twenty-one I used to have grand notions about improving my estates, and living patriarch of the country side, after the good old fashion. But all vanished in smoke. It's too late now."

"No good thing is ever too late. Did you not hear her saying so? She thinks you might carry out many of the Doctor's sanitary and educational schemes. She told me she wished you would."

"Did she? But I have not the power, and it isn't worth while. Let the world jog on as it likes, it will last my time. However, perhaps I may just hear what she says on the subject to-morrow."

I smiled to myself, and was satisfied.

"By-the-by, Alick, I altogether forgot to bid good-night to Jessie Corrie."

Substitution is the true theory of amendment. Knock a rotten substance out by driving a sound wedge in.

So thought I, when, two days after, I saw Austin making himself busy—at least as busy as a man can well be who is going through the water treatment—in this new interest, which perhaps was the only real interest he was capable of. It roused his best self—that for which nature intended him—the active, upright, benevolent country gentleman.

He took to plans, drawings, blue-books, works on political economy, and spent half the morning in that little parlor I so loved, with Dr. James Corrie and Miss Keir.

The former said to me, watching him—
"Here's a change in our friend Mr. Hardy. I fancy he, too, is participating in the spiritual water-cure."

"It appears so."

Nor did I grudge him that healing.

CHAPTER X.

It was a November day—November, yet so mild, so sunshiny, so heavenly calm, that but for the thinned trees, the brown heather, the withered fern, you would have thought it spring.

Her pony's feet were up to the fetlock in dead beech-leaves, making a soft rustle as we climbed the hill after her. We—that is, Miss Corrie, Hardy, Dr. James, and I. The old Dr. Corrie and his wife were a good way behind. They, too, had made a point of joining the triumphant procession which celebrated Miss Keir's return to the outer world; for every body loved her—every body!

She seemed to know and feel it—to sun herself in it almost as a child does. For, though thirty years old, there was still in her a great deal of the child. Trouble had passed over her, ripening, not blasting, and left her in the Indian summer of her days, a season almost as beautiful as spring. In that golden brightness, one of us at least lived, morning, noon, and eve, and half believed it was the return of May.

"This day seems made on purpose for you, Miss Keir," said Austin, as he struggled up the hill, assisting Miss Jessie kindly and courteously (perhaps more kindly and courteously than ever since his manner had gradually sunk to that and nothing more). The lady looked cross, and complained of damp leaves. In her was nothing of the Indian summer, but as affectation of girlishness, a frantic clinging to a lost youth, which is at once the saddest and most hateful thing I know.

"Eight hours since, when Hardy and I took our morning walk, this moor was all white with hoar-frost. Are you quite sure you are not cold, Miss Keir?"

"Let me run and get her my fur cape, Alick. Will you help Miss Corrie for a minute or two?"

"Mr. Hardy is certainly better; he has learned to run like any school-boy," said the doctor, with an amused satisfaction.

"And to fetch and carry like any spaniel," observed Miss Jessie Corrie, whose regard cooling down gave out a satirical spark or two occasionally. "Marvelous change! A month ago, he thought of nobody in the world but his dearly-beloved self."

"He was ill then," I said.

Laughing at my sharpness, she bent forward to a whisper of Miss Keir's, which she repeated aloud, with variations, afterward.

"Mr. Hardy, Ellice is much obliged. She says you run like a school-boy, and carry like a spaniel, and have learned at last to think of other folk in the house besides your beloved self."

"Did she say so?"

That hurt look on Austin's blasé visage was something new—new as the odd shyness with which he gave the fur to me to wrap her in—he, the erewhile officious squire of dames!

Ellice turned on him her bright, true, heart-satisfying smile.

"Jessie mistakes a little. I said that Mr. Hardy thinks of every body in the house except himself."

Austin showed that he could not only run, but blush like any school-boy; so pleasant seemed her praise.

On we went through the moorland, down in the ferny dell where those three cedars stood, huge and dark, with the faint sunbeams on their tops, and damp earthiness at their feet.

"This will not do," said Dr. James. "Very unsanitary spot. There's a wholesome breeze and a grand view half-way up Torbury Hill."

So we ascended, knee-deep in heather, in which poor Miss Jessie was stranded. Austin took her safely home, and came "tearing" back, his hair flying all abroad, and his clothes catching on furze-bushes. How his London friends would have stared! I told him so.

"Never mind. You are growing just as much of a boy yourself, old fellow! I think, Miss Keir, it must be something in the air of Highwood that makes one young."

He might have said, only he never made one of his pretty speeches to her, that she herself furnished no exception to the rule. For, in truth, her cheek had a girlish rosiness; a tint like the inside leaves of those delicate, peach-colored chrysanthemums she was so fond of. I think—oh, contemptibly-sentimental thought!

—I would like to have my grave planted with chrysanthemums. They come so cheerful and fair in the winter time, and they always remind me of Highwood and of Ellice Keir. She once said they looked like a handful of happiness gathered when one is growing old.

But we all eschewed age to-day—ay, even the doctor, whose general gravity was such that most of the patients looked upon him as more antiquated and reverend than his father. He threw off his antiquity now. He strode through the heather, led the pony, pointed out the sunset. He had always the keenest sense of natural beauty; his large gray eye softened and brightened as it turned on Ellice Keir.

"How strange, how sad it must be to have to seek out God in nature! To us all nature is but an emanation of from God."

I listened. He and she together—Christian man and Christian woman—had said some sweet, Christ-like words to me ere this; better still, had lived before me. It seemed strange now that I had ever cried out in that temporary insanity of unbelief with which this history begins. I stood "clothed, and in my right mind." It will be imagined the sort of feeling with which I often looked, as to-day, from one face to the other—what calm, noble, blessed faces they were!—especially hers.

Austin did the same. He had a great kindness for the doctor; and as for Miss Keir—

"Do you know," he said, stepping closer to her saddle, "this place is curiously like Netherlands. The country-side is all barren moor, just as this, dotted with tumble-down huts, where those brutes of riotous miners live. Ah! you smile. It shall not be so another year. Indeed, it shall not, Miss Keir. I'll see what I can do."

"Bravo! What you can do will be no little, Mr. Hardy."

"Thank you, doctor. And there, behind just such a fir-wood as that, the house stands. Poor old Netherlands, I have not been there these ten years. It is getting sadly dilapidated, my steward tells me—but then it's his interest to tell me lies—they all do. What were you saying, Miss Keir?"

He bent forward to hear her.

"I never thought of that," he answered, deprecatingly. Bless me, it never struck me my laziness was harming any body but myself; but for the future, I promise, and Fyfe knows I never break my promise. Doctor, you may well cry 'Bravo!' There's a good star rising over poor old Netherlands. You must come and see me there."

Then, in a lower tone,

"Will you come too, Miss Keir?"

She hesitated, colored slightly, or I fancied so; finally, gave a smiling assent. Austin thanked her, and stood looking toward the fir-wood, that lay in a black bank under the sunset.

"Poor old Netherlands—dear old Netherlands!" he murmured more than once, in the soft tone he had used years ago, when talking to my little sister, Mary.

I also was young then. Heavens! what it is to be young!

"Oh, my youth—my youth!" cried out my heart too, and seemed to catch at its last gleaming, even as each wave of moor, each stump of tree caught at the sun as he was going down, with a wild clutch, as knowing that this glimmer was indeed the last—that afterward there would be nothing but gloom. But he went down, and it was light still.

"This is the strangest winter evening," I said. "It will not grow dark. Did you ever see such a dainty, bright new moon?"

"We must go home for all that," insisted the doctor, smiling.

"Not yet—just one minute longer, Miss Keir."

I put my arm on her pony's neck. I could not see her face, but a fold or two of her gown —just enough to feel she was there. I fancied I heard her sigh. No wonder—every thing was so still and beautiful.

For me, my sigh was almost a sob. My soul was come into me again. I was no longer a wretched clod, passionless, brainless. I could feel, enjoy, create; I was again an author, a poet—greater yet, I was a man.

"Oh, thank God, this is like my youth! And I am young—I am only thirty-two. I might live my life out yet."

"Live it!" said the brave, kind voice of James Corrie.

"Live it!" said the silent smile of Ellice Keir.

"I will!"

Though the vow was then taken somewhat in blindness of what was, and was to come, still, God be witness, I shall never break it either to Him—or these.

CHAPTER XI.

"I've done it, Alick—I thought I could."

And Hardy, after a three days' absence—I supposed in London—burst into our sitting-room, a huge peripatetic snow-drift.

"Done what?"

"I forgot—you don't know yet. But I'll tell you in a minute, when I'm not out of breath."

"Did you come in by the six o'clock train, to-night?"

"Surely."

"Nobody expected you. You must have had to walk across the country."

"Of course I did."

"Tell it not at the Albany, lest Highwood should be inundated with a flood of bachelors seeking the water-cure! That I should have lived to see Austin Hardy, Esquire, taking a four-mile night-walk through a heavy Christmas snow!"

"Pshaw, don't make game of a fellow; it's only what a man ought to do, if he's any thing like a man."

He certainly looked every inch "a man." His languid affectations, his fashionable drawl, were gone. Even his dress—that Stultzian toilet once rivaling the Count himself—was now paid no more attention to than any decent gentleman is justified in paying. His hair frizzled, guiltless of Macassar; as for his oils and his perfumes, the water-cure seemed to have washed them all away. Altogether he was a very fine fellow indeed—in the physical line. My own small corporeality shrunk into insignificance beside him.

But I had been sitting for two hours looking direct into those eyes, which looked as steadily into mine, in bright and friendly communion— those eyes which always sent a deep peace, a quiet rest down to the very bottom of my soul. No; I did not envy Austin Hardy.

"Now, my good fellow, when you have shaken off your snow, sit down and inform me of this mighty deed."

"Oh, it's nothing—a mere nothing," with that air of positive shyness, which was in him so new and so comical. "First, is all well at Highwood?"

"Certainly. You surely did not expect any great internal convulsions to happen here in three days?"

"No; but when one is away, you know, one fancies things. How deliciously quiet this place seems, after knocking about for some hundreds of miles!"

"Some hundreds of miles! Why, where have you been?"

"To Edinburgh."

"To Edinburgh! You who grumble at a fifty miles' journey! In this snow, too! What important business dragged you there?"

"Oh, none. Only I thought I ought." (The amusing novelty of Austin Hardy's doing an unpleasant thing because he ought!) "I went to see young Harry Keir."

I was very much astonished.

"You see," he added, poking the fire hard, "I couldn't bear her sad looks when the young fellow and his doubtful prospects were mentioned. He is a real fine fellow—only wants giving a start in life, and he'd get on like a house on fire. Now, last week a thought struck me—"

"Will you kindly leave off striking showers of fir-wood sparks into my face?"

"I didn't like telling her beforehand, lest, if it failed, she should be disappointed. She loves that lad—though, by-the-by, he isn't exactly a lad; he took his doctor's degree this year, and is mighty clever, too—heigho! She is fond of him and he of her. And, by Jove! so he ought to be."

"But you have not yet told me—that is, if you were going to tell me—"

"Certainly, though there's little to tell. Merely, that I went to Edinburgh, found out the young man; then hunted up my friend, Lord C——, who is starting to Italy with his sick son. A tolerable hunt, too—followed him first to Yorkshire, and then to Bath. But it's all settled now. Keir is appointed traveling physician at £200 a year. Not a bad notion—ch, Alick? The young fellow is so glad—it quite does one good to think of him."

"Does she know?"

"Of course not."

"How happy she will be!"

And it was he who had the power to give her this happiness! For the first time in my life I envied Austin Hardy.

"When shall you tell her?"

"I don't know—I—I wish you would, Fyfe. You would do it so much better than I."

"No—no."

CHAPTER XII.

I was present when she was told—told in an awkward, unintelligible, and even agitated fashion, which no one would have expected from that finished gentleman, Mr. Austin Hardy.

She looked from one to the other of us vaguely. "I don't understand."

Hardy repeated the information—just the bare fact of her brother's appointment, which young Keir himself would confirm to-morrow.

She believed at last, asking pardon for her doubt. "But," with that rare tear, which showed how many could have, or had once flowed down her dear face, "Harry and I are not used to being so happy."

No more than this. Nothing in her of the tragic commodity—nothing that professional passion-mongers like me could study a scene out of. But my "studies" had gone to the winds weeks ago!

"And who has done me this kindness, for which I must be grateful all my days? Whom must I thank?"

He, generous fellow, had omitted that trifle. Of course, I told her all.

Miss Keir was very much affected. She held out both her hands to him.

"Thank you. God bless you!"

But Hardy had disappeared.

CHAPTER XIII.

THAT night, after the drawing-room was deserted, I sat alone there.

I leaned my cheek against the velvet arm-chair, which still seemed to keep the impress and even the perfume of her black hair. Long meditations seized me. All my past life glided before me in a moving picture—the latter half of it standing still like a diorama under my gaze. Then it began less to fade than to change—new forms mingling with the old, confusedly

at first. Gradually the old shapes melted out, without any sense of loss, and the new, the transcending beautiful and perfect scene stood out before me vivid as life itself.

I said in my heart: "Every man, at every great crisis of his existence, has a right, within reasonable and honorable bounds, to secure his own happiness, to grasp at the cup which he feels would be his soul's strength and salvation. It shall be so. Therefore, to-morrow—to-morrow."

Rising, I paced the room. My weak nervousness was gone—my spirit was strung up to its utmost pitch. I was able to remove mountains. My brain felt clear—my heart throbbed with all the warmth of my youth. Oh! what a youth was mine! In this moment it all came back. I could have written a great book, have lived a great life; have achieved the most daring exploit, have nerved myself to the most heroic sacrifice.

This was what she had made of me—she, and he, James Corrie, whom I honored with all my soul. But—I loved her.

Strange, solemn love—more solemn than in any young man's love—love that comes in autumn season—wild as autumn blasts—delicious and calm as autumn sunshine. Delicious, not merely as itself, but as the remembrance of by-gone spring—clung to as we cling to every soft October day that dies, knowing that afterward nothing can come, nothing will come, nothing ought to come, but winter and snows. This fatal love—I say fatal, simply implying that it came of fate, which means of God—was upon me, Alexander Fyfe, now.

I will not deny it, nor murmur at it, nor blush for it: I never sought it, nor rushed in the way of it—it was sent—and therefore was right to come.

Slowly, and rather loth, I went to my chamber. In our parlor I saw Austin Hardy. He was sitting over the fire. I should have passed him, but he turned round. Such a face —such a wan, haggard, wretched face—that I stopped.

"What have you been doing, so late up? Are you ill?"

"No."

"Has any thing happened? Come, tell me —we were lads together."

He groaned—"Oh, that I were a lad again! Alick, Alick, if you would help me to begin my life afresh, and make it in any way worthy of—"

"Of—out with it."

"Of Ellice Keir."

I had at times suspected this—had even tried to grasp at the possibility of it. Boldly too, as we dash at some horrible doubt that we know lies in wait for us—pin it to the ground and worry it—with a sort of hope that it will either vanish into air at our touch, or that we shall succeed in slaying it, leave it dead at our feet, and go on our way, safe and free.

But now, when the beast met me—when—pshaw! let me say it in plain English—when I knew that my cousin loved and wished to marry Ellice Keir, it drove me mad.

All kinds of insanities whirled through my brain. If I had any connected impulse at all, it was to fly at his throat and strangle him. But only—God be my witness!—because he dared to love *her*. Any certainty that she loved him, would—I feel it would—have sanctified him in my eyes; I *could* not have done him any harm.

Of course feelings like these subside, and one smiles at them afterward, as I smile now. But I would not like to live through that five minutes again.

It passed in total silence. I am thankful to say I never uttered a sound.

Austin at last raised his head, and looked at me. I steadily met his eyes. There was no mistaking mine.

"My God, Alick!—You too?—"

"Precisely."

We stood face to face, unblenching, for a full minute or more. Then I said—

"Strike hands. Fair fight—no quarter—or, if you will, let us both fly, and the devil take the hindmost."

For I was very mad indeed. Austin, on the contrary, was very quiet—nay, meek. We seemed to have changed natures.

"No," he said, at length, "Flying is useless; I should drop dead on the road. I'll take my chance. It must be as you say—a fair fight, and no quarter."

"It shall be."

Again a long pause.

"What do you purpose doing?"

"What do *you* purpose?"

Neither answered the other's question. Each looked in the other's face, savagely, and dropped his eyes in a sort of pity for the misery imprinted there.

"I wish it had not come to this, Alexander. We, that should have been brothers, if I had married little Mary."

That child's name calmed us. Both, looking aside, half extended an involuntary hand.

"Let us not be enemies yet. We do not know whether—"

"Tell me honestly, Austin, have you no belief in her preference—no tangible hope—?"

"Before Heaven, not a straw!"

I breathed freer. I did not refuse his hand; we had been friends so many, many years.

"Fair play, Alick?" said Hardy, almost piteously. "Is it fair play? You are a far cleverer fellow than I. You can talk with her and interest her. She likes you—respects you. Now, I—oh, what a wretched, trifling, brainless fool I must appear to her!"

Poor fellow!—poor open-hearted, simple-minded soul!

"Lad, lad,"—with my hand on his shoulder as when we used to stand fishing in the silvery Tyne—"do you think a woman only cares for brains?"

He shook his head, hopelessly. "I can't say.

I don't know. God forgive me"—with a bitter, remorseful humiliation—"till now I have hardly known any thing of *good* women. That's it," he added, after a pause—"it is not merely losing *her*, you see; if I lose her I shall lose myself—the better self she put into me. My only chance of a new life hangs on her. Think how she would help me—think what a man she would make of me. If I married her—Hold your hands off! Are you mad, Fyfe?"

"I am afraid so."

She married! Married!—sitting by another man's fireside; the wife of another man's bosom—the mother of another man's children! Reason could not take it in; imagination beat it off, even from the merest outworks of the brain. If once allowed to enter the citadel, there would have been a grand explosion—a conflagration reaching to the very heavens, burning down to such a heap of ruins that no man could rebuild a city thereon any more.

But this is what they call "fine" writing. Better say, in common polite phrase, that the idea of this lady's marriage—and to my cousin—was rather trying to a person of my excitable temperament.

I believe Austin was roused from his own feelings to contemplate mine. I have a vague recollection of his startled, shocked look, and the extreme gentleness of his tone. "Do sit down; there's a good fellow! I knew you didn't mean me any harm."

Also, I mind his watching me as I paced the room—watching with a disturbed, grieved air—and muttering to himself—

"Poor lad—he was always weakly. His mother used to say a great misfortune would kill him or turn his brain."

"I hope it would."

"Alick—don't say that." He turned upon me absolutely brimming eyes. Now, it so happened that, being her sister's child, Austin's eyes were not unlike my mother's. What could I do but come and sit down opposite to him, and try desperately to struggle against the strong tendency which I knew my mind had—which almost all minds similarly constituted, and hard worked, have likewise—to lose its balance, and go rocking, rocking, in a pleasant motion that seems temporarily to lull pain, till it plunges over, over—one hair-breadth, and it is lost in the abyss whence Reason is absent for evermore.

"That is right—sit down. I should be sorry if I wronged you, Alexander; sorry that any thing should turn you against me. You, the only fellow who never flattered nor quizzed me—who has stuck by me through thick and thin, for my own sake, I do believe, and not for my property."

And he was the only fellow who, ignorant of the gimcrackery of literature—disregarding my petty "reputation"—my barren "laurels"—loved heartily, and had loved from boyhood, not the "celebrated author," but the man Alexander Fyfe.

Such a friendship as ours, cemented by its

very incongruities, was rare—and precious as rare. Love could not, should not, annihilate it. "Austin, let's to bed. We shall see things clearer in the morning. Good-night. God bless you, my boy."

CHAPTER XIV.

NEVERTHELESS, it was a horrible night, and a horrible waking. Things stand so ghastly plain in the face of day.

Yet, blessings on you, friendly Aquarius, who came so welcomely at dawn, with pail after pail of icy torrents, cooling all the fever in my blood, leaving behind, on soul as well as body, a warm, heroic, healthy glow. I do believe half the passions, crimes, and miseries of humanity would be calmed down under the influence of water-cure.

In the hall, quaffing our matutinal glass, clear as crystal, refreshing as the *elixir vitæ*, my cousin and I met face to face—faces, strange, no doubt, and pallid still, but very different from last night.

No reference to that; temporarily the ghost was laid.

"Good-morning."

"Good-morning. Starting for your walk? 'Tis damp, rather."

"Very. Are you for the wood?"

"Probably. And you for the moorland?"

"Ay."

So tacitly we parted. Generally we walked together, but not now.

Up the hillside, through the mass of red beech-leaves her pony had trampled through; how dead and dank they now lay, slowly passing into corruption. Up, up—it is my habit never to rest till I have climbed as far as one can climb—up, steadily, till I came out on the level moorland.

It was all in a soft mist. Not a breath stirring; not a waft of cold December wind. The year had laid itself down to die patiently. It would not struggle any more. Only sometimes a great drop would come with a plash from some fir-tree hard by, like a heavy involuntary tear. But the leaden sky would not yield; the rain refused to fall.

I walked for a whole hour pondering. The text of my meditations was Austin's saying of last night—

"She is my better self. If I lose her, I shall lose my soul."

Now I, weak as my body was, had my soul in my own hand.

I might die—probably I should; but I did not believe that any stroke, however heavy, would drive out of my heart the virtue which her blessed influence had implanted there. Misery might kill me, or (possibly, though I trusted in God's mercy not!) might make me a lunatic, but it never would make me a criminal. Him, it might.

I took my determination—at least, for a time —till things altered, or till I saw some dim light. Oh no! Unless I sought for it, toiled for it, prayed for it, how could such a fellow as I hope to see the faintest love-light shining on me from her sweet eyes?

So no wrong to her in that determination of mine.

Again Austin and I met in the midst of a cluster of cheerful patients—somehow patients always are cheerful at the water-cure. We were cheerful, too. I felt, and something in his voice causing me to look at him hard, showed me he felt, too, an extraordinary calm.

He followed me to our rooms.

"Alexander, just one word. I have thought over last night, and somewhat changed my mind."

"So have I."

"I shall not speak to her—not just yet."

"Nor I."

Again we looked fixedly at one another— again, hand to hand, we rivals, yet almost brothers, closed.

"Thank you, Austin."

"You are a good fellow, Fyfe."

"I think," said I, brokenly, "this is right— this is how she would wish it to be. We must not hate one another for love of her, who has been a saving angel to us both."

"Ay, so she has."

"Let her be so still—let every thing go on as usual, till some chance gives either a sign of her regard. Then, each for himself! a fair struggle, and Heaven comfort the one who falls!"

CHAPTER XV.

DAY after day, during the whole of those strange two weeks, did things "go on as usual." That is, we met her at breakfast, at dinner, at supper; sometimes walked with her, drove with her, passed every evening in her presence, within sound of her voice, within brushing of her dress. Twice every day—fool! how one of us used to court and wait for the minute—we each touched her hand. And many times a day that same one—I will not answer for the other— would, standing by her, in serious fireside argument, or easy meal-time, look down, right down—she had a curiously steady, earnest, innocent gaze, when she was talking—into the infinitely tender depths, the warm, dark splendors of her eyes.

Yet neither of us, by word or look, sought to win, or by any word or look of hers could found a hope that we might win, her preference.

And, night after night, when the day's ordeal was over, we used to sit silent over the fire in our own room, sometimes by chance catching sight of one another's faces, and recognizing there the marvelous self-denial, the heroic self-control, which kept deferring, each for the other's sake, the delicious, the fatal day.

We sat—not unlike two friends drifting seaward in a crazy boat, incapable of a double freight, who sit sadly gazing—willing to prolong the time, yet knowing that, under certain definite circumstances, and within a certain definite time, one or the other *must* go down.

CHAPTER XVI.

SHE was sitting talking with me in Dr. James's study; no one there but our two selves —not a face to watch hers save mine—and those pictured faces on the walls, which she was so fond of—rare prints gathered by James Corrie on his wanderings:—grand old Buonarotti, the angelic, boyish Raffaelle, and Giotto, with that noble, irregular profile, serious, sweet, and brave.

"It is not unlike Dr. James himself, I fancy."

"Do you think so? So do I sometimes."

And Miss Keir sewed faster at her work—a collar or handkerchief for Harry, who had been at Highwood now for several days.

"What a pure nature it is!" continued I, and still looked at the Giotto, and thinking of James Corrie. "So very tender, for all its steadfastness and strength. I hardly ever honored any man as I do our friend the doctor. Do not you?"

"He has been the kindest friend in the world to Harry and to me."

"And to me, also. I must try to tell him so before I go away."

"You are not going away? Surely, not yet?"

That start—that look of earnest regret. What a leap my heart gave!

"I thought—I understood," with a slight hesitation, "that you were to stay at Highwood till after the New-Year?"

"Did James Corrie say so? And do you wish it?"

And that warm, soft color which, during all our talk, had been growing, growing, now seemed glowing into scarlet under my gaze. No; I would not take away my eyes. I would see whether they could not light up in hers some tithe of the hidden fire that I knew must be burning in my own.

I was right! She did tremble—she did blush; vividly, almost like a girl of fifteen— this calm, this quiet Ellice Keir.

"I ought; indeed I ought to leave. My book—you know—my—"

Stammering, I ceased.

She laid her work down, and looked me straight in the face, in her peculiar way, saying softly—

"No; you must not go. You are not strong enough. Besides, I want you to stay—just a week longer. Never mind your book."

"Miss Keir, you know I would thrust it and all the books I ever wrote into that flame this minute, if—"

I remembered my pledge. Ay, Austin—sacredly.

"If what?"

"If Miss Keir will tell me the reason why she wishes me to stay?"

I said this in an exaggeration of carelessness —even trying to make a joke of it. I did not expect to see that strange, unwonted blush rise again over face and throat, nor to see her very fingers tremble as she worked.

What was to become of me? One second more, and I should have forgotten all—she would have known all. Thank God it was not so.

I snatched up a book, muttered some vague apology, and rushed out of her sight.

No; this could not go on. An end must be put to it somehow. While she was indifferent, quiet, composed—merely the lady who smilingly shook hands with me morning and night, I could bear it. But to see her, as I saw her this morning—all the woman stirred in her, blushing, trembling—not Miss Keir, but Ellice —Ellice! It could not be. The crisis *must* come.

I made up my mind. But first I went in search of Austin Hardy—hesitatingly and slow; for involuntarily a wild conviction had forced itself on my mind (forgive me, thou essence of most simple and pure womanhood! but we men have such delusions sometimes) a conviction that Austin, at least, would never win Ellice Keir.

I went to meet him in the garden with a strange pity—even a sort of remorse. I found him walking, talking, and laughing with Harry and Ellice Keir.

"Yes, certainly, we will come, both Harry and I, and see all these wonderful changes and improvements at Netherlands. I am so happy to think of them all. You will not forget one of them. You promise?"

"I promise."

She spoke earnestly—Harry too: so earnestly that they did not notice me. They stood still under the great cedar. Harry Keir—what a gleesome face the young fellow had!—was tossing up and catching cedar cones.

"Yes; I will promise every thing. Netherlands shall begin a new life, like its master, please God! It shall hardly know its old likeness. It and the people belonging to it shall be the pattern of the whole country. Will that make you happy?"

"Very happy. Few things more."

"And—" Ay, dear Austin, I heard and honored the self-command which smoothed down to indifference that tremulous tone— "when will you do me that honor? It shall be quite a festival when you visit Netherlands. Fyfe—ah, my dear fellow, are you there?— Fyfe shall be asked, and all our good friends at Highwood."

"Bravo!" cried Harry, with a laugh, as he tossed up his biggest fir-cone; "and Dr. James, of course."

"Most certainly. Every one whom she cares for—every one who honors her. And now, Miss Keir, will you too promise?—When will you come to Netherlands?"

"I hope—some time—next year?"

Were my eyes dazzled by that red torrent which seemed to roll pouring in upon my brain; or did I again see, as an hour before, that same warm, tremulous, exquisite blush—such as is always coming and going in a woman's face when she loves, and is very happy?

Not a word more. She was gone. Austin and I stood under the heavy shade of the cedar. Was it that which made his face and my heart seem so dark and cold?

"Now, Hardy?"

"Well, I hear you. The time has come?"

"I think it has."

I saw him watching her on the terrace where she and Harry were walking merrily. The sun was shining there. As he looked all the gloom passed out of his countenance; it seemed to gather the sunshine too.

Jealousy! I had written pages on pages about it—learned "to throw myself into the feeling," as our literary cant goes—flattered myself I had sketched beautifully, to the very life, the whole thing. But now, to realize what I had described—and fancy indulged in a cruel spasmodic laugh to see how very real I had done it—now to feel the horror gnawing at me, like that fiend the old monk-painter painted, who afterward came and stood at his elbow till he died; to feel not only through my brain but in my heart that jealousy of which we poets prate so grandly—make into such pathetic novels, such withering tragedies—jealousy, which we say leads to hatred, madness, murder! I could believe it—I could prove it. I plumbed its lowest depths of possible crime in that one minute when I watched my cousin Austin watching Ellice Keir.

I had loved Austin—did so still. Yet for that one minute—happily it was only one—I hated him, loathed him. I believe I could have seen him shot down, and mounted over his dead body to the citadel of my frenzied hope—as our poor fellows are perhaps doing this day as I write, in the trenches before Sebastopol. But, "better is he that ruleth his spirit than he who taketh a city." I ruled mine.

"Austin, this must end."

"It must. When?"

"To-day if you will. There—look, she has gone within doors."

We stood—the crisis was at hand. Our life-boat reeled—quivered. Very pale sat we. Which would be the one to go down?

"Who is to learn his fortune first?" said Hardy.

"Let's draw lots." I laughed—I felt spurred on to any kind of insane folly. "Let's toss up, as the children do; or, since the coin of the realm is as dross to you, and as life's worth to me—let's take to the sentimental, the poetical. Here, choose."

I tore off a sprig of cedar and a sprig of a yew-tree hard by, and held out to him the two stems, the leaves being hidden.

"Now, which? Who is for his cedar-palace, and who for his branch of yew?"

I know Hardy thought I was losing my wits fast. He looked at me with pity. "No," he said, gently; "no child's play—we must be men. Go you in and speak to her first."

He leapt the hedge into the field. So it became my doom. Best, far the best.

The door happened to be fastened. I thought I would get into the house, as I often did, by the low windows of the doctor's study. Standing there I looked in.

James Corrie sat at his table, not writing, but thinking. His chin was on his folded hands—his eyes out-looking, calm and clear. What a noble face it was—the face of one who has gone through seas of trouble, and landed at length in serene, soul-satisfying joy.

Twice I knocked at the pane, and he did not perceive me. Then hearing me call, he came forward, smiling.

I said I would not interrupt him, as I was going to Miss Keir.

"Just stay one minute. I wanted to say a word to you—in fact, by the particular wish of Miss Keir."

I sat down.

James Corrie folded his newspaper, closed his desk, looked—something different from what James Corrie was wont to look, but happy, ineffably happy.

"I am waiting to hear—"

"Ay, and you shall hear, my old friend, for I know you will rejoice. Simply this. Miss Keir has told me you intend leaving us, and she wishes, most earnestly, that you would stay till after the New Year."

"And you?"

"Even if Alexander Fyfe were not welcome for his own sake, as he knows he is, still whatever adds to her happiness must necessarily add to mine.

He whom I knew she held—as in his simple goodness all good women might hold him—like a very brother; he who, she said, had been to her "the kindest friend in the world"—strange for him to speak to me thus! Perhaps, in spite of myself, I had betrayed my feelings. Did he think—did he guess—

"I see, Fyfe, you do not quite understand me. You do not know—in truth, being neither of us young, we were rather unwilling it should be known or talked about—that Miss Keir and myself have been engaged for two years. That, God willing, next Saturday, New-Year's morning, will be our wedding-day."

CHAPTER XVII.

No—I was right; it did not slay me. This misery passed by, and destroyed neither my life nor Austin's soul.

dle in her hand, and the baby asleep on her arm.'

" 'Did she speak ?' asked Mr. Everest, with another and rather satirical smile. 'Remember, you saw Hamlet last night. Indeed, sir—indeed, Dorothy—it was a mere dream. I do not believe in ghosts; it would be an insult to common sense, to human wisdom—nay, even to Divinity itself.'

"Edmond spoke so earnestly, justly, and withal so affectionately, that perforce I agreed; and even my father became to feel rather ashamed of his own weakness. He, a sensible man and the head of a family, to yield to a mere superstitious fancy, springing, probably, from a hot supper and an overexcited brain! To the same cause Mr. Everest attributed the other incident, which somewhat hesitatingly I told him.

" 'Dear, it was a bird—nothing but a bird. One flew in at my window last spring; it had hurt itself; and I kept it, and nursed it, and petted it. It was such a pretty, gentle little thing, it put me in mind of Dorothy.'

" 'Did it ?' said I.

" 'And at last it got well and flew away.'

" 'Ah ! that was not like Dorothy.'

"Thus, my father being persuaded, it was not hard to persuade me. We settled to remain till evening. Edmond and I, with my maid Patty, went about together, chiefly in Mr. West's Gallery, and in the quiet shade of our favorite Temple Gardens. And if for those four stolen hours, and the sweetness in them, I afterward suffered untold remorse and bitterness, I have entirely forgiven myself, as I know my dear mother would have forgiven me long ago."

Mrs. MacArthur stopped, wiped her eyes, and then continued, speaking more in the matter-of-fact way that old people speak in than she had been lately doing.

"Well, my dear, where was I ?"

"In the Temple Gardens."

"Yes, yes. Then we came home to dinner. My father always enjoyed his dinner and his nap afterward. He had nearly recovered himself now—only looked tired from loss of rest. Edmond and I sat in the window, watching the barges and wherries down the Thames. There were no steamboats then, you know.

"Some one knocked at the door with a message for my father, but he slept so heavily he did not hear. Mr. Everest went to see what it was; I stood at the window. I remember mechanically watching the red sail of a Margate hoy that was going down the river, and thinking with a sharp pang how dark the room seemed to grow in a moment with Edmond not there.

"Re-entering, after a somewhat long absence, he never looked at me, but went straight to my father.

" 'Sir, it is almost time for you to start' (oh! Edmond). 'There is a coach at the door; and, pardon me, but I think you should travel quickly.'

"My father sprang to his feet.

" 'Dear sir, wait one moment; I have received news from Bath. You have another little daughter, sir, and—'

" 'Dolly, my Dolly !' Without another word my father rushed away, leaped into the post-chaise that was waiting, and drove off.

" 'Edmond !' I gasped.

" 'My poor little girl—my own Dorothy !'

"By the tenderness of his embrace, less lover-like than brother-like—by his tears, for I could feel them on my neck—I knew, as well as if he had told me, that I should never see my dear mother any more.

"She had died in childbirth," continued the old lady after a long pause—"died at night, at the same hour and minute that I had heard the tapping on the window-pane, and my father had thought he saw her coming into his room with a baby on her arm."

"Was the baby dead, too ?"

"They thought so then, but it afterward revived."

"What a strange story !"

"I do not ask you to believe in it. How and why and what it was I can not tell ; I only know that it assuredly was as I have told it.

"And Mr. Everest ?" I inquired, after some hesitation.

The old lady shook her head. "Ah, my dear, you may perhaps learn—though I hope you will not—how very, very seldom things turn out as one expects when one is young. After that day I did not see Mr. Everest for twenty years."

"How wrong of him—how—"

"Don't blame him ; it was not his fault. You see, after that time my father took a prejudice against him—not unnatural, perhaps ; and she was not there to make things straight. Besides, my own conscience was very sore, and there were the six children at home, and the little baby had no mother : so at last I made up my mind. I should have loved him just the same if we had waited twenty years. I told him so ; but he could not see things in that light. Don't blame him—my dear—don't blame him. It was as well, perhaps, as it happened."

"Did he marry ?"

"Yes, after a few years ; and loved his wife dearly. When I was about one-and-thirty, I married Mr. MacArthur. So neither of us was unhappy, you see—at least, not more so than most people; and we became sincere friends afterward. Mr. and Mrs. Everest come to see me still, almost every Sunday. Why, you foolish child, you are not crying ?"

Ay, I was—but scarcely at the ghost-story.

A FAMILY IN LOVE.

This is the age of complainings. Nobody suffers in silence; nobody breaks his or her heart in secrecy and solitude: they all take "the public" into their confidence—the convenient public, which, like murder,

> Hath no tongue, but speaks
> With most miraculous organ.

Of course, it is neither the confider's fault nor yet the confidant's, if the winds sometimes whisper that King Midas has asses' ears.

Mine is no such confession. I have no gossip to retail of my neighbors: I am a very quiet gentleman, who prefer confining my interests and observations to my own household, my own immediate family. Ay, there lies my inevitable grief, there lurks my secret wrong; I am the unhappy elder brother of a family in love.

The fact dimly dawned upon me, widening by degrees, ever since I came home from India last year, and took upon myself the charge of my five sisters, aged from about— But Martha might object to my particularizing. Good little Patty! what a merry creature she was when she went nutting and fishing with me. And what ugly caps she has taken to wearing, poor dear! And why can't she speak as gently when scolding the servants, as I remember our sweet-voiced, pretty mother used always to do? And why, in spite of their mutual position, will she persist in calling Mr. Green, with a kind of frigid solemnity, "Mr. Green?" But he does not seem to mind it: probably he never was called any thing else.

He is a very worthy person, nevertheless, and I have a great respect for him. When my sister Martha—Miss Heathcote, as she has been called from her cradle—by letter announced to me at Madras that she intended to relinquish that title for the far less euphonious one of Mrs. Green, I was, to say the least of it, surprised. I had thought, for various reasons (of no moment now), that my eldest sister was not likely to marry—I rather hoped she would not. We might have been so comfortable, poor Patty and I. However, I had no business to interfere with either her happiness or her destiny; so when, the first Sunday after my arrival at home, a cozy carriage drove up the avenue, and a bald, rather stout little man got out, to be solemnly introduced to me as "Mr. Green," I submitted to the force of circumstances, and to the duties of a brother-in-law.

He has dined with us every Sunday since. He and I are capital friends; regularly, when the ladies retire, he informs me what the Funds have been at, day by day during the past week, and which is the safest railway to buy shares in for the week following. A most worthy person, I repeat; will make a kind husband, and I suppose Martha likes him; but—. However, poor girl, she is old enough to judge for herself, and it is no business of mine. Some time, before long, I shall give her away at the old parish church—quietly, without any show; I shall see her walk down the church-aisle with old Mr. Green—he in his best white waistcoat, and she in her sober gray poplin, which she insists on being married in—not the clear soft muslin and long lace vail I quite well remember seeing Patty working at and blushing over, we won't say how many years ago. Well, women are better married, they say; but I think I would rather have had Martha an old maid.

My second sister, Angeline, was fifteen when I left England; and the very loveliest creature I ever beheld. Every body knew it, every body acknowledged it. She could not walk down the street without people turning to look after her; she could not enter a room without creating a general whisper: "Who is she?" The same thing continued as she grew up to womanhood. All the world was at her feet; every one said she would make a splendid marriage—become a countess at least; and I do believe Angeline herself had the fullest confidence in that probability. She refused lovers by the dozen; every letter I got told me of some new slaughter of Miss Angeline's. I would have pitied the poor fellows, only she was such a dazzling beauty, and no man falls out of love so safely as a man who falls in love with a beauty. I never heard that any body died either by consumption, cord, or pistol, through the cruelty of my sister Angeline.

But, like most cruel damsels, she paid the penalty of her hard-heartedness; when I came home I found Angeline Heathcote, Angeline Heathcote still. Beautiful yet, beautiful exceedingly; a walking picture, a visible poem: it was a real pleasure to me to have such a handsome creature about the house. Though people did say, with a mysterious shake of the head, that, handsome as she was, if I had only seen my sister two or three years ago! And Angeline herself became tenacious on the subject of new gowns, and did not like it to be generally known whether she or Charlotte was the elder. Good, plain, merry Charlotte, who never thought about either her looks or her age!

Yet Charlotte was the first who brought me into trouble—that trouble which I am now called upon to bemoan. I had not been at home three months when there came a young gentleman—a very lively and pleasant young gentleman, too—who sang duets with the younger girls, and made himself quite at home in my family circle. I myself did not much meddle with him, thought him a good-natured lad, and no more—until one fine morning he astonished me by requesting five minutes' conversation with me in my study. (Alas! such misfortunes come not singly—my study has never been safe from similar applications and conversations since.)

I was very kind to the young man; when he blushed, I looked another way; when he trembled, I invited him to take a chair. I listened to his stammering explanations with the utmost patience and sympathy; I even tried to help him out with them—till he came to the last clause.

Now, I do say that a man who asks you for your purse, your horse, your friendship, after only four weeks' acquaintance, has considerable courage; but a man who, after that brief period since his introduction, comes and asks you for your *sister*—why, one's first impulse is to kick him down stairs.

Happily, I controlled myself. I called to mind that Mr. Cuthbert was a very honest young fellow, and that if he did choose to risk his whole future upon the result of a month's laughing, and singing, and dancing at balls—certainly it was his affair, not mine. My business solely related to Charlotte. I was just dispatching it in the quickest and friendliest manner, by advising the young fellow to go back to college and not make a fool of himself in vain, when he informed me that my consent only was required, since he and Charlotte had been a plighted couple for the space of three whole days!

I have always held certain crotchets on the paramount rights of lovers, and the wrong of interfering with any apparently sincere vows; so I sent for Lotty—talked with her; found she was just as foolish as he. That because he was the best waltzer, the sweetest tenor singer, and had the handsomest mustache she knew—our lively Charlotte was quite contented to dance through life with Mr. Cuthbert, and decidedly proud of having his diamond ring on her third finger, and being considered "engaged" —as indeed they were likely to remain, if their minds changed not, for the next ten years.

So, what could I do? Nothing but deal with the young simpletons—if such they were —according to their folly. If true, their love would have time to prove itself such; if false, they would best find out that fact by its not being thwarted. I kissed away Lotty's tears, silly child! and next Sunday I had the honor of carving for brother-in-law elect No. 2.

It never rains but it pours. Whether Angeline was roused at once to indignation and condescension by Charlotte's engagement—which she was the loudest in inveighing against—or whether, as was afterward reported to me, she

was influenced by a certain statistical newspaper paragraph, maliciously read aloud by Mr. Cuthbert for general edification, that women's chances of matrimony were proved by the late census to diminish greatly between the ages of thirty and thirty-five; but most assuredly Angeline's demeanor changed. She stooped to be agreeable as well as beautiful. To more than one suitor whom she had of old swept haughtily by did she now graciously incline; and the result was—partly owing to the gayeties of this autumn's election—that Miss Angeline Heathcote, the beauty of the county, held a general election on her own private account.

Alas for me! In one week I had no less than four hopeful candidates requesting "the honor of an interview" in my study.

Angeline's decision was rather dilatory—they were all such excellent matches; and, poor girl —with her beauty for her chief gift, and with all the tinsel adoration it brought her—she had never been used to think of marriage as any thing more than a mere worldly arrangement. She was ready to choose a husband as she would a wedding-gown—dispassionately, carefully, as the best out of a large selection of articles, each rich and good in its way, and warranted to wear. She had plenty of common sense, and an acute judgment; as for her heart—

"You see, Nigel," she said to me, when weighing the respective claims and merits of Mr. Archer and Sir Rowland Griffith Jones— "you see, I never was sentimentally inclined. I want to be married. I think I should be better married than single. Of course, my husband must be a good man; also, he should be a wealthy man; because—well!—because I rather like show and splendor: they suit me."

And she glanced into the mirror at something which, certainly, if any woman has any excuse for the vanities of life, might have pleaded Angeline's.

"But," I argued—half sorrowfully, as when you see an ignorant child throwing gold away, and choosing sham jewels for their pitiful glistering, "you surely would think it necessary to love your husband?"

"Oh, yes; and I like Sir Rowland extremely —perhaps even better than Mr. Archer—though *he* has been fond of me so long, poor fellow! But he will get over it—all men do."

So, though the balance hung for a whole week doubtful—Heaven forgive the girl! but true love was not in her nature, and how can people see further than their lights go?—I was soon pretty certain that fate would decide the marriage-question in favor of the baronet. As Lotty said, Angeline would look magnificent in the family diamonds as Lady Griffith Jones.

The Welsh cause triumphed; Mr. Archer quitted the field. He had been an old acquaintance; but—what was that to Sir Rowland and £10,000 a year?

After Angeline's affair was settled, there came a lull in the family epidemic—possibly because the head of the family grew savage as a bear, and for a full month his spirit hugged itself into fierce misanthropy, or rather misogyny, contemning the whole female sex, especially such as contemplated, or were contemplated in, the unholy estate of matrimony.

No wonder! I could not find peace in my own house; I had not my own sisters' society; not a single family fireside evening could I get from week's end to week's end; not a room could I enter without breaking in on some tête-à-tête; not a corner could I creep into without stumbling upon a pair of lovers. For a little while these fond couples kept on their good behavior toward me—preserved a degree of reserve toward each other out of respect to the head of the house, the elder brother; but gradually it deteriorated—ceased. Nay, I, who belong to the old generation—which was foolish enough to deem caresses hallowed things, that the mere pressure of a beloved woman's hand, not to speak of her sacred mouth, was a thing not to be made a public show of—never to be thought of without a tender reverence, a delicious fear—I, Nigel Heathcote, have actually seen two young men, strangers a little year ago, kiss my two sisters openly before their whole family—before their brother's very face!

My situation became intolerable. I fled the fireside; I took refuge in my study. Woe betide the next lover who should assail me there! Surely that fatality would not again arrive for some time. When the elder ones were once married and away, surely I, and Constantia, and little Lizzie, might live a few years in fraternal peace, unmolested by the haunting shadow of impending matrimony.

It occurred to me that in the interval of the weddings I would send for an old friend, a bachelor like myself—an honest, manly fellow, who worked hard from circuit to circuit, and got barely one brief a year. Yes, Will Launceston would keep me company; and we would spend our days in the woods, and our evenings in my study, safe out of the way of lovers, weddings, and womankind.

I had just written to him, when my sister Martha came in with a very serious face, and told me "she wished for a little conversation with me."

Ominous beginning! But she was not a young man, and could not well attack me concerning any more of my sisters. At least so I congratulated myself—alas, too soon!

My sister settled herself by the fire with a serious countenance.

"My dear Nigel."

"My dear Martha."

"I wish to consult you on a matter which has recently come to my knowledge, and has given me much pain and some anxiety."

"Indeed!" and I am afraid my tone was less sympathizing than eager, since from her troubled nervous manner, I thought—I hoped, the matter in question indicated the secession of Mr. Green. "Go on. Is it about"—I stopped

and corrected myself hypocritically—"about the girls?"

She assented.

"Whew!"—a disappointed whistle, faint and low. "Still, go on. I'll listen to any thing except another proposal."

Martha shook her head. "Alas, I fear it will never come to that! Brother, have you noticed?—but men never do—still, I myself have observed a great change in Constantia lately."

Now, Constantia always was different from the other girls—liked solitude and books, talked little, and had a trick of reverie. In short, was what young people called "interesting," and old people "romantic"—the sort of creature who, did she grow up a remarkable woman, would have her youthful peculiarities carefully and respectfully noted, with "I always said there was a great deal in that girl;" but who, did she turn out nothing particular, would be laughed at, and probably would laugh at herself, for having been "very sentimental when she was young." Nevertheless, having at one time of my life shared that imputation, I was tender over the little follies of Constantia.

"I think the girl reads too much, and sits with her eyes too wide open, Martha; is rather unsocial, likewise. She wanted to get out of the way of the weddings, and positively refused to be Angeline's bridesmaid."

"Ah!" sighed Martha, "that's it. Poor foolish child, to think of falling in love—"

I almost jumped off my chair. "I'll not hear a word of it—I declare I will not! I'll keep the young fellow off my premises with man-traps and spring-guns. I'll go back to India if you tell me of another "engagement."

"No chance of that;" and Martha shook her head more drearily than ever. "Poor child, I fear it is an unfortunate attachment!"

I brightened up—so much so, that my sister looked, nay, gently hinted, her conviction that I was a "brute." She expected I would have been as sorry as she was!

"No, Martha; I am rather glad. Glad, after my experience of these 'fortunate' love-affairs, to find that one of my sisters has the womanly courage, unselfishness, and simplicity to conceive an 'unfortunate' attachment."

Perhaps this speech hurt Martha, and yet it need not. She and I both knew and respected one another's youth; and if we differed in opinion concerning our middle age, why, I was as likely to be wrong as she.

She did not at first reply; and then, without comment, she explained to me her uneasiness about Constantia. The girl had long played confidante to Mr. Archer in the matter of Angeline, and, as often happens, the confidante had unwittingly taken too great interest in one of her principals, until she found herself envying the lot of the other. When Mr. Archer's dismissal finally broke off all his intercourse with our family, there was one of my sisters who missed him wearily, cruelly; and that was—not Angeline.

I was touched. Now, no doubt Constantia had been very foolish; no doubt she had nourished and encouraged this fancy, as romantic girls do, in moonlight walks and solitary dreams; hugging her pain, and deluding herself that it was bliss. Little doubt, likewise, that the feeling would wear itself out, or fade slowly away in life's stern truths; but at present it was a most sincere passion, sad and sore. Foolish and romantic as it might be, in itself and in its girlish demonstrations, I could not smile at it. It was a real thing, and as such to be respected.

Martha and I held counsel together, and acted on the result. We took Constantia under our especial charge; we gave her books to read, visits to pay, work to do; keeping her as much as possible with one or other of us, and out of the way of the childish flirtation of Cuthbert and Charlotte, or the formal philandering of Sir Rowland and the future Lady Griffith Jones. And if sometimes, as Lizzie told me—my little Lizzie, who laughed at love and lovers with the lightness of sixteen—Constantia grew impatient with Lotty's careless trifling, and curled her lip scornfully when Angeline paraded the splendors of her *trousseau*, we tried to lead the girl's mind out of herself, and out of dreamland altogether, as much as possible.

"But suppose," Lizzie sagely argued—"suppose, when Angeline is married, Mr. Archer should come back? He always liked Constantia extremely. Who knows but—"

I shook my head, and desired the little castle-builder to hold her tongue.

She was our sole sharer of the secret; and I must say, though she laughed at her now and then, Lizzie was extremely loving and patient with Constantia. After a time we left the two girls wholly to one another, more especially as my time was now taken up with my friend Launceston.

Oh the comfort, the relief, of the society of a man!—a real honest man—who had some sterling aim and object in life—some steady work to do—some earnest interest in the advance of the world, the duties and pursuits of his brother men; who was neither handsome, witty, nor accomplished; who rarely shone in ladies' society; in fact, rather eschewed it than otherwise. For, he said, nature had unfitted him to act the part of a mere admirer, and adverse fortune forbade him to appear in the character of a lover; so he held aloof, keeping his own company and that of one or two old friends like myself.

I was fond of Launceston; I wished my family to like him too; but they were all too busy about their own affairs. Evening after evening, I could not get any of my sisters to make tea for us, or give us a little music afterward, except the pale, dull-looking Constantia, or my bonny rose of June, little Lizzie. At last, we four settled into a small daily company, and went out together, read together, talked together continually. I kept these two younger ones as much as possible in our unromantic practical so-

ciety, that not only my mind, but Launceston's, in its thorough cheerfulness and healthiness of tone, might unconsciously have a good influence upon Constantia.

The girl's spirit slowly began to heal. She set aside her dreaming, and took with all the energy of her nature to active work—women's work—charity-school teaching, village-visiting, and the like. She put a little too much "romance" into all she did still; but there was life in it, truth, sincerity.

"Miss Constantia will make an admirable lady-of-all work," said Launceston, in his quaint way, watching her with his kindly and observant eyes. "The world wants such. She will find enough to do."

And so she did: enough to steal her too from my side, almost as much as the three *fiancées*. The circle in my study dwindled gradually down to Lizzie, Launceston, and me.

We were excellent company still, we three. I had rarely had so much of my pet sister's society; I had never found it so pleasant. True, she was shyer than usual, probably from being with us two, older and wiser people—men likewise—but she listened to our wisdom so sweetly—she bore with our dry, long-worded learning so patiently—that my study never seemed itself unless I had the little girl seated at my feet, or sewing quietly in the window-corner. And then she was completely a "little girl;" had no forward ways—no love notions, or, ten times worse, marriage-notions, crossing her innocent brain. I felt sure I could take her into my closest heart, form her mind and principles at my will, and one day make a noble woman of her, after the pattern of— But I never mention *that* sacred name.

I loved Lizzie—loved her to the core of my heart. Sometimes with fatherly more than even brotherly pride, I used to talk to Launceston of the child's sweetnesses, but he always gave me short answers. It was his way. His laconism in most things was really astonishing, for a man under thirty.

One day, when Angeline's grand wedding was safely over, and the house had sunk into a pathetic quietness that reminded one of the evening after a funeral—at least so I thought—Launceston and I fell into a discussion, which stirred him into more demonstrativeness than usual. The subject was men, women, and marriages.

"I am convinced," he said, "that I shall never marry."

It was not my first hearing of this laudable determination; so I let it pass, merely asking his reasons.

"Because my conscience, principles, and feelings go totally against the system of matrimony, as practiced in the world, especially the world of womankind. All the courting and proposing, the presents and the love-letters, the dinners to relatives and congratulations of friends, the marriage-guests and marriage-settlements, the white lace, white satin, and white favors, carriage, postillions, and all. Heigh-ho, Heathcote, what fools men are!"

I was just about to suggest the possibility of naming one, say two, wise individuals among our sex, when in stole a white fairy—my pretty Lizzie, in her bridesmaid's dress. Her presence changed the current of conversation; until from some remark she made about a message Angeline had left us to the proper way of inserting her marriage in the *Times* newspaper to-morrow, our talk imperceptibly fell back into the old channel.

"I, like you, Launceston, hate the whole system of love and marrying. It is one great sham. Beginning when miss, at school, learns that it is the apex of feminine honor to be a bride—the lowest deep of feminine humiliation to die an old maid. Continuing when she, a young lady at home, counts her numerous 'offers;' taking pride in what ought to be to her a source either of regret or humiliation. Ending when, time slipping by, she drops into the usual belief that nobody ever marries her first love; so takes the best match she can find, and makes marriage, which is merely the visible crown and completion of love, the pitiful dishonored substitute for it. I declare solemnly, I have seen many a wife whom I held to be scarcely better than no wife at all."

I had forgotten my little sister's presence; but she did not seem to hear me—nor Launceston either, for that matter. His earnestness had softened down; he sat, very thoughtful, over against the window where Lizzie had taken her sewing. What a pretty picture she made!

"Come here, my little girl," I said; "I should not like thee to go the way of the world; and yet I should be satisfied to give thee away some day, quietly, in a white muslin gown and a straw bonnet, to some honest man who loved thee—and was loved so well, that Lizzie would never dream of marrying any other, but would have been quite content, if need be, to live an old maid for his sake to the end of her days. That's what *I* call love—eh, my girl?"

Lizzie drooped her head, blushing deeply. Of course; girls always do.

Launceston said, in a tone so low that I quite started: "Then you do believe in true love, after all?"

"It would be ill for me—or for any human being—if I did not. And I believe in it the more earnestly because of its numberless counterfeits. Nay"—and now when, after this gay marriage-morning, the evening was sinking gray and dull, my mind inclined pensively, even tenderly, to the sister who had gone, the other two sisters who were shortly going away from my hearth forever—"nay, as since in the falsest creed there lurks, I hope, a modicum of absolute truth, I would fain trust that in the poorest travesty or masquerade of love, one might find a fragment of the sterling commodity. Still, my Lizzie dear, when all our brides are gone, let us congratulate ourselves that

for a long time we shall have no more engagements."

"You object to engagements?" said Lizzy, speaking timidly and downfaced—as I rather like to see a young girl speak on this subject.

"Why, how should you like it yourself, my little maid? To be loved, wooed, and wedded, in public, for the benefit of an amused circle of friends, neighbors, and connections. To have one's actions noticed, one's affairs canvassed, one's feelings weighed and measured; to be congratulated, condoled, and jested with. Horrible! literally horrible! My wonder is that any true lovers can ever stand it."

"Perhaps you are right," said Launceston, vehemently. "No man ought to place the girl he loves in such a position. Whatever it costs him, he ought to leave her free—altogether free—and offer her nothing until he can offer her his hand, at once, and with no delay."

"Bless my soul, Launceston, what are you in such excitement about? Has any body been offering himself to *your* sister? Because—you mistook me. Ask her, or Lizzy, or any good woman, if they would feel flattered by a gentleman's acting in the way you suggest? As if his hand—with the ring in it—were everything to them, and himself and his true love nothing at all!"

Launceston laughed uneasily. "Well, but what did you mean? A friend of mine would like to know your opinion on this matter."

"My opinion is simply—an opinion. Every man is the best judge of his own affairs, especially love-affairs. As the Eastern proverb says: 'Let not the lions decide for the tigers.' But I think, did *I* love a woman" (and it pleased me to know I was but speaking out her mind who years ago lived and died, in her fond simplicity wiser than any of these)—"did I love a woman, I would like to tell her so—just to herself, no more. I would like to give her my love to rest on—to receive the help and consolation of hers. I would like her to feel that through all chances and changes she and I were *one*; one, neither for foolish child's-play nor headlong passion, but for mutual strength and support, holding ourselves responsible both to heaven and each other for our life and our love. One, indissolubly, whether we were ever married or not; one in this world, and—we pray—one in the world everlasting."

Was I dreaming? Did I actually see my friend Launceston take, unforbidden, my youngest sister's hand, and hold it—firmly, tenderly, fast? Did I hear, with my own natural ears, Lizzie's soft little sob, not of grief certainly, as she slipped out of the room, as swift and silent as a moonbeam?

Eh! what? Good Heavens! Was there ever any creature so blind as a middle-aged elder brother!

Well, as I told Launceston, it was half my own fault; and I must bear it stoically. Perhaps, on the whole, things might have been worse, for he is a noble fellow, and no wonder the child loves him. They can not be married just yet meanwhile; Lizzie and I keep the matter between ourselves. They are very happy—God bless them! and so am I.

* * * * * *

P.S.—Mr. Archer reappeared yesterday—looking quite well and comfortable! I see clearly that, one day not distant, I shall be left lamenting—the solitary residuum of a Family in Love.

A LOW MARRIAGE.

CHAPTER I.

Mrs. ROCHDALE stood a good while talking at the school-gate this morning—Mrs. Rochdale, my mistress once, my friend now. My cousin, the village schoolmistress, was bemoaning over her lad George, now fighting in the Crimea, saying, poor body, "that no one could understand her feelings but a mother—a mother with an only son."

Mrs. Rochdale smiled—that peculiar smile of one who has bought peace through the "constant anguish of patience"—a look which I can still trace in her face at times, and which I suppose will never wholly vanish thence. We changed the conversation, and she shortly afterward departed.

A mother with an only son! All the neighborhood knew the story of our Mrs. Rochdale and her son; but it had long ceased to be discussed, at least openly, though still it was told under the seal of confidence to every new-comer in our village. And still every summer I used to see any strangers who occupied my cousin's lodgings staring with all their eyes when the manor-house carriage passed by, or peeping from over the blinds to catch a glimpse of Mrs. Rochdale.

No wonder. She is, both to look at and to know, a woman among a thousand.

It can do no possible harm—it may do good—if I here write down her history.

First let me describe her who even yet seems to me the fairest woman I ever knew. And why should not a woman be fair at sixty? Because the beauty that lasts till then—and it can last, for I have seen it—must be of the noblest and most satisfying kind, wholly independent of form or coloring; a beauty such as a young woman can by no art attain, but which, once attained, no woman need ever fear to lose till the coffin-lid, closing over its last and loveliest smile, makes of it "a joy forever."

Mrs. Rochdale was tall—too tall in youth—but your well-statured women have decidedly the advantage after forty. Her features, more soft than strong—looking softer still under the smooth-banded gray hair—might have been good; I am no artist—I do not know. But it was not that; it was the intangible, nameless grace which surrounded her as with an atmos-phere, making her presence in a room like light, and her absence like its loss; her soft but stately courtesy of mien in word and motion alike harmonious. Silent, her gentle ease of manner made every one else at ease. Speaking, though she was by no means a great talker, she always seemed instinctively to say just the right thing, to the right person, at the right moment, in the right way. She stood out distinct from all your "charming creatures," "most lady-like persons," "very talented women," as that rarest species of the whole race —a gentlewoman.

At twenty-three she became Mr. Rochdale's wife; at twenty-five his widow. From that time her whole life was devoted to the son who, at a twelvemonth old, was already Lemuel Rochdale, Esquire, lord of the manor of Thorpe and Stretton-Magna, owner of one of the largest estates in the county. Poor little baby!

He was the puniest, sickliest baby she ever saw, I have heard my mother say; but he grew up into a fine boy and a handsome youth; not unlike Mrs. Rochdale, except that a certain hereditary pride of manner, which in her was almost beautiful—if any pride can be beautiful—was in him exaggerated to self-assurance and haughtiness. He was the principal person in the establishment while he yet trundled hoops; and long before he discarded jackets had assumed his position as sole master of the manor-house — allowing, however, his mother to remain as sole mistress.

He loved her very much, I think—better than horses, dogs, or guns; swore she was the kindest and dearest mother in England, and handsomer, ten times over, than any girl he knew. At which the smiling mother would shake her head in credulous incredulousness. She rarely burdened him with caresses; perhaps she had found out early that boys dislike them—at least he did. To others she always spoke of him as "my son," or "Mr. Rochdale;" and her pride in him, or praise of him, was always more by implication than by open word. Yet all the house, all the village, knew quite well how things were. And though they were not often seen together, except on Sundays, when, year after year, she walked up the church-aisle, holding her little son by the hand; then, followed by the sturdy school-boy; finally, leaning proudly on the youth's proud arm—everybody said emphatically that the young squire was "his mother's own son;" passionately beloved, after the fashion of women ever since young Eve smiled down on Cain, saying, "I have gotten a man from the Lord."

So he grew up to be twenty-one years old. On that day Mrs. Rochdale, for the first time since her widowhood, opened her house, and invited all the country round. The morning was devoted to the poorer guests; in the evening there was a dinner-party and ball.

I dressed her, having since my girlhood been to her a sort of amateur milliner and lady's-maid. I may use the word "amateur" in its strictest sense, since it was out of the great love and reverence I had for her that I had got into this habit of haunting the manor-house. And since love begets love, and we always feel kindly to those we have been kind to, Mrs. Rochdale was fond of me. Through her means, and still more through herself, I gained a better education than I should have done as only her bailiff's daughter. But that is neither here nor there.

Mrs. Rochdale was standing before the glass in her black velvet gown—she never wore anything but black, with sometimes a gray or lilac ribbon. She had taken out from that casket, and was clasping on her arms and neck—white and round even at five-and-forty—some long-unworn family jewels.

I admired them very much.

"Yes, they are pretty; but I scarcely like to see myself in diamonds, Martha. I shall only wear them a few times, and then resign them to my daughter-in-law."

"Your daughter-in-law? Has Mr. Rochdale—"

"No" (smiling), "Mr. Rochdale has not made his choice yet, but I hope he will ere long. A young man should marry early, especially a young man of family and fortune. I shall be very glad when my son has chosen his wife."

She spoke as if she thought he had nothing to do but to choose, after the fashion of kings and sultans.

I smiled. She misinterpreted my thought, saying, with some little severity:

"Martha, you mistake. I repeat, I shall be altogether glad, even if such a chance were to happen to-day."

Ah, Mrs. Rochdale, was ever any widowed mother of an only son "altogether glad" when first startled into the knowledge that she herself was not his all in the world? that some strange woman had risen up, for whose sake he was bound to "leave father and mother and cleave unto his wife?" A righteous saying, but hard to be understood at first by the mothers.

It afterward struck me as an odd coincidence, that what Mrs. Rochdale had wished might happen did actually happen that same night.

The prettiest, and beyond all question the "sweetest," girl in all our county families—among which alone it was probable or permissible that our young squire should "throw the handkerchief"—was Miss Celandine Childe, niece and heiress of Sir John Childe. I was caught by her somewhat fanciful name—after Wordsworth's flower—which, as I overheard Mrs. Rochdale say, admirably expressed her.

I thought so too, when, peeping through the curtained ballroom-door, I caught sight of her, distinct among all the young ladies, as one's eye lights upon a celandine in a spring meadow. She was smaller than any lady in the room—very fair, with yellow hair—the only real gold hair I ever saw. Her head drooped like a flower-cup; and her motions, always soft and quiet, reminded one of the stirrings of a flower in the grass. Her dress—as if to humor the fancy, or else Nature herself did so by making that color most suitable to the girl's complexion—was some gauzy stuff, of a soft pale-green. Bright, delicate, innocent, and fair, you could hardly look at her without wishing to take her up in your bosom like a flower.

The ball was a great success. Mrs. Rochdale came up to her dressing-room long after midnight, but with the bright glow of maternal pride still burning on her cheeks. She looked quite young again, forcing one to acknowledge the fact constantly avouched by the elder generation, that our mothers and grandmothers were a great deal handsomer than we. Certainly, not a belle in the ballroom could compare with Mrs. Rochdale in my eyes. I should have liked to have told her so. In a vague manner I said something which slightly approximated to my thought.

Mrs. Rochdale answered, innocent of the compliment, "Yes, I have seen very lovely women in my youth. But to-night my son pointed out several whom he admired—one in particular."

"Was it Miss Childe, madam?"

"How acute you are, little Martha! How could you see that?"

I answered, rather deprecatingly, that from the corner where I was serving ices, I had heard several people remark Mr. Rochdale's great attention to Miss Childe.

"Indeed!" with a slight sharpness of accent. A moment or two after she added, with some hauteur, "You mistake, my dear; Mr. Rochdale could never be so uncourteous as to pay exclusive attention to any one of his guests; but Miss Childe is a stranger in the neighborhood." After a pause: "She is a most sweet-looking girl. My son said so to me, and—I perfectly agreed with him."

I let the subject drop—nor did Mrs. Rochdale resume it.

A month after I wondered if she knew what all the servants at the manor-house, and all the villagers at Thorpe soon knew quite well, and discussed incessantly in butlers' pantries and kitchens, over pots of ale and by cottage-doors—that our young squire from that day forward gave up his shooting, his otter-hunting, and even his coursing, and "went a-courting" sedulously for a whole month to Ashen Dale.

Meanwhile Sir John and Miss Childe came twice to luncheon. I saw her, pretty creature! walking by Mrs. Rochdale's side to feed the swans, and looking more like a flower than ever. And once, stately in the family-coach, which tumbled over the rough roads, two hours there and two hours back, shaking the old coachman almost to pieces, did Mrs. and Mr. Rochdale drive over to a formal dinner at Ashen Dale.

Finally, in the Christmas-week, after an interval of twenty lonely Christmases past and gone, did our lady of the manor prepare to pay to the same place a three-days' visit—such as is usual among county families—the "rest-day, the pressed day," and the day of departure.

I was at the door when she came home. Her usually bright and healthy cheeks were somewhat pale, and her eyes glittered; but her eyelids were heavy, as with long pressing back of tears. Mr. Rochdale did not drive, but sat beside her; he too seemed rather grave. He handed her out of the carriage carefully and tenderly. She responded with a fond smile. Mother and son went up the broad stair-case arm in arm.

That night the servants who had gone to Ashen Dale talked "it" all over with the servants who had staid at home; and every point was satisfactorily settled, down to the bride's fortune and pin-money, and whether she would be married in Brussels or Honiton lace.

Yet still Mrs. Rochdale said nothing. She looked happy, but pale, constantly pale. The squire was in the gayest spirits imaginable. He was, as I have said, a very handsome and winning young fellow; rather variable in his tastes and easily guided, some people said—but then it was always the old who said it, and nobody minded them. We thought Miss Celandine Childe was the happiest and luckiest girl imaginable.

She looked so when, after due time, the three-days' visit was returned; after which Sir John departed, and Miss Childe staid behind.

That evening—it was just the time of year when "evenings" begin to be perceptible, and in passing the drawing-room door I had heard the young master say something to Miss Childe about "primroses in the woods"—that evening I was waiting upon Mrs. Rochdale's toilet. She herself stood at the oriel window. It was after dinner—she had come up to her room to rest.

"Look here, Martha."

She pointed to the terrace-walk leading to the pool. There were the two young people sauntering slowly past—he gazing down on her, she with her eyes drooped low, low, to the very ground. But her arm rested in his, in a safe, happy, clinging way, as knowing it had a right there to rest forever.

"It is so, Mrs. Rochdale?"

"Ay, Martha. What do you think of my—my children?"

A few tears came to her eyes—a few quivers fluttered over and about her mouth; but she gazed still—she smiled still.

"Are you satisfied, madam?"

"Quite. It is the happiest thing in the world —for him. They will be married at Christmas."

"And you—"

She put her hands softly on my lips, and said, smiling, "Plenty of time to think of that— plenty of time."

After this day she gradually grew less pale, and recovered entirely her healthy, cheerful tone of mind. It was evident that she soon began to love her daughter-elect very much—as indeed, who could help it?—and that by no means as a mere matter of form had she called them both "my children."

For Celandine, who had never known a mother, it seemed as if Mrs. Rochdale were almost as dear to her as her betrothed. The two ladies were constantly together; and in them the proverbially formidable and all but impossible possibility bade fair to be realized, of a mother and daughter-in-law as united as if they were of the same flesh and blood.

The gossips shook their heads and said, "It wouldn't last." I think it would. Why should it not? They were two noble, tender, unselfish women. Either was ready to love any thing he loved—to renounce any thing to make him happy. In him, the lover and son, was their meeting-point, in him they learned to love one another.

Strange that women can not always see this. Strange that a girl should not, above all but her own mother, cling to the mother of him she loves—the woman who has borne him, nursed him, cherished him, suffered for him more than any living creature can suffer, excepting—ay, sometimes not even excepting—his wife. Most strange, that a mother, who would be fond and kind to any thing her boy cared for—his horse or his dog—should not, above all, love the creature he loves best in the world, on whom his happiness, honor, and peace are staked for a lifetime. Alas, that a bond so simple, natural, holy, should be found so hard as to be almost impossible—even among the good women of this world! Mothers, wives, whose fault is it? Is it because each exacts too much for herself, and too little for the other—one forgetting that she was ever young, the other that she will one day be old? Or that in the tenderest woman's devotion lurks a something of jealousy, which blinds them to the truth—as true in love as in charity—that "it is more blessed to give than to receive?" Perhaps I, Martha Stretton, spinster, have no right to discuss this question. But one thing I will say: that I can forgive much to an unloved daughter-in-law—to an unloving one *nothing*.

And now, from this long digression—which is not so irrelevant as it at first may seem—let me return to my story.

The year grew and waned. Mrs. Rochdale said to me, when it was near its closing, that it had been one of the happiest years she had ever known.

I believe it was. The more so as, like many a season of great happiness, it began with a conquered pang. But of this no one ever dared to hint; and perhaps the mother now would hardly have acknowledged, even to herself, that it had temporarily existed.

CHAPTER II.

The young people were to have been married at Christmas; but early in December the long-invalided Lady Childe died. This deferred the wedding. The lover said, loudly and often, that it was "very hard." The bride-elect said nothing at all. Consequently every lady's-maid and woman-servant at the manor-house, and every damsel down the village, talked over Miss Childe's hard-heartedness; especially as, soon after, she went traveling with poor broken-hearted Sir John Childe, thereby parting with her betrothed for three whole months.

But I myself watched her about the manor-house the last few days before she went away. Oh, Lemuel Rochdale, what had you deserved, that Heaven should bless you with the love of two such women—mother and bride!

Celandine went away. The manor-house was very dull after she was gone. Mrs. Rochdale said she did not wonder that her son was absent a good deal—it was natural. But this she only said to me. To others, she never took any notice of his absence at all.

These absences continued—lengthened. In most young men they would have been unremarked; but Lemuel was so fondly attached to his mother that he rarely in his life had spent his evenings away from home and her. Now, in the wild March nights, in the soft April twilights, in the May moonlights, Mrs. Rochdale sat alone in the great drawing-room, where they had sat so happily last year—all three of them.

She sat, grave and quiet, over her book or her knitting, still saying—if she ever said any thing—that it was quite "natural" her son should amuse himself abroad.

Once I heard her ask him, "Where he had been to-night?"

He hesitated; then said, "Up the village, mother."

"What, again? How fond you are of moonlight walks up the village!"

"Am I?" whipping his boots with his cane.

"Why, mother, moonlight is—very pretty, you know; and the evenings here are—so long."

"True." His mother half sighed. "But soon, you know, Celandine will be back."

It might have been my mistake, but I thought the young man turned scarlet, as, whistling his dog, he hastily quitted the room.

"How sensitive these lovers are!" said Mrs. Rochdale, smiling. "He can hardly bear to hear her name. I do wish they were married."

But that wish was still further deferred. Sir John Childe, fretful, ailing, begged another six months before he lost his niece. They were young; and he was old, and had not long to live. Besides, thus safely and happily betrothed, why should they not wait? A year more or less was of little moment to those who were bound together firm and sure, in good and ill, for a lifetime. Nay, did she not from the very day of her betrothal feel herself Lemuel's faithful wife?

Thus, Mrs. Rochdale told me, did Celandine urge—out of the love which in its completeness hardly recognized such a thing as separation. Her mother that was to be, reading the passage out of her letter, paused, silenced by starting tears.

The lover consented to this further delay. He did not once say that it was "very hard." Again Mrs. Rochdale began to talk, but with a tone of fainter certainty, about their being married next Christmas.

Meanwhile the young squire appeared quite satisfied; shot, fished, lounged about his property as usual, and kept up his spirits amazingly. He likewise took his moonlight walks up the village with creditable persistency. Once or twice I heard it whispered about that he did not take them alone.

But every one in the neighborhood so liked the young squire, and so tenderly honored his mother, that it was some time before the faintest of these ill whispers reached the ear of Mrs. Rochdale.

I never shall forget the day she heard it. She had sent for me to help her in gathering her grapes; a thing she often liked to do herself, giving the choice bunches to her own friends, and to the sick poor of her neighbors. She was standing in the vinery when I came. One moment's glance showed me something was amiss, but she stopped the question ere it was well out of my lips.

"No, nothing, Martha. This bunch—cut it while I hold it."

But her hand shook so that the grapes fell and were crushed, dyeing purple the stone floor. I picked them up—she took no notice.

Suddenly she put her hand to her head. "I am tired. We will do this another day."

I followed her across the garden to the hall-door. Entering, she gave orders to have the carriage ready immediately.

"I will take you home, Martha. I am going to the village."

Now the village was about two miles distant from the manor-house—a mere cluster of cottages; among which were only three decent dwellings—the butcher's, the baker's, and the school-house. Mrs. Rochdale rarely drove through Thorpe—still more rarely did she stop there.

She stopped now—it was some message at

the school-house. Then, addressing the coach-man—

"Drive on—to the baker's shop."

Old John started—touched his hat hurriedly. I saw him and the footman whispering on the box. Well I could guess why!

"The baker's, Mrs. Rochdale? Can not I call? Indeed, it is a pity you should take that trouble."

She looked me full in the face; I felt myself turn crimson.

"Thank you, Martha; but I wish to go myself."

I ceased. But I was now quite certain she knew, and guessed I knew also, that which all the village were now talking about. What could be her motive for acting thus? Was it to show her own ignorance of the report? No, that would have been to imply a falsehood; and Mrs. Rochdale was staunchly, absolutely true in deed as in word. Or was it to prove them all liars and scandal-mongers, that the lady of the manor drove up openly to the very door where—

Mrs. Rochdale startled me from my thoughts with her sudden voice, sharp and clear.

"He is a decent man, I believe. Hine, the baker?"

"Yes, madam."

"He has—a daughter, who—waits in the shop?"

"Yes, madam."

She pulled the check-string with a quick jerk, and got out. Two small burning spots were on either cheek; otherwise she looked herself—her tall, calm, stately self.

I wondered what Nancy thought of her—handsome Nancy Hine, who was laughing in her free loud way behind the counter, but who, perceiving the manor-house carriage, stopped, startled.

I could see them quite plainly through the shop-window—the baker's daughter and the mother of the young squire. I could see the very glitter in Mrs. Rochdale's eyes, as, giving in her ordinary tone some domestic order, she took the opportunity of gazing steadily at the large, well-featured girl, who stood awkward and painfully abashed, nay, blushing scarlet; though people did say that Nancy Hine was too clever a girl to have blushed since she was out of her teens.

I think they belied her—I think many people belied her, both then and afterward. She was "clever"—much cleverer than most girls of her station; she looked bold and determined enough, but neither unscrupulous nor insincere.

During the interview, which did not last two minutes, I thought it best to stay outside the door. Of course, when Mrs. Rochdale re-entered the carriage, I made no remark. Nor did she.

She gave me the cake for the school-children. From the wicket I watched her drive off, just catching through the carriage-window her profile, so proudly cut, so delicate and refined.

That a young man, born and reared of such a mother, with a lovely fair creature like Celandine for his own, his very own, could ever lower his tastes, habits, perceptions, to court—people said even to win—unlawfully, a common village-girl, handsome, indeed, but with the coarse blowsy beauty which at thirty might be positive ugliness—surely—surely it was impossible! It could not be true what they said about young Mr. Rochdale and Nancy Hine.

I did not think his mother believed it either; if she had, could she have driven away with that quiet smile on her mouth, left by her last kind words to the school-children and to me?

The young squire had gone to Scotland the day before this incident occurred. He did not seem in any hurry to return; not even when, by some whim of the old baronet's, Sir John Childe and his niece suddenly returned to Ashen Dale.

Mrs. Rochdale drove over there immediately, and brought Celandine back with her. The two ladies, elder and younger, were gladly seen by us all going about together in their old happy ways, lingering in the green-house, driving and walking, laughing their well-known merry laugh when they fed the swans of an evening in the pool.

There might have been no such things in the world as tale-bearers, slanderers, or—bakers' daughters.

Alas! this was only for four bright days—the last days when I ever saw Mrs. Rochdale looking happy and young, or Celandine Childe light-hearted and bewitchingly fair.

On the fifth, Sir John Childe's coach drove up to the manor-house, not lazily, as it generally did, but with ominously thundering wheels. He and Mrs. Rochdale were shut up in the library for two full hours. Then she came out, walking heavily, with a kind of mechanical strength, but never once drooping her head or her eyes, and desired me to go and look for Miss Childe, who was reading in the summer-house. She waited at the hall-door till the young lady came in.

"Mamma!" Already she had begun, by Mrs. Rochdale's wish, to give her that fond name. But it seemed to strike painfully now.

"Mamma, is any thing the matter?" and, turning pale, the girl clung to her arm.

"Nothing to alarm you, my pet; nothing that I care for—not I. I know it is false—wholly false; it could not but be." Her tone, warm with excitement, had nevertheless more anger in it than fear. Celandine's color returned.

"If it be false, mamma, never mind it," she said, in her fondling way. "But what is this news?"

"Something that your uncle has heard. Something he insists upon telling you. Let him. It can not matter either to you or to me. Come, my child."

What passed in the library of course never transpired; but about an hour after I was sent for to Mrs. Rochdale's dressing-room.

She sat at her writing-table. There was a firm, hard, almost fierce expression in her eyes, very painful to see. Yet when Celandine glided in, with that soft step and white face, Mrs. Rochdale looked up with a quick smile.

"Has he read it? Is he satisfied with it?" and she took, with painfully assumed carelessness, a letter newly written, which Miss Childe brought to her.

The girl assented; then, kneeling by the table, pressed her cheek upon Mrs. Rochdale's shoulder.

"Let me write, mamma, just one little line, to tell him that I—that I don't believe—"

"Hush!" and the trembling lips were shut with a kiss tender as firm. "No; not a line, my little girl. I, his mother, may speak of such things to him. Not you."

It did at the moment seem to me almost sickening that this pure fragile flower of a girl should ever have been told there existed such wickedness as that of which not only Sir John Childe, but the whole neighborhood now accused her lover; and which, as I afterward learned, the baronet insisted should be at once openly and explicitly denied by Mr. Rochdale, or the engagement must be held dissolved.

This question his mother claimed her own sole right to put to her son; and she had put it in the letter, which now, with a steady hand and a fixed smile—half-contemptuous as it were—she was sealing and directing.

"Martha, put this into the post-bag yourself; and tell Miss Childe's maid her mistress will remain another week at the manor-house. Yes, my love, best so."

Then, sitting down wearily in the large armchair, Mrs. Rochdale drew Celandine to her; and I saw her take the soft small figure on her lap, like a child, and fold her up close in the grave, comforting silence of inexpressible love.

It was a four-days' post to and from the moors where Mr. Rochdale was staying. Heavily the time must have passed with those two poor women, whose all was staked upon him—upon his one little "yes" or "no."

Sunday intervened, when they both appeared at church—evening as well as morning. With this exception, they did not go out; and were seen but rarely about the house, except at dinner-time. Then, with her companion on her arm, Mrs. Rochdale would walk down, and take her seat at the foot of the long dreary dining-table, placing Miss Childe on her right hand.

The old butler said it made his heart ache to see how sometimes they both looked toward the head of the board—at the empty chair there.

The fifth day came and passed. No letters. The sixth likewise. In the evening, his mother ordered Mr. Rochdale's chamber to be got ready, as it was "not improbable" he might unexpectedly come home. But he did not come.

They sat up half that night, I believe, both Mrs. Rochdale and Miss Childe.

Next morning they breakfasted together as usual in the dressing-room. As I crossed the plantation—for in my anxiety I made business at the manor-house every day now—I saw them both sitting at the window, waiting for the post.

Waiting for the post! Many a one has known that heart-sickening intolerable time; but few waitings have been like to theirs.

The stable-boy came lazily up, swinging the letter-bag to and fro in his hands. They saw it from the window.

The butler unlocked the bag as usual, and distributed the contents.

"Here's one from the young master. Lord bless us, what a big un!"

"Let me take it up stairs, William." For I saw it was addressed to Miss Childe.

Mechanically, as I went up stairs, my eye rested on the direction, in Mr. Rochdale's large careless hand; and on the seal, firm and clear, bearing not the sentimental devices he had once been fond of using, but his business seal—his coat-of-arms. With a heavy weight on my heart, I knocked at the dressing-room door.

Miss Childe opened it.

"Ah, mamma, for me, for me!" And with a sob of joy she caught and tore open the large envelope.

Out of it fell a heap of letters—her own pretty, dainty letters—addressed "Lemuel Rochdale, Esq."

She stood looking down at them with a bewildered air, then searched through the envelope. It was blank—quite blank.

"What does he mean, mamma? I—don't —understand."

But Mrs. Rochdale did. "Go away, Martha," she said, hoarsely, shutting me out at the door. And then I heard a smothered cry, and something falling to the floor like a stone.

CHAPTER III.

THE ladies did not appear at lunch. Word was sent down stairs that Miss Childe was "indisposed." I could not by any means get to see Mrs. Rochdale, though I hung about the house all day. Near dark I received a message that the mistress wanted me.

She was sitting in the dining-room without lights. She sat as quiet, as motionless as a carved figure. I dared not speak to her; I trembled to catch the first sound of her voice— my friend, my mistress, my dear Mrs. Rochdale!

"Martha!"

"Yes, madam."

"I wish, Martha—" and there the voice stopped.

I hardly know what prevented my saying or doing, on the impulse, things that the commonest instinct told me, the moment afterward, ought to be said and done by no one—certainly not by me—at this crisis, to Mrs. Rochdale. So, with an effort, I stood silent in the dim light— as silent and motionless as herself.

"I wish, Martha"—and her voice was steady now—"I wish to send you on a message, which requires some one whom I can implicitly trust."

My heart was at my lips; but, of course, I only said, "Yes, madam."

"I want you to go down to the village to the —the—young person at the baker's shop."

"Nancy Hine."

"Is that her name? Yes, I remember; Nancy Hine. Bring her here—to the manor-house; without observation, if you can."

"To-night, madam?"

"To-night. Make any excuse you choose; or, rather, make no excuse at all. Say Mrs. Rochdale wishes to speak to her."

"Any thing more?" I asked, softly, after a considerable pause.

"Nothing more. Go at once, Martha."

I obeyed implicitly. Much as this, my mission, had surprised, nay, startled me, I knew Mrs. Rochdale always did what was wisest, best to do under the circumstances. Also, that her combined directness of purpose and strength of character often led her to do things utterly unthought of by a weaker or less single-hearted woman.

Though a misty September moonlight, I walked blindly on in search of Nancy Hine. She was having a lively gossip at the bakehouse door. The fire showed her figure plainly. Her large, rosy arms, whitened with flour, were crossed over her decent working-gown. People allowed—even the most censorious—that Nancy was, in her own home, an active, industrious lass, though too much given to dress of Sundays, and holding herself rather above her station every day.

"Nancy Hine, I want to speak with you a minute."

"Oh! do you, Martha Stretton? Speak out, then. No secrets here."

Her careless, not to say rude, manner irritated me. I just turned away and walked down the village. I had not gone many yards when Nancy's hand was on my shoulder, and, with a loud laugh at my sudden start, she pulled me, by a back door, into the shop.

"Now, then?"

The baker's daughter folded her arms in a rather defiant way. Her eyes were bright and open. There was in her manner some excitement, coarseness, and boldness; but nothing unvirtuous—nothing to mark the fallen girl whom her neighbors were pointing the finger at. I could not loathe her quite as much as I had intended.

"Now, then?" she repeated.

I delivered Mrs. Rochdale's message word for word.

Nancy seemed a good deal surprised—not shocked, or alarmed, or ashamed—merely surprised.

"Wants me, does she? Why?"

"She did not say."

"But you guess, of course. Well, who cares? Not I."

Yet her brown, handsome face changed color. Her hands nervously fidgeted about, taking off her apron, "making herself decent," as she called it. Suddenly she stopped.

"Has there been any letter—any news—from young Mr. Rochdale?"

"I believe there has; but that is no business of—"

"Mine, you mean, eh? Come, don't be so sharp, Martha Stretton. I'll go with you, only let me put on my best bonnet first."

"Nancy Hine," I burst out, "do you think it can matter to Mrs. Rochdale whether you go in a queen's gown or a beggar's rags, except that the rags might suit you best? Come as you are."

"I will," cried Nancy, glaring in my face; "and you, Martha, keep a civil tongue, will you? My father's daughter is as good as you, or your mistress either. Get out of the shop. I'll follow 'ee. I bean't afeard!"

That broad accent, broadening as she got angry! those abrupt, awkward gestures! what could the young squire, his mother's son, who had lived with that dear mother all his days, have seen attractive in Nancy Hine?

But similar anomalies of taste have puzzled, and will puzzle, every body—especially women, who in their attachments generally see clearer and deeper than men—to the end of time.

Nancy Hine walked in sullen taciturnity to the manor-house. It was already late—nearly all the household were gone to bed. I left the young woman in the hall, and went up to Mrs. Rochdale.

She was sitting before her dressing-room fire absorbed in thought. In the chamber close by —in the large state-bed which Mrs. Rochdale always occupied, where generations of Rochdales had been born and died—slept the gentle girl whose happiness had been so cruelly betrayed. For that the engagement was broken, and for sufficient cause, Mr. Rochdale's answer, or rather non-answer, to his mother's plain letter made now certain, almost beyond a doubt.

"Hush; don't wake her," whispered Mrs. Rochdale, hurriedly. "Well, Martha?"

"The young woman—shall I bring her, madam?"

"What! here?" Words can not describe the look of repulsion, hatred, horror, which for a moment darkened Mrs. Rochdale's face. Perhaps the noblest human being, either man or woman, is born, not passionless, but with strong passions to be subjected to firm will. If at that moment—one passing moment—she could have crushed out of existence the girl who had led away her son—(for Nancy was older than he, and "no fool")—I think Mrs. Rochdale would have done it.

The next instant she would have done nothing of the kind; nothing that a generous Christian woman might not do.

She rose up, saying, quietly, "The young person can not come here, Martha. Bring her into—let me see—into the drawing-room."

There, entering a few minutes after, we found Mrs. Rochdale seated on one of the velvet couches, just in the light of the chandelier.

I do not suppose Nancy Hine had ever been in such a brilliant, beautiful room before. She was apparently quite stunned and dazzled by it; courtesied humbly, and stood with her arms wrapped up in her shawl, vacantly gazing about her.

Mrs. Rochdale spoke. "Nancy Hine, I believe, is your name?"

"Yes, my lady. That is—um—yes, ma'am, my name is Nancy."

She came a little forwarder now, and lifted up her eyes more boldly to the sofa. In fact, they both regarded each other keenly and long—the lady of the manor and the village girl.

I observed that Mrs. Rochdale had resumed her usual evening-dress, and that no trace of mental disorder was visible in her apparel—scarcely even in her countenance.

"I sent for you, Nancy Hine—(Martha, do not go away, I wish that there should be a witness to all that passes between this young woman and myself)—I sent for you on account of certain reports, more injurious to your character, if possible, than even to that of—the other person. Are you aware what reports I mean?"

"Yes, my lady, I be."

"That is an honest answer, and I like honesty," said Mrs. Rochdale, after a prolonged gaze at the face, now scarlet with wholesome blushes, of the baker's daughter. With a half-sigh of relief, she went on.

"You must also be aware that I, as the mother of—that other person, can have but one motive in sending for you here—namely, to ask a question which I more than any one else have a right to ask, and to have answered. Do you understand me?"

"Some'at."

"Nancy," she resumed, after another long gaze, as if struck by something in the young woman different from what she had expected, and led thereby to address her differently from what she had at first intended—"Nancy, I will be plain with you. It is not every lady—every mother, who would have spoken with you as I speak now, without anger or blame—only wishing to get from you the truth. If I believed the worst—if you were a poor girl whom my son had—had wronged, I would still have pitied you. Knowing him and now looking at you, I do not believe it. I believe you may have been foolish, light of conduct; but not guilty. Tell me—do tell me"—and the mother's agony broke through the lady's calm and dignified demeanor—"one word to assure me it is so!"

But Nancy Hine did not utter that word. She gave a little faint sob, and then dropped her head with a troubled awkward air, as if the presence of Lemuel's mother—speaking so kindly, and looking her through and through, was more than she could bear.

That poor mother, whom this last hope had failed, to whom her only son now appeared not only as a promise-breaker, but the systematic seducer of a girl beneath his own rank—between whom and himself could exist no mental union, no false gloss of sentiment to cover the foulness of mere sensual passion—that poor mother sank back, and put her hand over her eyes, as if she would fain henceforth shut out from her sight the whole world.

After a while she forced herself to look at the girl once more—who, now recovering from her momentary remorse, was busy casting admiring glances, accompanied with one or two curious smiles, around the drawing-room.

"From your silence, young woman, I must conclude that I was mistaken; that—but I will spare you. You will have enough to suffer. There now remains only one question which I desire—which I am compelled—to ask: How long has this—this" she seemed to choke over the unuttered word—"lasted?"

"Dunnot know what you mean."

"I must speak plainer, then. How long, Nancy Hine, have you been my son's—Mr. Rochdale's—mistress?"

"Not a day—not an hour," cried Nancy, violently, coming close to the sofa. "Mind what you say, Mrs. Rochdale. I'm an honest girl. I'm as good as you. I'm Mr. Rochdale's *wife!*"

Mr. Rochdale's mother sat mute, and watched the girl take from a ribbon round her neck a ring—an unmistakable wedding-ring, and slip it with a determined push on her large working-woman's finger. This done, she thrust it right in the lady's face.

"Look'ee, what do 'ee say to that? He put it there. All your anger can not take it off. I am Mrs. Lemuel Rochdale, your son's wife."

"Ah!" shrinking from her. But the next minute the true womanly feeling came into the virtuous mother's heart. "Better this—than—what they said. Better a thousand times. Thank God."

With a sigh, long and deep, she sat down, and again covered her eyes, as if trying to realize the amazing—impossible truth. Then she said, slowly, "Martha, I think this"—she hesitated what name to give Nancy; finally gave no name at all—"I think she had better go away."

Nancy, quite awed and moved—all her boldness gone—was creeping out of the room after me when Mrs. Rochdale called us back.

"Stay; at this hour of the night it is not fitting that—my son's wife—should be out alone. Martha, ask your father to see her safe home."

The baker's daughter turned at the door, and said, "Thank'ee, my lady;" but omitted her courtesy this time.

And Mrs. Rochdale had found her daughter-in-law!

CHAPTER IV.

ERE we knew what had happened the whole dynasty at the manor-house was changed. Mrs. Rochdale was gone; she left before her son returned from Scotland, and did not once see him. Mrs. Lemuel Rochdale, late Nancy Hine, was installed as lady of the manor.

Such a theme for gossip had not been vouchsafed our country for a hundred years. Of a surety they canvassed it over—talked it literally threadbare.

Mrs. Rochdale escaped it fortunately. She went abroad with Sir John and Miss Childe. All the popular voice was with her and against her son. They said he had killed that pretty gentle creature—who, however, did not die, but lived to suffer—perhaps better still, to overcome suffering; that he had broken his noble mother's heart. Few of his old friends visited him; not one of their wives visited his wife. He had done that which many "respectable" people are more shocked at than any species of profligacy—he had made a low marriage.

Society was harder upon him, harder than he deserved. At least, they despised him and his marriage for the wrong cause. Not because his wife was, when he chose her, a woman thoroughly beneath him in education, tastes, and feelings—because from this inferiority it was impossible he could have felt for her any save the lowest and most degrading kind of love—but simply because she was a village girl—a baker's daughter.

Sir John Childe said to Lemuel's mother, in a lofty compassion, the only time he was ever known to refer to the humiliating and miserable occurrence : "Madam, whatever herself might have been, the disgrace would have been lightened had your son not married a person of such low origin. Shocking!—a baker's daughter."

"Sir John," said Mrs. Rochdale, with dignity, "if my son had chosen a woman suitable and worthy of being his wife, I would not have minded had she been the daughter of the meanest laborer in the land."

CHAPTER V.

"Miss Martha!" called out our rector's wife to me one day, "is it true, that talk I hear of Mrs. Rochdale's coming home ?"

"Quite true, I believe."

"And where will she come to ? Not to the manor-house ?"

"Certainly not." I fear there was a bitterness in my tone, for the good old lady looked at me reprovingly.

"My dear, the right thing for us in this world is to make the very best of that which, having happened, was consequently ordained by Providence to happen. And we often find the worst things not so bad, after all. I was truly glad to-day to hear that Mrs. Rochdale was coming home."

"But not home to *them*—not to the manor-house. She will take a house in the village. She will never meet them, any more than when she was abroad."

"But she will hear of them. That does great good sometimes."

"When there is any good to be heard."

"I have told you, Martha, and I hope you have told Mrs. Rochdale, that there *is* good. When first I called on Mrs. Lemuel, it was simply in my character as the clergyman's wife, doing what I believed my duty. I found that duty easier than I expected."

"Because she remembered her position"— ("Her former position, my dear," corrected Mrs. Wood)—"because she showed off no airs and graces, but was quiet, humble, and thankful, as became her, for the kindness you thus showed."

"Because of that, and something more. Because the more I have seen of her the more I feel, that though not exactly to be liked, she is to be respected. She has sustained tolerably well a most difficult part—that of an ignorant person suddenly raised to wealth ; envied and abused by her former class, utterly scouted and despised by her present one. She has had to learn to comport herself as mistress where she was once an equal, and as an equal where she used to be an inferior. I can hardly imagine a greater trial as regards social position."

"Position ? She has none. No ladies except yourself will visit her. Why should they ?"

"My dear, why should they not ? A woman who since her marriage has conducted herself with perfect propriety, befitting the sphere to which she was raised ; has lived retired, and forced herself into no one's notice ; who is, whatever be her shortcomings in education and refinement of character, a good wife, a kind mistress—"

"How do you know that ?"

"Simply because her husband is rarely absent a day from home ; because all her servants have remained with her, and spoken well of her, these five years."

I could not deny these facts. They were known to the whole neighborhood. The proudest of our gentry were not wicked enough to shut their eyes to them, even when they contemptuously stared at Mrs. Lemuel Rochdale driving drearily about on long summer afternoons in her lonely carriage, with not a single female friend to pay a morning visit to, or suffer the like infliction from ; not even at church, when, quizzing her large figure and heavy gait — for she had not become more sylph-like with added years—they said she was growing "crumble," like her father's loaves, and wondered she would persist in wearing the finest bonnets in all the congregation.

Nay, even I, bitter as I was, really pitied her one sacrament day, when she unwittingly advanced to the first "rail" of communicants, upon which all the other "respectable" Christians hung back till the second. After that, the Rochdales were not seen again at the communion. Who could marvel ?

It was noticed —by some to his credit, by

others as a point for ridicule—that her husband always treated her, abroad and at home, with respect and consideration. Several times a few hunting neighbors, lunching at the manor-house, brought word how Mrs. Lemuel Rochdale had taken the mistress's place at table, in a grave, taciturn way, so that perforce every one had to forget entirely that he had ever joked and laughed over her father's counter with the ci-devant Nancy Hine.

For that honest old father, he had soon ceased to give any trouble to his aristocratic son-in-law, having died quietly—in a comfortable and honorable bedroom at the manor-house, too—and been buried underneath an equally comfortable and honorable head-stone to the memory of "Mr. Daniel Hine;" "baker" was omitted, to the great indignation of our village, who thought that, if a tradesman could "carry nothing" else, he ought at least to carry the stigma of his trade out with him into the next world.

Mrs. Rochdale came home to the only house in the neighborhood which could be found suitable. It was a little distance from the village, and three miles from the manor-house. Many, I believe, wished her to settle in some other part of the country; but she briefly said that she "preferred" living here.

Her jointure and an additional allowance from the estate, which was fully and regularly paid by my father—still Mr. Rochdale's steward—was, I believe, the only link of association between her and her former home. Nor did she, apparently, seek for more. The only possible or probable chance of her meeting the inhabitants of the manor-house was at Thorpe Church; and she attended a chapel-of-ease in the next parish, which was, as she said, "nearer." She fell into her old habits of charity—her old simple life; and though her means were much reduced, every one, far and near, vied in showing her attention and respect.

But Mrs. Rochdale did not look happy. She had grown much older — was decidedly "an elderly lady" now. Instead of her fair, calm aspect, was a certain unquiet air, a perpetual looking and longing for something she did not find. For weeks after she came to her new house she would start at strange knocks, and gaze eagerly after strange horsemen passing the window, as if she thought, "he *may* come to see his mother." But he did not; and after a time she settled down into the patient dignity of hopeless pain.

Many people said, because Lemuel's name was never heard on her lips, that she cherished an implacable resentment toward him. That, I thought was not true. She might have found it hard to forgive him—most mothers would; but did any mother ever find any pardon impossible?

She had still his boyish portrait hanging beside his father's in her bedroom; and once, opening by chance a drawer usually kept locked, I found it contained—what? Lemuel's child-ish muslin frocks, his boyish cloth cap, his fishing-rod, and an old book of flies.

After that, who could believe his mother "implacable?"

Yet she certainly was a great deal harder than she used to be; harsher and quicker in her judgments; more unforgiving of little faults in those about her. With regard to her son, her mind was absolutely impenetrable. She seemed to have fortified and intrenched herself behind a strong endurance; it would take a heavy stroke to reach the citadel—the poor desolate citadel of the forlorn mother's heart.

The stroke fell. None can doubt Who sent it, nor why it came.

Mrs. Rochdale was standing at the school-house door, when my cousin's lad, George, who had been to see the hunt pass, ran hastily in.

"Oh! mother, the squire's thrown and killed."

"Killed!" Oh, that shriek! May I never live to hear such another!

The tale, we soon found, was incorrect; Mr. Rochdale had only been stunned, and seriously injured, though not mortally. But—his poor mother!

CHAPTER VI.

For an hour she lay on the school-house floor, quite rigid. We thought she would never wake again. When she did, and we slowly made her understand that things were not as fatal as she feared, she seemed hardly able to take in the consolation.

"My bonnet, Martha, my bonnet! I must go to him." But she could not even stand.

I sent for my father. He came, bringing with him Dr. Hall, who had just left Mr. Rochdale.

Our doctor was a good man, whom every body trusted. At sight of him, Mrs. Rochdale sat up and listened—we all listened; no attempt at cold or polite disguises now—to his account of the accident. It was a simple fracture, curable by a few weeks of perfect quiet and care.

"Above all, my dear madam, *quiet*,"—for the doctor had seen Mrs. Rochdale's nervous fastening of her cloak, and her quick glance at the door. "I would not answer for the results of even ten minutes' mental agitation."

Mrs. Rochdale comprehended. A spasm, sharp and keen, crossed the unhappy mother's face. With a momentary pride she drew back.

"I assure you, Dr. Hall, I had no—that is, I have already changed my intention."

Then she leaned back, closed her eyes and her quivering mouth—fast—fast!—folded quietly her useless hands; and seemed as if trying to commit her son, patiently and unrepining, into the care of the only Healer—He "who woundeth, and His hands make whole."

At last she asked suddenly, "Who is with him?"

"His wife," said Dr. Hall, without hesitation.

"She is a good and tender nurse; and he is fond of her."

Mrs. Rochdale was silent.

Shortly afterward she went home in Dr. Hall's carriage; and by her own wish I left her there alone.

CHAPTER VII.

AFTER that dreadful day, every night and morning for five days I went up to the manor-house, and back again to Mrs. Rochdale's cottage, bringing tidings, and hearing the further report, never missed, which came to her through Dr. Hall. It was almost always favorable; yet the agony of that "almost" seemed to stretch the mother's powers of endurance to their utmost limit—at times her face, in its stolid fixed quietness, had an expression half-insane.

Late in the afternoon of the sixth day—it was a rainy December Sunday, and scarcely any one thought of stirring out but me—I was just considering whether it was not time to go to Mrs. Rochdale's, when some person, hooded and cloaked, came up the path to our door. It was herself.

"Martha, I want you. No, thank you; I will not come in."

Yet she leaned a minute against the dripping veranda, pale and breathless.

"Are you afraid of taking a walk with me in this rain—a long walk? No? Then put on your shawl and come."

Though this was all she said, and I made no attempt to question her further, still I knew as well as if she had told me where she was going. We went through miry lanes, and soaking woods, where the partridges started up—whirring across sunk fences, and under gloomy fir-plantations, till at last we came out opposite the manor-house. It looked just the same as in old times, save that there were no peacocks on the terrace, and the swans now never came near the house —no one fed or noticed them.

"Martha, do you see that light in my window? Oh, my poor boy!"

She gasped, struggled for breath, leaned on my arm a minute, and then went steadily up, and rang the hall-bell.

"I believe there is a new servant; he may not know you, Mrs. Rochdale;" I said, to prepare her.

But she needed no preparation. She asked in the quietest way—as if paying an ordinary call—for "Mrs. Lemuel Rochdale."

"Mistress is gone to lie down, ma'am. Master was worse, and she was up all night with him. But he is better again to-day, thank the Lord!"

The man seemed really affected, as though both "master" and "mistress" were served with truer than lip-service.

"I will wait to see Mrs. Lemuel," said Mrs. Rochdale, walking right into the library.

The man followed, asking respectfully what name he should say.

"Merely a lady."

We waited about a quarter of an hour. Then Mrs. Lemuel appeared—somewhat fluttered, looking, in spite of her handsome dress, a great deal shyer and more modest than the girl Nancy Hine.

"I beg pardon, ma'am, for keeping you waiting; I was with my husband. Perhaps you're a stranger, and don't know how ill he has been. I beg your pardon."

Mrs. Rochdale put back her vail, and Mrs. Lemuel seemed as if, in common phrase, "she could have dropped through the floor."

"I daresay you are surprised to see me here," the elder lady began; "still, you will well imagine, a mother—" She broke down. It was some moments before she could command herself to say, in broken accents, "I want to see —my son."

"That you shall, with pleasure, Mrs. Rochdale," said Nancy, earnestly. "I thought once of sending for you; but—"

The other made some gesture to indicate that she was not equal to conversation, and hastily moved up stairs—Nancy following. At the chamber-door, however, Nancy interrupted her, "Stop one minute, please. He has been so very ill; do let me tell him first, just to prepare—"

"He is my son—my own son. You need not be afraid," said Mrs. Rochdale, in tones of which I know not whether bitterness or keen anguish was uppermost. She pushed by the wife, and went in.

We heard a faint cry, "Oh, mother, my dear mother!" and a loud sob—that was all.

Mrs. Lemuel shut the door, and sat down on the floor outside, in tears. I forgot she had been Nancy Hine, and wept with her.

It was a long time before Mrs. Rochdale came out of her son's room. No one interrupted them, not even the wife. Mrs. Lemuel kept restlessly moving about the house—sometimes sitting down to talk familiarly with me, then recollecting herself and resuming her dignity. She was much improved. Her manners and her mode of speaking had become more refined. It was evident, too, that her mind had been a good deal cultivated, and that report had not lied when it avouched sarcastically, that the squire had left off educating his dogs and taken to educating his wife. If so, she certainly did her master credit. But Nancy Hine was always considered a "bright" girl.

Awkward she was still—large and gauche and underbred—wanting in that simple self-possession which needs no advantages of dress or formality of manner to confirm the obvious fact of innate "ladyhood." But there was nothing coarse or repulsive about her—nothing that would strike one as springing from that internal and ineradicable "vulgarity," which, being in the nature as much as in the bringing-up, no education or external refinement of manner can ever wholly conceal.

I have seen more than one "lady" of undeniable birth and rearing, who was a great deal more "vulgar" than Mrs. Lemuel Rochdale.

We were sitting by the dining-room fire. Servants came, doing the day's mechanical service, and brought in the tray.

Mrs. Lemuel began to fidget about. "Do you think, Miss Martha, she will stay and take some supper? Would she like to remain the night here? Ought I not to order a room to be got ready?"

But I could not answer for any of Mrs. Rochdale's movements.

In process of time she came down, looking calm and happy—oh, inconceivably happy!—scarcely happier, I doubt, even when, twenty-seven years ago, she had received her new-born son into her bosom—her son, now born again to her in reconciliation and love. She even said, with a gentle smile, to her son's wife,

"I think he wants you. Suppose you were to go up stairs?"

Nancy fled like lightning.

"He says," murmured Mrs. Rochdale, looking at the fire, "that she has been a good wife to him."

"She is much improved in many ways."

"Most likely. My son's wife could not fail of that," returned Mrs. Rochdale, with a certain air that forbade all further criticism on Nancy. She evidently was to be viewed entirely as "my son's wife."

Mrs. Lemuel returned. She looked as if she had been crying. Her manner toward her mother-in-law was a mixture of gratitude and pleasure.

"My husband says, since you will not stay the night, he hopes you will take supper here, and return in the carriage."

"Thank you; certainly." And Mrs. Rochdale sat down—unwittingly, perhaps—in her own familiar chair, by the bright hearth. Several times she sighed; but the happy look never altered. And now, wholly and forever, passed away that sorrowful look of seeking for something never found. It was found.

I think a mother, entirely and eternally sure of her son's perfect reverence and love, need not be jealous of any other love, not even for a wife. There is, in every good man's heart, a sublime strength and purity of attachment, which he never does feel, never can feel, for any woman on earth except his mother.

Supper was served; Mrs. Lemuel half-advanced to her usual place, then drew back, with a deprecating glance.

But Mrs. Rochdale quietly seated herself in the guest's seat at the side, leaving her son's wife to take the position of mistress and hostess at the head of the board.

Perhaps it was I only who felt a choking pang of regret and humiliation at seeing my dear, my noble Mrs. Rochdale sitting at the same table with Nancy Hine.

After that Sunday the mother went every day to see her son. This event was the talk of the whole village: some worthy souls were

glad; but I think the generality were rather shocked at the reconciliation. They "always thought Mrs. Rochdale had more spirit;" "wondered she could have let herself down." "But, of course, it was only on account of his illness. She might choose to be 'on terms' with her son, but it was quite impossible she could ever take up with Nancy Hine."

In that last sentiment I agreed. But then the gossips did not know that there was a great and a daily-increasing difference between Mrs. Lemuel Rochdale and "Nancy Hine."

I have stated my creed, as it was Mrs. Rochdale's, that lowness of birth does not necessarily constitute a low marriage. Also, that popular opinion was rather unjust to the baker's daughter. Doubtless she was a clever, ambitious girl, anxious to raise herself, and glad enough to do so by marrying the squire. But I believe she was a virtuous and not unscrupulous girl, and I firmly believe she loved him. Once married, she tried to raise herself so as to be worthy of her station; to keep and deserve her husband's affection. That which would have made a woman of meaner nature insufferably proud, only made Nancy humble. Not that she abated one jot of her self-respect—for she was a high-spirited creature—but she had sense enough to see that the truest self-respect lies, not in exacting honor which is undeserved, but in striving to attain that worth which receives honor and observance as its rightful due.

From this quality in her probably grew the undoubted fact of her great influence over her husband. Also because, to tell the truth—(I would not for worlds Mrs. Rochdale should read this page)—Nancy was of a stronger nature than he. Mild tempered, lazy, and kind, it was easier to him to be ruled than to rule, provided he knew nothing about it. This was why the gentle Celandine could not retain the love which Daniel Hine's energetic daughter won and was never likely to lose.

Mrs. Rochdale said to me, when for some weeks she had observed narrowly the ways of her son's household, "I think he is not unhappy. It might have been worse."

Thenceforward the gentry around Thorpe were "shocked" and "really quite amazed" every week of their lives. First, that poor Mr. Rochdale, looking very ill, but thoroughly content, was seen driving out with his mother by his side, and his wife, in her most objectionable and tasteless bonnet, sitting opposite. Secondly, that the two ladies, elder and younger, were several times seen driving out together, they two, alone! The village could scarcely believe this, even on the evidence of its own eyes. Thirdly, that on Christmas-day Mrs. Rochdale was observed in her old place in the manor-house pew; and when her son and his wife came in, she actually smiled!

After that every body gave up the relenting mother-in-law as a lost woman!

CHAPTER VIII.

Three months slipped away. It was the season when most of our county families were in town. When they gradually returned, the astounding truth was revealed concerning Mrs. Rochdale and her son. Some were greatly scandalized, some pitied the weakness of mothers, but thought that as she was now growing old, forgiveness was excusable.

"But, of course, she can never expect us to visit Mrs. Lemuel?"

"I am afraid not," was the rector's wife's mild remark. "Mrs. Rochdale is unlike most ladies; she is not only a gentlewoman, but a Christian."

Yet it was observable that the tide of feeling against the squire's "low" wife ebbed day by day. First, some kindly stranger publicly that she was "extremely good-looking;" to confirm which, by some lucky chance, poor Nancy grew much thinner, probably with the daily walks to and from Mrs. Rochdale's residence. Wild reports flew abroad that the squire's mother, without doubt one of the most accomplished and well-read women of her generation, was actually engaged in "improving the mind" of her daughter-in-law!

That some strong influence was at work became evident in the daily change creeping over Mrs. Lemuel. Her manners grew quieter, gentler; her voice took a softer tone; even her attire, down, or rather up, to the much abused bonnets, was subdued to colors suitable for her large and showy person. One day a second stranger actually asked "who was that *distingué*-looking woman?" and was coughed down. But the effect of the comment remained.

Gradually the point at issue slightly changed; and the question became:

"I wonder whether Mrs. Rochdale expects us to visit Mrs. Lemuel?"

But Mrs. Rochdale, though, of course, she knew all about it—for every body knew every thing in our village—never vouchsafed the slightest hint one way or the other as to her expectations.

Nevertheless the difficulty increased daily, especially as the squire's mother had been long the object of universal respect and attention from her neighbors. The question, "To visit or not to visit?" was mooted and canvassed far and wide. Mrs. Rochdale's example was strong; yet the "county people" had the prejudices of their class, and most of them had warmly regarded poor Celandine Childe.

I have hitherto not said a word of Miss Childe. She was still abroad. But though Mrs. Rochdale rarely alluded to her, I often noticed how her eyes would brighten at sight of letters in the delicate handwriting I knew so well. The strong attachment between these two nothing had power to break.

One day she sat poring long over one of Celandine's letters, and many times took off her glasses—alas! as I said, Mrs. Rochdale was an old lady now—to wipe the dews from them. At length she called in a clear voice, "Martha!" and I found her standing by the mirror smiling.

"Martha, I am going to a wedding!"

"Indeed! Whose, madam?"

"Miss Childe's. She is to be married next week."

"To whom!" I cried, in unfeigned astonishment."

"Do you remember Mr. Sinclair?"

I did. He was the rector of Ashen Dale. One of the many suitors whom, years ago, popular report had given to Miss Childe.

"Was that really the case, Mrs. Rochdale?"

"Yes. Afterward he became, and has been ever since, her truest, tenderest, most faithful *friend.* Now—"

Mrs. Rochdale sat down, still smiling, but sighing also. I, too, felt a certain pang, for which I blamed myself the moment after, to think that love can ever die and be buried. Yet surely the Maker of the human heart knows it best. One thing I know, and perhaps it would account for a great deal, that the Lemuel of Celandine's love was not, never had been, the real Lemuel Rochdale. Still—

Something in my looks betrayed me; for Mrs. Rochdale, turning round, said, decisively,

"Martha, I am very glad of this marriage, deeply and entirely glad. She will be happy —my poor Celandine!"

And happy she always has been, I believe. After Mrs. Rochdale's return from the wedding, she one day sent for me.

"Martha"—and an amused smile about her mouth reminded me of our lady of the manor in her young days—"I am going to astonish the village. I intend giving a dinner-party. Will you write the invitations?"

They were, without exception, to the "best" families of our neighborhood. Literally *the best*—the worthiest; people, like Mrs. Rochdale herself, to whom "position" was a mere clothing, used or not used, never concealing or meant to conceal the honest form beneath, the common humanity that we all owe alike to father Adam and mother Eve. People who had no need to stickle for the rank that was their birthright, the honor that was their due; whose blood was so thoroughly "gentle" that it inclined them to gentle manners and gentle deeds. Of such —and there are not a few throughout our English land—of such are the true aristocracy.

All Thorpe was on the *qui vive* respecting this wonderful dinner-party, for hitherto—gossip said because she could, of course, have no gentleman at the head of her table—Mrs. Rochdale had abstained from any thing of the kind. Now, would her son really take his rightful place at the entertainment? and if so, what was to be done with his wife? Could our "best" families, much as they esteemed Mrs. Rochdale, ever, under any possible circumstances, be expected to meet the former Nancy Hine?

I need not say how the whole question served

H

for a week's wonder; and how every body knew every other body's thoughts and intentions a great deal better than "other bodies" themselves. Half the village was out at the door or window, when on this memorable afternoon the several carriages were seen driving up to Mrs. Rochdale's house.

Within, we are quiet enough. She had few preparations—she always lived in simple elegance. Even on this grand occasion she only gave what cheer her means could afford—nothing more. Show was needless, for every guest was not a mere acquaintance, but a friend.

Dressed richly, and with special care—how well I remembered, that is, if I had dared to remember, another similar toilet!—Mrs. Rochdale sat in her chamber. Not until the visitors were all assembled did she descend to the drawing-room.

Entering there—she did not enter alone; on her arm was a lady of thirty; large and handsome in figure; plainly but most becomingly attired;—a lady to whose manners or appearance none could have taken the slighest exception, and on whom any stranger's most likely comment would have been, "What a fine-looking woman! but so quiet."

This lady Mrs. Rochdale at once presented to the guests, with a simple, unimpressive quietness, which was the most impressive effect she could have made—

"My daughter, Mrs. Lemuel Rochdale."

In a week, "every body" visited at the manor-house.

*   *   *   *   *   *

Perhaps I ought to end this history by describing the elder and younger Mrs. Rochdale

as henceforward united in the closest sympathy and tenderest affection. It was not so; it would have been unnatural, nay, impossible. The difference of education, habits, character, was too great ever to be wholly removed. But the mother and daughter-in-law maintain a sociable intercourse, even a certain amount of kindly regard, based on one safe point of union, where the strongest attachment of both converges and mingles. Perhaps, as those blessed with a superabundance of faithful love often end by deserving it, Mr. Rochdale may grow worthy, not only of his wife, but of his mother, in time.

Mrs. Rochdale is quite an old lady now. You rarely meet her beyond the lane where her small house stands; which she occupies still, and obstinately refuses to leave. But meeting her, you could not help turning back for another glance at her slow, stately walk, and her ineffably beautiful smile. A smile which, to a certainty, would rest on the gentleman upon whose arm she always leans, and whose horse is seen daily at her gate, with a persistency equal to that of a young man going a-courting. For people say in our village that the squire, with all his known affection for his good wife, is as attentive as any lover to his beloved old mother, who has been such a devoted mother to him.

One want exists at the manor-house—there are no children. For some things this is as well; and yet I know not. However, so it is; and since it is, it must be right to be. When this generation dies out, probably the next will altogether have forgotten the fact that the last Mr. Rochdale made what society ignominiously terms "a low marriage."

THE DOUBLE HOUSE.

"JAMES, the house is let."

"Which?" said Mr. Rivers, never looking up from his dinner—for a dozen patients, scattered over a dozen square miles, were awaiting him.

"The house—the Double House. The one that every body thought would never get a tenant. But it has got one."

"Who?"

"A Dr. Merchiston, a physician, but, luckily for us, he does not practice. He is a man of large fortune."

"Married?—children?"

"I really don't know. But I should rather think not. Most family men would object to that very inconvenient house. It might suit an eccentric bachelor, who could live alone in the one half, and shut up his domestics in the oth-

er, locking the door of communication between. But for a mistress and mother of a family—dear me!—one might as well live in two separate houses. One never could hear the children cry of nights, and the maids might idle as much as they liked without—"

Here I turned round, finding I was talking to the air. My husband had disappeared. It was in vain to attempt to interest *him* about the Double House, or the people that were coming there.

But as to the rest of our village—speculation ran wild concerning the new-comers. First, because a grave, dignified, middle-aged gentleman like Dr. Merchiston — of such composed and quiet manners, too—had chosen to live in this eccentric and uncomfortable mansion; for, as before stated, it went by the name of the

Double House, and consisted of two houses joined together by a covered passage and door of communication, each having its separate entrance, and being, in fact, a complete dwelling. Secondly, because, when the furniture was sent in, it was discovered to be the appointments of two distinct habitations; namely, two drawing-rooms, two dining-rooms, two kitchens, and so on. The wonder grew—when Dr. Merchiston, accompanied by an elderly person, "Mrs. Merchiston's maid," (there was a Mrs. Merchiston, then!) inducted into the establishment two distinct sets of domestics; two cooks, two housemaids, etc.

And now every body waited for the master and mistress, who, we learned, had to make a long journey from London by post—for all this happened when I was a young married woman, more than forty years ago. I had my hands empty then—possibly, my head, too, for I remember loitering about the whole day, and sitting lazily at parlor windows, just to catch the first sight of my new neighbors. Nay, I will confess that when the chaise and four thundered past our house I peeped from under the blind.

In the carriage I saw only the elderly female servant, and a figure leaning back. Dr. Merchiston was certainly not there.

Half an hour afterward he galloped past in the twilight to his own door, which closed upon him as quickly as it had, a short time before, closed upon the others.

"Well, they are come," said I to James that evening.

"Who?" he ejaculated, most provokingly.

"The Merchistons, of course. And nobody is a bit the wiser."

My husband put on his quaintest smile (a merry man, children, was your grandfather)—"Never mind—there's Sunday coming."

My hopes revived. I led a dull life in James's long absences, and had been really anxious for a neighbor—a pleasant neighbor—a true gentlewoman. Yes, of course, we should see the Merchistons at church on Sunday, for a large pew had been taken, cushioned and hassocked to perfection; besides, the doctor looked like a respectable church-going gentleman.

And sure enough, when service began, above the high pew, distinct to the eye of the whole congregation, rose his tall head and shoulders. He was in the prime of life, though his hair was already, as we say of a September tree, "turning." He had a large, well-shaped head, very broad across the crown, just where my grandson tells me lies the bump of conscientiousness; but we never thought of such folly as phrenology in my days. For the face—I do not clearly remember the features, but I know the general impression conveyed was that of a strong will, capable of any amount of self-control or self-denial. The eyes, though honest and clear, had at times much restlessness in them; when steady and fixed, they were, I think, the saddest eyes I ever saw. His countenance was sickly and pale, though he flushed up once or twice on meeting the universal stare—which stare increased tenfold when he actually repeated audibly and devoutly the responses which the Rubric enjoins on the congregation, and the congregation usually delegates to the charity-boys and the clerk.

Except this we could find nothing extraordinary in Dr. Merchiston's appearance or behavior. He sat in his pew alone; he went out as he had entered, silently, quietly, and alone. In another pew sat two of the house-servants and Mrs. Merchiston's maid. The lady herself did not come to church at all that day.

It was rather disappointing—since, by Apedale etiquette, no one could call on Mrs. Merchiston until she had appeared at church. But we heard during the week that the Rector had called on Dr. Merchiston.

I tried to persuade Mr. Rivers to do the same—it would be only kind and neighborly. After half an hour's coaxing, which, apparently, was all thrown away, he briefly observed,

"Peggy, I've been."

"Oh! do tell me all about it, from the very beginning. Which door did you knock at? The one with a brass plate, and 'Dr. Merchiston' on it?"

"Yes."

"And you saw him? You were shown up to the drawing-room or the library—which?"

"Library."

"Was he alone? Was he polite and pleasant? Did you see his wife?"

Two nods and a shake of the head were all the answer I received to these three questions.

"Dear me! How odd! I hope you inquired after her? How did her husband say she was?"

"Quite well."

"Nothing more?"

"Nothing more."

"Well—you are the most provoking man to get any thing out of."

"And you, my Peggy, are one of those excellent women who will never cease trying hard to get out of a man things which he absolutely does not know."

I laughed; for what was the use of quarreling? Besides, didn't I know all James's little peculiarities before I married him?

"Just one question more, James. Have they any children?"

"Didn't ask."

So the whole Merchiston affair stood precisely where it was—until the next Sunday. Then, in the afternoon, as I walked to church, I saw a lady come quietly out of the Double House, at the left-hand door—not the one with the brass name-plate—close it after her, and proceed alone across the road and down Church-alley.

She paused a moment in the church-yard walk, which was very beautiful in the May afternoon, with the two great trees meeting overhead, and throwing checkers of light and shade on the path leading to the porch. She looked around as if she admired and enjoyed this scene, with its picturesque groups of twos and threes—fathers and mothers, husbands and wives, lingering about and talking till the chime of bells should cease. She looked apparently with a kindly interest on them all, and then, as if suddenly conscious that they looked back inquisitively at her, dropped her vail and hurriedly entered the church.

I heard her asking the sexton in a low voice, which seemed to belong to a woman still young, "which was Dr. Merchiston's pew?"

She was shown in, and then—being small of stature—she entirely vanished from my gaze and that of the congregation.

Could it be that this was Mrs. Merchiston?

I do not exaggerate when I say that I had six successive "droppers-in" on the Monday morning—to my great inconvenience, for I was making my cowslip-wine—I should say, my first attempt at this potent liquor—and that the sole subject of conversation was Mrs. Merchiston.

"What a tiny woman!" "How plainly dressed! why, her pelisse was quite old-fashioned." "Yet somebody said she was young." "He does not seem above forty, either." "How strange that he should let her go to church alone—the first time of her appearance, too!"

Such were the comments, blended with a small quantum of lately-elicited facts, which reached me concerning my new neighbors. "Very odd people—exceedingly queer—ought to be inquired into," was the general conclusion. All the village began to discuss the Double House, the duplicate establishment, and the notable facts that, since their arrival, Dr. Merchiston had been seen out every day, Mrs. Merchiston never; that Dr. Merchiston had come to church, Mrs. Merchiston staying at home, and vice versa.

The result was, the Apedale ladies cautiously resolved to defer "visiting" the strangers a little longer, till assured of their respectability; and I being myself a new-comer, hating gossip, scandal, and censoriousness, with the virulence of warm-hearted, all-credulous youth, inly determined to call the next day.

But first, of course, I asked my husband's leave; and gaining it, hazarded a question or two further, since James, from his profession and long standing in the county, knew everybody and every thing.

"Who is he, Peg? I know no more than that he is Evan Merchiston, M.D., of the University of Glasgow."

"And Mrs. Merchiston?"

"Was Barbara, only child of Thomas and Barbara Currie, late of Apedale in this county, who were drowned at sea in seventeen hundred and—"

"Stop, stop! you are like an animated tombstone reading itself aloud. The very stone—I have seen it in our own church-yard. And so she was born at Apedale? That accounts for their coming to settle here."

"Precisely. Any thing more, Peg?"

"No, James;" for I was ashamed of my own doubts, as if that soft, mild face I caught a glimpse of under the vail, and the manly, benevolent head which I had watched the previous Sunday, did not prove, despite all gossip, that the Merchistons were "respectable"—even in my sense of the word, which was wider than that of my neighbors. "A respectable man"—as James once said when he was courting me—"a respectable man is one who is always worthy of respect, because he always respects both himself and other people."

Perhaps it was to prove my own "respectability" in this sense—and justly I might respect myself—namely, the happy woman who was James Rivers's wife—that I dressed myself in my very best muslin gown of my own working, and my pretty green silk spencer and hat that my mother gave when I was married, preparatory to calling on Mrs. Merchiston.

At the Double House arose a puzzle. There were two front doors, and which should I knock at? After some doubt, I thought I could not do better than follow in my husband's steps, so I gave a summons at the door with the brass plate on it.

A man, half valet, half groom, answered.

"Is Mrs. Merchiston at home?"

"I don't know, ma'am; I will inquire, if you please. Will you be so kind as to knock at the other door?"

Upon which, with some abruptness, he shut this one, and left me outside.

"Well," thought I, "what can it signify which door I go in at? though 'tis rather odd, too."

However, I did as I was bidden, and was shown by a neat maid-servant into a very handsome parlor—drawing-room you would call it now, but drawing-rooms had not then reached Apedale.

By the appearance of a recently vacated sitting-room you can make a very good guess at its occupant. I soon decided that Mrs. Merchiston was young, inclined to elegant tastes, especially music, that she had no children, was left a good deal alone, and probably found herself in that dreariest position for an active mind —that of a lady with nothing to do.

After a considerably long interval she appeared. Her welcome was courteous, even friendly, though not without a slight nervousness and hesitation.

It certainly had not been her toilet that kept me waiting, for she was in the simplest possible morning-gown of nankeen, and her hair would not have taken a minute's dressing, as it curled all round her head in natural, wavy curls like a child's. Very childlike, too, were both the figure and face; I could hardly believe that she must be, from the date of her parents' death on the tombstone, nearly, if not quite, thirty years old. She was not exactly pretty, but the expression of her blue eyes was very beautiful, perfectly simple, trusting, guileless, and gay. She was, in short, just the sort of woman that I should have expected a grave man like Dr. Merchiston to choose out from the world of much cleverer and lovelier women, and love deeply, perhaps even madly, to the end of his days.

I was quite satisfied, nay, charmed with her. When we parted, after a much longer chat than etiquette required, I invited her warmly to our house.

"I shall be happy to come in a friendly way, but I believe Dr. Merchiston does not wish for much visiting."

This was the first time the doctor's name had entered into our conversation, so I politely inquired after his health, stating that I had seen him in church, and hoping I should soon have the pleasure of an introduction to him. I expected she would take the hint, send for her husband, and perform the desired introduction now.

But Mrs. Merchiston did nothing of the kind; she merely answered my inquiries as briefly as civility allowed, and evaded the subject. Curiosity was too strong; I could not let it go.

"I hope sincerely that it is not on account of illness that Dr. Merchiston abstains from visiting. My husband thought he looked in rather weak health."

"Does he look so? In weak health? Oh no—oh no!"

All the wife was indicated in that start—that flush—that paleness. Yet she had answered indifferently when I inquired after him; and in her conversation and the surroundings of this room there was no more trace of Dr. Merchiston than if he never entered there, or indeed no longer existed. Likewise in her form of speech I had noticed not the habitual happy "we" which most married people learn to use, but the sad, involuntarily selfish "I" of spinsters and childless widows. It was incomprehensible.

I hastened to atone for my inadvertence. "Indeed, my dear Mrs. Merchiston, you need not be alarmed. It must be only his natural paleness which strikes a stranger; while you who see him every day—"

"Oh, that is it—that is it," she hurriedly answered, and took me to the window to show me her flowers. Very soon after, I departed.

Some weeks passed; she returned my visit, and, of course, I paid a second. Several of our village wives and mothers called likewise. It was always the same story: they had been received with courtesy, were delighted with Mrs. Merchiston, but no one ever saw her husband. And when the fathers of families, one after another, paid their respects to the doctor, they likewise returned well pleased, pronounced him a pleasant, good-hearted, gentlemanly fellow, but wondered that he never introduced them to his wife.

Two dinner-parties were made for the new-comers, and the invitations accepted; but ere

the first, Mrs. Merchiston was "slightly indisposed;" and at the second, Dr. Merchiston was "unavoidably absent on business." So that to both dinners each one came alone; nevertheless, the impression they severally left behind was that of "exceedingly nice people."

At this time I did not go out much; and some weeks after, your mother, children, was born. She cost me a long illness, almost my life; but she throve well, and at last I recovered. Mrs. Merchiston was among my first visitors.

I was glad to see her, for she had been very kind. Many a basket of fruit and flowers had come from the Double House to ours. I thanked her as warmly as I felt.

"And your husband, too—I do believe he has shot half the partridges in the county for my benefit—I have had so many; besides, it was he who rode twelve miles to fetch James that night they thought me dying."

"Was it?"

"Did you not know? Then do tell him, Mrs. Merchiston, how much I thank him for his goodness—for the comfort, the help he was to my poor James! Ah! he could understand what a husband feels when his wife is dying."

Mrs. Merchiston stooped over the new cradle with the little one asleep. She did not speak a word.

"But you will tell him," pursued I, earnest in my gratitude. "What an excellent man he must be!"

"He is," she answered, in a tone evidently steadied carefully down, even to coldness. "It is always a pleasure to him to do a kindness to any one. May I look at the baby?"

She walked up and down the parlor, lulling it on her arms. It nestled its wee face into her bosom.

"No, I am not your mother, little one. Ah, no!"

She gave the child back to me and turned away. Her eyes were full of tears.

Then taking a chair by me, and softly stroking baby's fingers, she said, "Children, I believe, are a great responsibility and a heavy care; but I think it is a sadder thing still never to have had a child. There can be no love, no happiness like a mother's; it often atones for the loss of all other love—all other happiness."

"Do you think so?"

"Yes, at times. Because motherhood must forever take away the selfishness of grief. How could a woman feel selfish or desolate—how could she indeed know any personal grief at all, if she had a child?"

"You are speaking less as a wife would feel than a widow. And you and I, Mrs. Merchiston, can not, need not, dare not, talk as widows."

"God forbid," she said, with a shiver.

I took an early opportunity of sending baby away, and talking of everyday things. I have great pity for a childless wife, unless, as rarely happens in this world, her marriage is so supremely happy that the brimming cup leaves not another drop to be desired. Yet even then its sweetness is apt to cloy, or become a sort of dual egotism, which feels no love, sympathizes with no sorrow, and shares no joy, that is not strictly its own. Forgetting, perhaps, that perfect wedded union is not meant for the satisfaction of the two only, but also that from their oneness of bliss they may radiate a wide light of goodness and blessedness out upon the world.

I rather wondered, knowing from report and from my own experience what good people the Merchistons were, that they did not both try more to live this life, which would certainly have made them happier than she, at least, appeared. Yet, as I said, I pitied her. No one can see the skeleton in his neighbor's house, or the worm in his friend's heart; yet we know, as our experience of life grows wider, that both must assuredly be there.

Mrs. Merchiston and I had a very pleasant chat; the baby had opened our hearts. We were growing better than acquaintance—friends. We planned social evenings for the ensuing winter, in which, when he came in, Mr. Rivers cordially joined.

"And I hope we shall see the doctor too, madam," continued he, breaking out into impressiveness, and discarding laconicism; "there isn't a man alive I respect more than your husband."

She colored vividly, but merely observed, "You are right—I thank you."

We were all standing at our door, she being just about to take leave. Suddenly she drew back within. At that moment there passed close by—so close that he must have touched his wife's dress—Dr. Merchiston.

He looked in, distinctly saw us all, and we him.

"Doctor—doctor!" cried my husband.

In crossing the street, Dr. Merchiston turned, bowed in reply, but did not stop.

"Excuse me, I had something to say to him," cried James, and was off, without a glance at Mrs. Merchiston.

But when I looked at her I was really alarmed. Her limbs were tottering, her countenance pale as death. I helped her back into the parlor, and made her lie down; but all my efforts could scarcely keep her from fainting. At length she said, feebly,

"Thank you, I am better now. It is very wrong of me. But I could not help it. Oh, Mrs. Rivers"—with a piteous, bewildered look —"if you had been his wife, and had not seen him for two whole years!"

"Him! Is it possible you mean your husband?"

"Yes, my own husband—my dear husband, who loved me when he married me. God knows what I have done that he should not love me now!—Oh me! what have I been saying?"

"Never mind what you have been saying, my dear lady, I shall keep it all secret. There now, it will do you good to cry."

And I cried too, heartily. It seemed very dreadful. That young, fond, pretty creature, to live under the same roof as her husband, and not to have seen him for two whole years. Here was explained the mystery of the Double House—here was confirmation entire of those few straggling reports which, when I caught them flying abroad, I had utterly quenched, denied, and disbelieved. I was greatly shocked, and, as was natural, I took the woman's side of the question.

"And I thought him so good, and you so happy! What deceivers men are!"

"You are mistaken, Mrs. Rivers, in one man at least," she returned, with dignity; "your husband spoke truly when he said there was no man living more worthy of respect than Dr. Merchiston."

"He has not lost yours, then?"

"In no point."

"And you love him still?"

"I do; God pity me—I do." She sobbed as if her heart were breaking.

There was then but one conclusion to be drawn—one only reason for a good man's thus mercilessly putting away his wife,—some error on her part, either known or imagined by him. But no! when I looked down on her gentle, innocent, childlike face, I rejected the doubt as impossible. Nor had I detected in her any of those inherent, incurable faults of temper or of character, the "continual dropping that weareth away the stone," which, if divorce be ever justifiable for any thing short of crime, would have justified it in some marriages I have seen.

"Does any body know? Not that I mind, but it might harm him. Mrs. Rivers, do you think any body at Apedale knows?"

"Alas, in a village like this, there can be no such thing as a secret."

She wrung her hands. "I thought so—I feared so. But he came to live in the country because the doctors said London air was killing me. I wish it had killed me—oh, I wish it had!"

I have seen the look of despair in many a wronged, miserable wife's eyes, but I never saw it so mournfully plain as in those of poor Barbara Merchiston. I took her to my arms, though she was older than I, and asked her to let me comfort her and be her friend, if she had no other.

"Not one—not one. But"—and she started back with a sudden fear—"you will not be my friend by becoming an enemy to my husband?"

"I have no such intention. I condemn him not: to his own Master let him stand or fall."

Probably this was harshly spoken, for she took my hand, saying, imploringly, "Pray do not misjudge either him or me. I was very wrong in betraying any thing. But my life is so lonely. I am not strong; and this shock was too much for me. How ill he looked—how gray he has grown! Oh, Evan, my poor husband!"

To see her weeping there, without the slightest anger or wounded pride, roused both feelings in me. I determined to fathom this mysterious affair; and, braving the usual fate of those who interfere between man and wife—namely, being hated by both parties—to try and remedy it if I could.

"Tell me, my dear Mrs. Merchiston—believe me it is from no idle curiosity I ask—how long has this state of things lasted?"

"For five years."

"Five years!" I was staggered. "Entire separation and estrangement for five years! And for no cause? Are you sure—oh, forgive me if I wound you—but are you sure there is no cause?"

"I declare before Heaven—none! He has never blamed me in word or deed."

"Nor given you reason to blame him?" said I, with a sharp glance, still strongly inclining to the rights of my own sex.

"Me—blame him?—blame my husband?" she answered, with a look of half-reproachful wonder. "I told you he loved me." •

"But love changes," continued I, very cautiously, for it was hard to meet her large innocent eyes, like a gazelle's, with your hand on its throat. "Men sometimes come to love other women than their wives."

She flushed indignantly all over her face. "You wrong him—you wickedly wrong him. His life is, and always has been, as spotless as my own."

Well, thought I, I give it up. Either she is extraordinarily deceived, and the hypocrisy of that man is such as never was man's before, or the problem is quite beyond my solving. Yet —one more attempt.

"Just a word. Tell me, Mrs. Merchiston, how and when did this sad estrangement begin?"

"Six months after our marriage. We married for love; we were both alone in the world; we were all in all to one another. Gradually he grew melancholy—I could not find out why; he said it would pass away in time. Then he had a fever—I nursed him through it. When he recovered—he—sent me away."

The brute! I thought. Just like a man!

"But how?" I said aloud. "What reason did he give? What excuse could he offer?"

"None. He only wrote to me, when away on a short journey, and told me that this separation must be—that it was absolutely inevitable—that if I desired it he would leave me altogether—otherwise, it was his earnest wish we should still live under the same roof. But never, never meet."

"And you never have met?"

"Very rarely—only by the merest chance. Then he would pass me by, never lifting his eyes. Once—it was in the first few weeks of our separation—I met him on the stair-case. I was different from what I am now, Mrs. Rivers; very proud, outraged, indignant. I flung past him, but he caught me in his arms. I would not speak; I stood upright in his clasp

like stone. 'We have been happy, Barbara.' 'But never can be again,' I cried, passionately. 'No,' he said; 'I know that—never again.' He held me close a moment or two, then broke from me. We have never met since."

Such was her story, which the more I dived into it, became the more incomprehensible. No condemnatory evidence could be found against the husband; in all things Mrs. Merchiston's comforts were studied, her wishes gratified. She said it often seemed as if an invisible watch were kept over her, to provide against her least desire. I could only counsel the poor wife to patience, hope, and trust in God.

She left me a little comforted. I asked her would she not stay? was she not afraid of meeting him in the street?

"Oh, no," she sighed, "he seems to know intuitively my goings out and my comings in. I never see him—never—not even by chance. I can not guess how it happened to-day. How ill he looked!" she added, recurring again to what seemed uppermost in her thoughts. "Mrs. Rivers, will you entreat your husband to watch over him—to take care of him? Promise me you will."

I promised her, poor tender thing! and inwardly determined to watch him myself with a closer eye than that of my simple-hearted husband, to whom, of course, I told the whole matter.

He, like me, was now fairly bewildered. "Peggy," he said, "hadn't you better let the thing alone?"

"Let it alone," I cried, "such cruel sorrow, such a flagrant wrong—never!"

"Well," kissing me, "perhaps you are right, Peg, my dear. Happy folk ought to help the miserable."

I set to work. Woman's wit is keen, and I had my share of the quality.

We invited Dr. Merchiston to our house; he came, at first rarely, then frequently. Of course Mrs. Merchiston was always included in these invitations, and, of course, we received duly the formal apology. Gradually this ceased, and he came still. He must have known that she came too, on other days: often he found books and work of hers lying about my table; yet his visits ceased not. He seemed to like to come. He and my husband became stanch friends, but as for me, despite his courtesy, my heart remained angry and sore against him.

Yet I must confess that we found him all his wife fondly believed; a man of keen intellect, high principle, generous and tender heart. If I had not known what I did know, I should have avouched, unhesitatingly, that the world did not contain a nobler man than Dr. Merchiston. Excepting, of course, my James.

For his manners, they were simple, natural, kind; not in any way eccentric, or indicative of vice or folly. Among our neighbors his character rose to the highest pitch of estimation; and when, at last, the fatal truth was known (alas! what household misery can ever long be hid, especially in a country place), all sorts of excuses and apologies were made for him.

And cruelly, mournfully—as it always falls on the weaker side—fell the lash of the world's tongue upon his wife.

But I—and one or two more who knew and loved her—stood boldly by Mrs. Merchiston through fair report and foul. And I believe, so great was the mingled awe and respect which the Doctor impressed upon all his acquaintance, that no portion of these calumnies against her reached her husband.

Three months slipped by without change, save that Mrs. Merchiston's sad lot grew sadder still. Her few acquaintance dropped her; it was so "extremely inconvenient." One lady was on thorns whenever Mrs. Merchiston called, lest Dr. Merchiston should chance to call likewise; another tried every conceivable diplomacy to bring about their meeting—it would be "so very amusing." Gradually the unfortunate wife could not walk down our village without being pointed at, or crossed aside from, till she rarely went out at all.

Dr. Merchiston, too, was seldom seen, except by his immediate friends, none of whom dared breathe a word to him concerning his domestic affairs, save the simple inquiries of courtesy after Mrs. Merchiston, to which he invariably answered in the customary form, as any other husband would answer. I think, in fact I know, that all this time he believed her to be living at peace; perfectly happy in her beautiful house in our cheerful village, and in a small society of her own choosing, of which I was the chief. He once hinted as much to me, expressing his great pleasure that Mrs. Merchiston and myself were fast friends.

I hardly know what possessed me that I did not then and there burst out upon him with a piece of my mind; any "woman of spirit"—as James sometimes called me—would have done it. What was he but a man?

Ay, there was the difficulty. His perfect manliness disarmed one; that quiet dignity of reserve, which, I have noticed, while women are ready enough to complain of their husbands, keeps nine men out of ten from ever saying a word against their wives. Then, too, the silent deprecation of his sickly mien, and of the ineffable, cureless melancholy which, the moment he ceased conversation, arose in his dark eyes. What could a tender-hearted woman do? Beginning by hating and despising, I often ended in pitying him, and every time I saw him all my determinations to attack him about his domestic wickedness vanished in air.

Besides—as James astutely observed—if a wife obstinately persists in blindly obeying her husband, never asking the why and the wherefore of his insane and incomprehensible will, and concealing from him that she is wasting away in slow misery, what business has a third party to accuse or even acquaint him of the fact?

Was no other plan to be tried? Yes; accidentally one was forced into my mind.

On a winter's afternoon, when I sat with my baby over our happy Christmas fire, Mrs. Merchiston came rushing in.

"Hide me—any where; let nobody find me. Mrs. Rivers, they hoot at me down the street. They say—oh, I dare not think what they say, and I dare not tell him. Perhaps—oh, horror! —perhaps he thinks so too."

Long shudders possessed her; it was some time before she gained the slightest composure. It was not difficult for me to guess the cause of her anguish.

"Never mind wicked tongues, Mrs. Merchiston, they will cease if let alone. Only live in peace and patience. Hope in God still."

"I can't," she said, with a wild look that I had not before seen. "How should I hope in Him? He has forsaken me; why should I live any longer? Oh! save me, save me! Let me go away from here, from my husband. I must go, their cruel tongues will kill me."

"You shall," I cried, with a sudden idea, as suddenly converted into a resolution, "you shall, and I will help you."

Whereupon I explained all to her; somewhat hastily, for I was afraid of Mr. Rivers coming home; he who had just a man's notion of marital authority, and the wickedness of conjugal rebellion. But this was a case in which I set even him at defiance—or rather, I trusted to my own influence to convince him that, acting from my conscience solely, I acted right.

Mark me, children, I would have a woman submit to any lawful authority, even unjustly and cruelly exercised, so long as the misery does not ruin her soul. When the torment goads her thus far—when, like Job's wife, the devil tempts her to "curse God and die," then, I hold, all duty ceases, except to her Maker and herself, the creature which He made; let her save her own soul and flee!

My counsel to Mrs. Merchiston was this: at once—openly if she could, secretly if that was impossible—to leave her husband, absolutely and entirely, exacting no maintenance, making neither excuse nor accusation.

It necessarily followed that she must earn her own bread; and she must immediately seek a position that would place her fair fame above suspicion, both now and at any future time.

This is how I planned it.

I had a sister, a well-jointured widow, with a large family. I proposed to place my poor friend with her as a governess. Mrs. Merchiston eagerly assented. She had been a teacher, she said, in her youth, so that the duty would be easy, and she could fulfill it well.

"And oh!" she cried, while the tears ran down her face, "I shall be in a household, a home among children. Perhaps the little things will love m'."

Poor desolate soul!

I will not detail the many evening lectures that were required to bring my husband to my own way of thinking. For one thing he inexorably held out, and finally I agreed with him that Dr. Merchiston should be openly and honorably informed of his wife's intended departure.

She wrote to him herself in our house. James and I both read the letter. It was as follows:

"DEAR HUSBAND.—Forgive my addressing you against your implied desire. Forgive my asking once more, and for the last time, what have I done to you? Why are you estranged from me? I can no longer sustain the life I lead. I desire to leave you. I am going to be a governess, as I was before we were married. Already all my plans are formed, but I could not part from you without this forewarning and farewell.

"Your wife, BARBARA."

This—the last and most carefully, even coldly worded, of the many letters she wrote and tore up—was left, to avoid remarks, by my own servant at Dr. Merchiston's door.

On the evening of that day Mrs. Merchiston came to my house. She looked white and shivering, but not with the cold. Her poor blue eyes, so warm and kind, had a frosty glitter in them that was strange and sad.

"No answer," she kept repeating; "no answer—none. Now I *must* go."

I replied that every thing was ready; our gig would be at the door in a minute; it was a bright moonlight night, and I myself would accompany her to my sister's house.

"It is not far—not so very far, Mrs. Rivers? Not so far but that I can always hear of him, or—if he should be ill at any time—"

"You can go home at once."

"Home!" she echoed, piteously. Then, as if stung into one desperate effort, the last struggle of her tender and feeble nature, she sprang into the gig, I following her.

I was scarcely seated, reins in hand, for I was determined that no other than myself should have the credit of eloping with Mrs. Merchiston, than I felt on my right arm a grasp like a vice.

"Mrs. Rivers, whom have you there? Is it my wife?"

"Yes, Dr. Merchiston," I cried, not in the least frightened by the look and tone; "yes, it is your wife. I am taking her to where she will live in peace, and not be killed by inches any longer. Stand aside; let me drive on."

"In one moment. Pardon me;" he passed in front of the horse to the other side. "Barbara? Is that you, Barbara?"

No words could describe the ineffable tenderness, the longing anguish of that voice. No wonder that it made her grasp my arm, and cry wildly on me to stop.

"It is not ten minutes since I received your letter. Barbara, grant me one word in the presence of this lady, by whose advice you are leaving your husband."

"By whose advice did you forsake your wife, Dr. Merchiston?" I began, boldly; but by the carriage-lamp I caught sight of his face, and it seemed like that of a man literally dying—dying of despair. "Mrs. Merchiston, suppose we re-enter my house for a while. Doctor, will you lift your wife down? She has fainted."

Soon the poor lady was sitting in my parlor, I by her side. Dr. Merchiston stood opposite, watching us both. He was neither violent nor reproachful, but perfectly silent. Nevertheless, I felt somewhat uncomfortable, and glad from my heart that James was safe ten miles off, and that I alone had been mixed up with this affair.

"She is better now, Mrs. Rivers. I may speak?"

"Speak, sir."

"I will pass over my present trying position. Of course, I perceive—in fact, I was already aware—that Mrs. Merchiston has acquainted you with our sad, inevitable estrangement."

"Why inevitable? When there has been no quarrel on either side? When, cruel as you have been to her, she has never breathed a word to your discredit?" (He groaned.) "When, as I understand, you have not the shadow of blame to urge against her?"

"Before Heaven, none. Have I not declared this, and will I not declare it before all the world? She knows I will."

"Then why, my dear sir, in the name of all that is good and honorable—nay, even in the name of common sense, why is your estrangement inevitable?"

He seemed to cower and shudder as before some inexpressible dread; once he glanced wildly round the room, as if with the vague idea of escaping. Finally, he forced himself to speak, with a smile that was most painful to witness.

"Mrs. Rivers, even though a lady asks me, I can not answer that question."

"Can you if your wife herself asks it? I will leave you together."

As I rose to go, Dr. Merchiston interposed. The cold sweat stood on his brow; he looked—yes, I thought so at the moment—like a possessed man struggling with his inward demon.

"For God's sake, no! For the love of mercy, no! Stay by her; take care of her. I will speak in your presence; I will not detain you long."

"You had better not. See," for the poor wife was again insensible. Dr. Merchiston rushed to her side; he chafed her hands; he fell on his knees before her; but as she opened her eyes he crept away, and put the room's length between them.

"Now may I speak? You wished to leave me, Barbara. To go whither?"

I told him, concealing nothing; he seemed greatly shocked.

"Mrs. Rivers," he said at length, "such a scheme is impossible. I will never consent to it. If she desires, she shall leave my house, for yours or any other. She shall have any luxuries she pleases; she shall be as free from me as if I were dead and she a widow. But that my wife should quit the shelter of my roof to earn her daily bread—I never will allow it."

From this decision there was no appeal. The wife evidently desired none; her eyes began to shine with joy, and even I took hope.

"But, Dr. Merchiston, can there be no

change? You loved one another once. Love is not yet dead ; love never wholly dies. Surely—"

"Madam, silence!"

Could it be his voice that spoke ; his once calm, low voice? I was now really terrified.

He rose and walked about the room; we two sat trembling. At last he stopped in his old position, with his hand on the mantle-piece.

"Mrs. Rivers, my extremely painful position—you will acknowledge it is such—must excuse any thing in me unbecoming, uncourteous."

I assured him he had my free pardon for any excitement, and I hoped he felt calmer now.

"Perfectly, perfectly ; you must see that, do you not?"

"I do," said I, with a sense of bitterness against the whole race of mankind, who can drive poor womankind almost out of their senses, while they themselves preserve the most sublime composure.

"I will now, with your permission and in your presence, speak to my wife. Barbara"—in a quiet equal tone, as if addressing an ordinary person—"I told you five years ago that it is not I who am inexorable, but fate, even if the life we then began to lead should last until my death. I repeat the same now. Yet, for these five years you have been at peace and safe. Safe," he repeated, with a slight pause, "under my roof, where I can shelter and protect you better than any where else."

"Protect her?" And then I told him—how could I help it?—of the slights and outrages to which their manner of life had exposed her. How every idle tongue in the neighborhood had wagged at her expense, and to both their dishonor. It was terrible to see the effect produced on him.

"Hush! tell me no more, or—Barbara, forgive me ; forgive me that I ever made you my wife. There is but one atonement ; shall I make you *my widow?*"

"Doctor Merchiston," I cried, catching his arm, "are you mad?"

He started, shuddered, and in a moment had recovered all his self-control.

"Mrs. Rivers, this is a state of things most terrible, of which I was totally ignorant. How is it to be remedied?—Granting, as you *must* grant, the one unalterable necessity?"

I thought a minute, and then proposed, to silence the tongue of all Apedale, that the husband and wife should openly walk to church together every Sunday, and kneel together in the house of God. And may He forgive me if in this scheme I had a deeper hope than I betrayed.

"I will do it," said Dr. Merchiston, after a pause. "Barbara, do you consent? Will you come home?"

"I will."

"But to the old life? In nothing changed —for changed it can not, must not be?"

"Under any circumstances I will come home."

"Thank you ; God bless you. It is better so."

There was a quiet pause, broken only by one or two faint sobs from her. At last they ceased. Dr. Merchiston took his hat to depart; as he was going, his wife started up and caught him by the hand.

"Husband, one word, and I can bear all things. Did—did you ever love me?"

"Love you? Oh, my little Barbara!"

"*Do* you love me?"

"Yes," in a whisper, sharp with intolerable pain ; "yes."

"Then I do not mind any thing. Oh no, thank God! I do not mind."

She burst into hysterical laughter, and threw herself into my arms. It was only my arms she could come to—her husband was gone.

She went home as she had promised, and the old life began once more. Without the slightest change, she told me—save that regularly on Sunday mornings he knocked at the door of communication between the double house, kept always locked on her side, by his desire—that she found him waiting in the hall, and they walked arm in arm, as silently and sadly as mourners after a corpse, to the church door. In the same way returning, he immediately parted from her, and went his way to his own apartments.

Apedale was quite satisfied, and circulated innumerable explanations, which had probably as much truth in them as the former accusations.

Dr. Merchiston came as usual to play chess with my husband, and no allusion was ever made to the night which had witnessed so strange a scene in our house.

Mrs. Merchiston improved in health and cheerfulness. To a woman the simple conviction of being loved is support and strength through the most terrible ordeal. Once sure of that, her faith is infinite, her consolation complete. After his "Yes," poor little Barbara revived like a flower in the sun.

Not so her husband. Every body noticed that Dr. Merchiston was wasting away to a shadow. On Sundays, especially, his countenance, always sallow and worn, seemed to me to have the ghastly look of one whom you know to be inwardly fighting a great soul-battle. You feel at once the warfare will be won—but the man will die.

And still, as ever, of all the impenetrable mysteries that life can weave, that man and his secret were the darkest.

At least to me. Whether it was so to my husband, whose reserved habits and wide experience of human nature helped to make him what, thank Heaven, he always was—much wiser than I—I do not know; but I often caught his grave penetrating eye intently fixed on Dr. Merchiston. So much so, that more than once the Doctor recoiled from it uneasily. But Mr. Rivers redoubled his kindness ; in truth, I never knew James, who was very undemonstrative, and usually engrossed between interest in his patients and his domestic affections, attach himself so strongly to any male friend out of his own home, as he did to Dr. Merchiston.

He seized every opportunity to allure our neighbor from his morbid, solitary in-door life to a more wholesome existence. They rode out together on the medical rounds—James trying to interest him in the many, many opportunities of philanthropy with which a country surgeon's life abounds. Sometimes—one day I especially remember—Dr. Merchiston said he thought Mr. Rivers had familiarized him with every possible aspect of human pain.

"Not all—I have yet to show you—indeed, I thought of doing so this morning—the blackest aspect human suffering can show. And yet, like all suffering, a merciful God has not left it without means of alleviation."

"What do you mean? I thought we were going to some hospital. For what disease?"

"No physical disease. Yet one which I believe, like all other diseases, is capable of prevention and cure—mental insanity."

Dr. Merchiston grew as white as this my paper. He said, in a confused manner, which vainly tried to simulate indifference—"You are right. But it is a painful subject—insanity."

I did not wonder that my husband tried to change the conversation, and his morning plan likewise. It was evident that in some way the topic strongly affected our friend. Probably he had had a relative thus afflicted.

It must be remembered that, forty years ago, the subject of insanity was viewed in a very different light from what it is at present. Instead of a mere disease, a mental instead of a bodily ailment—yet no less susceptible of remedy—it was looked upon as a visitation, a curse, almost a crime. Any family who owned a member thus suffering, hid the secret as if it had been absolute guilt. "Mad-house," "mad doctor," were words which people shuddered at, or dared not utter. And no wonder! for in many instances they revealed abysses of ignorance, cruelty, and wickedness, horrible to contemplate. Since then more than one modern Howard has gone among those worse than prisons, cleared away incalculable evils, and made even such dark places of the earth to see a hopeful dawn.

Throughout his professional career, one of my husband's favorite "crotchets," as I called them, had been the investigation of insanity.

Commencing with the simple doctrine, startling but true, that every man and woman is mad on some one point—that is, has a certain weak corner of the mind or brain, which requires carefully watching like any other weak portion of the body, lest it should become the seat of rampant disease, he went on with a theory of possible cure—one that would take a wiser head than mine to explain, but which effectually removed the intolerable horror, misery, and hopelessness of that great cloud overhanging the civilized and intellectual portion of the world—mental insanity. I do not mean the raving madness which is generally superinduced by violent passions, and which by-gone ages used to regard as a sort of demoniacal possession—which it may be, for aught I know—but that general state of unsoundness, unhealthiness of brain, which corresponds to unhealthiness of body, and like it, often requires less a physician than a sanitary commissioner.

This may seem an unnecessary didactic interpolation, but I owe it to the natural course of my story, and as a tribute to my dear husband. Besides, it formed the subject of a conversation which, the question being voluntarily revived by Dr. Merchiston, he and James held together during the whole afternoon.

It was good and pleasant to hear these two men talk. I listened, pleased as a woman who is contented to appreciate and enjoy that to which herself can never attain. And once more, for the thousandth time, I noted with admiration the wonderfully strong and lucid intellect with which Dr. Merchiston could grasp any subject, handle it, view it on all points, and make his auditors see it too. Even on this matter, which still seemed to touch his sympathies deeply, especially when he alluded to the world's horror and cruel treatment of insane persons—insane, perhaps, only on some particular point, while the rest of the brain was clear and sound—even there his powers of reasoning and argument never failed.

"Well," said Mr. Rivers, smiling, as they shook hands at the door, "I am glad to have found some one who can understand my hobby. You are certainly one of the clearest-headed men I ever knew."

"You truly think so? I thank you, Rivers," said the Doctor, earnestly, as he disappeared into the dark.

I remember this night's conversation vividly, because, in Heaven's inscrutable mercy—ay, I will write "mercy"—it was the last time Dr. Merchiston entered our house.

The next morning he bowed to me at the window, riding past on his gayly curveting horse, looking better and more cheerful than he had done for a long time.

That evening my husband was summoned to the Double House. Its master had been thrown from his horse, his leg and his right arm fractured. If all went well, James told me, and I had rarely seen him so moved—the patient would be confined to his bed, bound there hand and foot, helpless as a child, for three or four months. Poor Dr. Merchiston!

"Is his wife with him?" was the first question I asked.

"Yes, thank God, yes!" cried James, fairly bursting into tears. I was so shocked, so amazed by his emotion, that I never inquired or learned to this day how it came about, or what strange scene my husband had that evening witnessed in the Double House.

There was a long crisis, in which the balance

wavered between life and death. Life triumphed.

I went almost every day; but it was long before I saw Mrs. Merchiston: when I did, it was the strangest sight! Her looks were full of the deepest peace, the most seraphic joy. And yet she had been for weeks a nurse in that sick room. A close, tender, indefatigable nurse, such as none but a wife can be; as fondly watchful—ay, and as gratefully and adoringly watched, my husband told me, by the sick man's dim eyes, as if she had been a wife bound for years in near, continual household bonds, instead of having lived totally estranged from him since the first six months of union. But no one ever spoke or thought of that now. Dr. Merchiston slowly improved; though he was still totally helpless, and his weakness remained that of a very infant.

In this state he was when I was first admitted to his sick chamber.

Mrs. Merchiston sat at the window, sewing. The room was bright and pleasant; she had brought into it all those cheerfulnesses which can alleviate the long-to-be-endured suffering from which all danger is past. When I thought of the former aspect and atmosphere of the house, it did not seem in the least sad now; for Barbara's eyes had a permanent, mild, satisfied light; and her husband's, which were ever dwelling on her face and form, were full of the calmest, most entire happiness.

I sat with them a good while, and did not marvel at his saying ere I left—"that he thoroughly enjoyed being ill."

With what a solemn, sublime evenness is life meted out! Barbara has told me since that those five months following her husband's accident were the most truly happy her life had ever known.

"Look at him," she whispered to me one evening when he lay by the window, half-dozing, having been for the first time allowed a faint attempt at locomotion, though he was still obliged to be waited upon hand and foot—"Mrs. Rivers, did you ever see so beautiful a smile? Yet it is nothing compared to that he wore when he was very, very ill, when I first began to nurse and tend him; and he did nothing but watch me about the room, and call me his Barbara. I am here, Evan!—did you want me?"

She was at his side in a moment, smoothing his pillow, leaning over and caressing him. I think he was not aware of there being any one in the room but their two selves, for he fondled her curls and her soft cheeks.

"My Barbara, we have had a little ray of comfort in our sad life. How happy we have been in this sick room!"

"We have been, Evan?"

"Ay; but nothing lasts in this world—nothing!"

"Husband, that is like one of your morbid sayings when we were first married. But I will not have it now—I will not, indeed." And she closed his mouth with a pretty petulance.

He lifted his hand to remove hers, then sunk back.

"I am growing strong again; I can use my right arm. Oh, Heaven! my right arm! I am not helpless any longer."

"No, thank God! But you speak as if you were shocked and terrified."

"I am—I am. With strength comes—Oh, my Barbara!"

His wife, alarmed at the anguish of his tone, called out my name. Dr. Merchiston caught at it. "Is Mrs. Rivers there? Bid her come in; bid any body come in. Ah! yes, that is well."

After a pause, which seemed more of mental than physical exhaustion, he became himself again for the rest of the evening.

The next day he sent for me, and in Mrs. Merchiston's absence, talked with me a long while about her. He feared her health would give way; he wished her to be more with me; he hoped I would impress upon her that it made him miserable to see her spending all her days and nights in his sick room.

"What! in the only place in the world where she has real happiness?"

"Do you think so? Is she never happy but with me? Then Heaven forgive me! Heaven have pity on me!" he groaned.

"Dr. Merchiston! you surely do not intend to send your wife from you again—your forgiving, loving wife?"

Before he could answer she came in. I went away thoroughly angry and miserable. That evening I indulged James with such a long harangue on the heartlessness of his sex, that, as I said, he must have been less a man than an angel to have borne it. When I told him the cause, he ceased all general arguments, sat a long time thoughtful, burning his Hessians against the bars of the grate, finally sent me to bed and did not himself follow until midnight.

Dr. Merchiston's cure progressed; in the same ratio his wife's cheerfulness declined. He grew day by day more melancholy, irritable, and cold. By the time he was released from his helpless condition, the icy barrier between them had risen up again. She made no complaint, but the facts were evident.

My husband and I by his express desire spent almost every evening at the Double House. Very painful and dreary evenings they were. Convalescence seemed to the poor patient no happiness—only a terror, misery, and pain.

One night, just as we were leaving, making an attempt at cheerfulness—for it was the first time he had performed the feat of walking, and his wife had helped him across the room with triumphant joy—he said, breaking from a long reverie, "Stay—a few minutes more; Rivers—Mrs. Rivers—I want to speak with you both."

We sat down. He fell back in his chair, and covered his eyes. At length Mrs. Merchiston gently took the hands away.

"Evan, you don't feel so strong as usual to-night?"

"I do; alas, alas, I do," he muttered.—

"Would I were weak, and lay on that bed again, as powerless as a child. No, Barbara; look, I am strong—well." He stood up, stretching his gaunt right arm, and clenching the hand; then let it drop, affrighted. "My little Barbara, I must send thee away."

"Send me away?"

"Send her away?"

"Peggy," cried my husband, in stern reproof, "be silent!"

The poor wife broke out into bitter sobs. "Oh, Evan, what have I done to you? Dear Evan, let me stay—only till you are well, quite well."

For, despite what he said about his strength, his countenance, as he lay back, was almost that of a corpse. Barbara's clinging arms seemed to him worse than the gripe of a murderer.

"Take her away, Mrs. Rivers; take my poor wife away. You know how she has nursed me; you know whether I love her or not."

"Love her!" I cried bitterly; but James's hand was upon my shoulder. His eye, which with its gentle firmness could, they said at the Hospital, control the most refractory and soothe the most wretched patient, was fixed upon Dr. Merchiston. I saw the sick man yield; the bright hectic flush came and went in his cheek.

"Rivers, my good friend, what do you wish me to do?"

"A very simple thing. Tell me—not these poor, frightened women—but me, your real reason for acting thus."

"Impossible."

"Not quite. It may be I partly guess it already."

Dr. Merchiston started up with the look of a hunted wild beast in its last despair, but my husband laid his hand on his, in a kind but resolute way.

"Indeed, indeed, you are safe in telling me. Will you do it?"

The patient hesitated, held up his thin hand to the light with a wan smile, then said, "It can not matter for long; I will."

James immediately sent us both out of the room.

Mrs. Merchiston was a very weak woman, gentle and frail. She wept until her strength was gone; then I put her to bed in her maid's charge, and waited until Mr. Rivers ended his conference with her husband.

It was two hours before James came out. At sight of him my torrent of curiosity was dried up; he looked as I had sometimes seen him coming home from a death-bed. To my few questions he answered not a word.

"But at least," said I, half crying, "at least you might tell me what I am to do with poor Mrs. Merchiston."

"Yes, yes." He thought a minute. "She must go home with us; the sooner the better."

"You agree, then," I burst out, breathless; "you agree to this separation?"

"Entirely."

"You join with her wicked husband in his ingratitude—his brutality—"

"Peggy!" James caught me by the shoulders, with the sternest frown that ever fell on me in all our peaceful married life; "Peggy, may Heaven forgive you! You do not know what you are saying."

I was completely awed.

"Dr. Merchiston has told you the secret, and you are determined to keep it?"

"Implicitly, while his poor life lasts."

My husband was a man of inviolable honor. He never would tell a patient's secrets, or a friend's, even to me, his wife; nor was I the woman to desire it. I urged no more.

During the ten days that Mrs. Merchiston remained in my house, part of the time she was in a sort of low fever, which was the happiest thing for her, poor soul! I made not a single inquiry after her husband; I knew that Mr. Rivers was with him at all hours, as doctor, nurse, and friend.

One day, when Mrs. Merchiston was sitting in the parlor with me, he looked in at the door. She did not see him. He quietly beckoned me out.

"Well, James?"

"Speak lower, Peggy, lower; don't let her hear."

And then I saw how very much agitated he was; yet even that did not quite remove the bitterness with which I could not help mentioning the name of Dr. Merchiston.

"Peggy, Dr. Merchiston is dying."

I had not expected this; it was a great shock.

"I feared it would be so," continued James; "I have seen him sinking this long time. Now the mind is at peace, but the worn-out body—"

"His wife—his poor wife," was all I could utter.

"Yes, that is what I came to say. She must go to him; he wishes it much. Do you think she will?"

I smiled, sadly. "Ah! James, she is a woman."

"And you women can forgive to all eternity. Heaven bless you for it! Besides, she will know the whole truth soon."

I asked not what this "truth" was. What did it matter? he was dying.

"But are you sure, James, there is no hope of his recovery?"

"None, I believe, and am almost glad to believe it. There is no man I ever knew whom I so deeply pity, and shall so thankfully see gone to his last rest, as Dr. Merchiston."

These were strong words, enough to calm down every wrong feeling, and made me fit to lead the wife to her husband's sick—nay, death chamber.

How we brought her thither I forget. I only remember the moment when we stood within the door.

Dr. Merchiston lay on his bed, as for five long months he had patiently and cheerfully lain. He had something of that old quiet look now, but with a change—the strange, awful change which, however fond friends may deceive themselves, is always clearly visible to a colder gaze. You say at once, "That man will die."

When Barbara came into the room he stretched out his arms with the brightest, happiest smile. She clung to him closely and long. There was no forgiveness asked or bestowed; it was not needed.

"I am so content, my Barbara, content at last!" and he laid his head on her shoulder.

"Evan, you will not part from me again?"

"No; I need not now. They will tell you why it was. You believe—you will always believe how I loved you?"

"Yes."

"Stoop. Let me hold her close as I used to do—my wife, my little Barbara. Stoop down."

She obeyed. He put his arms round her, and kissed her with many kisses, such as he had not given her since she was a six months' bride; their memory remained sweet on her lips till she was old and gray.

Dr. Merchiston died at the next sunrise, died peacefully in Barbara's arms.

* * * * * *

Three days after my husband and I stood by the coffin, where, for the last few minutes on earth, the features, which had been so familiar to us for the last two years, were exposed to our view. James said—touching the forehead, which was placid as a dead baby's, with all the wrinkles gone—

"Thank the Lord!"

"Why?"

"For this blessed death, in which alone his sufferings could end. He was a monomaniac, and he knew it."

Before speaking again my husband, reverently and tenderly, closed the coffin, and led me down stairs.

The funeral over, and we two sitting quietly and solemnly by our own fireside, James told me the whole.

"He was, as I said, a monomaniac. Mad on one point only, the rest of his mind being clear and sound."

"And that point was—"

"The desire to murder his wife. He told me," pursued James, when my horror had a little subsided, "that it came upon him first in the very honeymoon, beginning with the sort of feeling that I have heard several people say that they had at the climax of happiness—the wish there and then to die—together. Afterward, day and night, whenever they were alone, the temptation used to haunt him. A physician himself, he knew that it was a monomania; but he also knew that, if he confessed it, he, sane on all other points, would be treated as a madman, and that his wife, the only creature he loved, would look on him with horror forever. There was but one course to save himself and her; he took it, and never swerved from it."

"But in his illness?"

"Then, being perfectly helpless, he knew he could not harm her, and in great bodily weakness most monomanias usually subside. His left him entirely. When he grew stronger it returned. You know the rest. His life was one long torture. Peace be with him now!"

"Amen!" I said, and went to comfort the widow.

The terrible fact, which Dr. Merchiston had desired should be told her after his death, did not seem to affect Barbara so much as we feared. Love to her, as to many other women, was the beginning and end of all things—sufficient for life, and even in death wholly undying.

"He loved me—he always loved me," she kept saying, and her days of mourning became the dawn of a perennial joy.

She lived to be nearly as old as I am now, remaining one of those widows who are "widows indeed," forever faithful to one love and one memory.

THE END.